death in a
delphi seminar

SUNY Series
The Margins of Literature

Mihai I. Spariosu, editor

death in a delphi seminar

---

a postmodern mystery

Norman N. Holland

state university of new york press

"The Snake" by Denise Levertov. *Collected Earlier Poems, 1940–1960*. Copyright © by Denise Levertov. First printed in *Poetry*. Reprinted by permission of New Directions Publishing Corp.

Published by
State University of New York Press

© 1995 State University of New York

For information, address the State University of New York Press,
State University Plaza, Albany, NY 12246

Production by Bernadine Dawes • Marketing by Nancy Farrell

Library of Congress Cataloging-in-Publication Data

Holland, Norman Norwood, 1927–
Death in a Delphi seminar : a postmodern mystery / Norman Holland.
p.   cm. — (SUNY series, the margins of literature)
ISBN 0-7914-2599-1 (HC : acid-free). — ISBN 0-7914-2600-9 (PB :
acid-free)
I. Title. II. Series.
PS3558.034857D43   1995
813'.54—dc20   95-2049
                                                 CIP

2   3   4   5   6   7   8   9   10

to Jane,

wonderful Jane

contents

afterward

State University of New York at Buffalo
Department of English

Mr. Bateson Winnicott
The Winnicott Agency
10 Astor Place
New York NY 10003

March 6, 1985

Dear Winn:

Here it is.

Whatever "it" is.

"It" is a mystery. More precisely, it is a postmodern mystery as I've de-fined that term in my serious writings. "In postmodernism, writers take as their subject matter the relationship between the book and its author or between the book and its audience."

So, is this "it" a thing-in-itself? Does it have people and events "in" it? Such confusions lie that way. Or is "it" just a thing, inert, a Sleeping Beauty waiting to be kissed into life by a loving reader—you, for example.

As my agent, you know, better than anyone, how I've thrashed around all these years with my questions about readers and reading. How does a book get from paper page to an experience in the mind? Do books mean or do readers make meaning? Do words constrain or just clue us?

If there was ever a book that followed the old maxim, Write about what you know, this is it. What I know is books and readers. Although, I suppose, if I knew, why would I have spent all these years trying to figure out how readers respond? So maybe this is a book about not knowing what you know.

Fact: in my seminar last year, one of the students was poisoned. I've built up a narrative out of the texts that this woman's dying, so to speak, happened in: transcripts of the police interviews with the people involved, student papers, some department memos, newspaper accounts, and parts of my journal of the events—a whole mix of different voices—narratives— "takes"—texts—on this event.

Just to be safe, I've changed the names. And my perception of these people and events is sufficiently idiosyncratic that we can truly make the customary claim that any resemblance to persons living or dead is purely coincidental.

There is one exception, sort of, to this fictionality (as literary critics term it). The hero, if he is the hero, is a professor whom I frankly call Norman

Holland. Is he fictional? Of course. Is he real? As the postmodern tradition of "the disappearance of the subject" takes hold, I am less and less certain.

Yours more or less truly,

/Norm/

From the *Buffalo Morning News Gazette,* March 8, 1984

Grad Student Dies, Poisoned in UB Class

Fingerprint All English Grad Students, Say Police

(CITY, March 7) A University at Buffalo student collapsed and died in an early morning class Wednesday, and Buffalo police say the young woman was poisoned.

Patricia Hassler, a 22-year-old graduate student, said to be from Iron Springs, Georgia, took her seat and "instantly keeled over," said Dr. Norman Holland, whose class Hassler was attending. When campus police and paramedics arrived, she was already dead, according to campus police spokesperson, Sgt. Herman Gehring.

Hassler arrived late for the class, where she was to give a presentation. "I was terribly shocked," said Paul Penza, a classmate. "Poor Trish. She had a marvelous mind and, as a writer, a distinctive voice."

Lieutenant Norman ("Justin")

Rhodes of the Homicide Unit, MBPD, is in charge of the investigation of Hassler's death. He has asked for all graduate students in the English Department to be fingerprinted.

At first, students and others who had seen Hassler collapse described her death as due to a stroke or heart attack. Lt. Rhodes' announcement that police had found she was poisoned was unexpected.

It was Medical Examiner Robert Welder, said Rhodes, who established that the victim was poisoned. He declined to comment further on the case except to say that police were not yet disclosing the name of the poison.

Patricia Hassler was a first-year graduate student who had begun working toward her Ph.D. at UB in the fall semester of 1983. She earned her bachelor's degree in English at Yale University in New Haven.

UB Dean of Students, Reynard Overten, said that the University has been unable to locate the victim's family, because the addresses on her application appear to be out of date.

"She was a student in whom we all saw a great deal of promise," said Dr. Romola Badger, chair of the English Department. "We all regret this tragic event, and we extend our deepest sympathies to all her parents and friends."

Dr. Holland is a specialist in "literature-and-psychology." He applies psychology to literary problems, and his class is noted at UB for its unusual teaching technique. Students write about one another's reading and writing styles in papers that "are as frank as what you'd hear in a psychiatrist's office," according to an English Department official.

But the teacher said the unusual style of the class could not possibly be related to Hassler's death. "I've been giving this kind of seminar for years, and we've never had any kind of trouble."

Ironically, Lt. Rhodes is no stranger to writing and dramas. In addition to his work as a detective, he is well known as a playwright. Lt. Rhodes is a native of Buffalo and son of Mr. George Rhodes and Mrs. Henrietta ("Pookie") Goodrich, the former Mrs. Rhodes, both of West Eden.

wednesday

Metropolitan Buffalo Police Department

Tape Transcription   Homicide Unit

Body: *Hassler, P.*   Tape No. *840307.007*
Place: *Rhodes Hall, UB West Campus*   Time: *9:46 a.m.*
Persons present: *Det. Sgt. M. Yorrick; N. N. Holland*

                                                        Transcribed by: *S. Moreno*

SGT. YORRICK: Don't be nervous, Professor. These things happen, particularly in Buffalo.

HOLLAND: I've never seen anything like this.

SGT. YORRICK: There has to be a first time, doesn't there, as the bridegroom said to the bride. You know, it really is like sex. You never get entirely used to it. Anyway, just speak into the tape recorder, Professor.

HOLLAND: Yes, Sergeant. *[Pause.]* This is awful. Mortality. I need a minute to calm down.

SGT. YORRICK: Take your time.

HOLLAND: *[Pause. Clears throat.]* I knew this session of the seminar would be different from the others. Today was the day Trish Hassler was going to respond to the things the other students had written about her—or, more accurately, had written to her about their perceptions of her style of reading and writing. I'm sorry that that's so complicated, but that's what this seminar is about: people reading one another and writing to one another about one another.

Anyway, Trish had bumped me out of my regular seat. Characteristic. You see, the seminar table is one of those long, narrow, boat-shaped ones. If you're the teacher, if you sit at the side, you wear your neck out, swinging your head back and forth to maintain eye contact. So it's understood in the seminar that I sit at the head of the long table.

SGT. YORRICK: Professor. About the death?

HOLLAND: I'm sorry, Sergeant.

This morning Trish had put her books at my seat at the window end of the table. That seems to me something you probably want to know.

You see, she wasn't there when I came in.

I put my notebook and papers down at the other end of the table, near the door, and I wandered over to the window. Collecting my thoughts. When this was a private house, this must have been a pleasant enough room, but . . .

SGT. YORRICK: Professor . . .

HOLLAND: Do we have to talk in the hall right next to the classroom where she is still lying?

SGT. YORRICK: I'll have to keep you here until His Nibs, the lieutenant, gets here. Now you just go on and don't worry about all that.

HOLLAND: I was dreading Trish's responses to the other students. She'd been a problem from the beginning of the semester—disruptive, combative, just plain nasty. I just went on hoping it wouldn't be so bad this time.

This morning she'd evidently come in early. She'd put her stack of books down to reserve a spot at the table, my spot, and then she had gone back out.

I suppose I could have pushed her books aside, but I didn't want to—for all kinds of reasons. So I put my notebook down at the other end of the table, by the door. The students were all milling around out in the hall, talking, laughing, taking last drags.

I remember looking out at March. Grimy snow, grass the color of old grocery bags. Behind me I could smell the oldness of this old house. Rhodes Hall. You see, Sergeant, the English Department building, is the Rhodes family's mansion, donated to the university and made over into classrooms and offices.

SGT. YORRICK: The lieutenant comes from a rich family.

HOLLAND: I could smell the wet wool smell of the student coats and scarves heaped up on an extra chair over by the radiator. I thought, Oh God, wouldn't it be nice, just once, to look out at some palm trees? Students who wear shorts and not those big down jackets that make them look like Monsieur Michelin. You can't even tell the men from the women. Yes, Sergeant, I'll stop rambling.

I sat down at the door end of the seminar table. By this time, it was 9:10, and some of the students were already sitting there. The rest of them came in. They were all there. Not Trish. She was already ten minutes late. I remember that Anne Glendish wondered who would be "it" for next week. Paul Penza told me about some story contest he was entering. Barry Ireland was kidding around with Max Ebenfeld about taking steroids. Suddenly, I could feel cold air behind me. I twisted my neck around and looked up, too.

Trish Hassler was a mountain of woman, Sergeant, a mountain of always angry young woman. She was wearing the orange scarf we'd all grown to recognize, over a maroon sweater and an immense wraparound skirt of brown corduroy. Earrings, beads, bracelets, all her ragtag stuff. She snatched off her gloves and her stocking cap so that her blond hair fell back down around her face in long damp strings. She looked around the room, and she looked at each one of us one by one. For a moment, she looked scared, panicky almost. I remember wondering what she was going to say in the seminar, dreading it.

She had a way of looking at me with her eyes focused high on my forehead so that I always had the feeling that she was staring at my bald head. She marched down the side of the table where Barry was sitting, took her coat off as she went, and sat down.

No. Wait a minute. I'm leaving something out. All the students *weren't* there. While she was standing in the doorway, Christian Aval pushed past her and came in and sat down. God, I'm confused. Then, while she was walking to her seat, she paused behind his chair, and she said something. She said, "This is the one I was talking about. Him." Then, she marched down to her end of the table. She tossed her big sheepskin coat over onto one of the chairs with a pile of coats on it. She plunked herself down in her chair. She gave us another long, slow glare around the table—it seemed an eternity—and then she just keeled over.

God! Her eyes closed, her jaw clamped shut as if she were going to say something but had decided very hard not to say it. She just sort of settled in on herself. Then her head tipped over on her right side, and she leaned over. Her jaw fell open as if she were surprised by something, and she slid to her right side and collapsed between the chair and the table leg. When her head hit the floor there was a tremendous thump. I didn't know bone could sound like that.

We were all terribly startled. Paul Penza was sitting next to her—on her right side—so that she was right there at his left arm. He pushed his chair back and knelt over her. He felt her throat for a pulse. "She's dead," he said.

SGT. YORRICK: And no one has moved her.

HOLLAND: I don't think anybody *wanted* to touch her. I told Penza to find a phone and call the university police, and I took the seminar to the classroom across the hall. I didn't think they should stay in the room with the body. I had Max Ebenfeld stand in the doorway of the seminar room and keep people from going in. Suddenly there were a lot of people milling around in the hall. They must have heard Penza telephone.

SGT. YORRICK: Well done, Professor.

HOLLAND: I was numb. Affect block. Anyway, Security came very quickly—to my surprise. They brought a team of paramedics with them, and they started pushing and poking and listening to Trish Hassler. After a while, they too announced she was dead. The paramedics called back to their headquarters. Evidently somebody told them to leave the body where it was and call the city police. The university police told us to stay in that empty classroom. You came and took me out here and asked me to make this statement.

SGT. YORRICK: Yes. Now you just wait in the classroom with your students, Professor. Lt. Rhodes is going to be in charge of this case. I have no doubt he'll be here shortly and he'll be telling you what he wants. Sure as Joseph and Mary, he's going to want to talk to all of you.

HOLLAND: He's the playwright, isn't he? That's appropriate.

SGT. YORRICK: D'you think so, now? Oh, one thing, Professor. Where's your office?

HOLLAND: On the third floor, where the small rooms are. At the head of the stairs. They made the bigger rooms on the first and second floors into classrooms like this and the department offices. The smaller rooms on the third floor they made into faculty offices and the mailroom. Faculty with pull have their offices and classrooms on the new campus in Fiedler Hall.

SGT. YORRICK: You don't have pull?

HOLLAND: No.

SGT. YORRICK: Why is that, Professor?

HOLLAND: Badger, the chair, doesn't like what I do.

SGT. YORRICK: Chair?

HOLLAND: Chairperson. Chair. What we used to call a chairman.

SGT. YORRICK: I see. A woman. Could we use your office as an interrogation room?

HOLLAND: That sounds grim. Sure.

SGT. YORRICK: Professor, there are only seven coats here, but there were nine people in the room when Hassler died.

HOLLAND: Wally Sisley—he's the other faculty member in the seminar—probably left his coat in his office, as I did.

SGT. YORRICK: Thank you, Professor. Would you go across the hall now?END OF THIS SECTION OF TAPE END OF THIS SECTION OF TAPE END

Metropolitan Buffalo Police Department

Tape Transcription   Homicide Unit

Body: *Hassler, P.*   Tape No. *840307.008*

Place: *Rhodes Hall, UB West Campus*   Time: *10:05 a.m.*

Persons present: *Det. Lt. Norman Rhodes, Det. Sgt. M. Yorrick; see below*

Transcribed by: *J. Cipperman*

Civilians Present: Professor Norman Holland, Professor Wallace Sisley, Anne Glendish, Christian Aval, Max Ebenfeld, Amelia Lemaire, Barry Ireland, Paul Penza. *[Confused hubbub.]*

LT. RHODES: Listen up, people. All right, quiet down, quiet down. You're upset and grieved and probably frightened by Patricia Hassler's death. I understand. Your feelings are perfectly natural.

I'm Lieutenant Justin Rhodes.

I want to explain something to you at this early stage. You shouldn't draw any inferences from the presence of me and my people from the Homicide Unit. The city and county require the police, and specifically the Homicide Unit, to investigate any death unless and until we can show its cause is illness or accident or suicide—that it's not a homicide. We're here strictly as a routine legal requirement.

Our investigation is beginning in the other room right now. My people are photographing the scene and checking for evidence, and the medical examiner is making his on-the-scene examination of Ms. Hassler's body. Then he'll take the body to the county hospital for autopsy. Again, don't jump to any conclusions. Since we don't know the cause of death, we have to do an autopsy.

You'll notice that I've put on the table a miniature tape recorder, the kind they use in offices for dictating. This is something new. The Police Department has decided to use on-the-scene tape recordings. That way we shift paperwork from police and detectives, who ought to be in the field, onto professional transcribers. Also, tape recordings would also meet the worries about police brutality from the A.C.L.U. and the Civilian Review Board.

This morning, I want to establish what happened in the room across the hall at 9:10 a.m. and who and what Patricia Hassler was. What you all were doing here. To that end, I'd like to interview each of you who saw her die. Professor Holland has volunteered his office, and you can wait in this seminar room until I can get to you. Professor Holland first, then the rest of you one by one. Questions?

IRELAND: Do we have to stay here?

GLENDISH: We've been sitting here for nearly an hour.

LT. RHODES: I think it better for all kinds of reasons if you stay. Do you *have* to stay? I *could* detain you all, but I'd appreciate it if you'd just cooperate without my having to do that. Okay? Right.

Professor Holland, will you get me settled in your office?END OF THIS SECTION OF TAPE END OF THIS SECTION OF TAPE END OF

from the journal of Norman Holland

[I suppose it's all right if I put this useful section in here, although I actually wrote it about an hour later Wednesday morning. As Sam Shepard, a play-wright better known than Justin Rhodes, has rewritten Aristotle, "A play should have a beginning, middle, and end, but not necessarily in that order." A perfect definition of the postmodern.]

Yes, she's dead, utterly and completely and irrevocably dead. It felt to me like a sudden, cold exhalation, as if we had opened the door of a mausoleum. Did the students feel, as I did, overwhelmed with our own mortality? Or were they feeling guilty because they really didn't like her and were glad to see her gone? Again, like me.

Amy seemed genuinely moved and saddened at her death. Glendish less so. Ireland just seemed sobered. After all, as he keeps telling us, he saw a lot of death in Vietnam. Aval, who may have had the most reason to wish her out of the way, looked quite shocked. Frightened, I would say. I couldn't tell whether the students were responding to the manner of her death or the fact of it. Curiously, Wally Sisley seemed surprised rather than moved or fearful. I don't remember the others, because I got busy getting them out of the seminar room and making a statement.

I desperately wanted to call Jane—for sympathy and wisdom. But she was in Philadelphia, seeing her mother through yet another stage on her slow glide toward the last letting go. It being morning, Jane was at the hospital. I had no time to track her down.

And why did she die? Was that what the students were wondering? Or were they hit by the sheer fact of death itself? This person who was so ornery and vital is now—over. Finished. I've heard a saying: When a person dies a library burns. How especially true for Trish.

I can barely pretend to be sorry. It's like the old joke, Why are you hitting yourself on the head? It feels so good when I stop. Now she has stopped—been stopped.

Her dying raises hell with the seminar. Should we just meet next week in the ordinary way? Should we memorialize Trish somehow? Would that be hypo-critical? The other students didn't like her any more than I did. I believe.

What did she mean? "This is the one I was talking about." I guess she's referring to the plagiarism. A problem in interpretation that I, the literary critic, ought to be expert at.

I feel like writing something about this event. That would be one way of coming to grips with this painful ambivalence, the awfulness of her dying but also the awfulness of the relief I feel. That's why I'm typing this into my trusty Tandy laptop as we all wait around.

Some of the police wore uniforms, others—detectives, I suppose—mufti. A Sergeant Yorrick (one of the ones in civvies) interviewed me. He looks like Gary Cooper in the process of aging into Scarlett O'Hara's father.

Finally the lieutenant arrived and took over. He was tall, six feet anyway, with grey eyes and fine, straight, brown hair, neatly parted and brushed flat on his suitably dolichocephalic head. Mid-forties. He has a long, pointed nose and large, almost droopy ears. I thought right away, Bloodhound! Or Sherlock Holmes (at least the Basil Rathbone version). No bad thing for a detective, I should think. He smiles comfortably, but I don't feel he gets close to people. When he speaks you can hear the upper-class drawl.

He sauntered in wearing a tweed cap, a camel's hair overcoat, brown leather gloves—unlined! Nobody wears unlined gloves in this climate. You could see that his hands and fingers were long. Later, when he took off his overcoat, he was wearing a double-breasted navy blue blazer, grey flannels, blue oxford shirt, and rep tie—a whole preppie uniform. The only unusual thing was the Timberland waterproof shoes, a necessary concession to the snow piled everywhere this March. Preppitude in, of all places, the police department. WASP ivy among the ethnic polyester that the other detectives were wearing.

Rhodes strolled off the elevator that must have been installed for some decrepit forebear into our second-floor hubbub. (It has a big sign, "For Handicapped Only," but I suppose the police have their privileges.) His assistant, Yorrick, had already finished questioning me.

Capable. He moved in on Hassler's death with efficiency and tact. He sent the fingerprint experts, the "scene guys," and sundry patrolmen here and there. With a fast dose of facts, he calmed the anxious prof and his flock of students. Within minutes he had us being interviewed, while he waits for a report from the "M.E.," the medical examiner, a Dr. Welder, on the cause of death.

I saw that worthy come bustling in, a small roly-poly tweedy man with prominent rubbery lips, thick glasses, and a big, black doctor bag. Ver-r-ry serious. But surely it takes no expert come from the grave to tell us she died because she was in such wretched physical shape, overweight, a heavy smoker, always angry and stressed. A heart attack, presumably, or a stroke.

There was a piece about him in the News-Gazette *last spring. Norman ("Justin") Rhodes is a detective who's also an amateur playwright. (Homicide detectives, I've read somewhere, are the intellectuals of any police department.) He writes plays that get performed by church groups and community players who can't afford the royalties on regular plays. Small casts, simple sets, ordinary clothes for costumes. Published by Samuel French, circulated in small editions. It's his hobby, he said in the interview, but he's not exactly an amateur. He's had at least one play produced Off Broadway.*

I've read it. It looks at first like drawing-room comedy. Ordinary people, rather like the rich of Buffalo, but then he experiments with strange dramatic frames and stories within stories. I'm not being very precise. He writes about people dominated by their money, their ancestry, their upper-classness. You'd think you were in your own home looking at your own relatives—if you had that kind of wealthy home. But at the same time he carefully calls attention to the play-ness of the play you are watching. Somerset Maugham with a touch of metatheater. The few reviews I've read say he realistically portrays the life of upper-class WASPs. No, no. I think he's much more postmodern than that.

He has an M.A., I read, in playwriting—from the Yale School of Drama, no less! He'll understand the vagaries of an English department. If anybody can.

The newspaper article said that he went to some East Coast prep school and on to Harvard. He is the "scion," as the newspaper here likes to put it, of the Buffalo Rhodeses, one of the last few in a rapidly thinning aristocratic family or, at least, from what passes for aristocracy in this provincial city. They have not heard of Rhodeses in Boston or New York, but here they are a mainstay among the old families that, after the Civil War, were going to make Buffalo one of a progression of jewels strung along the waterways of a newly industrialized America. Cleveland, Chicago, Cincinnati, St. Louis—and Buffalo among them. Ah, the dreams of men.

They laid out the parks, paid for the art museums, built the libraries, and were rewarded by having everything in town named after them. Then the old families were swamped by floods of the very immigrants they had imported to make them rich in their factories. They huddled together in their private clubs, private schools, and very private dancing classes, private except when their quiet adulteries went public.

When you say Old Money, you've said all there is to say about the Rhodeses. In fact this university is partly built on land they sold to the state. This very building, the English Department's building, was, once upon a time, the Rhodes family mansion. They built out here instead of downtown with the rest of them.

Big? Oh my, yes. I don't know how many bedrooms it had originally, because "Rhodes Hall" has been deconstructed to make offices and classrooms. Out of this one family's house, we got about ten classrooms and seminar rooms, ten small offices, and a big departmental office with quarters for one secretary. There is even a ballroom with a lovely cut-glass chandelier that became a small lecture room for poetry readings and the like. The building as a whole has the look of a Victorian family's mansion still. It's a pleasant change from the relentlessly "modern" (and cheap) cinderblock construction of the rest of the university.

Our detective is one of these Buffalo Rhodeses, but he chose not to go into the banking business or whatever Rhodeses currently do to manipulate their own and other people's money. The family put up with his M.A. in creative writing—that was Yale—but when he went to New York and majored in criminal investigation at John Jay College, that was too much. Young Norman or "Justin," as everybody calls him (god knows why!), had decided to become a detective. A detective?! And, even worse, a playwright! And one who exposes the secret idiosyncrasies of rich, midwestern WASPs!! I read between the lines in that newspaper story that the family regards him as something of a black sheep or a rebel, despite the blue blazer and his grey flannels and his clubby accent. He married an agreeable woman, I heard, another "scion" of the city's upper classes, but they divorced. It was a mean one, people said. He wouldn't let her go—couldn't. They had an ugly legal melee, a jousting of the best local talent in divorce law.

Rhodes had a long interview with me, and I rambled on about this seminar and reader-response theory. He seemed interested. Now, as I tap this into my miraculous little Tandy 100, he is interviewing the students one by one.

A new police department regulation requires that he tape everything. I couldn't help wondering if he was getting dialogue for a new play, maybe a mystery based on the death of Patricia Hassler. Is our cast small enough, our setting inexpensive, our clothes ordinary?

He must find us (me?) a strange lot. There's no percentage in academia in bringing matters to a swift, decisive conclusion. The more you can keep juggling the ideas, the more possibilities you can keep open, the longer the discussion lasts, the more likely you are to get an article out of it and the less risk you will exhaust the subject. We put a premium on indecisiveness. How different this man is.

Metropolitan Buffalo Police Department

Tape Transcription   Homicide Unit

Body: *Hassler, P.*   Tape No. *840307.008*

Place: *Rhodes Hall, UB*   Time: *10:15 a.m.*

Persons present: *Det. Lt. Rhodes, Norman Holland*

    Det. Sgt. Yorrick, Romola Badger, Anne Glendish, Christian

    Aval

Transcribed by: *J. Cipperman*

HOLLAND: Welcome, Lieutenant. Take the swivel chair. Let me move those books. I'll sit across, where the students usually sit. Students! What's going to happen to the seminar now? This death's going to change everything.

LT. RHODES: It usually does. Anyway, thanks for lending me your office.

HOLLAND: There's something I want to say right off about this investigation. Hassler's death must have come from something like a heart attack. She was in terrible shape physically, overweight, a heavy smoker, angry and stressed most of the time.

LT. RHODES: Angry? You said that in your statement, too. Angry about what?

HOLLAND: She was just angry in general. In this seminar, she was terribly disruptive.

LT. RHODES: Disruptive? Shooting rubber bands and flying paper airplanes?

HOLLAND: No, intellectually disruptive. She was having a running battle with me about theoretical assumptions. She insisted all the time on talking deconstruction.

LT. RHODES: Whatever that is. I've listened to your taped statement. She just walked into the seminar, sat down, and collapsed. Is that it?

HOLLAND: Yes, that's all I saw.

LT. RHODES: I'll have to go over the same ground with the students, though. Do you have a class list or something I can keep track with as I interview them?

HOLLAND: Sure. Here's one.

LT. RHODES: Include this, will you, whoever is transcribing this?

Class List—

Aval, Christian
Ebenfeld, Max
Glendish, Anne
Hassler, Patricia
Ireland, Barry
Lemaire, Amelia
Penza, Paul
Sisley, Wallace

HOLLAND: Why don't I just go down it alphabetically? Christian Aval—he's the small, lively, dark one, with those brown, sparkling eyes and the close-cropped hair. And, of course, an accent. He's French. He went to Yale as an undergraduate, like Trish Hassler. He would agree with her on theory, but he doesn't seem to have come away with the same fanaticism.

Second, the one with the Arnold Schwarzenegger build—Ebenfeld, Max Ebenfeld. Well, not really. He's not as tall as Schwarzenegger. He talks about delts and lats and pecs, but he's a good-hearted fellow and moderately intelligent.

Next, the aptly named Anne Glendish.

LT. RHODES: Why aptly named?

HOLLAND: Because she really is a dish, a sight to gladden the eyes of the aging professor. You won't have any trouble recognizing her when you go in the next room. A blue-eyed blonde, slim, above-average height. Very stylishly dressed. No jeans for Ms. Glendish, not unless they are Gloria Vanderbilt jeans. Very intelligent and, as far as I can tell, very nice. Old, rich family. Another southerner—like Hassler. Ambitious. Strong.

Next, Barry Ireland. You'll recognize him as the one with the red hair and pock marks. Oh, and today he's wearing a bandanna round his forehead. A problem child, one of the Vietnam vets who got into trouble. He has an alchohol problem—he's told us that in seminar—and I suspect he may do other drugs as well. Sometimes he scares me with the way he talks about killing. Basically a nice guy, but unstable, and with a truly startling indifference to violence.

Amelia—Amy—Lemaire. A particularly likable person. She's the one who's older than the regular students, about thirty-five, I'd say. Small, stocky, with dark hair cut close to the head, brown eyes. The other students in the seminar depend on her to be the peacemaker when Trish and I get locked into theoretical argument. When students say uncomfortable, risky things, she's always the one who comes up with the right support and reassurance. I've often wondered why she never married and had children—she seems a natural for that role. I'd say she's a born teacher, maybe because she's a born mother. That's what she wants to do when she gets her Ph.D.—teach. I worry how she'll deal with the profession's demands for research and publication. Not her thing.

Next comes Penza. Paul's a creative writer—fiction. I think he just uses this seminar in literary theory as time to write his fiction. That is, sometimes he doesn't talk about the poem or the story we read at all, he just writes his own story. They can be quite good, but unfortunately for Paul he's supposed to be writing responses made up of free associations, not short stories. Or unfortunately for me, because he's testing me as Trish was. There is no way, after all, I can say his story isn't a free association— some random set of words that came into his mind. He's got me.

LT. RHODES: Are you telling me that's what you do in this seminar? Free associate?

HOLLAND: Sort of. This is a seminar in reader-response theory.

LT. RHODES: I can guess what that is from the phrase, but explain.

HOLLAND: Not in a few words, Lieutenant. It involves a lot of literary theory. Do you really have time for that?

LT. RHODES: Probably not. Okay, Penza.

HOLLAND: He has a wonderful imagination, and he can be very witty. But I don't feel he's committed the way some of the others are. He's just playing around so that he has time to write. He's the good-looking, blond young guy, slim, not the muscle man.

Oh, and I suppose I should have mentioned him first, the other prof in the seminar, Wally—Wallace Sisley.

LT. RHODES: Is that usual? To have two professors teach one seminar?

HOLLAND: Actually, Wally isn't teaching it, although it's nice to have another professor present, particularly when you have to manage a seminar as difficult as Hassler has made this one. I'm doing all the teaching. Wally is, if you get right down to it, like another student.

From time to time, I get other professors taking my Delphi seminars.

LT. RHODES: Delphi seminar?

HOLLAND: We call it a Delphi seminar, because that was the first great commandment on the temple of Apollo at Delphi, *gnothe seauton*. Know thyself.

LT. RHODES: This is a seminar about knowing yourself?

HOLLAND: In more modern language, it's a seminar where the student learns his or her "cognitive style."

LT. RHODES: That's not helping me.

HOLLAND: This is a seminar in which people learn about their personal styles of reading or writing. That's what we study.

YORRICK: Lieutenant, Dr. Welder wants to take the body now.

LT. RHODES: Okay, take it. I saw whatever I could see when I came in. Now, back to Sisley.

HOLLAND: Sometimes other professors take this Delphi seminar. They may want to learn about their own styles. They may want to try out the Delphi method with an eye to using the technique themselves. I guess Wally might come under both headings.

He's perfectly capable, but not one of the outstanding people in the department. He's coming up for tenure soon, and he's an iffy case. Like a lot of people these days, he has a problem publishing.

LT. RHODES: Ah yes, publish or perish. Out here in what is euphemistically called the real world, I had forgotten the rules for professors.

HOLLAND: Wally withdraws a bit. In one of the responses he wrote for the seminar, he said he felt in the shadow of his older brother, his twin. You'll spot Wally easily enough. He's the one who's older, like Ireland, but he looks tweedy and professorial. He's a quite intelligent person, a good teacher, and a solid worker on committees. He's in his forties, the tall one with the brown hair going gray around the edges.

That's all of us— Oops. I almost forgot. We have a mystery student. This has never happened to me before, but this semester we have an interloper.

LT. RHODES: Tell me what you mean.

HOLLAND: I'll have to explain the mechanics of the seminar, and that could take some time.

LT. RHODES: I probably need to know.

HOLLAND: It works this way. We write these free associative responses to various poems, stories, whatnot. Two to three pages. We're all supposed to circulate these papers to the other people in the seminar the Monday before the Wednesday meeting. That gives us time to read and ponder what the others have written.

Each of us puts his or her response in the others' mailboxes in the department mailroom. You write your response, you make however many copies—nine for this year's seminar—and you stick them in the boxes. The squibs—

LT. RHODES: Squibs?

HOLLAND: That's what the students call these free writings, squibs.

Anyway, we circulate these squibs to one another and analyze them. And I do them myself, of course. I have to do what they do, otherwise they feel threatened.

The squibs for a given week are supposed to be in all the seminar members' mailboxes by Monday noon so that we'll have enough time on Monday afternoon or all day Tuesday to read everybody else's writing before the seminar meets at 9:00 a.m. Wednesday.

LT. RHODES: Now tell me about this mystery student.

HOLLAND: After the first meeting of the seminar, I circulated in the mailboxes of the group a list of the people in the seminar to let them know which mailboxes to put responses in. I include on this list everybody's phone number so that we can reach one another if there's some problem about getting papers or if the seminar is canceled or whatever. Evidently, he got hold of that list. Ever since, he's been filching responses out of the boxes and putting in his own—in general, mixing into the seminar. That wouldn't be hard, because the mailboxes are just pigeonholes, open to everybody. Faculty, students, and secretaries are in the mailroom all the time putting stuff in the boxes or taking stuff out.

LT. RHODES: You said "he."

HOLLAND: We know it's a he, because the three women in the seminar got anonymous phone calls. The caller tried to get them to go out with him. They say they haven't. It's very annoying, but, I believe, nothing serious. They tell me his language doesn't go beyond the flirtatious, the ineptly flirtatious. I have no idea who he is, but you'll have to include him in the seminar group, I suppose, Lieutenant, although obviously he wasn't there this morning.

LT. RHODES: Is that so obvious? Wouldn't it be easy for one of the regular people to pretend to be this interloper? That might be why you haven't seen this person putting things in the boxes.

HOLLAND: I guess that would be possible, Lieutenant. It hadn't occurred to me that anyone would want to. After all, if you're in the group, you can say just about anything you want in our discussions. This guy is doing most of the work for the seminar but getting no academic credit. And he's another disruptive element, like Hassler.

LT. RHODES: You've had your troubles this semester. Well, while I wait for the M.E.'s report, I might just as well work down your list. That means I start with Aval. Would you go downstairs and send him up here?

HOLLAND: Sure.END OF THIS SECTION OF TAPE END OF THIS SECTION OF TAPE END OF THIS SECTION OF TAPE END OF THIS SECTION

LT. RHODES: *Comment.* Just for the record, Holland is in his mid-fifties, I'd say, about 145 pounds, very bald, hazel eyes, bifocals, big, long nose, unusually small ears. No marks that I could see. Dark brown Harris tweed jacket, worn suede boots, blue workshirt, no tie. I guess that's a thing of the past.

I wonder why he's pushing the idea that Hassler died a natural death. The paramedics said it looked fishy, not your ordinary stroke or coronary. I wish Robbie Welder would hurry up.

It's weird being back in an English department. It all comes washing back over me from college. Phrases, quotations, names, voices, mannerisms. I'm being taken over. I'm beginning to talk like Holland. I'd better not. I won't have any credibility in the unit if I start sounding like an English teacher. But how different this place is from the School of Drama.

Yes, come in, Sergeant.

SGT. YORRICK: Christian Aval, Lieutenant.

AVAL: Good morning, sir. Here are my passport and my identity papers, also my student visa and my social security card. They are all in order, I believe.

LT. RHODES: M. Aval, it doesn't work quite that way here. In this country, we don't have a dossier, like the system of identity papers in France. Here we are more interested in you than your papers. Just sit down and tell me what you witnessed this morning. But first, would you be so kind, M. Aval, as to indicate that you accept that you are being tape recorded.

AVAL: Forgive me, Lieutenant, may I be permitted a slightly ironic assertion of my theoretical position? I would make the claim that I cannot be recorded in the mode you indicate. That is, language flees, leaving behind only traces of disparate and destabilized meanings. No effort to fix it can succeed. But in your sense, not mine, you are indeed tape-recording me, and I accept that.

LT. RHODES: Thank you for that clarification, M. Aval, or should I say obfuscation? If I may be ironic myself.

Tell me what you saw this morning.

AVAL: We had assembled for this rather strange seminar. You must understand, Lieutenant, that there is absolutely nothing like this in French literary studies, nothing like these reader-response theories of Professor Holland. Absolutely. Patricia Hassler was to be the focus of the discussion, and she was late. All the rest of us had placed ourselves around the table. Finally she appeared in the frame of the door and looked down at all of us.

I felt uncomfortable as she stood there. I wished to be someplace else. I wondered, as I often did with Patricia Hassler, How am I to situate in my thinking this woman who is so big, so fat, so unhealthy, so angry? I always felt about her that she stood for some trick, some contradiction, here, in American life or American literature or the American relations between the genders. I was a little curious to explore her secret. Although I know that that is impossible, finally. We cannot even know ourselves, to say nothing of other people. Whatever Professor Holland says.

In any case, she looked at us all. She walked to the end of the table where she had put her books. She sat down. She fell over. She was dead. Just like that. It was fast, just like that.

LT. RHODES: When did you come into the room?

AVAL: Actually, she was already standing in the doorway when I came up the stairs to the seminar, and I had to budge past her to get to the table and sit down.

LT. RHODES: She spoke to you as she sat down, didn't she?

AVAL: Ah yes, Lieutenant, I forgot to mention that. Perhaps she was speaking to me. More probably, she was speaking about me to the others. She stood for a moment behind my chair, and she said, "Him. He is the one."

LT. RHODES: What did she mean?

AVAL: I do not know what she meant. I am sorry I did not mention it.

LT. RHODES: *Why* did you not mention this?

AVAL: You must forgive me, Lieutenant, my mind is such that it neglects what it cannot grasp. It, as you say, slipped my mind. I am sorry, but, of course, you have heard about it from others. That is obvious, isn't it? I could not possibly have hidden this event from you. It is in the range of forgetting honestly, if there can be such a thing.

LT. RHODES: Do you have any idea if anyone might have wanted to kill her?

AVAL: *Merde!* You think this was murder? But how?

No assuredly, I do not know that anyone wanted to kill her. She was not at all an agreeable person, you understand, but we cannot kill people for that reason.

LT. RHODES: What else can you tell me about Patricia Hassler?

AVAL: Lieutenant, I have told you all I know. To me she remains a mystery, a mystery I did not penetrate.

LT. RHODES: No pun intended.

AVAL: What? Oh. Well, it would be indiscreet of me, Lieutenant, to answer that with either of the two possibilities. Unless you insist.

LT. RHODES: I will not insist.

AVAL: You should realize, Lieutenant, that she was not so heavy at Yale.

LT. RHODES: That's right! You two were at Yale together. Did you know her there?

AVAL: Again, I assume, you do not intend the biblical sense of that verb in English. Certainly, I knew her by sight. I tended to keep apart, to myself, while I was at Yale. She did also.

LT. RHODES: Can you tell me anything about her career at Yale?

AVAL: She worked in literary theory, as I did, but then everyone was doing that at Yale. The place was famous for it.

LT. RHODES: Not the School of Drama.

AVAL: What?

LT. RHODES: Nothing. Go on.

AVAL: We were in two seminars together. She was well thought of by the profs, and one of the papers I heard her give in one seminar was very good. But when it came time for us to do our senior theses, she did not present a thesis at all. That caused her some trouble.

LT. RHODES: What kind of trouble?

AVAL: You see, she had signed up to write a thesis. If she were not going to write one, she would have had to do other work in its place. By failing to turn one in, she had evaded some requirements. She was not able to continue in graduate work at Yale.

LT. RHODES: How do you happen to be in Buffalo, New York?

AVAL: My name is Christian Aval. I was born in Cassis, December 7, 1961. I attended the local schools, and I took my *bachot* at the Lycée Alphonse Thiers in Marseille. I came to Paris to university, Paris Eight, as we called it, the radical branch of the University of Paris, where one could study with some of the most brilliant figures to evolve from the *événements* of 1968, Jacques Lacan, Hélène Cixous, Julia Kristeva—do these names mean anything to you, Lieutenant?

LT. RHODES: Sorry.

AVAL: In the course of my studies, I read some American theorists, and in 1980, I applied to Yale University to come over here and study American literary theory. And then I shifted once more and came here to SUNY/Buffalo to continue my studies. Yes, I, at least the pronoun I, am truly, as we say in structural linguistics, a shifter.

LT. RHODES: If I knew anything about structural linguistics, I might enjoy your wit, M. Aval. But Cassis, Paris, New Haven, Buffalo—you have indeed shifted your ground. Why didn't you stay on at Yale?

AVAL: Because the people I had come to study with were all dispersed. Paul de Man died. There were rumors that Hillis Miller was looking for a different university. Geoffrey Hartman and Harold Bloom began to do more of their work in New York. I shifted to this university because it was, in many ways, a more interesting department than Yale had become.

LT. RHODES: An unusual career move.

AVAL: I am always a shifter. As Baudelaire said, "Il me semble que je serais toujours bien là où je ne suis pas."

LT. RHODES: Do I have that right? I would translate it, It seems to me that I will be always happy in the place where I am not.

AVAL: Yes, that is a good translation. If I were translating it, I think I would be both more free and more severe. "Wherever I am not is the place where I am happy." To my ear that sounds more of today. Yours is a more gracious translation. Perhaps we would say in American, "mellow." But is that all, Lieutenant?

LT. RHODES: Yes, M. Aval. Do not leave the city without informing the police. That's particularly important for you, because you are here on a student visa. Here's my card. Please telephone me if anything occurs to you that you think would assist the police in their investigations.

AVAL: Thank you, sir. Good day.

LT. RHODES: *Comments.* The Aval interview. He's an ingratiating young man, but, to use his own word, shifty. He certainly dodged round the question of their relationship at Yale. And the way he hinted at sex, and then canceled it out. In describing the events of the morning, he omitted two things that bear on himself. That Hassler accused him of something—if that's what her speech means. That he had to brush right by Hassler when he came in. Well, we don't know yet that this is homicide. There's only that paramedic's saying that this doesn't look like a heart attack or stroke. But she's young for those things. Not your basic senior citizen.

For the record, he's about five foot seven. About 140 pounds. Dark brown hair cut short and his eyes are dark brown. Wears aviator-style glasses. No marks, no facial hair. A scar over his right eyebrow. And a French accent, of course.

He knew her before she came here. How well? Does that make any difference anyway? Then Hassler's troubles at Yale. They might have some bearing.

How touchy Aval was about the tape recorder and his phrasings and translating the Baudelaire. And how involved they all are in this literary theory! END OF THIS SECTION OF TAPE END OF THIS SECTION OF TAPE END OF THIS SECTION OF TAPE END OF THIS SECTION

SGT. YORRICK: Lieutenant, there's one serious-looking lady out here insists on seeing you. Says she's Professor Romola Badger. Says she's "chairperson" of this department.

LT. RHODES: Send her in, Sergeant.

BADGER: Lieutenant Rhodes, I hate to break in on your interrogations, but rumors are *flying* around the department, the whole building, the whole university for all I know. The Homicide Unit in Rhodes Hall! Please, I need your help in calming the situation. What can I *say* to quell these rumblings?

LT. RHODES: Sit down, Professor Badger. You'll notice that I'm tape-recording you—a new departmental rule.

BADGER: Your department no doubt establishes its routines as my own does.

LT. RHODES: A few minutes after eight this morning, Patricia Hassler walked into Professor Holland's seminar, sat down, collapsed, and died. Homicide has to investigate until we can show definitely that this was not a homicide. This is purely MBPD routine.

BADGER: But what can I tell the students and faculty?

LT. RHODES: What I've just told you.

BADGER: *Surely* there is more.

LT. RHODES: It's scarcely an hour since Hassler died.

BADGER: You cannot imagine, Lieutenant, how rumors *race* around a campus. They can utterly poison the university's image or the department's. That's why it's so important to keep them in bounds. Particularly in view of Professor Holland's *peculiar* teaching methods.

But I am sure you will do everything you can to help, Lieutenant. Is there anything I can do for you?

LT. RHODES: Not at the moment, Professor Badger, but I'd be grateful if you could remain available in your office.

BADGER: Certainly, Lieutenant. That is my morning habit, in any case. Should I put out a memorandum stating what you have just told me?

LT. RHODES: If you wish, Professor Badger. I will talk to you again later, as soon as we know more. Sergeant, bring in Max Ebenfeld.

BADGER: Surely, you can't suspect Max Ebenfeld!

LT. RHODES: Anybody and everybody, Professor Badger.

LT. RHODES: *Comment.* I remember reading in the paper about this statuesque lady when she was appointed chair. Well, I suppose she can't have had much to do with Patricia Hassler, first-year graduate student.

Here comes Ebenfeld. I'd better put in a new tape. END OF THIS SECTION OF TAPE END OF THIS SECTION OF TAPE END OF THIS

Metropolitan Buffalo Police Department

Tape Transcription   Homicide Unit

Body: *Hassler, P.*   Tape No. *840307.014*
Place: *Rhodes Hall, UB*   Time: *10:56 a.m.*
Persons present: *Det. Lt. Rhodes, M. Ebenfeld, A. Glendish*

Transcribed by: *B. J. Saik*

LT. RHODES: Come in, Mr. Ebenfeld. Sit down, if you would. This shouldn't take long.

EBENFIELD: Yes, sir, Lieutenant.

LT. RHODES: "Max." Is that short for Maximilian?

EBENFELD: No, Maxfield. That was my mother's maiden name. I have one name from her and the other from my father.

LT. RHODES: Say, in your own words, what happened this morning.

EBENFELD: Well, we all got to the seminar on time. We'd figured today to be pretty unruly, with Trish going to give us all hell probably, for what we had written to her about her responses. We were sitting around chatting, fidgeting a little, I suppose. She finally appeared and stood in the doorway, looking us over. She was a big woman, was Trish. I think she must have been about six feet with weight to match, more than two-twenty easy.

LT. RHODES: You yourself are no shrimp, Mr. Ebenfeld.

EBENFELD: Six even. Just a hundred and eighty-three pounds. I keep my weight down with workouts, and I do weights.

Anyway, she stood there, big, heavy Trish, and she marched down the room. Then there was something I didn't understand. She stopped behind Christian Aval's head and said something like, "He's the one. He's the one," and then she squeezed herself down in her chair. Holland's chair, really, but Trish had put her books there. She was going to be boss today. I could hear the floor creak as she went by. Clump, she sat down. I could almost feel it. She couldn't have sat there for more than twenty seconds or so, before she fell. Her head hit the table, and she fell over onto the floor. I wanted to pick her up or at least straighten her out. I couldn't stand the way she was lying there all every which way. Norm, Professor Holland, that is, stopped me. Rightly so.

LT. RHODES: What do you think caused her death, Mr. Ebenfeld?

EBENFELD: Stroke. Heart attack. Something sudden like that. Trish looked unhealthy, as though her parents had given her all the wrong stuff when she was growing up. Fats and carbs. Poor people's food. She wrote once about her family being poor. I always felt she was in bad health. All that weight. And she smoked. I don't imagine she ate the right food at all, and I never saw a sign of any exercise. Full of hostility.

LT. RHODES: What happened after she fell over?

EBENFELD: We all crowded round her body. Paul checked the pulse in her throat—he's had CPR training—and he said, "She's dead." Norm kept pushing us away from the body. Finally he took the seminar across the hall and closed the door to the seminar room. He sent Paul off to call Security, and he put me in front of the door to the seminar room. I kept the gawkers out.

LT. RHODES: What did you think of her?

EBENFELD: Well, I didn't like her, that's for sure. None of us did. But I feel sad about her dying this young. I don't think she had had much of a life. She could have been good-looking if she had done something about her weight and if she wore some decent-looking clothes. She was always bundled up—well, you have to bundle up in this climate—but she wore huge rolls of scarves and woollens.

LT. RHODES: Do you think anyone might have wanted to kill her, Mr. Ebenfeld?

EBENFELD: I think she was taking her frustrations out on the rest of us. You could be angry at her for that, but it was better to be sorry for her. I can't think that anyone would want to kill her.

Holland must have disliked her more than any of us. She was really unpleasant to him, bordering on downright rudeness. But surely that wasn't enough to tip the scales and make someone actually act against her—kill her.

LT. RHODES: Tell me about these arguments with Holland.

EBENFELD: She argued with Holland a lot about theory. In the seminar she was always dragging the discussion off onto her deconstructionist stuff. Not my thing. Too thin and airy for me.

LT. RHODES: And what is your thing? Tell me a little about yourself.

EBENFELD: There's not much to tell, Lieutenant. With me, what you see is what you get. I grew up in Olean, about 75 miles south of here, almost down to the Pennsylvania border. When I came here as an undergraduate, I really went in for sports. I majored in phys. ed., but then in my junior year I began to face up to reality. I wasn't going to make a living at sports—I just wasn't in that league. I thought I might like to teach, but I'd rather teach in a school than a college or university. I like the idea of being both a teacher and a coach. I suppose you'd call it shaping both the body and the mind. So I thought I'd go on for my M.A., probably in American lit.

Then I took a seminar in the eighteenth century—English—and I got hooked on Gray, Collins, Goldsmith, Dr. Johnson, Miss Burney. I liked their quiet steady style, their morality, their seriousness. It was not only a great literary period, looking forward to Austen and the romantics, but the beginning of the industrial revolution. Up there in Scotland, they were putting coal and water and ore together and building these pumps and steam engines and beautiful cast iron bridges. There was the antislavery movement. The Scottish aestheticians. It was a great period—that's all I can say.

LT. RHODES: And this seminar? It's not in the eighteenth century.

EBENFELD: This seminar is perfect for me, because it doesn't wander off into a lot of fancy theory. I'm getting to understand the way people read things, and that's what I need to know if I'm going to teach in a high school. Leave the theory and the fancy criticism and the esoteric literary history for the guys that want to teach graduate students. I like to think of myself molding young minds and bodies. That may sound old-fashioned, but it's what I want to do. And I think I could persuade high school kids to like Dr. Johnson. Maybe you think that's silly.

LT. RHODES: Who's to say, Mr. Ebenfeld? You can go now, but stay with the seminar group in the room across the hall, please. And would you ask the next person—Anne Glendish—to step down here? Thank you.

EBENFELD: Yes, certainly, Lieutenant.END OF THIS SECTION OF TAPE END OF THIS SECTION OF TAPE END OF THIS SECTION OF TAPE END

LT. RHODES: *Comment.* Dr. Johnson! Would you believe! Dr. Johnson for today's adolescent. Will Dr. Johnson ever replace Nintendo? Metallica? Hip-hop?

Okay, Mr. Maxfield Ebenfeld. Is that an oxymoron? Jewish? Half-Jewish? A real straight arrow, anyway. He told me: six foot, 183 pounds. Big muscles, big features—that nose! Wiry black hair. No marks, except for his whole body. He really stands out.

What you see is what you get, he says. Maybe so. He looks like the kind of person you take one look at and you trust him. In later life, he's the one they choose to raise money for the symphony or to direct the United Way Campaign. Or he turns that solid look into a con and sells phony bonds.

Yes?

GLENDISH: I'm Anne Glendish, Lieutenant.

LT. RHODES: How do you do. Please sit down.

GLENDISH: Thank you.

LT. RHODES: Would you acknowledge, please, Ms. Glendish, that this interview is being tape-recorded?

GLENDISH: You're taping me. Is that what you wanted me to say?

LT. RHODES: Precisely. Ms. Glendish, please say in your own words what happened in the Delphi seminar this morning.

GLENDISH: I came in and I sat down. Then—

LT. RHODES: Just a moment. Who else was in the room when you came in?

GLENDISH: No one. When Paul and I came in, no one.

LT. RHODES: You came in with Paul—is it Penza?

GLENDISH: Yes. To both. It looked nice out, so Paul and I left the apartment early.

LT. RHODES: This was your apartment or his?

GLENDISH: Mine, but Paul lives with me.

LT. RHODES: Well. About this morning. You were the first to arrive.

GLENDISH: Yes. No. There was nobody there when Paul and I came in, but there was a stack of books on the table. I assumed it was Norm's—

LT. RHODES: Professor Holland's?—

GLENDISH: —yes, Norm's, because it was where he usually sits at the head of the table. Later, when Paul and I came back, I realized they were Trish's books. I remember thinking, I wouldn't do that, but Trish would. It's just part of her nastiness, and then I thought, maybe not. Maybe she's just trying to change things round a little, and that's all right. I could do that. And it's her day to be "it," so maybe she's entitled to shake the seminar up a little. She always does, anyway.

LT. RHODES: What do you mean, "It was her day to be 'it'"?

GLENDISH: Did Norm tell you how this seminar works?

LT. RHODES: No.

GLENDISH: It's pretty complicated. You better get him to explain the theory. In practice, it works this way. For the first six or seven weeks, he assigns various poems and stories. He has us write responses to them and we put them in mailboxes for the rest of the seminar. We're supposed to, I guess you'd say, free associate. He says, Say whatever comes into your mind. He *doesn't* want us to do the regular kind of literary analysis that we do in other classes. In fact, he marks you down if you do that.

Let me tell you, that part is pretty strange. Nobody had ever asked me to do that before in a literature class, just say any old thing. I think we were all a little frightened to be revealing so much of ourselves. But, after a while, that part of the seminar got to be fun.

LT. RHODES: What's this about Hassler being "it"?

GLENDISH: That's the second half. That's when it gets touchy. About the middle of the semester, he turns the process around. Each week the text we write about is what one of the people in the seminar has written. We call that being "it,'" like in hide-and-seek. This week Trish was "it."

LT. RHODES: I understand, I think. All right, what happened this morning? Who came in after you and Paul Penza?

GLENDISH: I'm not sure. You see, once Paul and I came in and put our books down at our places, we went out.

LT. RHODES: Why was that?

GLENDISH: We thought it was a nice day for a walk.

LT. RHODES: You've got to be kidding. March in Buffalo and you go for a walk?

GLENDISH: To me, today was a study in gray and black and white. There's the gray sky, the black of the bare tree trunks, the gray of the old snow dusted with the black dust they make us breathe, the white of the new snow . . . You're looking at me oddly.

LT. RHODES: That way of looking out a Buffalo window in winter would not have occurred to me.

GLENDISH: Sometimes I like to imagine these gray landscapes as the setting for a fashion photograph. Some glamorous model in a brilliant red gown standing in front of the black tree trunks or the different grays in the stone blocks of the older buildings, like this one.

LT. RHODES: When did you come back to the seminar room?

GLENDISH: At 9:00 sharp. I was watching the time.

LT. RHODES: Penza came with you?

GLENDISH: Yes.

LT. RHODES: And who was there then?

GLENDISH: By then they were all there. No, not all. Trish came last, of course. We had to wait for her. More nastiness, I thought. I remember, when all the students had come in, Norm was standing by the window, as he often does. He sat down. Then Trish suddenly appeared in the doorway. She stood there in her usual theatrical get-up and looked us all over. She was so angry! I remember I couldn't stand to look at her, and began shuffling books. And then I thought, What the hey! A cat can look at a king—or a queen. Then she whipped off her coat—that's the only word for it, "whipped," and tossed it on top of the pile of coats in the corner. We all watched her walk the length of the table and sit herself down. She stopped behind Chris's chair, and she said, "Him. Him. He's the one I was talking about."

LT. RHODES: Aval?

GLENDISH: Yes. Wait a minute. I almost forgot. As Trish was standing in the doorway, Chris came past her and into the room and sat down.

LT. RHODES: So he had not been in the room when she appeared in the doorway.

GLENDISH: No. He squeezed past her and sat down. She watched him do that. Then she took off her coat, walked to her chair, and sat down. The minute she sat down, she looked at us in this funny way. I'd say she looked at us as though we were way off in the distance somewhere. Then she pitched forward and onto the floor. She lay there like a great messy pile of old clothes. I remember the sound her beads made when she fell.

LT. RHODES: What happened then?

GLENDISH: Paul—he was sitting at her right—bent over her and felt her pulse and after a minute or so he looked up and he just said, "She's dead," and she was. Paul has had some first-aid and CPR training. We all sat there, scared, shocked. Nobody knew what to do. Then Norm said, "Everybody stay where you are. Paul, go find a campus phone and call Security." Paul got up and went out into the hall. I could hear him talking to somebody in an open office and telephoning. He came back, and we just sat there and waited.

A bunch of campus policemen came in—suddenly the room was full of them. And a couple of guys in white uniforms, paramedics, I guess. They rolled her over— Oh God, her face was awful. Her mouth was drawn up in this awful crazy-looking smile. The paramedics checked her and just looked at one another. You could see they had decided she was dead. It was numbing, the feeling that she would never look at you again, never speak to you again, never again be a presence. They were going to roll her over onto a stretcher, but one of the campus cops stopped them.

LT. RHODES: Okay, Ms. Glendish. The rest is history or at least public knowledge.

As I explained in the other room, Ms. Glendish, we don't know yet what caused Patricia Hassler's death. Do you know of anyone who would want her dead?

GLENDISH: I don't know anybody who would kill her, but, let's face it, I don't know anybody who liked her, either. She was a pretty horrible person. She made a mess of this seminar, taunting Norm and arguing with him, and she was hard on the rest of us. Very hard.

The time she took up! Oh, I remember us all sitting on those hard old Windsor chairs and thinking, Why won't she stop! Why won't they stop! They put a little rubber mat on those chairs, you know, but it really doesn't help. Your fanny gets sore, and the slats dig into your back.

Aside from the seminar, I didn't know her. In fact, I gave her a wide berth. Oops! You're smiling. That wasn't meant as a joke, honest, although I guess it's funny. She was god-awful fat.

LT. RHODES: Would you mind telling me where you're from, what you're studying, why you're in this seminar, things like that?

GLENDISH: Originally, I'm from Richmond, Virginia. I wanted to get out of the East, so I went to Berkeley as an undergraduate. I was a theater major, but I couldn't make it work for me, so I gave it up. Meanwhile, I'd gotten interested in literary criticism and theory. I decided I would look good to the admissions committee here, even though my grades were not the greatest. Well, I'll be frank. I figured I could get in here, so I applied. I got interested in this seminar, because it reminded me of acting, trying to find the inner life of the character as we used to say in the Theater Department. Yes, I like this seminar, and I hated what Trish was doing to it. But not enough to kill her.

LT. RHODES: Thank you, Ms. Glendish. Here's my card. Call me if anything important occurs to you.

GLENDISH: I can remember the sound her beads made when she fell. I can hear it now, ticky-tick, and then a long scrape against the table. That's an odd thing to remember, isn't it?

LT. RHODES: Oddity is, like beauty, in the eye of the beholder, Ms. Glendish.

GLENDISH: A gracious sentiment and very reader-responsy.

LT. RHODES: Would you ask Mr. Ireland to step down here?

GLENDISH: Sure, Lieutenant.END OF THIS SECTION OF TAPE END OF THIS SECTION OF TAPE END OF THIS SECTION OF TAPE END OF THIS

LT. RHODES: *Comment.* Again the same story. Hassler antagonized everybody. Okay, okay. But I don't see any real motives here.

Description for the record. I'd put Glendish in her early twenties, about 5' 9", straight blonde hair cut in a short, sharp-edged bob, about 120 pounds, blue eyes, straight nose, thin lips. Proper tidewater accent. No marks. Black blouse, long sweeping blue skirt. Black boots with high heels. Holland is right, a dish indeed.

SGT. YORRICK: Dr. Welder on the phone for you.

LT. RHODES: Too bad. I was enjoying sitting and chatting about literature with an attractive blonde. Robbie'll put an end to that.

Metropolitan Buffalo Police Department

Tape Transcription   Homicide Unit

Body: *Hassler, P.*   Tape No. *840307.014*
Place: *Telephone call, Rhodes Hall, UB*   Time: *11:40 a.m.*
Persons present: *Det. Lt. Rhodes, Robert Welder, M.D., M.E.*

Transcribed by: *B. J. Saik*

LT. RHODES: Doc, give me a minute to hook up this dingus. *(Unrecorded dialogue from telephone.)* Okay, tell me what you've got.

DR. WELDER: As long as you're recording this, Justin, let's do it by the book. This is Dr. Robert Welder, and I'm calling from the morgue where I've been examining the body of Patricia Hassler, case number 840307/1. The victim was a large white woman in her early twenties, height 1.80 meters, 5 feet 11, weight 106 kilograms, 233 pounds. Hair dark blonde, eyes brown. No distinguishing marks. Nothing unusual about the body except for that obesity. The density of the lipoproteins suggests that the obesity was acquired recently.

This is a preliminary report only, preliminary for reasons that will become clear in a moment. I've got bad news for you, Justin, and good news. I'll give you the bad news first. She was poisoned.

LT. RHODES: Poisoned!

DR. WELDER: I'm pretty certain of it, although I'm going to have to do some special tests to be absolutely sure. Her body showed no signs of a stroke or heart attack. None. Instead, she was the victim of one of the neurotoxins. That is, she was hit with a poison that simply shut down her CNS—sorry, central nervous system. Heart, lungs, brain, everything came to an abrupt stop.

LT. RHODES: Damn! I thought they'd given me an easy one, natural death. Okay, tell me how the killer got the poison into her.

DR. WELDER: He didn't feed it to her, although I know that's what you think when you hear the word "poison." Envenomation took place through a small puncture wound, about one millimeter in diameter, on the right buttock on the dorsal surface nearest the hip joint.

LT. RHODES: You mean we're dealing with a pinprick?

DR. WELDER: Yes, that's all it takes with the purified forms of these neurotoxins. A couple of milligrams will do it. And they are fast. If the dose was large enough, we're talking a minute or two, maybe less than a minute. Maybe even half a minute.

LT. RHODES: Half a minute! But that's the minimum. Max time?

DR. WELDER: Max, about five minutes. At the absolute outside.

I found something else odd on the body, Justin. In the same area as the puncture by which the poison entered the bloodstream, that is, on the right buttock, there was another puncture wound, like the fatal one, but this one was almost healed. Was she an addict? First thing you think of. I don't think so. Not in this location. Injection at that point would not give as good a "high," and it would be hard to reach the needle around, since the lady was so fat. Although, I suppose, she could have had a fellow user do the actual injection. I leave this for you to figure out, Justin. You're the detective. I'm just the medical examiner.

LT. RHODES: Let me get this straight. You're telling me that it was nothing more than a pinprick that killed her and that she died within a minute or two of the wound.

DR. WELDER: Or even less. I'll be able to tell you more when I complete the analysis. But you should realize there's a lot of mystery around these neurotoxins. Because they work fast and use a minimum dose, they have their political uses.

RHODES: A minute or less! Then it must have been somebody in that seminar room. No, it could have been out in the hall, just before she came in.

DR. WELDER: I suppose so. Your job, not mine. If you're through with me, Justin, I'll split. I've got to get back to my cold companions here.

LT. RHODES: Hey, wait a minute! That was the bad news. What about the good news?

DR. WELDER: I almost forgot. These neurotoxins are not your rat poisons or weed killers. We're talking curare here, nerve agents, saxitoxin, tetrododoxin. These are not something you buy at the corner pharmacy or the garden supply store. The upside, then, is that once you learn who had this stuff, you've got your killer. At least that's the way I'd go on this case. Of course, you're the detective, not me.

LT. RHODES: Okay, what's the poison then? Maybe you'd better spell it for me. Let me get a pencil— God, how can anybody work at a desk this messy—

DR. WELDER: I wish I *could* spell it for you. That's some more bad news, Justin. The tests for these things are tricky, and they take time. Also, this stuff requires some special equipment that I don't have. I need to do an HPLC, and I have to have an autoanalyzer. I'll try at the university. Pop Vernor has one, I know.

LT. RHODES: What's an HPLC? What's an autoanalyzer, for that matter?

DR. WELDER: Do you really want to know?

LT. RHODES: No.

DR. WELDER: Then let me get on with the analysis, and you can get started detecting. It's going to take me at least five hours to identify the poison for you, because the tests take that long.

LT. RHODES: Five hours!

DR. WELDER: Yes, if this stuff is what I think it is, we have to try it on an actual mouse. That's *after* we've done the preliminary molecular analysis.

You know, I keep telling the commissioner the department ought to have its own autoanalyzer, and he keeps telling me he doesn't have budget for it. Now, if I could get some help from you people who would really benefit from an autoanalyzer—

LT. RHODES: Sure, Robbie. Next time I have a chance. The commissioner always does what I tell him to.

DR. WELDER: No sarcasm, please.

LT. RHODES: Doc, call me as soon as you can with the specific name, will you?

DR. WELDER: Did you think I wouldn't?

LT. RHODES: No, not really.

DR. WELDER: Okay. So I'll call you sometime this afternoon. Later rather than sooner, though.

LT. RHODES: Thanks, Doc. Later then.END OF THIS SECTION OF TAPE END OF THIS SECTION OF TAPE END OF THIS SECTION OF TAPE END

LT. RHODES: *Comment.* Poisoned! All right, that means premeditation and murder one. We're off. And I thought Robbie was going to send me back to headquarters.

Just a pinprick. Hard to believe. Am I supposed to find a pin? Still I've got to try. I don't have enough yet to search these eight people, and if we're dealing with something as small as a pin, the murderer has surely gotten rid of it by now. Even if we found it in a wastebasket, we couldn't connect it to one of them in particular. And if the murderer has gone to the john . . . But, but, but—we've got to check the room again on the odd chance.

When? Robbie says it could not be more than five minutes before death. Okay, the jackpot question. By whom? If it's within five minutes of death . . .

Opportunity. How was said pinprick administered? We're looking at the people who had contact, close physical contact with Patricia Hassler in the five minutes—five minutes maximum!—before she collapsed. Probably less. That means the people in this seminar surely, but also anyone she might have met out in the hall. Or Aval, brushing past her, could have done it. I guess. Wouldn't she have squawked?

Wait a minute. She came in before anybody else—as far as we know. She put her books down and disappeared for a good twenty minutes, so it could have been anyone or anywhere. Where did she go when she went out? Whom did she meet?

Motive. Everybody and nobody. Nothing on motive yet.

Means. Who had access to the poison? First we have to know what it is. So my best move—God, my only move!—is to wait for Welder to identify the poison. He's surely right. If it's some fancy neurotoxin, it's got to be easy to trace. Until he identifies the poison, I'm thrown back on motive, so I think I do best to continue this low-key questioning. These interviews at least keep the students all in one place. Damn, I wish I had more physical evidence to go on.

Ireland must be waiting in the hall.

LT. RHODES: Come in, Mr. Ireland, sit down.

IRELAND: Yes sir, Lieutenant. Damn. It's been a bunch of time since I called anybody that.

LT. RHODES: You were in Vietnam?

IRELAND: Fuckin' A. I was over there when being a lieutenant wasn't the safest thing you could be. Safer here in peaceful old Buffalo. Where you were, right, Lieutenant?

LT. RHODES: Buffalo might surprise you, Mr. Ireland. Would you mind saying you know you're being tape-recorded?

IRELAND: Hell, yes, I mind. What the fuck ever happened to privacy and minding your own business in this country?

LT. RHODES: You mind. Do you refuse?

IRELAND: Would it do me any good if I did? What's the use? Go ahead, Lieutenant. You've got your job to do, as the saying goes.

LT. RHODES: What did you do after Vietnam?

IRELAND: I spent twenty-seven months in a V.A. hospital. Detox and dry-out. I'm an alcoholic, you see, in remission. One day at a time, if that. Don't get me wrong. It wasn't Nam that did it to me. I was doing drugs and booze before I enlisted. Saigon just gave me a wider arena for my activities. As wide as the fat lady at the circus. As wide as Trish Hassler. I guess that's what I was thinking of. Holland gets you listening to yourself, and I did a lot of that in that V.A. hospital. Group therapy.

After I got out and got dried out, I worked for another vet, a guy who dealt army surplus. He liked me. Charlie Ackerman. Charlie Ack-ack, everybody called him. His war was Korea. I put the money I had on discharge into the business, and we branched out into junk. Mostly cars and car parts, but other stuff too. Old machine tools, farm equipment.

LT. RHODES: The occasional weapon?

IRELAND: Hell, Lieutenant, you know that'd be ille-e-e-e-gal. We wouldn't do that.

LT. RHODES: Continue.

IRELAND: That is one tough business. Competitive? You wouldn't believe. I think old Ack-ack got some of his stock out of our competitors' yards at night. They sure as hell tried to get some of theirs out of our lot. After a while Ack-ack decided to retire, and by that time, 1983, I'd made enough to buy him out.

LT. RHODES: What on earth brought you to graduate school in English?

IRELAND: In the early days Ack-ack and I were short of money. I doubled up as night watchman. The dog and I'd sit around the yard all night. That's how I know about our competition trying to steal from us. Trying, not succeeding. I'd had plenty of practice listening to people try to sneak up on me.

After Nam, I couldn't sleep well, and I shouldn't have been sleeping anyway. So I'd read, and I really got into it. Liked it. No TV either. Found I could care about books and ideas. Debate. Rebut. I like to argue. It's fun.

I guess I can make a living at it once I get out. If not, well, it's back to the junkyard. I've got a guy who manages it while I'm in school. It pays my way.

LT. RHODES: An unusual form of financial aid. Tell me what you saw this morning.

IRELAND: Not much to tell. Trish was "it."

LT. RHODES: "It."

IRELAND: Didn't Holland explain that to you? This was Trish's day to chew us all out for what we wrote about her. We all got there early. You bet we did. We were sitting around the table, making that innocent-sounding small talk that grad students do when they're nervous. Did anybody tell you, Lieutenant, how competitive this place really is? Sweetness and light it's not. Some of these people would do *anything* to make it big in this teeny-tiny litcrit world. Trish was one of those, a wild card in our little troop, wildly ambitious, wildly bitchy.

Anyway, Trish came to the door. She'd staked out Holland's chair by putting her gear there. She looked down at him. Then she looked down at the rest of us. I tell you, Lieutenant, if looks could kill, you'd have had eight body bags going out that door, not just one.

Then she stood behind Frenchy's chair and she pointed a finger at him like a revolver, you know? Bang, bang. She said something like, "He's the one," like he was the mark and she was the holdup man. Then she sat down, and pitched over dead. Like a sniper took somebody out. You just watch and they're gone. I haven't seen anything like that in a while.

LT. RHODES: Would anybody have any reason to kill her?

IRELAND: Every damn one of us, but we weren't going to, were we? Poor old Holland. She'd ride him something terrible. She was always laying deconstruction on him, Derrida, all that French crap. Decockstruction, I call it.

God, she was piss and vinegar. There were times when I thought he'd blow his stack. I sure as hell would have. Frag her. Fuck her. She was one prize bitch.

LT. RHODES: Well, on that note, Mr. Ireland . . .

IRELAND: Happy hunting, Lieutenant.

LT. RHODES: Tell Amy Lemaire to come down here.

IRELAND: Yes, *sir!* END OF THIS SECTION OF TAPE END OF THIS SECTION OF TAPE END OF THIS SECTION OF TAPE END OF THIS SEC

LT. RHODES: *Comment on Ireland interview.* Smiling and grinning, but all that hostility! The hair, the red bandanna—he comes right out of Elizabethan psychology: Harry Hotspur, the choleric man. Five-six, 140, red hair, blue eyes, ruddy complexion, some acne scars, muscular. He swings between hair-trigger reactions and studied casualness. Weapons, sniping, wasting, fragging, fucking. He could have killed Hassler as coolly as he'd step on a cockroach. He wouldn't change the expression on his face from that grin that half says, "I could be real mean to you, friend," and half, "I don't care enough to bother." But he's not the poisoning type. And motive?

I guess I need another tape.

Metropolitan Buffalo Police Department

Tape Transcription   Homicide Unit

Body: *Hassler, P.*   Tape No. *840307.019*
Place: *Telephone call, Rhodes Hall, UB*   Time: *11:58 a.m.*
Persons present: *Det. Lt. Rhodes; A. Lemaire, Professor N. Holland, P. Penza*

Transcribed by: *M. Windham*

LT. RHODES: Please sit down.

LEMAIRE: Thank you, Lieutenant Rhodes.

LT. RHODES: Let's do the formalities, Ms. Lemaire. Say that you're letting yourself be taped.

LEMAIRE: I'm letting myself be taped.

LT. RHODES: Now, tell me a bit about yourself.

LEMAIRE: I'm a graduate student here. I'm taking Professor Holland's seminar. That sort of thing?

LT. RHODES: Yes.

LEMAIRE: But now I'm stuck. What do you want me to say?

LT. RHODES: How long have you been a student here? What did you do before you were a student?

LEMAIRE: You've noticed that I'm a bit older than the other students. More than a bit, I guess, and I only went to a community college, not a regular four-year school. After I got out of Erie County Community College, I took a job at USAir as a flight attendant—stewardess, we called ourselves then. They trained me, and I worked for them for eleven years.

I liked it. I liked taking care of people, feeling that I was the person responsible for their safety and well-being, and I liked the travel. I liked being part of a comradeship of the air. I can see you think that's a corny phrase, and it is, but can you think of a better way of saying it? It was the feeling of coming into a strange airport, and there'd be the locker rooms for the crew, and I'd have instant friends—pilots, engineers, other flight attendants, all part of a big, friendly club. It was like having family wherever you were.

After I'd been with USAir for eleven years, I'd built up some leave time and some airfare, and I took a sort of sabbatical. I spent six months in England, and that was where I got interested in teaching literature.

You could say it all started with moss. There was something so green about England, and finally I decided it was the way, in that damp climate, moss or lichen would grow just about anywhere. There'd be this gray stone, on a cathedral, say, and all over it, lichen growing or moss among the headstones. Nowadays you'd say that it was just Thatcherian decay, but then I felt it was a sort of kindness, that out of something as cold as stone could come that gentle green. It symbolized for me something about England and especially something about English education. I got interested and I made some contacts, and I was able to see how they taught in English schools and colleges. I was pleased with the tutorial system, the professor working with students one on one or one on two or three. I was fascinated with the Leicestershire system of teaching in schools, where the kids who learn the lesson first teach it to the ones who're slower. It all seemed so— what shall I say?—giving. It was certainly different from Erie County Community College, let me tell you, where the teachers were just doing their job, and the students were just trying to fill requirements. This was a companionable kind of learning and teaching. I was interested and impressed, and I decided to do something about it when I got back to the States.

I worked for some more years until I built up my savings, and then I quit. The State University of New York had a program where they gave you credits for "life experience," and on that basis I managed to enter SUNY/ Buffalo and finish my bachelor's degree in two semesters. I headed on to graduate school to get a master's and teach, maybe in a community college—anyway, someplace where I could try to put into practice the kind of teaching I'd admired in England. That's what I'm doing in graduate school.

As for this seminar, I heard that Holland was a pretty big name, so I decided to take his course. And it's been fascinating. Really mind-opening. I think I'm finally understanding something about the way people read, how they take a book inside them, what goes on in their heads. Other seminars, they talk a lot about reading, but it's all made up.

LT. RHODES: "Made up"?

LEMAIRE: Speculation. They talk as though they know what goes on when people read poems or stories, but they don't really know. Here, we look at real readers. Anyway, that's what I'm doing in this seminar. I think I gave you more than you bargained for.

LT. RHODES: I don't mind, Ms. Lemaire. To the inquiring mind, it's all interesting, and I like getting people to talk about themselves. Now, what did you see this morning?

LEMAIRE: I could see that Trish's books marked out her place at the table, really Norm's place—Professor Holland's place. I wouldn't have done that myself, but that was Trish, always pushing, always testing, and she must have felt particularly pushy today, because she was "it." We'd all settled into our seats before she arrived. She stood for a long minute, framed by the door. She looked at us, and we looked at her. She walked around the table. Then she stopped behind Chris's chair—Christian, he's the French student in the seminar—and she said, "Him. He's the one I'm telling you about." Then she sat down where her books were. And then it was as though her mouth caved in. And her body, her big body, she was tall and, oh, so fat—all of her just caved in. Folded in on herself.

LT. RHODES: How did you feel?

LEMAIRE: Shaken. I thought to myself, That poor, wretched woman. She was emotionally unhealthy. She seemed angry all the time, and everyone was graveled by her.

LT. RHODES: Would anyone have any reason to kill her?

LEMAIRE: Kill her? I think we all killed her. Trish was a very troubling person, and we all ran away from her. Someone should have put her arm around Trish and just held her and said, "Trish, it's all right. It's going to be all right." She needed support, but we didn't give it to her. We couldn't. She wanted us to hate her, and we did. We couldn't help it, and she played on that. I think she felt that if we hated her, then she was justified in hating us and being as nasty to us as she was. We shouldn't have, but I don't see how we could help it. That's why I say we all killed her. And Trish herself, most of all.

LT. RHODES: Thank you, Ms. Lemaire. That'll be all.

LEMAIRE: Shall I send the next person down? If you're proceeding alphabetically, that would be Paul Penza.

LT. RHODES: No. As it happens, I want to ask Professor Holland some things. thank you. Would you ask him to come back here?

LEMAIRE: Sure.END OF THIS SECTION OF TAPE END OF THIS SECTION OF TAPE END OF THIS SECTION OF TAPE END OF THIS SECTION OF TAPE END OF THIS SECTION

LT. RHODES: *Comments on Lemaire interview.* Moss! I've got a body on my hands, and I'm sitting here listening to this lady tell me about moss.

    Amy Lemaire. Five-two, 120, brown hair, brown eyes, stocky build. No distinguishing marks. No motive evident, at least no more than anyone else's. I sense a real motherliness in this small, round woman. I wonder why she never got married. It seems an almost inevitable role for her, and she's certainly attractive enough. I have the feeling I'd like to protect her from the ugliness of the Hassler woman and her death, and I suppose most men would feel that way. A feeling to be distrusted.

LT. RHODES: I got you back, Professor, because there are some things I don't understand. Your students refer to Hassler as being "it." She dies on the day she's "it." They tried to explain it to me, but I'd like to hear from you how this seminar works.

HOLLAND: I warn you, this involves some literary theory. Do you really want to get into this?

LT. RHODES: I think I have to.

HOLLAND: Okay, here goes. This is a seminar in reader-response theory. We try to observe how people read and respond to stories, poems, movies—yes, plays, too. That sounds complicated, but it starts from a very familiar phenomenon.

    You and I go to see a play, say, *The Taming of the Shrew.* You come out of the theater with a certain feeling toward the performance, a certain opinion about it, a certain understanding. How does that happen? And why? How can we think about it?

LT. RHODES: Tell me.

HOLLAND: Differences, but, of course, there are a lot of samenesses, too. Everybody who went to the play would agree that the stars are called Katherine and Petruchio, that Petruchio pushes Katherine around a lot, that Katherine becomes a dutiful wife, and so on. Everybody hears the same lines and sees the same sets and business on stage, but reads them differently.

LT. RHODES: We see it the same. We see it differently. You're telling me the obvious.

HOLLAND: We critics need a psychological model to explain both the samenesses and the differences. The model we work with in this seminar is that members of the audience share certain techniques for understanding *The Taming of the Shrew.* Those shared techniques account for the samenesses. At the same time each person *uses* these techniques so as to meet personal needs. So they hear the lines differently. Barry Ireland may enjoy the roughhouse in the play. Amy Lemaire may enjoy the way the heroine submits at the end. Anne Glendish may enjoy the way Katharine is the center of attention.

LT. RHODES: Okay. We all respond differently, but the important things we agree about. That the heroine is named Kate. That she starts out bitchy and ends up defeated.

HOLLAND: "Defeated" is your term. Do you think Amy would see it the same way?

LT. RHODES: You tell me.

HOLLAND: I'll say it in one professorial sentence for you. Our feelings guide us as we use our language skills to make a satisfying experience out of the play. That experience is in some ways like everybody else's and in some ways like nobody else's and in some ways like some people's and not others'.

LT. RHODES: Okay, back to the seminar. People respond to literature out of personal concerns. And you teach that?

HOLLAND: For the first part of the semester, I assign various poems, stories, essays, sometimes a movie if we can arrange it. I ask the students just to write freely in response to these writings. No analysis. Just say whatever comes into their minds in connection with some particular text.

LT. RHODES: I never had a literature class like this.

HOLLAND: Most people haven't. These students get quite disconcerted, but pretty soon they get the hang of it, and then they start writing freely. It's amazing the kinds of things they'll talk about: childhood, parents, lovers, other literature, other profs. It's a little like a Rorschach test. What comes to your mind when you see this inkblot? What comes to your mind when you read this novel?

LT. RHODES: My plays as inkblot? You're saying my plays are only inkblots?

HOLLAND: No, only that what we're looking for are what a psychoanalyst would call free associations, just as if we were doing a Rorschach test.

LT. RHODES: Aren't you forcing these kids to expose very private things to one another?

HOLLAND: I always tell them to censor touchy material. We're looking for themes in their lives, not facts, not what actually happened. A Delphi seminar gets these future teachers sensitive to the patterns in their own and other people's heads when they read a story or a poem.

LT. RHODES: How do you work this out in practice?

HOLLAND: Each week each of us circulates these free responses—squibs, the students call them—to everyone else in the seminar. After a few weeks, we can all see that each of us has a characteristic way of responding. One student will relate everything to the body, another to looking, another to being looked at.

LT. RHODES: So everything is relative.

HOLLAND: Yes. Different people see different things in a poem because, to different people, different things matter. Once you collect a set of these free responses, you'll never again believe in fixed meanings or literary facts or inherent structures. At least I didn't.

LT. RHODES: So the text disappears. Are you one of these deconstructionists we used to hear about over in the School of Drama?

HOLLAND: Just the contrary, in fact. The text is very much there, because it's what your perceptions, your way of knowing things, is working on. And that's what the students learn in this seminar, their cognitive style.

LT. RHODES: By cognitive style, then, you just mean how some individual sees things as opposed to some other individual.

HOLLAND: Right. When you state the aim as cognitive style, you can see that the seminar works with very general principles of how we know things. You could use the same technique in any class, even one in homicide investigation. Wouldn't you like to know what personal needs and characteristics you bring to your work?

LT. RHODES: You're assuming I don't know.

HOLLAND: That's probably not true in your case.

LT. RHODES: So, what exactly did the students mean when they said Hassler was "it"?

HOLLAND: That's the second part of a Delphi seminar. In the first part, we write free responses to literary texts. Everybody reads everybody else's response. Then we talk about them.

At a certain point in the semester, we shift. The students call this move the "Delphi twist." Instead of a poem or story, we use, as the text to respond to, the writings that one of the individuals in the seminar has produced. We circulate free responses to those writings. The idea is to let Chris or Trish or whoever hear what the others see them bringing to the act of reading. Today was Trish's turn. She was "it," as the students say.

LT. RHODES: You mean you were going to have the rest of the students in the seminar tell this hostile, rather repellent person, what they thought of her?

HOLLAND: Not the way you make it sound. We're writing not about the person as such but about the writings they've produced. The students say things like "Trish, you use a lot of statements referring things to yourself."

LT. RHODES: Except that people tend to see what they write as extensions of themselves.

HOLLAND: True, but the students are pretty protective both of the person being studied and of themselves. After all, if you're responding to a story by some long-dead author, you can say anything you want, and no one's the worse for it. So associations and evaluations go all over the place. But if you're writing about somebody who's sitting right there in front of you, you're going to be a lot more careful, more rational, more to the point, more tactful.

LT. RHODES: It still sounds pretty touchy-feely to me.

HOLLAND: It can get a little bit that way, but only a little bit. We stay quite close to the surface. No one is going to say, This comes from your toilet training at the age of two. And no diagnoses. Nothing like, You're paranoid. Everything we say is about cognitive style, and that's pretty far removed from the kind of thing you get into in psychoanalysis or even in psychotherapy.

LT. RHODES: What you're saying, then, is that you think you can bring even a fairly disturbed student like Hassler through this process unscathed.

HOLLAND: I've done it. And they really have learned something about their personal styles of reading, writing, and teaching, and perhaps their ways of relating to other people.

LT. RHODES: What precisely was Hassler going to do this morning?

HOLLAND: I don't know.

Usually we get into discussions about what this or that interpreter saw in the writings. We do stay pretty close to the writing.

Some people write a squib about themselves and hand it in on Monday. Penza did that. The week he was "it," he wrote a hilarious sketch of himself as the mad poet starving in an attic somewhere, shouting out the windows, trying to get an audience. But that's not required. Amy Lemaire didn't, and evidently Trish didn't. Otherwise, we'd have gotten a squib from her on Monday.

LT. RHODES: Ebenfeld and Ireland tell me Hassler was driving you crazy.

HOLLAND: Yes, Trish was a devout deconstructionist. "Devout" is the only word for it. She was going to convert us all. She was religious about it. Coming from Yale, you must know about deconstruction and contemporary literary theory.

LT. RHODES: I know there was a lot of this going on at the college, but not at the School of Drama. I have to think about what will move audiences. So, what's deconstructionism?

HOLLAND: The deconstructionists hold that everything is language, and everything in language is built out of a series of linguistic differences. That is, every word means what it means because of its differences from other words. *D-o-g* is *dog,* because *d-o-g* isn't *c-a-t.* And *dog* means dog, because it isn't *cat* or *fire hydrant.* A word means what it means only because it's different from all other words. But you're aware of these other possibilities. Every time you hear or read *dog,* it's in the nature of language that you're also aware of *cat* or *fire hydrant.* Therefore every text is going to be inconsistent with itself. *Dog* will mean at the same time both *dog* and *not-dog.* And it's in the very nature of language, particularly literary language, to develop and reveal this inconsistency.

LT. RHODES: So nothing means anything?

HOLLAND: So everything means everything. Each text has built into it all these other possibilities of meaning. The language creates all these conflicted meanings. The human reader is a merely a kind of receiver of a process that has already been done by the language.

LT. RHODES: That's quite different from your seminar.

HOLLAND: Right. Exactly different. You catch on quickly.

If you take this position far enough, you end up saying there are no writers or readers. Language does it all.

Hassler was passionately committed to this intellectual position, which is squarely opposed to the way this seminar works—worked. She was fanatical about it.

Instead of saying to herself, I've signed up for Holland's seminar. I'll get out of it what I can— And why the hell did she sign up for it if she was so opposed? Well, she explained that in one of her squibs.

Anyway, she kept us arguing all the time about basic premises.

LT. RHODES: You got pretty angry. How about the students?

HOLLAND: The other students didn't quite know what to do about her. Even among graduate students, we have the old schoolboy loyalty. Schoolperson loyalty? Students stick together against the teacher. If I'd come down hard on her, they'd have resented that. They could see she was monopolizing the seminar, spoiling it for them, but I couldn't be sure that they'd back me up if I tried to force her back in line.

LT. RHODES: Now, what precisely was she doing?

HOLLAND: She was trying to convert us. Every time I'd try to make a point, she'd drag us back over basic assumptions. Again and again, we'd have to argue about the nature of language, Saussure versus Chomsky.

I could see the other students' eyes glaze over when Trish would ask these first-day questions. I was losing them. We couldn't get on with the readings and writings I wanted—and I think the other students wanted—to talk about.

LT. RHODES: They were annoyed, then.

HOLLAND: Yes, but she did it to annoy *me*. Constantly Trish would quote my colleagues at me. "But Professor So-and-so says . . ." She'd smirk, as if to add, And you know how smart or talented or celebrated or famous *he* is. I don't want to say what I really think, which is that Professor So-and-so has his head up his— in the clouds. So I have to be nice and calm and try and get the seminar back on track. "Well, let's look at what Anne or Max has said about this poem." I'm letting off steam.

LT. RHODES: She really got to you, didn't she? Was that why, a few minutes ago, you picked *The Taming of the Shrew* for your example?

HOLLAND: You *are* clever. Yes, probably. She was an absolutely maddening person. Maddening! I wanted to kick her out. But then I'd stop myself. "No, that isn't professional. That isn't what you do in a Delphi seminar. Whatever she says, you have to let it come out, and you have to face it and discuss it rationally."

LT. RHODES: That's Hassler as a student. Tell me what you know about her life. What's her story?

HOLLAND: A sad one. I could be sorry for her, if she weren't so damned irritating. I suppose that's one reason she was so hostile—to keep people from pitying her. In the papers she wrote for this seminar, she told us some things about her family and herself. She was brought up in some strict and tiny southern town, a Bible-thumping, flag-wagging, gun-toting family.

Was she the way she was because of sexual abuse or brutality? Or simply what she had to watch going on between her father, her mother, and half a dozen brothers and sisters, living in those close quarters in a tiny, broken-down double-wide. I could never decide.

Maybe it was because home was so awful that she turned out to be so good in school. Brilliant, in fact. She dazzled her teachers, and they worked hard for her. She became the first student from that pathetic rural high school not only to get admitted but to get a scholarship to an Ivy League university, Yale. That was where she started on this deconstruction stuff. Derrida, Miller, de Man, Hartman, Bloom—surely you know these names.

LT. RHODES: Of course I heard them bandied about when I was at Yale, but over in the School of Drama we didn't pay a whole lot of attention to literary theory.

HOLLAND: As soon as Trish heard about the self-contradicting text and the rest of it, it became a kind of faith to her. The Yale people were making a playful, witty, creative kind of literary criticism. Trish made it hard and serious and hateful, mean-mouthed like the Bible for her family. Like a revivalist preacher, she couldn't stop proclaiming the gospel. She'd talk deconstruction to anyone anytime all the time.

The seminar got to be like a class in grade school. One student starts testing the teacher, and the other students get drawn into the game. I can't stand that sort of confrontation. I just want to go back to my word processor and write in peace.

LT. RHODES: You sound as though it wasn't just the confrontation you hated. You hated her.

HOLLAND: *[Pause.]* Yes, I did. *[Pause.]* At the same time I was sorry for her. I could see that what she was doing was her way of dealing with her childhood. It was wrecking this seminar, though.

LT. RHODES: You know, you're doing something like a playwright in this class. A playwright puts a lot of people in, say, a drawing room and makes them relate to one another. In an odd way, you've got your students writing their own play. You put all these different identities in a room and make them interpret each other.

HOLLAND: Inside every critic is a frustrated writer.

LT. RHODES: It's something of a treat for me, being put back in the academy this way. I like seeing what people do now. I'll be honest with you—I find it quite strange. But I'd better get back to interviewing eyewitnesses. Would you send Paul Penza down?

HOLLAND: My pleasure, Lieutenant.END OF THIS SECTION OF TAPE END OF THIS SECTION OF TAPE END OF THIS SECTION OF TAPE END

LT. RHODES: *Comments.* I'd forgotten what a strange place an English department is. For a few minutes there, I felt like a student again, being lectured by Holland. Once he gets started talking . . . He's *so* wrapped up in his ideas about reading and this strange seminar of his. I suppose that's the university world. You invest yourself in your ideas, and that makes you vulnerable. You can't draw a line between intellectual disagreement and personal attack. That's why he hated Hassler so.

He's a passionate man, our mild-mannered, good-humored Professor Norman Holland, with his strange, wordy, introspective seminar. That nose! Strong features, and yet his manner wasn't strong. He was yielding, really, making concessions to me, to the students. He seemed afraid of something. What? Something to do with the death? Or is that just what academia does to people? Being pushed around by administrators, parents, students.

Clearly, Holland is one of the keys to this death, although I doubt very much if he himself had anything to do with it. He probably couldn't climb out of his texts long enough. But still, I'll have to keep him on the suspect list. And I'll have to be careful not to tell him more than I should. That would be all too easy, because I like talking literature with him, even this theory. He seems decent company, but God!, he's *so* wound up in reading and texts and literary theory.

LT. RHODES: Come in please, Mr. Penza.

PENZA: Thanks. Let me say right off, I've read about you. You're the detective-playwright. I haven't read you, but I've read about you, and that's nearly as good, isn't it?

LT. RHODES: Nearly. Does the microphone bother you?

PENZA: No, although I'm for the written word myself.

LT. RHODES: Do you want to tell me a bit about that, about yourself?

PENZA: I write short stories. That is, I try to.

LT. RHODES: Why are you taking Holland's seminar, then? It sounds like something for a critic, not a writer.

PENZA: Zap! Right on the mark, oh how right you are. Maybe I shouldn't be in school at all, I should just write. Nowadays, though, even with fiction, you need the contacts you can get from your instructors in a creative writing program. Sure, you learn things from them, but basically you need their pull to get your stuff placed. Was it that way when you were starting out? But plays are different. Plays are especially hard to get started with, because you have to get a theater and actors and all that. How did you get started? Where did you get your contacts from?

LT. RHODES: Some other time, Mr. Penza. Right now, I'm looking into the death of Patricia Hassler. Why are you in this seminar?

PENZA: That's easy. They require creative writers to take some regular academic litcrit. In this seminar you don't have to produce a "critical paper." You get to write pretty much as you please, because Holland wants you to write "free associations." What are my free associations? To what does my mind turn if I don't direct my thoughts? To the story I'm working on. Today I'm writing a sketch of a woman meeting first her lover then her husband in two different train stations, the lover in Dijon, the husband in Paris. A woman all in white. Well— Holland has to accept whatever you turn in—they're your free associations, after all—so I can sneak in drafts of short stories as if they were responses. Likewise, I'd rather talk to you about publishers and agents and outlets than about Trish Hassler.

LT. RHODES: But that's why I brought you in here. What did you see this morning?

PENZA: What did I see? I saw Trish Hassler come to the door of the seminar—

LT. RHODES: Wait a minute. Who was there already?

PENZA: We all were. Holland too. Trish had taken his seat, I guess as a sign that this was her day to talk. But who wanted to listen? All she wanted to do was badger Holland. Anyway, we were all sitting desultorily around the table. That's a word I like, "desultorily." She marched up to the door of the classroom, swathed in her scarves and beads. She always reminded me of the caterpillar in *Alice*. Caterpillar? She was one big woman. I wonder what it would have been like to make love to her. Six foot and nearly 300 pounds. Well, 200 then. Whatever. Anyhow, I'm for daintier game myself. There she stood and looked at us all for a minute like a rhinoceros ready to charge. What a look! Zzzzzzt! I felt like a mosquito in one of those ultraviolet traps. As if she was going to fry me.

Trish's bark was worse than her bite, though. At least she was always fairly decent to me. This morning she walked over to her seat, sat down— No. Hold on a minute. She hovered behind Chris's chair, like some great prehistoric bird, like a pterodactyl waiting to pounce, and she said, "You! You're the one I'm writing about." What was that supposed to mean? I don't know. Anyway, then she walked to her seat at the head of the table, sat down, and then she seemed just to cave in on herself. That whole big bulk sagged, as if your shot had finally killed the charging rhino, and she rolled over onto the floor. Another victim of the poachers. End of story.

LT. RHODES: Do you think somebody might have tried to kill her?

PENZA: To know Trish was not to like Trish—that's for damned sure. We could all have done without her, especially in this seminar. She made herself a nuisance here, monologuing, always trying to get Holland's goat. I used to tune her out when she started ranting about her deconstructive bullshit. (Or rhino shit.) Who needs it? I'd think about more useful things.

But what makes you imagine she was killed? I thought she just collapsed. She must have been sixty pounds overweight, a smoker, no exercise that I ever heard of. And angry. Breathing fire all the time. I thought she died out of sheer self-destruct. Like Margaret Hamilton in *The Wizard of Oz* when she just pops off in a puff of smoke.

LT. RHODES: Not this time, Mr. Penza. Trish left a body behind, and the autopsy will tell why. In the meantime, we've finished, and you can go back. Stay with the others in the seminar room, please.

PENZA: Aren't you going to say, "And don't leave town"? Detectives always say that in the movies.

LT. RHODES: Okay, Mr. Penza. Don't leave town. End of interview.

PENZA: Sure, Lieutenant. That was easy. Maybe we can talk publishing sometime.

LT. RHODES: Maybe. But right now, would you send in Professor Sisley?

PENZA: Right-o. Ciao, Lieutenant.END OF THIS SECTION OF TAPE END OF THIS SECTION OF TAPE END OF THIS SECTION OF TAPE END OF

LT. RHODES: *Comment on Penza interview.* Single-minded about his writing. I ought to be more so, but then there's my job— Was that why I felt irritated with him?

Six foot, slim, 150 maybe, blond, straight hair, blue eyes, regular features, no distinguishing marks. A self-confident young man and egotistical. I could even say downright self-centered. No hint of a motive, though, and not the type, I'd say. A creature of fantasy rather than action, particularly so planned an action as a poisoning must be. And how was this one planned? Come on, Welder, come on.

"Penza." Italian? Spanish? Portuguese? But with those blond WASP fine features and good looks. Oh well.END OF THIS SECTION OF TAPE END OF THIS SECTION OF TAPE END OF THIS SECTION OF TAPE

Metropolitan Buffalo Police Department

Tape Transcription   Homicide Unit

Body: *Hassler, P.*   Tape No. *840307.023*
Place: *Rhodes Hall, UB*   Time: *12:47 p.m.*
Persons present: *Det. Lt. Rhodes, W. Sisley*

Transcribed by: *J. Cipperman*

LT. RHODES: Come in, Professor Sisley.

SISLEY: Right, Lieutenant.

LT. RHODES: Would you acknowledge my tape recorder?

SISLEY: You're holding a tape recorder.

LT. RHODES: And I'm recording what you say.

SISLEY: You're recording what I say.

LT. RHODES: It's all part of this new procedure in the department.

SISLEY: Just what you needed. First Miranda, now tape recorders. I don't see how they expect you to have time to collar any perps.

LT. RHODES: Actually, to my surprise, the procedure has been a great success. It's been a couple of weeks since I've had to do anything more than sign off on my written reports. *[Thanks, Boss—JC.]*

But down to this case, Professor Sisley. Tell me what happened this morning.

SISLEY: When I got to the class some of the students were already there, sitting at the table. Norman and I came in, and we said hello. I took a chair, and we all chatted a bit. One of those uncomfortable chairs, a hard wooden seat with a thin rubber mat that only reminds you of what a cushion is like. I think they must keep the seats uncomfortable so the students will stay awake.

LT. RHODES: It's the same in police stations. Public sector.

SISLEY: I'll bet there are other parts of the public sector that sit on comfortable cushions. Higher priority parts.

LT. RHODES: Higher priority rumps, at least. You're no doubt right, Professor Sisley, but let's get back to this uncomfortable seminar room.

SISLEY: As I say, Dr. Holland and I came in, sat down, and he started chatting up the students. I didn't try to remember what he said. Eventually, the others drifted in. Actually, I made a diagram of where everyone was sitting.

LT. RHODES: You did! I'd like to have that.

SISLEY: Sure. Let me just mark in the door and the window to get you pointed right. And the two piles of coats. Here.

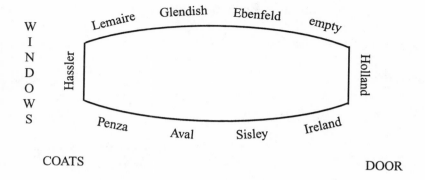

COATS   DOOR

LT. RHODES: Why did you make the drawing? That's my job, isn't it?

SISLEY: It will help you to keep track of who's who and who sat where. After all, you've got nine new people to get straight in your head.

LT. RHODES: Very considerate. Do you also happen to remember the order people came in?

SISLEY: Of course, I do—at least from the time I came in. I walked in with Holland—I can't remember who went through the door first. When we came in, the big fellow—

LT. RHODES: Ebenfeld?

SISLEY: —yes, Ebenfeld was there and the veteran, Ireland. Then, a few minutes after Holland and I came in, Ms. Lemaire came in and sat down—where you see on the diagram. Nobody changed seats. Then Anne Glendish and Paul Penza came in after a minute or two. Finally Hassler came and stood in the doorway. While she stood there, the French student—

LT. RHODES: Aval—

SISLEY: made his way past her—she pretty well filled the doorway. After he sat down, Hassler herself came in.

LT. RHODES: Tell me about Hassler's arrival.

SISLEY: She walked up to the doorway, and stood there. She took just about all the space. She was a big woman. 5' 11" at least, maybe six feet—I was sitting down. Long stringy blond hair. Brown eyes. I'd say between 230 and 240 pounds, but it was hard to tell because she was bundled up in a lot of scarves and wraps—hippie stuff. Beads. She stood there in the doorway and stared at the class. I'd say she looked angry about something. After maybe half a minute, she walked forward down the left side of the table, and she stopped behind the French student, Aval. She looked at the group and said, "Him. He's the one. Don't you care? He's the one." Then she walked to her seat at the end of the table. As soon as she sat down, the expression on her face changed, and she collapsed forward, hitting the left side of her head on the table as she went down. She ended up between her chair and the right table leg, right from her point of view, left from mine. I noticed how quickly she died. My guess is that she'd had a stroke. The students jumped up, so I couldn't see much, and then Holland told us all to sit down, and he sent one of the students out to call for security. He led us across the hall into the other room and stationed somebody in front of the room where the body was, to keep the tourists out. I thought he handled the situation well.

LT. RHODES: Professor Sisley, would tell me a little about yourself? In particular, why you're taking this seminar?

SISLEY: Well, Lieutenant, I'm just about due to come up for promotion to associate professor and tenure, and I'm not going to breeze through the process. I've had some trouble publishing. I'm a good teacher, as good as anyone in the department, but as you know, you don't get promoted for teaching. That's dumb. After all, what they pay professors for is to teach the young of the State of New York. But you can't fight the system. So I thought this seminar might help me get on with my career, with publishing articles and books. There's a lot of ready-made material in one of these seminars, and people are interested in reader-oriented criticism.

LT. RHODES: I've seen you in another context besides professing, though, haven't I? Holding the mirror up to nature?

SISLEY: Excuse me?

LT. RHODES: "The purpose of playing, whose end, both at the first and now, was and is, to hold as 'twere the mirror up to nature." Not bad, eh?

SISLEY: You've got quite the memory.

LT. RHODES: It's actors who have the memories. Maybe you'll be learning some of my lines someday.

SISLEY: I do community theater. I like to act.

LT. RHODES: I hear you're quite good.

SISLEY: People are generous to amateurs.

LT. RHODES: They certainly have been generous to my plays. Professor Sisley, thank you for being candid about your academic situation. Would you wait with the other members of the seminar, please?END OF THIS SECTION OF TAPE END OF THIS SECTION OF TAPE END OF THIS SECTION

LT. RHODES: *Comment.* What's happening to English professors these days? He acted as though he didn't recognize Hamlet's advice to the actors, and he an actor himself. Don't they even read Shakespeare any more? Well, what can you expect? He's in American literature. And now *I'm* making academic jokes.

There's something else odd here. He was so forward about his diagram of who was sitting where, but he seemed to blank on Ebenfeld's and Aval's names.

Wally Sisley. About thirty-three, I'd say. Five-ten,140. Brown hair, graying slightly. Glasses. No marks. Slight build, but I have the impression of some kind of force or determination underneath. He was certainly efficient about the crime with his diagram of the seating and his description of Hassler. Very professional. But my profession, not his.

Well, it's time to shepherd my little flock of suspects.

State University of New York at Buffalo
Department of English
- Memo -

Date: Wednesday, March 7, 1984
To: All Faculty and Graduate Students
From: Romola Badger, Chair

Many of you will have heard by now of the dreadful tragedy that has come upon us. Patricia Hassler, one of our most brilliant and promising graduate students—she came to us from Yale—has died under mysterious circumstances just as Professor Norman Holland's group was beginning this morning at 8:00. "Sweets to the sweet, farewell." She is dead, dead ere her prime, Patricia is, and hath not left her peer—if I may paraphrase.

We are, of course, shocked and grieved by this painful event, yet even in our grief, we must remember and share the even greater grief of Patricia's parents and her brothers and sisters. Their address is: Mr. and Mrs. Harley Clyde Hassler, R.F.D. #6, County Road 23, Iron Springs, Georgia, 31797. We expect the funeral to take place in Iron Springs, but, as a department, we will of course have a memorial service here for Patricia as soon as circumstances permit. Should you choose to write Patricia's parents, it would be a kindness and an indication to them, to everyone, that we care. Trish's fellow students care. This department cares. SUNY/Buffalo cares.

In addition, the department has set up a scholarship fund in her honor. I encourage you to make a contribution in memoriam to the Patricia Hassler Scholarship Fund.

Metropolitan Buffalo Police Department

Tape Transcription   Homicide Unit

Body: *Hassler, P.*   Tape No. *840307.023*
Place: *Rhodes Hall, UB West Campus*   Time: *1:06 p.m.*
Persons present: *Det. Lt. Norman Rhodes, Det. Sgt. M. Yorrick*
Civilians: *See below*

Transcribed by: *J. Cipperman*

Civilians Present: Professor Norman Holland, Professor Wallace Sisley, Christian Aval, Max Ebenfeld, Anne Glendish, Barry Ireland, Amelia Lemaire, Paul Penza

LT. RHODES: . . . recording again. Please, please.

> *[J.C.: I get just a confused hubbub of voices with over them the Lieutenant calling, "Settle down, settle down now." Impossible to distinguish voices. After some quieting—]*

LT. RHODES: Thank you for waiting here. I've now gotten the medical examiner's preliminary report. I have to tell you this isn't a case of natural death or accident. Patricia Hassler was poisoned.

> *[J.C.: More hubbub. "Poisoned!" "I can't believe it." Etc. Impossible to distinguish voices.]*

LT. RHODES: Yes, this is now a homicide, and we'll all have to act accordingly. First of all, don't leave the city without informing me or Sergeant Yorrick.

HOLLAND: Are you saying, Lieutenant, that you think someone in this seminar did it? *[General talk.]*

LT. RHODES: No—quiet down, quiet down!—I'm not saying that. You all were, however, witnesses to her dying. The medical report isn't complete yet, but we believe the poison would have had to have been administered a short time before the seminar began. Therefore the people in this seminar had a known opportunity. That fact moves you closer to the center of the investigation. Please, therefore, if you discover—or remember—anything that would throw any light at all on this poisoning, tell me. You can reach me at any hour by calling 392-7332 and asking for Lieutenant Justin Rhodes. They'll beep me.

HOLLAND: Maybe she poisoned herself. Maybe she committed suicide.

LT. RHODES: From what we know about the way the poison was administered, that isn't likely.

LEMAIRE: If you're considering people in the seminar, shouldn't someone mention the mystery student? He's certainly someone suspicious.

GLENDISH: Our very own Peeping Tom. He looks to me like somebody to watch. No pun intended.

PENZA: On target, ladies—sorry, women. I *knew* our crazy was going to be good for something. He's the one you should be looking for, Lieutenant.

GENERAL: Yes, yes.

GLENDISH: Look, this guy committed verbal violence on the women in the seminar.

LT. RHODES: Verbal violence?

GLENDISH: What else do you call it when someone is secretly watching you and intruding into your space with his phone calls and trying to have sex with you? I call it rape.

LT. RHODES: Surely that's a little premature, Ms. Glendish.

GLENDISH: You're taking this lightly, Lieutenant. Let me assure you that, to the women in the seminar, this is something we think you should be looking at very carefully.

LT. RHODES: What do you think I should do?

GLENDISH: I think you ought to find out who this guy is.

LT. RHODES: I agree with you completely, Ms. Glendish, and, let me assure *you,* I don't take this man at all lightly. When was the last time you got a telephone call from him?

GLENDISH: Not since the end of January. I blasted him good the last time he called—I keep a police whistle by the phone for obscene callers—and he never called back after I blew it in his ear.

LT. RHODES: You, Ms. Lemaire?

LEMAIRE: He seemed to me a lonely, troubled person, and I urged him to find therapy. We talked a couple of times before I realized he was just playing on my sympathies to keep me talking to him. Finally I told him in no uncertain terms that he wasn't going to get anything at all out of me, and I haven't heard from him since—I'd say—mid-February.

LT. RHODES: And Trish Hassler? Did she say anything about these calls?

LEMAIRE: Trish mentioned 'way back—I'd say, in January—that she had gotten some calls from this guy. I don't remember her mentioning it again. Do you, Anne?

GLENDISH: No.

LT. RHODES: As far as the women in the seminar are concerned, then, the calls stopped in mid-February. But he has been turning papers in since then?

HOLLAND: Yes, every week, although he doesn't really do what I'm asking. He just makes wisecracks and occasionally offers conclusions without any backup.

LT. RHODES: I want to find out who this man is ASAP, Ms. Glendish. The only way I have is to check the papers he turned in for his fingerprints. I'll bet that some of you are not quite as conscientious about reading all these papers before seminar meetings as you might be. Is that possible? *[Silence.]* Just possibly then, there may be some unsmudged fingerprints of the interloper on the protocols he turned in. Partials at least.

Okay, then. I want to check the papers you got from him. If we're to get fingerprints, it's important that they not be touched any more than they have been. The sergeant has tweezers for the purpose.

SGT. YORRICK: Tongs, I'd call them, Lieutenant.

LT. RHODES: All right, Mort, tongs. Will you let us check your briefcases and book bags and extract the interloper's response for this week?

SISLEY: I think the lieutenant is exactly right. We should cooperate totally with him. I for one will go along with his request to search my books and papers, and I urge you all to do the same.

HOLLAND: I will also.

EBENFELD: I've got nothing to hide, Lieutenant. You're welcome to the responses for this week. I have those with me. I don't think you realize, though, how much paper this seminar generates. All the papers for all the sessions so far comes to—let's see, eight sessions times nine respondents times three pages each—that's more than two hundred pages. Most of us don't want to lug all that around. I just bring to seminar the papers that came in for this week or the ones we're going to discuss. The rest I keep at home.

LT. RHODES: That presents us with a problem. As for this week, I'm interested in two responses, the mystery student's and Patricia Hassler's.

HOLLAND: She didn't write this week.

LT. RHODES: You told me that. Yes. What about the interloper?

HOLLAND: He turned in a squib this week. I'll get it.

LT. RHODES: NO! Put down those papers! Remember, I want those fingerprints. Don't touch those responses, anybody! Sergeant Yorrick will go round the room and use his tongs to pick up the papers from our unknown friend. Sergeant, as you get these papers, put them in glassine envelopes one by one.

SGT. YORRICK: Ms. Glendish? *[Pause.]* Mr. Penza. *[Pause.]*

LT. RHODES: Sergeant, give me one of those envelopes, will you? I want to read what he said. *[Pause.]* Good God, Holland, this is supposed to be a paper for an English class for Ph.D. students?

HOLLAND: No, Lieutenant. It's not at all typical of what I expect, or what I get, from my students. I told you that.

LT. RHODES: Joan or whoever, I'll read this into the tape recorder so you can transcribe it.

"To the Happy Campers Seminar from the Spy Who Came In From the Cold.

"Hah, hah. Trish Hassler's week to tell you all off. Trish will turn this seminar inside out. I wish I were going to be there to see it.

"How do I read Trish? How do I read thee, let me count the ways? Sorry, campers, I'm not going to play Holland's little game and carefully ferret out themes from Trish's papers. I feel I know her too well for that. I'll just say that Trish says right out what the rest of you think, but hide. But I suppose I'm an odd one to be talking about hiding. I'm not hiding, though, so far as Trish is concerned. She's a soothsayer in the original sense of the word if anyone remembers it in these decadent times. She speaks the truth, although, come to think of it, given her passion for deconstruction, she'd vigorously deny what I just wrote. Which is why she's a soothsayer. Ho, ho, ho, campers, keep the mysteries coming."

I don't get anything out of that. Does anyone else? It sounds as though he knew something about Hassler or with Hassler or something like that.

HOLLAND: Quite possibly. He's always obscure, hinting at things. I at least never know what they are. He suggests he knows something that the people he's writing to don't.

SGT. YORRICK: Who haven't I collected from yet?

PENZA: I'm ready for you, Sergeant. Tong away, or is it tweeze? [Pause.]

SGT. YORRICK: Consider yourself both tonged and tweezed, Mr. Penza. Mr. Ireland? [Pause.]

Ireland: Sure, Sarge.

LT. RHODES: Professor Holland, you say your copy is in your office?

HOLLAND: No, I have the one for this week here. The preceding weeks' papers are in folders in my office. I can bring the folder for the mystery student back without touching any of the responses.

LT. RHODES: No doubt you can, but I'll walk down to your office with you later. I want to ask you some more questions. Professor Sisley, are your responses in your office too?

SISLEY: No, they're at home, but, if you don't mind, could I step down to my office for a minute? I've got an important phone call to make.

LT. RHODES: Not now, Professor Sisley. Stay put, everybody, until I get the collecting of the interloper's responses organized. Anybody else? Are all the other interloper squibs at home? [A chorus of yesses.]

SGT. YORRICK: Mr. Ebenfeld? *[Pause.]* Dr. Sisley? *[Pause.]* No, that's right, yours
are at home. Let's see. Who haven't I collected from yet? I've got Glendish,
Penza, Ebenfeld, Ireland. Ms. Lemaire, can you show me where you've
got this intruder?

LEMAIRE: The paper is in here, Sergeant, there, right between those other two.

SGT. YORRICK: Thank you, miss. You now, Mr. Aval?

AVAL: Here it is, Sergeant, where I'm pointing. *[Pause.]*

LT. RHODES: Do all of you live in those apartment buildings just north of campus? Across Main Street? *[Chorus of yesses.]*

SGT. YORRICK: I've got everybody's, Lieutenant, everybody's except this stack of
books and papers here. I don't know who they belong to.

LT. RHODES: Whose books are these? *[Long silence.]* Whose books *are* these?

SISLEY: I'll bet they're Hassler's.

LT. RHODES: Hassler's! What are they doing over here? How did they get from
the room where the body was? Who brought them over here? *[Long silence.]* I said, Who brought them over here? *[Long silence.]*

IRELAND: Evidently, whoever did it is not saying.

LT. RHODES: I want to know. *Who brought these books across the hall? [Long
silence.]* All right, you're sitting next to them, Penza, and you, Aval.

PENZA: Not me. I never carry more than I have to.

AVAL: Nor do I know anything, sir, about these books and papers.

LEMAIRE: Lieutenant, probably somebody just picked them up absentmindedly
when we all came over here. There was a lot of confusion at that point. I
expect the person just doesn't remember.

IRELAND: Or just maybe your yelling and trying to intimidate us a minute ago
made them clam up.

GLENDISH: Right!

LT. RHODES: I think the silence is more serious than that. We now know something we didn't know five minutes ago. But there will be time enough for
us to go over that.

Yorrick, get a plastic bag for Hassler's books. Stack them alongside
the other things we've got to take down to headquarters. I want to go over
them.

We've got all of the interloper's squibs for today at this point, haven't
we? All except Professor Holland's set and Professor Sisley's. Now, I'd
like to get the interloper's squibs for previous weeks from wherever you've
got them. At home, you say, all except for Professor Holland. What do you
want, Professor Sisley?

SISLEY: Lieutenant, I've *got* to go to the bathroom.

LT. RHODES: You really are determined, aren't you. Go, then.

I want to check the rest of the intruder's responses for prints. I'll send Sergeant Yorrick with each of you in turn to collect all the papers you have received from him. When we get to your home or office or whatever, please be so kind as just to locate the papers for the sergeant. Point them out, don't touch them. What I want to get, obviously, are his fingerprints, not yours. Let the detective do all the handling. Is that all right? *[Yesses.]*

Now I should point out that you don't have to admit Sergeant Yorrick to your living quarters without our obtaining a search warrant, but as Ms. Glendish has said, we owe it to the women in the seminar to identify this interloper as soon as possible.

PENZA: You can enter our place, of course, Lieutenant.

GLENDISH: Thanks, Paul. *My* place, Lieutenant. Men!

LEMAIRE: You can come to my apartment, too, Lieutenant.

EBENFELD: Mine, too. *[General chorus of permissions.]*

LT. RHODES: Yorrick, I think the easiest way to do this is to have headquarters send one of their minibuses. Get Bill Hoyt and Tony Masiello to ride with you. We can load you and them and these people in the bus and you can go with them to their homes or apartments or wherever and collect the interloper's papers. Give them a call downtown for a bus.

Is that clear to everybody? Yorrick will ride with you in a police bus. He'll walk in with each of you to your apartment and collect the intruder's papers. If anyone has any objection, please tell me now. *[Silence.]*

LEMAIRE: I haven't had lunch yet.

LT. RHODES: Yorrick, on the way, buy Ms. Lemaire a slice of pizza from Bocce's, will you?

SGT. YORRICK: Pepperoni or mushroom, or maybe you're preferring double cheese, Ms. Lemaire?

LEMAIRE: Lieutenant, can I just get a salad at the cafeteria? Doesn't anybody else need lunch? I don't know about the rest of you, but I think some food might help me to digest this awful thing. Oops! I'm sorry.

PENZA: Identity, identity, Amy. *[Voices: "Yes, yes." "Food..." Laughter. "That's our Amy."]*

LT. RHODES: All right, all right. Time out for a cafeteria stop.

Professor Sisley, you're back already. Ms. Lemaire has got us stopping at the cafeteria in the next building. Then we'll pick up the rest of the interloper's responses from people's homes.

SISLEY: It turned out I had them in the office, Lieutenant. Here they are, in this file folder. I didn't touch them.

LT. RHODES: Sisley, are you going to be something of a nuisance? You know I wanted those to be collected by the sergeant with his meticulous tweezers.

SISLEY: I didn't touch them, Lieutenant, I promise you.

LEMAIRE: Are you all right, Wally? You look pale.

SISLEY: This thing has shaken me terribly. If I'm honest and come right out with it, I'd have to say I'm scared.

LEMAIRE: I think we all are, Wally.

LT. RHODES: On that note, I'll turn off this tape and we can break for lunch. Take over, Sergeant. Don't forget, everybody, we'll meet again, right here, tomorrow at 9:00 a.m. Professor Holland, I'll join you in your office.

SGT. YORRICK: All right, people, let's go next door and see if they've got anything besides the salad Ms. Lemaire prefers. Maybe a little corned beef and cabbage. Or will they only have that ten days from now?

IRELAND: What's so special about ten days from now?

SGT. YORRICK: Ah, Mr. Ireland, I can see that, despite your fine name, you're no Irishman.END OF THIS SECTION OF TAPE END OF THIS SECTION OF TAPE END OF THIS SECTION OF TAPE END OF THIS SECTION

LT. RHODES: *Comment.* Whew! We know where we stand now. Somebody brought her books over, and the somebody isn't telling.

It would have been possible, after all—not easy but possible—for some of the people milling around in the hall after Penza's telephone call to have stepped in and picked up Hassler's books, got what they wanted, and put them down among the books of the people in the seminar. Just possible.

But I think not. Somebody is guilty about something—and it's somebody in that room, not somebody outside in the hall. I think it's a safe bet at this point to home in on just the eight people in the seminar. Probably. But I don't think I should make it too obvious that that's what I'm doing.

There's still the interloper. Conceivably, he could be someone in this group playing a double role. More likely he's someone outside the group.

Looking for those responses will give Yorrick a chance to get a look round in their apartments, no more than a look, but even that's useful. He'll be going in with them, so they won't have a chance to hide anything. I thought that was pretty artful, getting Glendish worked up so that she'd insist on discovering the interloper. None of them would insist on a warrant after that.

There's something fishy about Sisley, the way he stepped forward to support my searching their papers and then the way he came back from the john, all pale and scared. And he hadn't gone to the john. He went to his office, because he brought the interloper's responses from his office.

The game's afoot, as the master says.

Metropolitan Buffalo Police Department

Tape Transcription

Homicide Unit

Body: *Hassler, P.* Tape No. *840307.023*
Place: *Rhodes Hall, UB West Campus* Time: *1:19 p.m.*
Persons present: *Det. Lt. N. Rhodes, Professor R. Badger*

Transcribed by: *J. Cipperman*

BADGER: *So* sorry to keep you waiting, Lieutenant Rhodes. I had an urgent call from the National Endowment about a review panel I'm chairing.

LT. RHODES: I only need a few minutes of your time, Professor Badger. I want to tell you something, and then I need you to do something. As before, I'm taping our conversation.

BADGER: I shall of course cooperate in every way I can, including acquiescing in your recording our conversation.

LT. RHODES: I have to tell you that Patricia Hassler was poisoned.

BADGER: I can't be*lieve* it. How could she have been poisoned?

LT. RHODES: We don't know that yet.

BADGER: What an awful thing for the department!

LT. RHODES: Also awful for Ms. Hassler.

BADGER: Of course, Lieutenant, of course. I had already thought of Patricia. You may have seen the memo I sent out to the faculty, students, and staff this morning. I *won*der if I have let my feelings show too much.

LT. RHODES: Surely, at a time like this, we're all going to show our feelings.

BADGER: Murdered! I can't believe it. I had *such* hopes for her.

LT. RHODES: Yes, she was murdered. That seems quite definite.

BADGER: That, I take it, was what you had to tell me, Lieutenant. What is it you want me to do?

LT. RHODES: What I've found out so far leads me to believe it was someone connected with that particular seminar. It'll be easy enough to obtain the prints of those formally registered. Holland and the other professor in the seminar—

BADGER: *Sis*ley. *Wal*lace *Sis*ley.

LT. RHODES: —Holland, Sisley, and the remaining six students have already agreed. They've all been most cooperative, by the way. What you may not know is that there was an interloper in Holland's seminar. The way the seminar works, the students circulate—

BADGER: Yes, yes, Lieutenant, I know the complicated inter*weav*ing of the paper chase in Professor Holland's seminar.

LT. RHODES: What you may not know is that, this semester, someone was taking advantage of these papers being circulated in open mailboxes to introduce his own comments and papers and, in general, to intrude into the seminar.

BADGER: Professor Holland told me about this. I've already put out word that I will expel from the graduate program whoever is doing this *des*picable thing. I suppose it was only a matter of time before something like this happened. But you said "he."

LT. RHODES: Because he telephoned the women in the seminar, at least, the two who can tell us about it. He commented to them on their papers, tried to make dates with them, made sexual remarks, and so on. I believe this man could be involved in Hassler's death. I want to find out who he is and question him. I think it probable that he's a graduate student in English, not a faculty member, and not someone from another department. If I can fingerprint the graduate students in English and compare those prints to the partials on the papers this person handed in, I should be able to identify him.

BADGER: But you're asking for fingerprints from all graduate students, both men and women.

LT. RHODES: This is only part of the bigger search—for the murderer—and the murderer could be a woman. The fingerprints will help us in both searches.

BADGER: I want to help in *every* way I can, Lieutenant. I'll get a memo out right away to the department, asking them to cooperate. How will you manage?

LT. RHODES: If it's all right with you, I'll station two of the fingerprint people in the office here. The students can just come by and be fingerprinted.

BADGER: Very straightforward. I'll get the memo out as soon as we finish. Incidentally, *let* me assign you a mailbox. That will give us an easy, fast way to communicate with you or your men.

LT. RHODES: Thanks. That could be very useful. Something else I need. Head shots of the students in Professor Holland's seminar and of Professors Holland and Sisley.

BADGER: Are you saying one of *them* did this dreadful thing?

LT. RHODES: Not at all. The pictures are just routine.

BADGER: I'll have my secretary get the student photographs from the registrar's office. As for the professors, the university's public relations office keeps pictures of them. In case they do anything newsworthy.

LT. RHODES: Thank you, and I'll be on my way.

BADGER: Oh, please, Lieutenant, one more minute. As long as you're here, Lieutnant, *may* I ask you a favor? Trish's death being a murder presents the department with a public relations problem.

LT. RHODES: How urgent is this, Professor Badger? Could it possibly wait? Just now, at the very beginning of the investigation, I have to confine myself to the most urgent matters.

BADGER: I understand, Lieutenant. *May* I talk to you about it tomorrow perhaps?

LT. RHODES: Perhaps. Believe me, Professor Badger, I'll try to be as helpful to you as you're being to me, but right now, you must let me get the investigation started. I'll excuse myself now, if I may.

BADGER: Certainly, Lieutenant.END OF THIS SECTION OF TAPE END OF THIS SECTION OF TAPE END OF THIS SECTION OF TAPE END OF

LT. RHODES: *Comment*. God, she talks like a college president already. If I were this dean, I'd watch my—back. She's as cold and tough as a madam at 5 a.m.

My simile tells me I'm wondering about her personal life—well, let's be blunt, about her as a sexual being. But she shows nothing but executive. I don't think she could be more than forty. A tall, graceful, statuesque woman, five-eleven,145, with prematurely gray hair. She wears a highly professional-looking black suit, and her blouse has a bow at the neck right out of the ads for professional women's suits in the *Times*. Every inch the chair of the department, but I can't help remarking that her breasts are unusually large. I just keep noticing. Maybe that's some kind of saving grace in this tight little office she runs—superficially courteous, but stingy inside, like the thin, mean smile on the secretary's lips.

When she mentioned Sisley's name, she looked as though she had bit on a piece of gristle, to say nothing of what she thinks of Holland. I'm glad I don't have to be them in this department.

Well, as long as I get my fingerprints.

Metropolitan Buffalo Police Department

Tape Transcription   Homicide Unit

Body: *Hassler, P.*   Tape No. *840307.026*
Place: *Rhodes Hall, UB West Campus*   Time: *1:28 p.m.*
Persons present: *Det. Lt. Norman Rhodes, Professor*
       Norman Holland

Transcribed by: *S. Moreno*

HOLLAND: God! *[Pause.]* I don't want this, I just don't want it. I want to go off and sit in front of my word processor and work and not have it. *[Pause.]* I can't imagine who in our group would commit murder. Or why.

LT. RHODES: You think it must have been someone in the seminar?

HOLLAND: I have this seminar on the brain. I suppose it could have been anybody in the English Department. Or anybody at all from anywhere.

LT. RHODES: I didn't say that. I asked you why you assumed it had to be someone in the seminar.

HOLLAND: I suppose I was just thinking automatically of this small world I inhabit. Now that I think of it, I have to tell you something that may have a bearing on—the case. *[Pause.]* I was going to say "the death," but I guess we have to think of it as "the case" now or even "the murder."

LT. RHODES: Tell me. Incidentally, acknowledge the taping.

HOLLAND: Of course, the ever-turning reels of fortune. All right, if we have to be legalistic, of the tape recorder. What I have to tell you is about Christian Aval.

LT. RHODES: The Yale connection?

HOLLAND: You've already picked up the plagiarism! I'm impressed. You *are* good!

LT. RHODES: Plagiarism! All I learned—and it was from you—was that he and Hassler had attended Yale at the same time.

HOLLAND: You didn't get the other, then. I'm not surprised, because we've treated it as confidential, on a need-to-know basis. That sounds dramatic, but plagiarism is always a serious business in the academy.

LT. RHODES: Tell.

HOLLAND: I should say that all this is quite confidential. I happen to know about it because I was serving on the admissions committee when both Trish Hassler and Chris Aval wrote us. They applied very late in the year, practically in May. They were both strong applications, though, and we waived the deadline.

We were a little puzzled, though, why neither of them, in the space where you're supposed to list the other places to which you're applying, listed Yale. They were both interested in literary theory—Yale is very strong in that—and their undergraduate records at Yale were both good, but odd.

Hassler's started off strong, but then fell off in the last year because she failed to write a senior thesis. Aval's grades weren't as high as hers up to the last year, but then they picked up. He did turn in a thesis, and it got very high marks.

We noticed an odd reticence in some of the letters of recommendation. The admissions committee asked me to ask a friend of mine at Yale, who'd written a letter for Hassler, what the story was.

I called my friend, whose name I'd rather not mention, and I pressured her into telling me the real story.

Hassler claimed that Aval had stolen her honors thesis the night before it was due. She said that Aval had wormed his way into her confidence. Once they'd become friends, he managed to steal her paper. According to Hassler, he got into her computer and erased every file related to her thesis, notes, outlines, early drafts, final drafts, everything. He even got hold somehow of her paper notes and print-outs. Then he printed it out on his own machine and turned in the thesis as his own.

LT. RHODES: Whew! Does that sound probable to you?

HOLLAND: Frankly, no. At the time, I didn't see how someone could steal each and every trace of someone else's writing. There are always notes and drafts around. And then, once I got to know Hassler and her anger, it seemed even less likely.

Nevertheless, one thing tended to confirm Hassler's accusation. Aval had handed in a most brilliant thesis, a distinct cut above his previous work.

LT. RHODES: That sounds pretty flimsy to me.

HOLLAND: Her case rested entirely on the Yalies' judgment that she had done outstanding work as contrasted to Aval's much more ordinary performance.

LT. RHODES: No circumstantial evidence?

HOLLAND: She was unable to come up with *any* notes, *any* drafts, *not the slightest scrap of paper,* to indicate that she'd been working on a thesis like the one Aval handed in.

A check by Yale's computer people found no trace of her thesis in her computer—surely an odd state of affairs—and they could see that some files had been erased with more than usual care, as if someone was trying to leave no traces. But, as the computer people pointed out, Hassler could have done that herself, to support her claim.

LT. RHODES: How did Aval answer the accusation?

HOLLAND: He said that they'd been having an affair (and, according to my friend, some students had seen the two of them going into or out of Hassler's room). If that sounds strange, my friend assured me that Hassler had been much more attractive at that time, that she put on a lot of extra weight after all this. Aval claimed his work had suffered because of his involvement with Trish—that was why his earlier grades didn't demonstrate the same ability as the thesis. He said he'd broken off the affair for that and other reasons. She was terribly angry about the breakup and had been unable to write her thesis. Now, he said, she was accusing him of plagiarism out of revenge and, perhaps, as a way of making up for her not having written a thesis. He pointed out that he'd discussed his project with his adviser several times before theses were due. His adviser confirmed the discussions, but said he'd received no notes or drafts from Aval.

LT. RHODES: How did the Yale people decide the case?

HOLLAND: Essentially they saw it as an authorship problem. Who wrote the thesis in question? Like the claim that Shakespeare didn't write Shakespeare. In deciding issues like that, there are two kinds of evidence, intrinsic and extrinsic.

Intrinsic evidence rests on the text alone or inferences from the text. Like the people who say that Shakespeare couldn't have known about kings or Denmark or armies. Extrinsic evidence is evidence from outside the text in question, like the twenty-some contemporaries who said that he wrote one or another of the plays attributed to him.

LT. RHODES: That's like the distinction we draw between direct evidence and evidence of motive, say. One confession or one eyewitness who saw the killing outweighs evidence about who disliked whom or who would profit from the death.

HOLLAND: I guess. I know the principles of my game. I don't know the principles of yours. With us, in factual questions, it's a fundamental principle that extrinsic evidence is much stronger than intrinsic. The twenty-some witnesses far outweigh any inferences from Shakespeare's plays about how much the author knew about court life or Latin grammar.

LT. RHODES: Direct evidence—extrinsic evidence—of course, isn't just eyewitnesses anymore. It has to include chemical analyses of poisons, say, blood types, DNA identifications, fingerprints, all the things the lab guys do. They deal in probabilities so high that they're as conclusive as eyewitness testimony. More so, given the unreliability of eyewitnesses.

HOLLAND: We rarely get physical evidence in literary questions.

LT. RHODES: But in this case you had evidence that someone erased Hassler's computer.

HOLLAND: Who, though? The Yale people had no way to tell. As for extrinsic evidence, they had two totally conflicting and inconsistent narratives, each somewhat shaky. There was no way to choose between them. If only they could have found a file or a print-out with Hassler's name on it or her notes and drafts, but she couldn't produce anything like that. Aval, however, had notes and drafts aplenty.

As for intrinsic evidence, that was inconclusive, too. The style of the thesis looked like Hassler's earlier papers, but it also looked like Aval's earlier papers. They had, after all, been taking the same seminars, reading the same books, playing with the same ideas. In fact, they wrote rather alike, and I'd have to confess that a lot of the high-flying theory that literary people write these days sounds all alike to me.

The Yale people were baffled by the problem. Aval's account was not convincing, but not obviously false. They had no basis for denying him the thesis and awarding it to Trish.

LT. RHODES: So how did the two of them fetch up here?

HOLLAND: Yale decided, finally, on a kind of compromise. Neither student would be admitted to graduate school at Yale. Both should go someplace else for at least a year and then reapply to Yale, if they wished, based on their record in the interim.

   The Yale people urged them to bury the matter. No good would come to Patricia by her continuing her accusations, and obviously no good could come to Aval from this under any circumstances. The best thing for both of them would be to put this behind them and concentrate on doing good work in the future.

LT. RHODES: That's ridiculous! Guilty or not guilty—you have to decide.

HOLLAND: Not in academia. Now, no one was satisfied with this compromise, to be sure, but no one could see anything else to do. My own opinion is that the Yalies did the best they could. The whole effort in a case like this isn't so much to punish as to stop the behavior. One tries to prevent future plagiarism and rescue the fledgling career. The Yale people, for their part, promised to put the matter behind *them* and not to report it in their letters of recommendation or when they reapplied. That was the reason my friend was so reticent.

LT. RHODES: You reported this back to your admissions committee here?

HOLLAND: Yes, and to the chair of the department, Romola Badger. Our committee was very leery of the whole thing. We felt that Yale was just passing the problem on to the next school—us—and we should have none of it. Why were they both coming here anyway? You'd think they'd want to put as much distance between them as possible. Our seven-person committee stood five to two against admitting either one of them. Then Romola stepped in.

LT. RHODES: Stepped in? How?

HOLLAND: This was a great opportunity for us, she said. This was a chance to get two outstanding graduate students from a top-ranking undergraduate school. She'd be able to point to these two and say to the dean that these first-rate students had chosen to leave the program at Yale and come to us for graduate work in English. She could turn this into prestige and even, maybe, money for the department.

   Her argument didn't prevail, so Badger just overruled the rest of us. She sent out letters on her own, accepting the two and even giving them scholarships. It was a fait accompli. The five against admission couldn't do anything. Although all seven of us greatly resented Romola's action, we could hardly call up Hassler and Aval and take their admissions and scholarships back.

We decided the best thing we could do would be to follow Yale's lead. We'd try to get the two students beyond this crisis. We agreed to keep what we had learned from the Yale people confidential, and we didn't tell Trish or Chris that we had learned of the plagiarism affair from Yale. We reasoned that they ought to think—and it was true, after all!—that they were getting a fresh start. That may have been a mistake, however.

LT. RHODES: Why?

HOLLAND: Trish didn't, unfortunately, take the Yale people's advice. When she arrived here, she promptly went to Romola and repeated the same accusation. Three months later, it was even less possible for her to back it up. Furthermore, she said, Aval had followed her here to harass her and block her career in some new way. She behaved toward Romola in an angry and difficult way, and by this time she'd become pathologically fat. (Both those things would count against her with Romola.)

Romola advised her—indeed Romola told me she virtually threatened her—to put this thing behind her and concentrate on building a positive record here. I guess Trish did. At least that's the last I've heard about it. She hasn't spread the accusation among any of the other students or faculty, as far as I can tell, just Romola. As for Aval, he has kept very quiet. He may not even know that she accused him here as she had at Yale.

LT. RHODES: Badger seems to have had a lot to do with Hassler. What's the story? Tell me about Romola Badger.

HOLLAND: Romola may have seen in Hassler a kindred spirit. Humble origins, you could say. Badger started out as a secretary in the Harvard English department back in Cambridge. Far from being intimidated by all those academic stars, she seized on the idea of becoming a professor herself. She worked her way through graduate school and a Ph.D. at Boston University, making all the right contacts. There she wrote a quite conventional and conservative dissertation, on English motifs in Yeats' poetry, in which she forcefully argued the Anglo-aristocratic side of Yeats. Somebody who has read it told me she downplayed all the more obvious Irishness, and that was just what some proper Bostonians among her former employers at Harvard wanted to hear. No friends to the local Irish, they. In due course, the thesis was published, by Harvard University Press, no less. Her pals at Harvard, who would never dream of hiring her themselves, wrote strong letters for her. These earned her an entry-level job at Buffalo, partly because we were more adventurous than most departments in hiring. We hired women before it became the fashionable, and even mandated, thing to do. We liked the idea of a late bloomer, whom conventional departments would have ruled out.

Her predecessor as chair here, and the one who hired her, was Anselm

Agger. During his six-year term, the state was pouring in money, and Ansie built the department from thirty-five to sixty-five people. In that growth period, he made a series of adventurous and glamorous appointments, and Buffalo received considerable local and national visibility. The department could boast of a Pulitzer and a National Book Award, but it also antagonized the town because some of these same leading lights got into trouble for getting drunk, smoking dope, sniffing cocaine, and staging some particularly unsavory homosexual parties.

LT. RHODES: In fact, among my more conservative friends, the university is practically a dirty word. But go on about Badger.

HOLLAND: During Agger's tenure, Badger taught and published steadily if unremarkably. Others at the junior levels fell by the wayside, but after the canonical seven years, she had risen to associate professor and gotten tenure. Then four years ago we got a new governor, the state money dried up, and Badger made her move. She'd built up enough votes to create a kind of palace revolt, the dean intervened, Agger was suddenly out—but got a job at Santa Cruz—and newly tenured Badger was in as chair. Chairperson. She's a political animal, Justin. She wants an administrative career, and I think she's going to have one, worse luck for us.

LT. RHODES: I got the impression, talking to her, that she didn't care for either you or Sisley.

HOLLAND: I'm in the liberal, Agger wing of the department. She's very conservative, both politically and intellectually. She wanted Hassler and Aval because they're right in the conventional main line of the profession.

LT. RHODES: Are you saying deconstruction is conventional?

HOLLAND: Yes, very much so.

LT. RHODES: All this makes a tangled tale, but as you tell the story, the plagiarism, if plagiarism there was, seems to me to give Hassler a motive for killing Aval—revenge. It doesn't give Aval a motive for killing Hassler. If he did plagiarize, he's gotten away with it.

HOLLAND: I hadn't thought of it that way. You're right, of course, but the episode does leave a sort of general suspicion in the air. That's why I thought you ought to know.

LT. RHODES: And why *did* both of them come to UB? I'd sure like to know that. Incidentally, Aval didn't mention a word of this to me. In fact, he went out of his way to give me the impression he scarcely knew Hassler.

HOLLAND: I can understand that. Hassler's accusation could ruin him.

LT. RHODES: I think this plagiarism business must have been what Hassler meant when she said, "He's the one." Or "He's the one who did it." Or whatever she said. So far, I've got eight different versions of what she said. Eyewitnesses!

HOLLAND: Justin, you know, that thought flashed through my mind as she was saying it, but she didn't finish her sentence. "This is the one"—*who? what?* And then when she collapsed and fell, I guess I got distracted and forgot about it. Or I repressed the thought. I don't want to think that of any of my students.

LT. RHODES: You don't want to think *what* of any of your students?

HOLLAND: That one might be a murderer.

LT. RHODES: So now you think that Hassler was accusing Aval of murdering her. The problem with that is, the murder hadn't taken place yet. How could she accuse someone of murdering her if she was still alive?

HOLLAND: So maybe she was accusing him of the plagiarism. But how was the seminar supposed to know that that was what she was talking about? Or maybe that was what she was going to do in the seminar. She was, as you've found out, "it" today.

LT. RHODES: You know, I keep having the feeling that I ought to be able somehow to use the special features of this seminar to expose Hassler's murderer. Something's nagging at my brain.

Let me go over it again. Papers go in mailboxes before Monday noon. Each student reads what the others have written before the seminar meets on Wednesday morning.

HOLLAND: Except that—as you pointed out—they don't all read what they're supposed to.

LT. RHODES: So, it's all done indirectly, not face to face.

HOLLAND: Right.

LT. RHODES: Then, what happens when the seminar meets? If they've written out their responses, what's left for people to say?

HOLLAND: That gets kind of dicey. A lot of times, we're just quiet. People don't know what to say. But what I like to do is this. I like to ask each student to take another student's response and, so to speak, pass it back through the poem so as to generate a new reading. That way, you open the poem or the story up to all kinds of new ways of experiencing it.

LT. RHODES: I'm not sure what that means, but maybe I don't have to know. Papers are in the mailboxes by noon on Monday—Did everyone hand in a response this week?

HOLLAND: Yes.

LT. RHODES: What about Hassler? Does the person who's "it" write a response?

HOLLAND: That's dealer's choice, as the students say. On the week you're "it," you can do what you want. You can write a response to your own writings, stating what you see as your own style, a response like the other students' statements of your style. Most people, however, want to respond to the other students' comments on their writing. There's really only time to do that orally, in the actual seminar meeting.

LT. RHODES: Which did Hassler choose?

HOLLAND: We haven't seen a response from her this week, so I assume she planned to respond face to face. That would be like her.

LT. RHODES: If Hassler had written a response, would it have been possible for someone to take it out of the mailboxes? The interloper, for example. Could he have snitched her replies to the other students?

HOLLAND: I suppose so. It would take awfully precise timing, though. He'd have to steal the responses between the time Trish put them in and before any of the other eight came in to pick them up.

LT. RHODES: So we can be fairly sure that Hassler didn't put a response in the mailboxes.

I keep wondering about that interloper. I wish I knew how he fits into this case.

HOLLAND: I just wish he'd go away. He's been one more thing in this semester's seminar making it unusually difficult.

LT. RHODES: There *must* be some way I could use the kind of insight you're getting in this seminar. Cognitive style, you call it.

HOLLAND: Right. You can take that deeper, if you want. In a psychoanalytic sense, we're getting at their identities. That is, you can imagine a person as having a central theme, the way a piece of music has a theme. Whatever's constant about that person. Whatever you mean when you say, "That's so like Norm." Call it an "identity theme."

The different things that person does we can think of as variations on that theme. An individual walks, talks, writes, reads, makes love—whatever—all with a certain personal style. Then you can read any of those diverse activities as expressions of "identity themes."

LT. RHODES: You can get at these identity themes in a seminar?

HOLLAND: Sort of. You become intensely aware of all these various personal styles in the room with you. You *hear* them as identities. You say to yourself, There goes Amy again. The way the students laughed at her wanting lunch.

It's an uncanny sensation. It's as though the room is full of spirits crowding in on you. It's what it must be like to stand onstage in an octet in an opera. You hear the Don sounding his theme, then Donna Anna sounding hers, and so on. Each sounds distinctive, yet each forms part of this complex, interacting whole. It's like being in the middle of a work of art.

LT. RHODES: I'll say it again. You're like a novelist or a playwright. You say "identity." I'd say you have to find these people's *voices*. Once you can hear them, *really* hear them, you can put them all in a room together and make them interact and they'll sound, somehow, real.

HOLLAND: Maybe. I'm pretty good at reading identities, but I'm not sure I could write a novel or a play.

LT. RHODES: You hear their voices. You know what they're going to say and even how they're going to see and feel. Damn! There must be some way to use this seminar to solve the crime.

HOLLAND: You're going too far, Justin. This theme-and-variation way of reading a person tells you style, but not content. I can't say anything factual about these people on the basis of their identity themes, any more than an understanding of an author's style, *how* an author writes, would let you predict *what* that author will write.

LT. RHODES: You can't predict from these themes . . .

HOLLAND: You can only look backwards. Once my students have done something, I can show you how that's "in character," that is, how it fits their identity theme or, alternatively, how one has to alter one's statement of that theme to fit the new event.

LT. RHODES: So, you could say that so-and-so's murdering Hassler would—or would not—fit so-and-so's theme.

HOLLAND: But that wouldn't prove anything, would it?

LT. RHODES: I'd still like to try and use your seminar. Can I look at these responses and see if I can get any clues?

HOLLAND: You're welcome to look, Lieutenant, but you have to realize that they've written an awful lot. They each write two or three single-spaced pages each week. Do you really want to work your way through a hundred sixty pages of people's free associations?

LT. RHODES: Not me, you.

HOLLAND: Wait a minute. That's what I do in this seminar, but I do it bit by bit over five or six weeks. It takes time to analyze twenty—or sixteen—pages of somebody's writing as closely as this kind of interpretation requires. I'm not sure I can do it all at once.

LT. RHODES: Look, we have a murder on our hands. Give it a try. Let's pick, say, three people and see what you can tell me about them that might open up this killing. What facts can you learn that might be relevant? And what in their style or their identity might have a bearing? If it doesn't work, it doesn't work. You'd only be doing what you have to do for the seminar anyway.

HOLLAND: All right, but I'll just be giving you style. The only facts I can offer you will be what they allege as facts in their squibs.

LT. RHODES: That's plenty right there. Now, which three? I'm very curious about that interloper. Can you tell me anything at all about him from his responses? I'd also like you to tell me what you can about the victim, Patricia Hassler. And, since there's this plagiarism thing between them, what can you tell me about Christian Aval?

HOLLAND: I'll do my best.

LT. RHODES: As soon as you've got something, give me a call.

HOLLAND: Yes. But this is a bigger job than you evidently think.

LT. RHODES: In the meantime, I've got to work though Hassler's papers and search her apartment.

HOLLAND: Can I help?

LT. RHODES: No. Do this other thing. That's something only you can do.END OF THIS SECTION OF TAPE END OF THIS SECTION OF TAPE END OF

LT. RHODES: *Comment.* What do you think of that last question? "Can I help?" Evidently he thinks he's not a suspect. But he has the strongest motive I've uncovered yet, the woman's harassing him, messing up his seminar, humiliating him. He wants to work alongside me, and I wouldn't mind that. He's intelligent, and he can guide me around this strange world. But I've got to remember that he's still a suspect himself.

If that plagiarism took place, it would give Hassler a motive for killing Aval, but how would it give Aval a motive for killing Hassler? Am I missing something here?

There's a discrepancy between their theory and their practice, Hassler and Aval, and the Yale profs. It's just these postmodern types, according to Holland, who believe that the author doesn't matter, that the author has disappeared, that there is no author. But they make all this fuss about plagiarism.

And with what care Holland lectured me on his theories! Couldn't we just say, Personal identity is to style as personal history is to content? That makes sense.

He thinks style won't tell me who did it. He could be wrong.

Anyway, it's useful to keep Holland busy, and who knows? I might learn *some*thing.

I wonder what *his* identity is. Or does that take us into a hall of mirrors?

Metropolitan Buffalo Police Department

Tape Transcription   Homicide Unit

Body: *Hassler, P.*   Tape No. *840307.024*

Place: *24 Masling Blvd.,Apt. 4-K*   Time: *2:04 p.m.*

Persons present: *Det. Sgt. M. Yorrick, A. Lemaire*

Transcribed by: *S. Moreno*

SGT. YORRICK: . . . lots of stairs, Miss Lemaire.

LEMAIRE: They keep my weight down, Sergeant. Let me get these double locks. There. Come in and sit down, won't you? While I fetch those papers.

SGT. YORRICK: But don't touch, remember? And I've turned on this accursed tape recorder, Miss Lemaire.

LEMAIRE: Okay, I understand, but do make yourself comfortable.

SGT. YORRICK: Oof!—I don't know if I can get up out of this chair. Oo-oo-oh, that feels good. I came on at six this morning.

LEMAIRE: Can I offer you a cup of coffee? Tea? Soft drink? Real drink?

SGT. YORRICK: That'd be nice, but the others are waiting in the bus downstairs. This is a real attractive apartment, Miss Lemaire. You've got real furniture in your apartment, not like most of these student places we see. You have this deep armchair, a real maple bureau.

LEMAIRE: Thank you, Sergeant.

SGT. YORRICK: I like the pink and brown colors.

LEMAIRE: The other students have homes they go to. This *is* my home.

SGT. YORRICK: Complete with brown teddy bear, affectionately worn.

LEMAIRE: I've had Mr. Huggins since I was a baby. He looks it, don't you think? Did you know that the psychoanalysts would call Huggins a "transitional object"? I learned that in this seminar.

SGT. YORRICK: I'm just a humble sergeant, Miss Lemaire. And that's your computer, is it? The big box under the flowered cloth? You've put a slip cover over your computer. I suppose that'll be to keep the dust off.

LEMAIRE: It humanizes it a little, too. I know it's wonderful for rewriting and outlining and checking the spelling and all the rest. I feel odd, though, that it's doing all those things for me, and yet it's not a person. It's just a thing, a machine.

SGT. YORRICK: And a bird feeder on the windowsill! And do you get many birds, Miss Lemaire?

LEMAIRE: Mostly in spring. Cardinals, bluejays, nothing special, but I like to do what I can to take care of them in this cruel climate.

SGT. YORRICK: I hope you don't mind my asking it, Miss Lemaire, but how can you afford so nice an apartment?

LEMAIRE: My nest egg, Sergeant. As I told the Lieutenant, I was a flight attendant for eleven years. I saved up enough to take care of me through the Ph.D. and until I get started teaching.

Speaking of which, will you reconsider my offer of coffee or tea? You see, I haven't lost the knack.

SGT. YORRICK: Sorry. The others are waiting. Can you point me to this interloper's papers? Let me do the handling.

LEMAIRE: I keep the Delphi responses in these folders, Sergeant. They're

alphabetical by first name. I call the one you call "the interloper" the out-
sider. He's under O, just after Norm, just before Paul Penza.

SGT. YORRICK: I don't get it. You've got Hassler after Penza. Patricia after
Paul?

LEMAIRE: No, Trish after Paul. I guess they're really alphabetical by nickname.

SGT. YORRICK: Okay, got'em. Well, Miss Lemaire, thank you for letting me in.

LEMAIRE: Who's next?

SGT. YORRICK: Let's see. This is Masling Boulevard, isn't it? You're number 24.
Barry Ireland is 48, further down the street. So long for now.END OF THIS
SECTION OF TAPE END OF THIS SECTION OF TAPE END OF THIS

SGT. YORRICK: *Comment.* Charming little Miss Lemaire has quite a dear apartment for herself. Her "nest egg" must be substantial. There's a photo on
her bureau of a man in uniform, but I couldn't tell what the uniform was.
Not an American military uniform. I didn't think this was the time to ask
her about him. She might have misunderstood.

Metropolitan Buffalo Police Department

Tape Transcription   Homicide Unit

Body: *Hassler, P.*	Tape No. *840307.026*
Place: *48 Masling Blvd., Apt. 3-E*	Time: *2:00 p.m.*
Persons present: *Det. Lt. Rhodes*	
	Transcribed by: *G. de Santis*

LT. RHODES: I'm about to enter the deceased, Patricia Hassler's apartment, apartment 3-E, 48 Masling Boulevard. I'm using the key from her book bag,
although I scarcely need it. This is just an old-fashioned room lock that a
dime store skeleton key would open. There.

Ugh! Books, books, books, everywhere. Boards and bricks for book
shelves. What a mess! A desk made out of plywood laid over packing boxes,
and she's put more books in the boxes. Books stacked on the floor, on the
one chair. So many books, so few papers. A couple of stacks on the desk, a
couple more on the floor. That's it.

Brown plastic garbage bags tacked up for curtains—I've never seen that one before. It's as though she's going to show us what it's like to live in classic student poverty.

Nothing on the wall but more papers. Oh, I see. They're notices of lectures and courses and conferences. She must have taken them off bulletin boards and pinned them up here.

A toaster oven in the corner. It sits on top of one of those little cube refrigerators. Could so meager a kitchen support so fat a woman? Maybe she was trying to reduce.

I don't see a bed. No bed?? How do you live without a bed? Oh, there it is, behind the wardrobe and the bookshelves. It's as though it's set off from the rest of the room, hidden away. A little narrow cot all neatly made up. Hospital corners. And, oh my God!, a child's stuffed animal on the pillow. A cat! A child's toy cat all soft and floppy and rubbed and worn that must have come from childhood here through all her troubles, come to rest on her pillow all hidden away from that chaos of books in the rest of the room.

What's in the wardrobe? Whew! A smell, that's for sure. A few clothes, very few. She's only got two dark shapeless skirts in here. Four blouses on hangers. Underwear in the drawers on the side. Two pair of same on the floor. People said she looked awful in these floppy shapeless clothes.

A tiny bathroom, not much bigger than a closet. I wouldn't be surprised if that was what it was, and that's why she has to use a wardrobe. These landlords! Medicine cabinet. Very neat. Aspirin. Tampax. Birth control pills! But look how old the prescription is—these go back to last spring. And the doctor is in New Haven. No perfume? A razor. Yes, she did shave her legs. Why, you wonder. Nothing much here. The bed and the bathroom are almost impersonal. Except for the cat. I'm touched by that, I have to admit.

Back to the rest of the room and the papers. What is all this stuff on the wall? "Chaucer Deconstructed, a lecture by B. J. Whiting, Harvard University." Here's a sign that just says, "Please Post." Just "Please Post"? Some kind of academic joke, I guess. "Henry Fielding as Feminist" by somebody from the Bunting Institute, Radcliffe. That must have been a short lecture. "Lesbian Science Fiction: Toward the Twenty-Fifth Century?" What would Buck Rogers say or, more to the point, Wilma? It's as if she lived facing a bulletin board. The wall would constantly talk to her, spurring her on in her professional ambitions.

Speaking of which, where are the papers for her courses? Here's one notebook. "Feminism, Film, and Psychoanalysis. Spring 1984." A ringed notebook—these look like class notes. No paper—it's still midsemester, so she hasn't written a paper. "Introduction to Cultural Criticism. Spring 1984."

Okay, so the materials for Holland's seminar should be here too, but where are they? I've got the stuff she took to class, and I've glanced through it. That first look turned up a notebook with notes, very few of them, on past classes in Holland's seminar, but nothing for this one, the March 7 meeting. And I don't see any notes here for today's seminar. There's no accumulation of papers, either—that's what she should have. The rest of them have these file folders full of the papers they've all been circulating to one another, but I don't see any such thing here.

Boy, it could take a week to search this place right. I'll have to get someone who knows this seminar to check it out. Holland? No, he's interpreting the suspects' identities. Sisley? No, he's a suspect, like Holland, for that matter. I need somebody who knows something about the seminar and the university. Badger? I don't trust her. Am I stymied?

And Hassler's computer! I almost forgot. I'm just not used to these things. How do I turn this on? Here. What is this circle and line? Why don't they use on-off like normal people? Wait a minute. Okay. It's humming and beeping like a proper little computer should. Wait. It says, "Operating System Not Installed. Insert Reference Diskette." I've got to get somebody who knows something about computers down here. Maistry? She got a computer science degree from UB, and she's a lot closer to being a student than I am. Maistry could probably search her papers as well as anyone. I'll call headquarters from the cellular downstairs, then get back to the English Department.

—No! I'm at 48 Masling Boulevard, and somebody else in the group lives here. Ireland. That means Yorrick has to be coming by with his busload of seminarians. I'll catch up with them. END OF THIS SECTION OF TAPE END OF THIS SECTION OF TAPE END OF THIS SECTION OF TAPE

Metropolitan Buffalo Police Department

Tape Transcription   Homicide Unit

Body: *Hassler, P.*   Tape No. *840307.024*

Place: *48 Masling Blvd., Apt. 4-H*   Time: *2:20 p.m.*

Persons present: *Det. Sgt. Yorrick, Det. Lt. Rhodes*

    Barry Ireland

Transcribed by: *M. Windham*

IRELAND: Welcome to the hootch, Sarge. Man, it's good to see a sergeant again. Sergeants are real.

SGT. YORRICK: Detective Sergeant. It matters.

IRELAND: It does if you make such a point of it.

SGT. YORRICK: You must like cats, Mr. Ireland. Four in this one-room apartment.

IRELAND: Hey, man, you must be a detective. Yes, I like cats. Love 'em in fact.

SGT. YORRICK: That'd solve the mouse problem in an old building like this.

IRELAND: Yeah, no mice in this apartment, except the ones I bring in myself.

SGT. YORRICK: You do what?

IRELAND: I've got a Vietnamese friend who works in a toxicology lab, where they use a lot of mice. Did you know that's how they measure a lethal dose of a poison? In mouse-units. They really call them that. The amount it takes to kill one twenty-gram mouse in fifteen minutes. They use up a lot of mice that way, and my girlfriend gives me the extras. Keeps the cats in trim. It's the only way I've figured out to keep them from getting to be lethargic pussies instead of real, working cats.

SGT. YORRICK: I guess. But I'm not sure I'm all that cold-blooded, to take a little mouse and turn him loose for these four to chase and torment. They don't kill quick, I'll bet.

IRELAND: Hey, Sarge, don't be squeamish. You got to learn to take your fun where you find it. It's all instinct, anyway. They're just doing what comes natcherly. So far as the mouse is concerned, it's the farm either way, and I'll bet some of those poisons in that lab don't give him too easy an ending. At least my cats are killing for food.

SGT. YORRICK: You've got some souvenirs from Nam—bayonet, Viet Cong flag, cartridge belt, one photo—but alongside it you have this one picture. Is it Greek?

IRELAND: Right on, Sarge. The Charioteer of Delphi. The first time I saw that photograph of the old charioteer, it spoke to me. Ours was a messier war than his—if he was in a war at all and not just a race. I like the way he stands there all obedient, neat vertical lines, poised to do just what they've told him to do. His coach or his officer, whoever. No emotions, just readiness. And stillness. The eyes. The blank whites of the eyes somehow preserved through all these centuries. In Nam, we called that the thousand-yard stare. He looks straight ahead, and what does he see? All the time between him and us stretched out in front of him? Or just the race he's about to run? He sees and he doesn't see, you see, Sarge.

SGT. YORRICK: You mention seeing. I came here to see those papers from Holland's seminar.

IRELAND: Yes sir. [A knock on the door.]

IRELAND: Come in!

LT. RHODES: Gentlemen.

IRELAND: I don't know as there's any here, Lieutenant.

LT. RHODES: If you say so, Ireland. Sergeant, I did some talking up at the English Department, and I took a quick look at Hassler's apartment, which is just down the hall. I think it might be useful if I go around with you collecting the interloper's papers.

Four cats! Does your landlord let you do that?

IRELAND: He does now. One of the other tenants objected, so the landlord got on my case. *[Pause.]*

Then he got off it. *[Pause.]*

SGT. YORRICK: I was just about to get the papers, Lieutenant. Just point, Mr. Ireland. Don't touch.

IRELAND: They're in this stack. I throw all the responses together in one folder, and I only sort them when I need to. I marked his *S* for spy. I doubt if you'll find my prints on them. I'm not the greatest one for reading what I don't have to. If I have to comment on somebody, like with Hassler this week, then I read their papers. But this weirdo? I don't figure we're going to have to write about him.

I'll do what Holland wants, but on my own timetable.

LT. RHODES: Speaking of which, I'd like to go over your timing this morning with you. Hassler lived in this same building, didn't she? And even on the same floor.

IRELAND: Just two doors down the hall.

LT. RHODES: I noticed. Were you ever in her room?

IRELAND: No way. She kept to herself and just as well. Like most people, I didn't care one whole helluva lot for our Trish.

LT. RHODES: When I went through her belongings a few minutes ago, I didn't find any of the papers for this seminar. I also think somebody has tampered with her computer.

IRELAND: Hunh!

LT. RHODES: I think it must have been done this morning between the time she left her apartment and the time everybody was present at the seminar. It wouldn't have been hard to get in—she had an easily defeatable lock. As you do. You live just down the hall from her. Can you account for your movements during that time?

IRELAND: Hey, back off, Lieutenant. I didn't have anything to do with that lady, and I could care less about somebody else doing her. But I didn't dislike her enough to whack her, if that's what you're thinking.

LT. RHODES: Your movements, Mr. Ireland?

IRELAND: I don't know when she left, but I left at my regular time. I allow time enough before seminar for coffee and Danish out of some vending machines on the way. About 8:45. Hell, I can prove it. I saw Hassler on the corner of Main Street, and I gave her the high sign. She didn't answer. Just like her.

LT. RHODES: And what was she doing there?

IRELAND: Doing? I don't know. She was just standing there, in a doorway, with a cigarette in her mouth and her hands stuck in her pockets. She saw me and looked away. I think she didn't want to see anybody. It was cold this morning at 8:45.

SGT. YORRICK: She can't be a witness for your movements, she's dead.

IRELAND: Sorry about that. I forgot for a moment.

LT. RHODES: Which side of the street was she on?

IRELAND: North side.

LT. RHODES: Anybody else see you?

IRELAND: When I got up to the machines, Max Ebenfeld was there.

LT. RHODES: When was that?

IRELAND: As long as it takes to walk up Masling Boulevard, cross Main Street, and walk up to Rhodes Hall—you figure it out.

LT. RHODES: Six or seven minutes?

IRELAND: That sounds about it.

LT. RHODES: Have you got those papers, Sergeant?

SGT. YORRICK: All tucked away.

IRELAND: You through with me, Lieutenant? If you are, I'll just stay here. I've got some work to do.

LT. RHODES: Don't forget, I've asked the seminar to meet tomorrow morning at 9:00 to go over what we've found so far.

IRELAND: You say be there, I'll be there.

LT. RHODES: One more question. You kept on walking up to the English Department, right?

IRELAND: Yeah.

LT. RHODES: Was Hassler still standing there?

IRELAND: Yes.END OF THIS SECTION OF TAPE END OF THIS SECTION OF TAPE END OF THIS SECTION OF TAPE END OF THIS SECTION

LT. RHODES: *Comment.* Just two doors down the hall. That gives Ireland plenty of *other* opportunities. So "doing" her in the seminar, if he could manage it, would make it look as though somebody else did it. *If* he was the killer.

    Ireland would surely have been capable of killing Hassler, if he'd wanted to. But he says he had no reason to, and so far, I don't see that he did. But living so near Hassler . . . Could he have erased her disks this morning? Probably not involved with Hassler. The Charioteer of Delphi. Could he be gay? The cats. An enigma. What we did to people in that war . . .

SGT. YORRICK: Something that might be important, Lieutenant. He told me he has a girlfriend who works in a toxicology lab. A Vietnamese girlfriend. Maybe he could have gotten her to give him this rare poison we're supposed to be looking for.

LT. RHODES: Damned right that could be important! Do we get after him now on that connection? No. I think I'd better wait until Robbie Welder can be definite on what kind of poison it is. But that's an important point, Sergeant.

SGT. YORRICK: He says he saw Hassler just standing around on the corner of Main and Masling.

LT. RHODES: That's puzzling, isn't it? Why would she go to the seminar, then leave in order to stand around in the cold? That's like Glendish and Penza going for a walk. But she wasn't even walking. If he's telling the truth.

State University of New York at Buffalo
Department of English
-Memo-

Date: March 7, 1984
To: All Faculty and Graduate Students
From: Romola Badger, Chairperson
Subject: The tragic death of Patricia Hassler

Earlier today I sent you a memo regarding the demise of Patricia Hassler. I am writing now to correct and add to that earlier notice. I suggested that you write to her family. I am now informed by the Dean of Students that, on trying to contact her parents, the Dean's Office has found that the address in their (and our) files is erroneous. Even as I write, Dean Overten's office is making every effort to ascertain the correct names and address. Until he succeeds, we will have to delay writing our letters of condolence. It is still possible, however, to make a contribution to the memorial scholarship fund the department has set up.

Our grief must be deepened by the shocking news that the police fear her death may well be a homicide. This is a frightful development for our department. I can only hope that this early hypothesis will prove not to be correct. In the meantime, though, it is imperative that we all, students and faculty alike, cooperate fully with the police in their investigation. How we now act is momentous for the way the city and other English departments will perceive us.

We are fortunate that Lieutenant Justin Rhodes has taken charge of the case. Because of his association with the building in which we carry on our work, I think of him as one of us, really, as Rhodes of Rhodes Hall. He is someone who understands the special atmosphere and concerns of an English department. He is on our side in this.

Because of our responsibilities to the community's law enforcement processes, Lt. Rhodes's investigation will take priority over other activities of the department. If his investigation requires the presence of any faculty member or student, that will take precedence over either classes taught or classes attended. If you will notify me of any such requests from Lt. Rhodes, I stand ready to make alternative arrangements, either to have someone else teach the class or to obtain notes or excuses or extensions for students taking classes.

As Lt. Rhodes's investigation has taken shape, he informs me that some problems of identity have arisen concerning graduate students. He has instructed me to tell you that all graduate students are to be fingerprinted. For this purpose, two officers, Hy Rollins and Fred Bowers, will be stationed in the department headquarters with fingerprinting equipment.

Because of the urgency and importance of Lt. Rhodes's fingerprinting order, I am having this memorandum placed immediately in your mailboxes. In addition, I am asking our ever-helpful secretaries to telephone all faculty and graduate students to read you this memorandum if you have not been able to obtain it for yourselves.

Please welcome officers Rollins and Bowers and cooperate with them. The whole business of fingerprinting takes only a minute or so for each individual. I have tried to indicate the department's eagerness to cooperate by being myself the first to be fingerprinted. I found it easy to clean off the ink afterwards.

Again, I know that I speak for every faculty member and student in the department when I speak of our deep sorrow at the passing of Patricia Hassler. As soon as Lt. Rhodes's investigation permits, we shall have a memorial service in which to share our loss and our grief.

Metropolitan Buffalo Police Department

Tape Transcription   Homicide Unit

Body: *Hassler, P.*   Tape No. *840307.029*
Place: *14 Slatin Parkway, # 4*   Time: *2:41 p.m.*
Persons present: *Det. Lt. Rhodes, Det. Sgt. Yorrick; Anne Glendish,*
        Paul Penza

                                             Transcribed by: *M. Windham*

SGT. YORRICK: . . . tape recorder.

PENZA: Hey, sure I see it. Don't you think I love the idea of someone taking down my every sparkling word and carefully transcribing them and treasuring them in files forever and ever? That's immortality, faster than I'll ever see it as a writer.

SGT. YORRICK: And it's okay if I come in and get those extra papers?

PENZA: Sure, those too.

GLENDISH: Hey, Paul, that's for me to say, but, yes, Sergeant, it's okay.

SGT. YORRICK: Nice place.

GLENDISH: Glad you like it.

PENZA: Two can live cheaper than one, they say. Two below poverty level are only half as far down in the soup—or something.

SGT. YORRICK: I don't think I've ever seen so many mirrors in one place.

GLENDISH: They make a small apartment look like a big one.

LT. RHODES: There's hardly any room left for pictures or posters. Is this a poster of you in a production?

GLENDISH: Yes, *School for Scandal,* my sophomore year. I played Maria.

LT. RHODES: The ingenue.

GLENDISH: But—you're a playwright, aren't you? As you'd point out, the interesting part is Lady Teazle. She requires some real acting.

LT. RHODES: As I remember, the older woman whose adultery is exposed, who reforms, and is forgiven.

GLENDISH: Right. That was the part I really wanted.

SGT. YORRICK: I think I could go a little crazy seeing myself everywhere.

PENZA: You have to like yourself a lot, Sergeant.

LT. RHODES: You're frank, Mr. Penza.

PENZA: No, Paul.

LT. RHODES: Oh, come on . . .

PENZA: I couldn't resist, Lieutenant.

LT. RHODES: Try.

SGT. YORRICK: Anyhoo, we came here for the interloper's papers, didn't we? Where do you keep the papers for Holland's seminar?

PENZA: I've got mine over at this desk.

GLENDISH: And mine are here.

LT. RHODES: You keep two sets.

PENZA: Might as well. We get two sets.

SGT. YORRICK: Let's take yours first, Mr. Penza. Let me do the looking and you tell me what to look for. I'm going to handle these sheets by the edges with plastic gloves so as not to smudge any prints. Okay?

PENZA: I keep these in alphabetical order by first names. Just to be different. The mystery student I call a jerk, so he's under *J*.

SGT. YORRICK: Okay, here are the Amys, the Annes, the Barrys, the Christians—and here are the Jerk's. I'll use the tongs to get them in the plastic folder. You marked them in the upper right corners?

PENZA: Yeah. I like to keep them all neatly nicely nestled in order.

GLENDISH: I did that, too. In this seminar there are so many papers to look back and forth at, that you'd go crazy if you didn't arrange them in some kind of order. Yes, that's my stack, but I used last names, and I called this guy the Stranger. That puts him on the bottom where he damn well belongs. There, you've got them.

LT. RHODES: Mind if I look around as long as I'm here?

PENZA: Go ahead. It's all on display.

LT. RHODES: King-sized water bed.

PENZA: Yeah!

LT. RHODES: Two desks.

PENZA: Yeah.

LT. RHODES: I can picture the two of you working here. I like it. Crowded, but maybe you help each other out on assignments. You're the writer, Mr. Penza . . .

PENZA: Yeah.

LT. RHODES: . . . and you're the critic, Ms. Glendish. Nice combination.

GLENDISH: Thank you, Lieutenant.

LT. RHODES: Can I ask, who do you think killed Patricia Hassler?

PENZA: That's your job, not ours.

SGT. YORRICK: Easy, Penza.

GLENDISH: No, Paul's right. You're asking us to cast suspicion on our fellow students. As I see it, we *should* dodge your question.

LT. RHODES: Let me put it the other way round then. Who do you think *didn't* do it?

PENZA: Hah! Artful!

GLENDISH: Yes, clever, but doesn't it come to the same thing?

LT. RHODES: Not really. I'm just looking for a name or two, and there are at least nine suspects.

PENZA: Sorry, Lieutenant, gambit declined.

LT. RHODES: Well, would you listen to the way I size it up? I'm still at the stage of looking for motives or just suspicious behavior. For example, someone behaved very oddly this morning.

PENZA: Who?

LT. RHODES: Professor Sisley.

PENZA: Wally? Cut it out! Wally wouldn't squoosh a cockroach.

LT. RHODES: . . . and Professor Holland had a strong motive . . .

GLENDISH: Holland! Why him?

LT. RHODES: Because she was ruining his seminar, challenging his authority, making him look ridiculous. You know how sensitive professors are. Their whole careers rest on other people's ratings. Besides, Professor Badger was already giving him grief for running this seminar. Hassler was making that much worse.

PENZA: Cool it, Lieutenant. We all resented what Trish was doing to the seminar. It wasn't just Norm.

LT. RHODES: That's what you all tell me. First, everybody disliked Hassler, and then you all add, "But not enough to kill her." Somebody did.

GLENDISH: Dammit, Paul, I'm going to tell him. Rather than his thinking Wally or Norm did it, he's got to know.

PENZA: Now you've torn it! I got that in confidence.

GLENDISH: Not the first part. Not what *you* did, you bastard. Yes, Lieutenant, I'll tell you about somebody's motive. Max Ebenfeld. Good old solid, stolid Max. Trish did a number on him, Trish and Paul here, and I'll venture that he hated her more than anybody. Being Max, he wouldn't show it, of course.

PENZA: Don't, Anne.

LT. RHODES: Quiet, Penza. She has to tell the rest or risk getting into trouble. Go on, Ms. Glendish.

GLENDISH: Look, I can see—everybody can see—that Max is a very decent person. He didn't kill Trish Hassler—I'd stake my life on that. I just want you to realize that other people have motives besides Norm and Wally.

Please don't ever let this get out unless you have to, but he was dating one of his students. Well, one of his ex-students. Like the rest of us grad students, Ebenfeld was teaching a section of freshman comp. There was this freshman girl in his class, Candy Quail, a foxy little bitch away from home for the first time and into recreational fucking. Ebenfeld didn't know that, of course—it was Paul here who found *that* out.

Ebenfeld was smitten. That's the only word for it. A man like Max can commit totally to a woman, and sometimes it's the wrong woman. He was absolutely crazy for Candy, but being honorable old Max Ebenfeld, he didn't try to date her while he was teaching her. He waited for the semester to end. Then when she came back after Christmas, he telephoned her very properly and asked her for a coffee date. (By the way, the dean's office would still look askance at what he was doing. And Ma Badger would have his neck.) She was flattered by this big older—and old-fashioned—graduate student, and off they went to the Pub. Who should be there but Trish Hassler?

Why don't you tell the story, Paul? After all, you were right there in the flesh, you son of a bitch.

PENZA: Always Johnny on the spot to say nothing of Jack of all trades, Lieutenant. Annie, I hate going over all this again.

GLENDISH: Think of Norm and Wally.

PENZA: I was there, at another table, trying to coax myself through another afternoon of literary criticism. Trish Hassler could be amazingly effective with people sometimes. She sized up Ebenfeld and his crush on this little baggage, or somehow maybe she knew about it beforehand. She sat down with the two of them, and she started teasing Ebenfeld. He's a sober, serious kind of fellow, not very good at people games. Pretty soon Trish was playing off Candy against Max, teasing. Did he fix your comma splices? Isn't he the solid, marriageable one? Aren't you finding a father in him? Is he the first Jewish guy you've dated? Trish was quick and nasty, and Max was fumbling for repartee. At least, I think that's the way it must have been. My table was too far away for me to hear every word, but I got most of it. Trish said all kinds of things to make Max look dull and silly. Then Trish sort of scooped Ms. Quail up and took her over to my table. Here's metal more attractive, says Trish, although I doubt if little Candy got the literary allusion.

Well, she was on the make, and Annie and I'd been fighting, and I was teasing and funning with her, and first thing you know she's asking me back to her room. Yes, I felt on my mettle, and Candy was—is—very cute and very willing, and so I went, and I ended up spending most of the weekend in that freshman dorm.

GLENDISH: Paul's Original Rent-A-Penis Agency. You son of a bitch. You have the morals of an alleycat.

PENZA: Look, we went through all this at the time, Anne. Lieutenant, she was as mad as if I'd given her herpes or something. I used a condom!

GLENDISH: You asshole! As if that makes it all right. Yes, we patched it up, Lieutenant, but I can still get angry about it. What a humiliating experience! That dim twit of a freshman! You made me look ridiculous. I guess what keeps me from throwing you out is knowing that I'd just look more ridiculous if I did. This is only temporary anyway.

LT. RHODES: Temporary?

GLENDISH: You have to recognize something about Paul and me. We're not a permanent thing. We're not a big Romance with a capital *R*. We're realists with a capital *R*. Paul takes a realistic view of me, and I take a realistic view of Paul. I like Paul, maybe even love him, but I don't have any illusions about him. He's too much of a cocksman to settle down. Our relationship is strictly temporary.

I couldn't stand you permanently, Paul, and you know that. We have a good thing between us, but it's going to end. I'm going to get my degree and go someplace, and you're going to get your degree and go someplace else. Once a year I'll see you at the Modern Language Association meetings in December. I'll have some fond memories to share with you—and some rotten ones—and that'll be that. I don't want to marry you, and we've had this settled for a long time.

PENZA: I feel I ought to say something smart—defend myself—but you're right, Anne. I'd only be pretending if I tried to do the rose-covered cottage bit. But then, I do like to pretend.

GLENDISH: Pretenses aside, Lieutenant, we don't place great expectations on our relationship. But poor Max—he's not like us.

PENZA: Don't, Anne. I learned this in confidence.

GLENDISH: I don't care. It's got to come out. Paul was working at the Crisis Center one night . . .

PENZA: Goddammit, Annie.

LT. RHODES: Crisis Center?

GLENDISH: Goddammit yourself, Paul. Paul answers telephones at the local crisis center . . .

PENZA: All right, Anne, have it your way. I'll tell it. My thing, my fling, with Candy just lasted that one weekend right after New Year's. Can you have a two-night stand? Well, that's what we did. Max saw us leave the cafeteria, and he heard about the weekend. I don't know how much he blamed me— Max has said to me that he doesn't think I'm the kind of person you can hold responsible—should I be flattered?—but he sure as hell blamed Trish.

How do I know? Because I was on the telephones at the Crisis Center one lousy, snowy February night, and a call came in. George Ames, one of the other volunteers, took it. Thank God it wasn't me. That was some kind of luck! I heard George's end of the call, the names that George was feeding back, "Candy," "Paul," "Trish," and I began to realize that this was Max on the phone. Max was telling George this same charming story that Anne has just told you.

You've got to realize, Lieutenant, I'm not proud of what I did. I was just tomcatting, and that's the way I am, but I didn't mean any harm. Candy was sleeping with every man that took her fancy—why not me? It isn't as though Annie and I were engaged or anything. Candy didn't want Max, and she'd have made Max utterly miserable if they'd connected, so that was that.

I cut my line in to George's and I listened. Max had been drinking, and I think he'd done some pills, too. That's not at all like Max, which tells you how upset he was. This was a whole month after the Candy thing happened. Me he was still furious at, but absolutely enraged at Trish. He saw her as setting out just to do a mean thing to him for no other reason than to do a mean thing, and I have to say he was probably right. He said she'd been teasing him about it, and she said she was going to write a gossipy piece for the student newspaper. That would have utterly humiliated Max.

He was raving about killing her or killing himself. I wrote on George's pad to find out where Max was and go talk him down. I was able to tell George some things about Candy that I figured he could use to help Max cool out and get over her. Despite the weather, George did go over to Max's apartment, and he telephoned me several hours later that he had in fact calmed Max down. He's been his stoical, heroical self ever since that night.

I apologized and told him I didn't know that he felt that strongly about her, which was sort of true, but that she wasn't a good bet for him. I told him how promiscuous she was, and so on. I think Max isn't angry at me anymore or at least not very. I think he feels contempt for me, although it hurts to admit that.

Knowing Max, I think he's probably calmed down toward Trish, too. Certainly, he'd never act on his anger. That's just not Max. You don't even have to know him well to know that. There was just that one night when he was bombed. Max is innocent, I'm absolutely stone-cold sure, and I'd never have told you all this if Anne hadn't forced my hand.

LT. RHODES: When did all this happen, this two-night stand?

PENZA: January 13.

LT. RHODES: And when did Max call the Crisis Center?

PENZA: Let's see. February. A Saturday night. There's a calendar—it must have been the 11th.

LT. RHODES: Less than a month ago.

GLENDISH: I know what you're thinking—that Max is still mad enough at Trish to have killed her. No. That's all wrong. We're telling you this so that you'll realize that some people in that seminar had a stronger motive than just being angry about what was happening in the seminar. You can't settle on Norm or Wally or anybody else for just that.

LT. RHODES: Incidentally, Ms. Glendish, doesn't this episode give you a motive too? Weren't you angry at Trish? "Mad as if I'd given her herpes" was Paul's phrase. That's pretty mad. Did Trish know about your relationship with Paul?

GLENDISH: Of course. Everybody knew.

LT. RHODES: But she used Paul in her little games anyway.

GLENDISH: Trish never liked me. Look, be realistic. We're both Southerners, but from opposite ends of the scale. Trish comes from poor rural white—I was about to say "trash," but that's snotty. I come from well-to-do parents in Richmond. Trish is fat and homely. I'm not. I know from things she's said that Trish looks at me with a good deal of resentment. I've seen it in her eyes.

LT. RHODES: She got back at you, didn't she, by throwing Paul and this freshman together?

PENZA: Freshperson?

GLENDISH: I can't deny that I was damned angry at both her and Paul at the time, but, as you see, wisdom prevails. I'm clearer in my head now about Paul, and I probably wouldn't have been without this.

LT. RHODES: I see. And Paul, what Anne is telling me now is that you and she would have a more serious relationship if Trish hadn't succeeded in using you to get at Max. Trish managed to change your relationship into a definitely temporary one. It sounds to me as though in one maneuver she scored off Ebenfeld, you, and Anne . . .

PENZA: She was one clever bitch.

LT. RHODES: . . . and so you had a motive, too. Revenge, like Anne, and like Max.

PENZA: I was awfully mad for a while, but then I was awfully mad at myself too, and I haven't done myself in, and have no plans to do so.

LT. RHODES: Well, as the old melodramatists used to say, the plot thickens. I appreciate your telling me all this. I'm hoping we can close the case soon. Tomorrow morning I'll have the seminar in for that 9:00 a.m. meeting, and, if I have anything definite, I'll tell you.END OF THIS SECTION OF TAPE END OF THIS SECTION OF TAPE END OF THIS SECTION OF

LT. RHODES: *Comment.* More motives, Sergeant: a motive for Ebenfeld, one for Glendish, one for Penza, but none of them sounds strong enough to do it. I'm just not hearing any *passion* from these people. Interesting that they're so loyal to the two profs in the seminar.

What an intriguing woman Glendish is. The way she turned Penza's story around to make herself, not Ebenfeld, the center of attention. Subtle.

And what's a lightweight like Paul Penza doing in a Crisis Center?

Still no hard facts! Oh well. Who's next, Sergeant?

SGT. YORRICK: Ebenfeld. He lives further down on Masling Boulevard.

LT. RHODES: And he's waiting. Let's go. I guess it wouldn't be much use running the recorder in the bus.

SGT. YORRICK: *I* didn't.

Metropolitan Buffalo Police Department

Tape Transcription   Homicide Unit

Body: *Hassler, P.*   Tape No. *840307.029*

Place: *131 Masling Blvd., Apt 3*   Time: *3:05 p.m.*

Persons present: *Det. Lt. Rhodes, Sgt. Yorrick, Max Ebenfeld*

Transcribed by: *M. Windham*

LT. RHODES: Whew! That's a lot of weights, Mr. Ebenfeld. I don't envy whoever lives on the floor below you. And you've got machines anchored to the wall, too. Did your landlady go along with that?

EBENFELD: I promised her I'd spackle the holes when I moved out, and she trusts me, and I will.

LT. RHODES: I can remember impoverished student days, when the only pictures I could afford were tacked-up reproductions. You've got a portrait bust, a head, and I like it. It's usually identified as Julius Caesar's, isn't it?

EBENFELD: Yes, so they say.

LT. RHODES: Although that seems fairly improbable, I suppose.

EBENFELD: I don't know. Somebody as important as Caesar—there must have been some genuine likenesses.

LT. RHODES: But is this one? Or is it just some handsome older Roman gentleman?

EBENFELD: Whoever it is, I like the leanness and severity of the face. It works by contrast, as I read it. The strong, downward lines at the mouth, lines of judgment and decision. Then see how they're balanced by the horizontal furrows across the brow, marks of thought and concern. Altogether, it's the face of a man with all the pagan virtues. I'm afraid I don't have all the pagan virtues, and my jaw is too big. I have too much hair to look like Caesar. But I like to imagine myself someday, when I'm older, having a face like that.

LT. RHODES: Older, yes. It seems to me an odd, elderly choice of art for a young man. I would've expected a pin-up or something postmodern.

EBENFELD: People sometimes tell me I was born middle aged.

LT. RHODES: But this other picture, this girl, seems little more than a child. This from a newspaper?

EBENFELD: The campus paper was reporting on a beauty contest they held among the freshmen women. Joe College stuff, but this girl was in the section of freshman comp I was teaching last semester.

LT. RHODES: Is this Candy Quail, the one that Paul Penza spent the weekend with? [Pause.]

EBENFELD: You don't miss much, Lieutenant. How did you hear about that?

LT. RHODES: Anne Glendish told me.

EBENFELD: I think Anne was a lot more bothered about what Paul did than she lets on. Anyway, I was taken with Candy Quail. It's as straightforward as that. Your mind can do strange things to you, staring at a pretty young blonde all semester and knowing she's taboo. And they flirt, of course. They figure it can't do their grade any harm to flirt a little with the instructor. I think now I was rather a fool. I keep the picture on the wall as a cautionary reminder. Perhaps too because I'm still not over it.

It's an old story, as old, I suppose, as Samson and Delilah.

LT. RHODES: How about King Kong and Fay Wray? "It was Beauty killed the Beast."

EBENFELD: I don't fancy myself a beast, Lieutenant.

LT. RHODES: Ms. Glendish said the one who broke up your romance was Trish Hassler.

EBENFELD: Yes. Of the three of them, she was doing it just out of meanness. Candy was, well, hell, she was just being the way she was—is. Penza you can't blame for screwing her any more than you can blame a cat for killing a bird. But Hassler spoiled it just for the sake of spoiling it, of showing her power and her—meanness.

LT. RHODES: They tell me you were angry—furious—at Hassler for her interfering.

EBENFELD: I won't deny it. I was angry at her, angry at Penza, angry most of all at myself. Did I kill her? No, of course not. How does getting revenge weigh against ruining my life? No. I'll get over it. I was infatuated. I misread her. I wasn't rational. Now I am. It's that simple, Lieutenant.

LT. RHODES: You understand, I have to consider every possibility. Now, can we find those papers from the interloper?

EBENFELD: Here they are— I keep them separated from the rest of the seminar papers.

SGT. YORRICK: Don't touch, just point to them. Okay. Into the glassine with you.

EBENFELD: Do you think he did it?

LT. RHODES: That I don't know, but until we can force him out into the open, we're not going to know everything we should know about Patricia Hassler's death.

EBENFELD: Is that all you need me for, Lieutenant? I've got work to do.

LT. RHODES: Yes, Mr. Ebenfeld. Thank you for your cooperation.END OF THIS SECTION OF TAPE END OF THIS SECTION OF TAPE END OF THIS

LT. RHODES: *Comment.* He sounds too damned rational. Why would he still keep her picture on the wall? Is he fueling his anger? He says not. He seems calmed down, but he'd be formidable if you had to fight him. Poison? He doesn't seem the type—he seems more physical than that—but the interview leaves me uncertain. I think if he were angry, he could be enraged—all that rationality would fall away. But we're dealing with a poisoning here, and an esoteric poison at that, premeditation and lots and lots of planning. Ebenfeld would fly off the handle and then calm down—I think. Hyperrational, perhaps, after the cooldown.

But I can't be sure. I need some piece of direct evidence. Who's next, Sergeant?

SGT. YORRICK: Aval. He's the last one in the bus. 7 Sanes Terrace. Back towards Main Street.

LT. RHODES: These streets cross one another like ski trails.

SGT. YORRICK: Let me put a new tape in the machine. END OF THIS SECTION OF TAPE END OF THIS SECTION OF TAPE END OF THIS SECTION

Metropolitan Buffalo Police Department

Tape Transcription   Homicide Unit

Body: *Hassler, P.*   Tape No. *840307.031*

Place: *7 Sanes Terrace*   Time: *3:30 p.m.*

Persons present: *Det. Lt. Rhodes, Sgt. Yorrick*

        Christian Aval

                                                Transcribed by: *S. Moreno*

SGT. YORRICK: No, not just a nod—could you say something?

AVAL: Ever the logocentric, are we not? Yes, Sergeant. I acknowledge that you are recording our search for the papers—the squibs—of this so-called mystery student. In fact, Sergeant, it will take no time at all, because I have got them in their proper, special place. You can see the folders for this seminar on that shelf over the desk. I have kept the mystery student's squibs in a folder marked X. I think it is on the bottom . . .

SGT. YORRICK: Let me handle the papers, Mr. Aval.

LT. RHODES: I think I mentioned, M. Aval, that we're looking for fingerprints.

AVAL: I understand, Lieutenant, and I hope you find them. It grieves me very much what happened to Patricia Hassler, and I hope you find out who did it.

LT. RHODES: That is, as we say, the aim of the game. You have a pleasant apartment here. I like your choice of art.

AVAL: I can only afford cheap reproductions.

LT. RHODES: But they interest me for all that. Escher: the birds turning into fishes and the hand drawing itself. And Magritte's picture of the pipe with the words, *Ceci n'est pas une pipe*. You do like paradoxes, don't you? But this object I don't recognize. This is an original, not some reproduction. It looks like a million doors—how does it do that?

AVAL: I am very fond of this work. It was given me by the artist, who is a young woman I used to know in Paris. Sylvie Japrisot is her real name, but she signs her work Boum. Simply Boum. What she did here was make a wire construction of a door and hang it between two mirrors that are at a very slight angle to each other. An angle both in the horizontal plane and the vertical plane. The result is that you see a spiral of transparent doors leading up and down from the frame.

LT. RHODES: Every door leads to another door, you could say. It could be a motto for a detective.

AVAL: It fits everyone, I think, Lieutenant. She has dramatized the path of the signifier as described in the teachings of Jacques Lacan.

LT. RHODES: The signifier?

AVAL: Loosely, the word. Each word leading to another word, never to a definite meaning.

LT. RHODES: But you could simply say each door is empty, an image. Even the first one, you must admit, is only a volume created by wires. So it could say something else: that each door is itself an illusion.

AVAL: I could not have put it better myself, Lieutenant. An excellent reading.

SGT. YORRICK: This is quite the computer you've got here, my lad.

AVAL: My one luxury. I love computers. I love to play games with them. I love to program them. They seem to me the most marvelous toys that anyone ever invented.

SGT. YORRICK: This is a PS/2 70. Those are just out, aren't they? State of the art— verr-ry nice.

LT. RHODES: And verr-ry expensive.

AVAL: The one indulgence I can give myself. I am crazy about computers. To me, they are an extension of my being into hyperspace. They project me out into millions of bytes in files upon files and, when I use my modem, out into the universe. I can of course use e-mail and BITNET for letters, but I can even talk—or talk-on-the-typewriter—with my friends in France through the CompuServe network here which interfaces—that is a verb, is it not?—to Minitel, the teletext that runs on the French telephone system. I do not have a car, and I live cheaply otherwise. Accordingly, I simply added another thousand dollars to what I would have had to spend anyway. I think I mentioned to you that I had a small inheritance from my father's sister.

Just a minute! What is this? There is something here in the computer that does not belong here, something wedged between the monitor and the central processing unit. It is a vial. It has a label. This is a word I do not know! S-A-X- . . .

LT. RHODES: What does that label say? Saxitoxin? Saxitoxin. Where have I heard that word before?

AVAL: If it ends in "toxin," it must be a poison. *Toxine* in French.

LT. RHODES: Right! I remember now. That was one of the poisons Robbie Welder mentioned, one of the possibilities in the killing of Patricia Hassler. For God's sake, Aval, be careful! Put that down very gently on the table. *NO!* Don't try to open it. Just put it down.

SGT. YORRICK: That's it, Aval. On the table.

LT. RHODES: Yorrick, bag it. Use tweezers. There may be fingerprints. This is our first solid evidence. M. Aval, you and I have to have a talk.

AVAL: But this is not mine. I have never seen it before. I do not know what it is doing there stuck into my system.

LT. RHODES: I don't know either, and that's why you're going down to headquarters—to explain.

AVAL: But this is an outrage! How can I explain? I have never seen this vial before. I have never laid hands on it. This is not normal! I never heard of this stuff, whatever you call it, sexy toxin.

LT. RHODES: Saxitoxin.

AVAL: You are mounting an attack on me. I am being boxed!

LT. RHODES: You mean framed—that's the idiom you've heard in the *films noirs*. Nevertheless, M. Aval, I am going to have to bring you down to headquarters for questioning.

AVAL: You cannot be arresting me!

LT. RHODES: Actually, I can. I have enough evidence. As for motive, there was the plagiarism problem with Patricia at Yale.

AVAL: But nothing was ever proven! And now you are accusing me of murder! You irrational Americans, you are making me into a criminal, because you do not think logically.

LT. RHODES: Something else. During our first interview, you pretended you hardly knew Hassler. But you went through that whole plagiarism investigation at Yale with her, and, if we believe her, you were lovers.

AVAL: I said nothing false. Your recording tapes, in which you rely so much, will tell you that.

LT. RHODES: When you said that you knew her by sight, you certainly implied that you scarcely knew her at all, and that was false.

AVAL: That was true. I did know her by sight.

SGT. YORRICK: Mither o' God, this is our murderer!

LT. RHODES: Stop playing games, Aval. Another thing. I've checked Hassler's apartment and her computer was wiped. Just the way it was at Yale. Now I find that you know enough about computers to have done that. And this vial. How did you get this poison?

AVAL: I did not get it! I never saw that bottle before. After all, it was I who pointed it out to you. Would I do that if I were the murderer? I know nothing about erasing her computer. You cannot arrest me. If you arrest me you make me a criminal. Even if I can prove my innocence, the Immigration will send me back to France.

LT. RHODES: M. Aval, I could arrest you on the strength of this bottle. I think I could even convict you . . .

AVAL: No!

LT. RHODES: . . . with what I now have, but if you'll come willingly to headquarters for questioning, I won't have to make a formal arrest. You must admit, the circumstances make you look very guilty.

AVAL: What are these "circumstances"? This is nothing but your accusation. Mere psychologizing!

LT. RHODES: Be precise, M. Aval. My *suspicion* of you—not my accusation, not my arrest—rests on my interpretation of certain well-established facts—

AVAL: Facts! This is simply formalist-humanist psychologizing hypostatized . . .

LT. RHODES: Be quiet. You and Patricia Hassler had a terrible quarrel less than a year ago. The accusations you exchanged were nearly enough to destroy both your careers. There's a motive in that exchange. We find in her apartment that her computer's hard disk has been erased. The same thing happened last year at Yale. You're expert with computers. Now I find in your apartment a vial of the same kind of poison that the medical examiner tells me killed her, a neurotoxin. Granted, these facts say nothing in themselves. It's my interpretation that leads me to you. It's also my interpretation that could very well convict you of her murder. It's my interpretation that leads me to keep you at headquarters until we can establish your relation to the murder of Patricia Hassler.

AVAL: You are ontologizing these suspicions, Lieutenant. These facts say something entirely different. They say that someone is trying to cast suspicion on me. I have no way of getting into Patricia Hassler's apartment to do things to her computer. And why would I do that, anyway? What does that have to do with her death? I have no way of obtaining such a chemical. Certainly, if I were going to hide this bottle, I would pick a better place. And why would I keep it around, anyway?

LT. RHODES: For future use. For another attempt if the first wasn't successful.

SGT. YORRICK: Because we didn't give you a chance to get rid of it, after you used it this morning to kill Patricia Hassler.

AVAL: No, Sergeant, no! I did not kill Patricia! Yes, there was a bad feeling between the two of us. But it was she who hated me. I did not hate her. I do not understand what happened between us. I have never understood the situation in which I found myself with her at Yale.

LT. RHODES: All these matters, M. Aval, I'd like you to go over with us at headquarters. If you insist, I'll arrest you, but, as you point out, that could cause you difficulties with Immigration. I'd prefer that you come with us, so to speak, willingly. If you do so, I'll keep your visit to headquarters quiet. If not . . .

AVAL: Willingly! You give me no choice!

LT. RHODES: I didn't intend to give you a choice, M. Aval, but I do intend to deal fairly with you. If you didn't kill Patricia Hassler, we'll find that out, too. Did you send that minibus back to headquarters, Yorrick?

SGT. YORRICK: No, Lieutenant. It should still be downstairs.

LT. RHODES: Then take him to headquarters, Yorrick. Wait a minute while I wind this up.END OF THIS SECTION OF TAPE END OF THIS SECTION OF TAPE END OF THIS SECTION OF TAPE END OF THIS SECTION OF

LT. RHODES: *Comment.* Aval is right, of course, but I have to bring him in. If I didn't, given the evidence we have, the papers would be all over me and probably the captain too.

Aval found the vial, and he didn't have to. We could easily have missed it. The most telling point is that he'd surely have found a better place to hide it. For God's sake, he could just have chucked it out of the window into the bushes behind this rooming house!

But a vial of saxitoxin! A neurotoxin of the type that Welder says killed her. No way can I ignore that.

The computer wiped at Yale and wiped here. I've got to get Maistry to look at it! Damn! Why doesn't she call back?

I'll go down to headquarters with Aval and Yorrick to set up the interrogation. I think Yorrick and Wakowski can handle it, since it's pro forma. I'll go back to the English Department for Holland's analyses.

Metropolitan Buffalo Police Department

Office of the Medical Examiner

Case: *Hassler, P., #840307/1*   March 7, 1984

To: *Det. Lt. Norman Rhodes*

Department or Unit: *Homicide*

From: *Robert Welder, M.D.*

Second Report

The victim was a large, white woman in her early twenties, height 1.80 m. (5' 11"), weight 106 kg. (233 lbs.). Hair dark blonde, eyes brown. No distinguishing marks. There was nothing unusual about the body except for her obesity. The varying density of the lipoproteins suggests that said obesity was recently acquired.

Time of death was established by external evidence at 9:10 a.m., Wednesday, March 7. Preliminary examination at the scene took place at 9:51 a.m. Autopsy began at 10:50 a.m. and was completed at 11:35 a.m.

Examination during autopsy of the esophagus and stomach indicated that the victim had consumed no food since the previous night.

My conclusion on initial pathological examination of the body (conveyed by telephone to Det. Lt. Rhodes at 11:40 a.m.) was correct. Death was by poisoning, and the poison was one of the alkaloid neurotoxins. Envenomation took place through a puncture wound on the right buttock on the dorsal surface nearest the hip joint. Judging from the traces of poison we found in the wound, I would estimate the dose at about 15 mg.

The alkaloid neurotoxins break down the sodium-channel conduction of nerve impulses to the muscles. As a result, the muscles of the heart and diaphragm abruptly cease to function. The victim stops circulating blood, stops taking in oxygen, and death follows very rapidly, sometimes in less than a minute. The process is, as these things go, fairly painless.

Identifying this type of poison requires an up-to-date autoanalyzer and high-pressure liquid chromatography. Because this department has not been budgeted for a recent-model autoanalyzer, it was necessary to carry out these preliminary tests at the laboratory of Professor Harold Vernor of the College of Pharmacy at the State University of New York at Buffalo. Further tests were required to place this poison specifically among the dibenzoxazepines. I conducted with Professor Vernor an application of the specimen obtained from the victim's body to mouse blastoma cells, and we were able to establish that this poison was saxitoxin or one of its close variants.

This poison is not easy to obtain. Discovery of who obtained it and how could be decisive in solving this homicide.

Notable: In the same area as the puncture wound by which the poison was introduced into the bloodstream, that is, on the right buttock, there was one similar puncture wound, partially healed.

I leave this matter and the obtaining of the saxitoxin to the detectives on the scene.

/Robert Welder/

Metropolitan Buffalo Police Department

Tape Transcription   Homicide Unit

Body: *Hassler, P.*   Tape No. *840307.031*
Place: *Telephone call*   Time: *5:16 p.m.*
Persons present: *Det. Lt. Rhodes to Medical Examiner*
    Robert Welder, M.D.

Transcribed by: *G. de Santis*

[Dial tone, ringing]

LT. RHODES: Robbie! Is that you? What're you doing to me? What is this saxitoxin stuff? Explain, explain.

DR. WELDER: Ah, Justin, dear boy. It's always a pleasure to chat with my distinguished colleague from the Rhodes family, and I had an idea my report might get a rise out of you. By the way, are you taping this? So that I won't have to write it all out?

LT. RHODES: Of course, Robbie. You know the drill. Just tell me about this re-markable poison.

DR. WELDER: Patience, patience, dear boy. I've been enjoying the leisurely pace and the relaxing charms of academe today, and it's hard to come back to your intensive speed.

    Justin, I had quite the fascinating afternoon. All those women! Don't you ever get the feeling we ought to retire to the university? Ah, it was so good to get this aging body out of my cold basement shop and into a bright, cheerful top-notch university lab for a change. Where, by the way, I met the most charming Vietnamese girl—

LT. RHODES: Yes, I'm sitting in the English Department right now, and it's charm-ing, utterly charming. But I want to know about this saxitoxin.

DR. WELDER: What's the hurry? I heard down here that you'd made an arrest.

LT. RHODES: Not an arrest. We brought one of the students in for questioning. Pro forma. He didn't do it—at least not on the evidence we have. Anyway, I'm back in academe, you're not, and now, dammit, tell me about saxitoxin.

DR. WELDER: You're always in a hurry, Justin, always ordering people around. But if you insist on haste, my friend, you shall have it. As soon as I got Hassler's body down here and found the tiny amount it had taken to kill her, I realized that this poison was a little beyond the capabilities of our humble lab. Justin, if you have any pull at all with the commissioner, tell him we really need that new autoanalyzer . . .

LT. RHODES: Please!

DR. WELDER: I called "Pop" Vernor, a well-known toxicologist at the university. His research is on neurotoxins, and his specialty is tetrododoxin, you know, the poison from those puffer fish the Japanese eat. The danger adds to the whole eating experience. However, our poison here wasn't tetrodotoxin, it was saxitoxin, but that turned out to be close enough so that Vernor could test for it and establish its identity.

LT. RHODES: Go on.

DR. WELDER: Saxitoxin is quite an ancient poison, actually. It's what people who live by the sea call a "red tide." Tiny organisms color the water and also concentrate in the stomachs of certain shellfish, which makes them abso-lutely lethal to eat. You can get sick just from smelling this stuff. It's a disaster both for tourism and the fishing industry. That's why there's been a lot of research on it.

    Primitive peoples have known and feared this phenomenon for a long time, but it wasn't until 1927 after a San Francisco outbreak that the organ-ism was identified by a very brilliant man, Hermann Sommer. It was one of the great breakthroughs in our knowledge of marine animal poisons, and I hope you're being properly reverent, Justin.

LT. RHODES: Come to the point, Robbie.

DR. WELDER: That's exactly what I'm coming to, the point. You're too young to remember this, Justin, but Eisenhower and Khrushchev were all set to have a summit meeting sometime in the late fifties, when the Soviets managed to shoot down a spy plane flying way up in the stratosphere somewhere. Eisenhower claimed the U.S. wasn't involved, but the Soviets called him a liar and scuttled the summit by putting the pilot on TV—one Gary Powers, a CIA freelancer.

LT. RHODES: The point, Robbie.

DR. WELDER: The Russians also showed on TV a lucky piece they had found in Powers's pocket. It looked like a regular silver dollar, but when you slid back the figure on the coin, a small chromium needle stuck out. The Russians tried the pin on a dog, which went into convulsions and died almost instantly. The needle was grooved, and in the grooves was the captured spy's friend, saxitoxin. Evidently Powers was supposed to use the suicide coin, but didn't, and that's how saxitoxin emerged on the international scene.

Nowadays the CIA has much purer forms with much higher lethality. The victim goes "out like a candle," to quote one of the military documents Vernor showed me. That's how your poisoner could do it with a single pinprick.

LT. RHODES: Who'd have this stuff, Robbie?

DR. WELDER: Most obviously, the CIA. Congress caught the agency with a huge amount, and its sole use is assassination. Naughty, naughty, Congress said, get rid of it—burn it. But what really happened to it, nobody knows, of course.

LT. RHODES: Robbie, be serious. You don't think the CIA killed Patricia Hassler.

DR. WELDER: As a good liberal, mayn't I even entertain the thought?

LT. RHODES: Robbie, please. How or why would somebody besides the CIA have saxitoxin?

DR. WELDER: A medical researcher might have it. Vernor told me that it's used to research the "voltage-gated sodium channel" by which nerves transmit impulses. The drug blocks it completely, so you can, in effect, turn the channel on and off.

In fact, that's how we tested for it. Vernor explained it to me. They used to test the unknown substance on a live mouse, but this new test just uses a few mouse blastoma cells that you watch reacting in a microscope. Chemically, you increase the cells' permeability to sodium so they begin to swell up and die. You then administer the unknown substance. If it's saxitoxin, that blocks the sodium, and the cells stop swelling and survive. This new test is a honey, a lot cheaper, a lot more reliable. The shellfish industry is delighted. And so are the mice.

LT. RHODES: Welder, you're being professorial.

DR. WELDER: Naturally. I've been around the university all afternoon, Justin. Besides, you know how I get interested in the science of it and lose sight of the case.

LT. RHODES: But I don't have that luxury. What does the fact that saxitoxin was used tell us about this case?

DR. WELDER: One thing. Hassler had a remarkably quick and easy death.

LT. RHODES: All right. What else?

DR. WELDER: Nothing, except, given where and how and when this took place, given the point of envenomation, given the amount, I've got a beautiful guess as to how it was done.

LT. RHODES: Save your guess, Robbie. Not yet. I don't want it on this tape. We've found what you call "the means of envenomation," and I've had what I'll bet is the same idea, but I want to keep it very quiet. I'm going to spring it on the seminar tomorrow and see who's surprised and who isn't. Yorrick is on his way down to your lab with it.

DR. WELDER: I'll be here for another fifteen minutes—no more, Justin. If you're going to test for saxitoxin, though, take it directly to Vernor at the university. Remember, we don't have an up-to-date autoanalyzer here. Please, I know you know the commissioner. Tell him—

LT. RHODES: Okay, Robbie, okay. The next time the commissioner asks me how to spend his budget, I'll tell him to buy you a—what is it?

DR. WELDER: An autoanalyzer.

LT. RHODES: Will do. Thanks for the lesson, proto-prof. I've got some new words in my vocabulary. Catch you later.END OF THIS SECTION OF TAPE END OF THIS SECTION OF TAPE END OF THIS SECTION OF TAPE

LT. RHODES: *Comment.* Progress on two fronts. One, we have an esoteric poison that apparently only the CIA or some highly specialized medical researcher would possess. Hence one line for us to follow is, Who had access to saxitoxin? Who actually possessed it? Once we've traced it, we've got our killer. I think I'll start with this Professor Vernor. Let him check the vial that the killer planted in Aval's apartment. And I've got to get him to check the "means of envenomation," anyway.

Point two, I think we may have gotten the way she was poisoned. If we're right, it has to have been someone who was in that room this morning, someone who was there after she came in and went out again. Probably not Aval.

Things are narrowing nicely. As long as I'm here in the English Department, I'll ask Holland how he's coming along with his analyses of the student papers.

Metropolitan Buffalo Police Department

Tape Transcription   Homicide Unit

Body: *Hassler, P.*   Tape No. *840307.031*

Place: *Rhodes Hall, West Campus, EB*   Time: *5:28 p.m.*

Persons present: *Det. Lt. Rhodes, N. N. Holland*

Transcribed by: *J. Cipperman*

LT. RHODES: *[Knocks at door.]* Rhodes here. Can I come in?

HOLLAND: Sure, come in. If you can fit. At least I've got a window with a view of Main Street. Let me get some books off this chair, and you can sit down.

LT. RHODES: I have to tell you something. We've taken Christian Aval down to headquarters.

HOLLAND: Chris! Chris killed Trish Hassler?

LT. RHODES: No, I'm distinctly not telling you that, and that's why I'm not noising this fact around. Let me explain. We found evidence in Aval's apartment that I simply cannot ignore. We found an empty vial of the poison that killed Hassler stuck under his computer monitor.

HOLLAND: I can't believe this!

LT. RHODES: I took Aval in because I had to. The newspapers and the captain would have my a— my neck, if I ignored a piece of evidence like that. I don't mind telling you, though, Norman (and, for that matter, putting it on tape) that I'm not convinced the evidence proves he's guilty.

    Strictly speaking, we didn't arrest him. He was worried about Immigration, so I made him come down quote—voluntarily—unquote. The real reason I wanted to interrogate him was to make him tell us what actually happened at Yale. But we're not getting anywhere with that either.

HOLLAND: You mean this questioning is going on right now? While we talk?

LT. RHODES: Yes.

HOLLAND: Why aren't you down there?

LT. RHODES: I did hang around for an hour or so.

HOLLAND: And you left?

LT. RHODES: Because I don't think he killed Hassler. Because Yorrick and Wakowski are good at this kind of thing. Because it takes a lot of time. They could be at it until midnight. They'll alternate. They'll grill him for a while, hard about the poison and Hassler's computer and sidewise about what happened at Yale. Then they'll let him cool his heels for half an hour or so, working up a little anxiety. Then they'll grill him again, good-cop–bad-cop style. Yorrick plays the good guy, your genial Irishman, while Wakowski looks very threatening, kind of like a skinhead, which sometimes I suspect he is.

HOLLAND: This is rotten.

LT. RHODES: All very legal, Professor, and we do have a murder to solve.

HOLLAND: Has he got a lawyer?

LT. RHODES: He's an alien. No Miranda rights. And he hasn't been arrested.

HOLLAND: But you're putting him through this, and you don't even think he did it!

LT. RHODES: Think about it. I've got to make sure, haven't I? For Aval's sake as well as everybody else's. Right now this case is a long way from being closed. Speaking of which, tell me, How are you coming with analyzing those responses for me?

HOLLAND: You're asking me to do about a week and a half's work, all told, in a day.

And I got interrupted, too. A reporter from the *BMNG*. She wanted to hear all about the seminar, and that took a while. She was convinced that the seminar caused the murder, and it took me a while to convince her otherwise. I hope.

But I've done two sets of responses, and I've nearly finished Aval. The first ones took longer, because I had to figure out how to do the interpretation so it would be of use to you. Here's what I did. It's all written out for you. I'm afraid it's fairly long, but I can continue to work on Aval while you're reading it—them.

LT. RHODES: Okay, whoever is transcribing this— put in the file at this point Professor Holland's letter dated March 7, 1984.END OF THIS SECTION OF TAPE END OF THIS SECTION OF TAPE END OF THIS SECTION

State University of New York at Buffalo
Department of English

March 7, 1984

Dear Justin:

You asked me to interpret the seminar responses from the mystery student, from Patricia Hassler, and from Christian Aval. You asked me to give you my idea of the kind of person they are or, more precisely, my reading of their cognitive styles. Let me remind you again that all I can claim is that once they've done something, whatever they've done will very likely fit the themes I've found. (But not necessarily; maybe we'd have to revise the themes.) *Caveat detector.*

Something else. Identity is a way that one person interprets another person. You can't take these interpretations as some final reading of Trish or our mystery student or Aval. They're only the opening of a discussion that, in principle, can never end. The perfect academic interpretation.

As I looked back through the students' writings, it seemed to me the best way to go about this would be to recognize that you're no slouch as an interpreter yourself. You could do worse than read the responses on your own.

But you're in the middle of a murder investigation and pressed for time. What I'll do is give you here just two of their responses, the same two for each. That way, you can compare. Incidentally, that's what took the time this afternoon: going through the responses and choosing the two I'd photocopy for you.

One of the responses I chose is to a poem by Denise Levertov. Because it's about a snake, a lot of them wrote about poison, and I thought you might find that relevant. Also, it's quite a clear illustration of the method we use in the seminar. Here's the poem:

TO THE SNAKE

Green Snake, when I hung you round my neck
and stroked your cold, pulsing throat
      as you hissed to me, glinting
arrowy gold scales, and I felt
      the weight of you on my shoulders,
and the whispering silver of your dryness
sounded close at my ears—

Green Snake—I swore to my companions that certainly
      you were harmless! But truly
I had no certainty, and no hope, only desiring
      to hold you, for that joy,
            which left
a long wake of pleasure, as the leaves moved
and you faded into the pattern
of grass and shadows, and I returned
smiling and haunted, to a dark morning.

I think it's quite a poem. I've used it for a couple of years in these Delphi seminars, and I find it tends to bring out the students' fantasies or wishes.

The other paper I chose was in response to the following assignment. "Describe for us," I asked them, "a feature, characteristic, or trait of yours that you'd like the other members of the seminar to know." You'd think this assignment would lead to a lot of self-revelation, but it makes students nervous. Hence, they tend to show their psychological defenses.

You asked me to look first at the mystery student. Now, since he's outside the seminar, his responses aren't typical, but here are the two I mentioned. In his case, though, I'm going to start with a third, his very first, in which he introduced himself to the seminar. Don't worry. It's short.

As you read, Justin, notice how he's fascinated by his own hiding. Hiding gives him power. Nobody can reach him, not even the police.

English 6121   Jan. 18, 1984

Wheee!

Our very own seminar to play around in--yours and now mine. Coz now I've got a little list of you, phone numbers and all. I'll be the not-so-silent partner in your business here. I'll be leaving messages in your boxes (no pun intended). I'll be calling you on the tellyphone, some of you, anyway. Hey, let's gas, gang.

Call me the Interloper. Call me the Meddler. Call me the Eavesdropper. Call me the Pest. Call me the Intruder. Call me what you like. What the Joker was to the Batman, I am to you. I'm the antagonist you need in order to turn on your imagination. I'm a mole doing counter-intelligence, counter your intelligence, somebody deeply hidden but able to wreak havoc in the big real world outside. Power, that's what I have, paper power, anyway. Do any of you have more than that?

Don't you wonder who I am? What's my name? What do I look like? How do I walk, talk, smoke, joke, wear, stare, make love? That, says the Dutchman, you'll be able to figure out from these writings of mine. Maybe so, Holland's students, maybe so. But do you think all the Mad Doctor's analysis of styles is going to tell you any simple fact, like who I really am?

How will you find out? Patrol the mail room? Call the fuzz? Don't you wish you could stop me? How about you, Norm, don't you wish you could crack a ruler across my

palm? Hey, easy, gang, be cool. It's rap time at the
ranch. Later, gator. But all that chatter aside, Emily
said it straight:

>   This is my letter to the world,
>   That never wrote to me,--
>
>   Yore frend.

Power in hiding. It's like the hidden identities in the Batman or Super-
man comics. I look like a weak, mild-mannered reporter or an indolent play-
boy—or just a kid—but I have secret *POWER!* Hidden, underneath, a mole,
he can be anything—Joker, counterspy, lover.

But being not that all sure of himself, he recognizes that these are only
things he does on paper. In that same vein, there are the "poor me" lines
from Emily Dickinson. Well, that's for openers.

Here's what our mystery student says about the snake poem. You can
hear again the theme of power-from-hiding in his opening words. That makes
something else important to him: being in the group or out of it. What's
inside, hidden, as against what's outside, public.

English 6121   February 15, 1984
To the identity-mongers
From The Soothsayer.

I don't have to do this, you know. From my special
vantage point on this seminar, I can do or not do, just
as I please. But this squib I wanted to do, because the
poem irritated me, it was so phony.

Levertov would like us to think this is some moment of
perfect communion between her and the wild, wild wet. She
picks up that snake, she strokes it, she lets it embrace
her, she lets it poke into her ear . . . Pretty obvious
what's going on here, isn't it, Holland? We Freudians
know, don't we. Bullshit.

This poem's a scam. She puts in those companions, as
if she were talking to them, as if she were concealing
her fears and uncertainties from them, and communing only
with that snake, but that's not what she's concealing.
What she's concealing is you and me. She isn't saying
anything at all to those companions. She's publishing a

poem to be bought and read and admired by the public.
"You," she says, as if she were talking to the snake. But
"you" is you, yew, yoo-hoo--the population of English
6121 and all her other devoted readers.

When you realize that, you realize how phony this poem
is. This is a poet posturing as though she had had some
mystical charmed moment of intimacy. There probably never
were any such thing as those "companions." For all I
know, there was never any snake, either. The thing should
really end, "I returned, smug and self-satisfied, to a
dark morning, having written this classy self-aggrandiz-
ing poem." She oozes the same kind of self-satisfaction
Holland probably feels after one of your seminar meetings, all full of commyewnication and shayring and
touchy-feely and phony intimacy. Am I right, or am I
right? Right here, anyway. I'm always here, and from my
vantage point you can show these things up for what they
really are. Sooth means truth, and that's not just a
rhyme, kids. You, yew, yoo-oo-ou. Yoo-hoo! Who who what?

As you can imagine, Justin, it's no fun coming across these in your
mailbox of a Monday morning and realizing that your students are reading
the same thing. *They* don't write this way, only Trish and this guy.

He comes across somewhat more decently in the last one I've photo-
copied for you. This one talks about a trait he wants us to know about himself.

English 6121   Feb. 8

To: The Speckled Band, about to be discovered by
      Sherlock Holland
From: An honest, hardworking traitsman.

Tell us, sez the Man in that hopelessly earnest boojwa
way of his, something about yourself that you'd like the
rest of us to know. Hey, how can I pass this up?

I'll tell you all something about me that I want you
to know. I hate philosophy. I'm studying literature because it's just the opposite. There we have Heidegger and
Hegel torturing the language and clambering around logical ladders to try to get at something and missing it.
And here we have Homer or Hardy or Hemingway telling

lies, making it all up. Did you know Hemingway was sitting around back in St. Louis when the retreat from
Caporetto was going on? But he wrote the truth about that
wretched shambles. Somehow out of the fictions and
imaginings and downright lies, Shakespeare and Chaucer
and Milton and the rest of the boys and girls made
truths. As ever, Emily said it nicely.

> Tell all the Truth but tell it slant--
> Success in Circuit lies

Isn't that lovely? And true, how true! There she was,
poor old crazy, heartbroken Emily, hidden away in that
tiny town in her little bedroom and her prim white
dresses, lowering cookies out the window. There was Emily
living no life at all, the Belle of Amherst ho, ho, ho,
while the rest of the Dickinsons went on with their
church politics and college fund-raising and discreet
adulteries.

> I'm Nobody! Who are you?
> Are you--Nobody--Too?
> Then there's a pair of us?
> Don't tell! they'd advertise--you know!
>
> How dreary--to be--Somebody!
> How public--like a Frog--
> To tell one's name--the livelong June--
> To an admiring Bog!

That's what <u>they</u> were doing, and what was poor benighted
Emily doing? Hey, let's have some more poetry. It's a
commodity in all too short supply in our oh-so-theoreti-
cal studies--

> To make a prairie it takes a clover and one bee,
> One clover, and a bee,
> And revery.
> The revery alone will do,
> If bees are few.

They could make a noise and a fuss, but she could make a
prairie, couldn't she, out of nothing but As and Bs, and
not even those? Isn't that the art of her? That her poems

go off into nothing, and then they are most present? The
myth of presence, our French friends call it.

    That's why I'm present, here in cold old Buffalo,
studying literature and interpretation and thee-ry and
ree-eeding and all the rest. That's why I'm here in your
seminar, or not here, depending on how you look at it.
This is my letter to the world, That never wrote to me--
I'm here to watch you make a prairie. And maybe even some
cookies.

He's the imagination inside, like Emily Dickinson's frog or revery.
He's hiding somewhere inside while we are public like the open, empty,
vast prairie or the admiring bog. He imagines Emily Dickinson cooped
up in her bedroom while the real doings of the family went on outside.
But these real doings are prosaic and boring while inside is Dickinson's
wonderful imagining of the prairie or Hemingway's or Hardy's. Imagination inside, facts outside. Facts are boring, like public frogs or great flat
prairies. Imaginings can be wondrous, lovely. So he wants to be hidden
in the world of imagination, but he also wants to change the outer world.
Us.

    How to put this together into his "identity"? I'd say our mystery stu-
dent was someone who imagines a precious, imaginative inside hidden
away from a worthless outside. He imagines that the inside has power.
When it comes out or just influences the outside, it transforms that outside.

    I haven't the vaguest idea, Justin, what you can do with this kind of
abstract theme. So far as extrinsic evidence is concerned, our mystery student has been very careful indeed. I couldn't find a clue in his writings to his
identity as it would appear on his driver's license or his social security card.
As for his identity in my sense, my interpretation of him as a theme and
variations, that's all over the place.

    Trish Hassler's responses are also not the usual sort. Unlike the mys-
tery student, she tells us a lot about her childhood and her life, but, like him,
she's angry. Indeed, she's a lot angrier than he is, and her squibs are very
unusual.

    Here's her reponse to the Levertov poem. The first thing you'll notice is
her tremendous anger. It's involved with food. She's furious because, as
she sees it, I'm not feeding her good stuff to work on. She wants to take
things in and then put them out. When she can do that, she's happy. When
she can't—as in my seminar—she spits like an angry cat.

English 6121   Feb. 15
                                                      Trish

To the psyche wigglers--

   You sure can pick 'em, Norm. Who feeds you this stuff?
And why do you feed it to us? Can't you ever pick anything we might <u>like</u> to write about, that we might even
write intelligently, sophisticatedly, theoretically,
about? But I almost forgot. We're not supposed to write
intelligent and sophisticated and theoretical things in
this seminar. We're supposed to say whatever comes to
mind about this poem. The first thing that comes to mind
is that this is one lousy poem.
   Well, I'll tell you what comes to mind. The snake
handlers. Holy Rollers. Jesus Onlys. You Yankees don't
get a chance to see these people much, but when I was a
kid they had a church right down the road.
   Have any of you ever heard speaking in tongues? These
weird high-pitched voices, and the tongue flickering like
the snake's tongue, and the sounds pouring out: kla-bi-
gub-oloh . . . It could be ancient Egyptian or Aramaic or
patristic Greek or Old Church Slavonic--I'm damned if I
know. Who needs education if you can talk all these lan-
guages just by letting the spirit of our Lord Jesus
Christ flow through you? Greatest argument for ignorance
ever invented.
   Then come the rattlers and the copperheads. "They
shall take up serpents." Another sign of the true be-
liever, Jesus said. The minister brings them out in wooden
boxes with airholes on the sides. The Jesus Onlys open the
boxes and sway and croon as the snakes slither out onto the
floor. The women, women mostly, but some men, would pick
them up and wrap them around their arms and necks and
heads. Why don't they get bitten? Again, damned if I
know. (And I probably am damned. They'd sure think so.)
   The spirit is in them, they say. They don't get poisoned because they have conquered Satan, the forked
tongue, the narrow fellow in the grass. He twines round
her neck, around my neck, like a lover, a false lover
inside my cunt. Oh yes, Norm, I didn't forget--the snake
is a phallic symbol. Duplicity. Deception. Falsity. "The
serpent beguiled me, and I did eat." Truer than you know.

I know what was in the woman's mind. Rage, rage, rage if your mind has been pierced and poisoned by lying patriarchal language.

And what was in the snake's mind? His alien eyes focus on the woman. He opens his pink mouth and shows his fangs. Snake and woman are one in that moment, face to face, one in the raw, red instinct. They have penetrated to that final, pure animality deep inside them. But she is the powerful one. She feels his weight, but it's nothing compared to the strength in her hands around his throat. Does he know that? Is that why he's afraid to bite? Is that why he can only bite in treachery, hidden in the grass, lying with his forked tongue?

"Now the serpent was more subtil than any beast of the field which the Lord God had made," but he's no match for me. I have strong hands and a heavy body and a mind far subtler even than any snake. I could crush the snake, I'm tempted to say I <u>shall</u> crush him. I'd squeeze its pulsing throat and watch it writhe and twist itself round my arm until it suffocated and stopped moving and hung, limp, lorn, lifeless.

I don't believe the pleasure at the end. "A long wake of pleasure" is just tacked on. It doesn't break through to what really is happening between the woman and the snake face to face, desire to desire, hunger to hunger. I believe it ends in numbness, nothing, all passion spent, as I feel after reading this poem.

LT. RHODES: Norman, I have to break in here. All that anger! Whew! I can almost feel her rage, it's expressed in such physical, tactile terms. She'll bite, squeeze, crush, strangle. It's almost sexual the way she comes to a kind of climax in the next to last paragraph, and the snake goes limp, and she's exhausted. It's like an orgasm. Or am I reading in?

HOLLAND: No, I think you're reading her very well. Sex, but all tangled up with anger so that the sex becomes distorted and cruel.

LT. RHODES: This is fascinating, sort of, and more than a little repulsive.

HOLLAND: Go on. Read some more. It gets even wilder in the squib about the trait. This seminar brought out all this hostility.

LT. RHODES: Have you figured out why?

HOLLAND: She tells us. Why don't you go back to reading? You'll get more of a sense of her from the other squib. I'll go on entering my Aval reading in my laptop. As you read her, keep watching food and mouths. Watch the bound-

aries come down between her and her surroundings.END OF THIS SEC-
TION OF TAPE END OF THIS SECTION OF TAPE END OF THIS SEC

English 6121   Feb. 8
                                                Trish

To the navel inspectors--

"Tell the other members of the seminar something about
yourself that you want them to know." (Jesus H. Christ!
if that doesn't sound like something they'd assign you in
high school!) You said, Norm, <u>Doctor</u> Holland, that we can
write whatever we want, that we <u>should</u> write whatever we
want, that we <u>have</u> *to* write whatever we want, so I'm
going to do just that.

Why I hate this seminar

It's really very simple. There's nothing <u>in</u> this
seminar. There's nothing I can sink my teeth into, and,
as you all must have noticed by now, I like to sink my
teeth into things. It's empty, flat, deflated. I want
ideas, information, texts, theories, stuff that I can put
in my mind and work with. I want to write papers. I want
to publish. I want to take this profession by storm. Why
else are we here in grad school?
You know my story from my squibs. I was born into a
poor family in rural Georgia, never mind where, and I
haven't had any dealings with them in years. School--one
teacher, really--was everything to me, my whole life.
When I was a senior, she gushed, she wrote, she pleaded,
and she got me a scholarship to Yale. And, as if that
were the one bright spot in her life, she promptly died.
Smart move on her part. I don't think she'd approve of me
now. I failed.
I don't have family, I don't have money, I don't have
looks, I don't have friends, I don't have lovers. I have
brains, a certain kind of literary brains. I'm going to
be the <u>one</u> in our little game of literary criticism and
literary theorizing--that's my life. I am words, themes,
publishing, argument. You take that away from me, you take
away my life. That's why I don't like this seminar--it
doesn't let me do what I can do, want to do, have to do.

Phil Feder's Theory of Fiction--now <u>there's</u> a seminar.
I've scarcely begun to digest it all. Phil can recite
reams of <u>Finnegans Wake</u>, theorize any critical position,
analyze rock and roll, problematize pro wrestling, for
God's sake--he can do <u>anything</u>. And I thrived on that diet
of hard work. God, did we work! A novel every week <u>plus</u> a
book-length work of theory. I wrote beautiful papers for
Phil, intricate, subtle, theoretical pieces, because I
got so much to work with. I like just saying his name.

And here? No theory. No ideas. One poem a week, maybe
one short story a week. But, of course, we're supposed to
study these things we write, these "free writings" (like
high school!), these "responses," these "squibs," whatever the hell you want to call them. Is anybody going to
publish them? Is anybody but us ever going to read them?
But they are a fine way of staring into our navels. Way
down in there, past all the lint and crud I can see a
little, squirming identity theme.

Do you really believe in some "I" behind what we've
written? All you have in your notebooks is words, just
words, self-contradictory words, words that subvert and
marginalize and destabilize the very thing they signify--
or don't signify. Language is only a system of
differenced signifiers and signifieds, and being only
difference, it cannot tell my truth or your truth or any
truth at all.

That's why these squibs are ridiculous. Yes, I'm
talking to you, Holland. You think they say something
about us, but the person you're talking about is already
in a different place, a different discourse, turning on
you, giving you back in spades what you haven't yet even
begun to suspect.

Language is difference, <u>différance</u>, really (but sssh!,
we're not supposed to mention that), and language is all
any of us has. Since everything is discourse, you can
never know me. I can never know you. All any of us can
know is the discourse we shove at each other. And as
Foucault and Barthes have so deliciously proved, there is
no author. The subject is dead. I'm dead, and so are you.

To steal my language is the ultimate crime, because it
takes from me the only thing that any human being truly
has. Do you really think you can "read" me better than I
can read myself? Try to tell me something? I'll give it
back plus something of my own. Try to teach me something?
I'll learn on my own and learn more than you ever thought

you could teach me. I suppose you'll tell me that's what
I've done in this squib.

So, <u>Doctor</u> Holland, I don't believe your theories, and
I don't like writing your squibs, and I don't give a
flying fuck for this seminar. But, for now, I've done
exactly what we were supposed to do, tell you *one* thing
about me I want the rest of you to know. Happy now? Fulfilled? Everything all shared? Okay, give me my A. I'm
entitled.

LT. RHODES: Jesus, Norman, why do you let her write stuff like this?

HOLLAND: What am I supposed to do? As she points out, I tell them they are
supposed to write whatever comes into their mind. This is what comes into
her mind.

The Delphi method is like the psychoanalysts' free association. On
the couch, if thoughts about the analyst come to mind—and they could
hardly *not* come to mind—you have to say them. The patient is free to tell
the analyst what he or she thinks of the analyst. Indeed, the patient is required to do just that. The patient can't hold back even the most insulting
thoughts, so long as he or she thinks them.

In this seminar they're supposed to write whatever comes to mind.
When she hits out at me that way, she's doing what she's supposed to do.
That doesn't make it any easier to take, of course.

LT. RHODES: Did she talk like this in seminar?

HOLLAND: Not quite so brutally, but almost, and she does—did—lots of talking,
too. She would dominate discussion until I'd have to tell her to let the
others get a word in edgewise. She's a very bright, capable student, who's
boiling with hostility.

LT. RHODES: I can see why you, and maybe a lot of other people, wouldn't mind
seeing her dead.

HOLLAND: That doesn't mean I murdered her, though.

Look, you've read as far as my interpretation. Try it. See if it suggests
anything useful to you. END OF THIS SECTION OF TAPE END OF THIS
SECTION OF TAPE END OF THIS SECTION OF TAPE END OF THIS

First, she's in a rage like a hungry newborn's furious crying. She talks
about my choice of poems as "Who feeds it to you?" And then I "feed it to"
the seminar. The snake looking at the woman was "hunger to hunger." In
Feder's seminar, "I thrived on that diet." "I've scarcely begun to digest it all."
She wants to take in and to give out again in the form of beautiful work,

as she calls it, with language. When that happens, she feels fulfilled and no longer angry, as in Phil Feder's seminar. Lucky Phil. He filled her. In the snake poem, she sees hunger facing hunger. That leads, she says, to rage, then numbness, an indifference that she identifies with her feeling toward the snake, the poem, this seminar, and me.

From a psychological point of view, when you eat something you break down the boundary between you and it. Notice how Trish projects herself into the mind of the poet, into my mind (when she complains about the poem), into the minds of the snake-wagglers, and most fascinating of all, into the snake's mind. That's something of a tour de force, almost the way Keats could imagine himself enjoying, as a billiard ball might, its roundness, smoothness, and rapidity. But the anger makes it all chaotic. There were times when she seemed to me what the psychiatrists call a borderline personality, someone whose boundaries between self and others are very shaky and often tangled up with uncontrollable anger. Do you remember Alex in the movie *Fatal Attraction*? That anger-mixed-with-sexuality? Trish is like that.

She talks here about being penetrated, sexually, in the stuff about the snake as a phallic symbol, and linguistically, when she talks about patriarchal language. I see the penetration as the physical equivalent of the boundaries breaking down, her mixing into other minds, taking thoughts out of them or putting her own angry thoughts in.

That's the psychological basis, I think, for her intellectual commitment to deconstructionism. She believes that language is by its very nature duplicitous. One never is fed by words, so to speak, rightly or truly or enough. In that sense, Trish can think of her anger as justified. It's not her fault. It's language. It's life. The boundaries are all down.

All this, as I say, is my interpretation. It's probably no help at all with the external facts. She says that she's read this poem, has seen snake wagglers—that's about it. I feel that she's about to say something in the fifth paragraph of that response when she remembers, "'The serpent beguiled me, and I did eat'." Then she breaks off with "Truer than you know." Maybe she was going to write something about the plagiarism business at Yale. But that's just my hunch.

That's her pattern. She gets done to, and now she will do to. If I were Aval, I'd be worried about her trying to attack me somehow. Don't forget, Justin, that he read these responses. He knew what she was thinking.

Does this analysis help? Perhaps some sense of Hassler's style is useful. I hope so.

Yours,
/Norm/

LT. RHODES: That's a fascinating document, the whole thing, I mean, the squibs and your interpretation.

HOLLAND: Themes are the best way I know to talk systematically about people's identities, even though they are very abstract. The students learn pretty quickly how to do it, too.

LT. RHODES: I'd be curious to see what they had to say about Hassler. I really should, shouldn't I?

HOLLAND: None of us, I'm afraid, will give you any extrinsic evidence. Especially with someone as explosive as Trish Hassler, they stuck pretty close to her writings. I've been through all her responses and found nothing that would help with the case.

LT. RHODES: Would it be worthwhile for me to go through her papers myself?

HOLLAND: I don't think so. I checked, but I didn't see anything.

LT. RHODES: How about the papers the students wrote about her, the papers that the seminar was going to talk about today?

HOLLAND: Again, Justin, it's a lot to read. Lots of quotations from her responses. Do you have the time?

LT. RHODES: Will it be worthwhile?

HOLLAND: Look, I have my copies here and my outline for managing the discussion in class. Let me give you the key ideas.

LT. RHODES: Fine. Aval first. That should be interesting.

HOLLAND: I'm afraid not. He was very subdued—and brief. Basically he makes only two points. "Why are you in this seminar?" He asks the question in different ways. "Why are you here in Buffalo?" "Why do you take this seminar when you dislike it so?"

His second point is complicated. He says she is deconstructing herself.

LT. RHODES: Can you do that?

HOLLAND: This is his argument. First, he points to her urgent need to establish herself through critical writings. Second, he points to the impossibility of doing that, the usual postmodern dismissal of the idea that there's a "transhistorical core of being." "The subject," writes Chris, "is only a complex and variable function of discourse."

LT. RHODES: Tell me what that's supposed to mean.

HOLLAND: The idea is that we are only what we say and think—language. Discourse. And that is out of our control, because we don't make the rules of discourse. So discourse speaks through us, regardless of our wishes.

Even in her critical writings, then, Chris argues, Patricia Hassler can only express the dominant discourse, not herself as such. She is self-contradictory, because she is trying to establish herself, although she (and he) no longer believe that there's an essential self to establish. In contradicting herself, she deconstructs herself.

He goes on to say that therefore her anger is not really anger.

LT. RHODES: Whoo-ee! Do you believe that?

HOLLAND: No.

LT. RHODES: Did he say anything about Yale?

HOLLAND: Not a word. *[Pause.]* Shall I go on to Max Ebenfeld?

LT. RHODES: Sure.

HOLLAND: Ebenfeld talks about her body. "You have every right to be angry," he writes. "The world treats fat people miserably and unjustly." Then he turns to her mind. "You have a large body, Trish, and it is the outward, visible sign of a great mind inside. You're one of the most brilliant people I've ever met. You need to balance that powerful mind with a healthy body." And he goes on to prescribe diet and exercise for her.

LT. RHODES: This is *some* kind of literature class. That brings us to Anne Glendish.

HOLLAND: Anne made three points, basically, maybe four. First, she pointed to Trish's anger. "The way you use your anger," she writes, . . . END OF THIS SECTION OF TAPE END OF THIS SECTION OF TAPE END OF

Metropolitan Buffalo Police Department

Tape Transcription   Homicide Unit

Body: *Hassler, P.*   Tape No. *840307.032*

Place: *Telephone call, Rhodes Hall, UB*   Time: *6:06 p.m.*

Persons present: *Det. Lt. Rhodes, N. N. Holland*

Transcribed by: *J. Cipperman*

LT. RHODES: . . . usually catch those before the tape runs out. Okay, go on. Glendish.

HOLLAND: Start now? Okay. Trish's anger. Glendish wrote, "The way you use your anger guarantees that we are aware of you practically to the exclusion of everything else in the seminar. It guarantees you the spotlight."

LT. RHODES: She's right about that.

HOLLAND: Then, like many students writing this kind of touchy response to another student, she placates Hassler by finding something they share. "We're

both from the South," she writes, "but from different ends of the socio-
economic spectrum. I know you resent that, and I hope that's the only reason you don't think much of my mind. Nevertheless, we both want the
same thing. We want to be admired for our work and our brains, and both
of us are willing to work very hard to gain that admiration." Finally, she
says she admires and envies Patricia's freedom, her ability to say "whatever the hell you think no matter who's listening." At the same time, Anne
writes, "You see things for what they are, and you say what you see, holding back nothing." And Anne says these are qualities she hopes she has or
can emulate.

LT. RHODES: That seems both mild and true, quite mild for someone as abrasive
as Hassler.

HOLLAND: The students tend to be protective of their maimed colleagues.

LT. RHODES: Go on.

HOLLAND: Barry Ireland next. He's easy. He simply typed out—or got his computer to type out—a whole page of messages like, "Don't mess with me."
"Don't cross me." "Don't fuck around with me." "Don't shit me." "Don't
give me any trouble." Over and over again.

LT. RHODES: What's *that* all about?

HOLLAND: Just a guess. When we were discussing one of Barry's earlier papers,
it came out that he thought Hassler was responsible for causing him some
trouble with their landlord about his cats—you knew that he kept cats?

LT. RHODES: Yes, incongruous though it may be.

HOLLAND: So maybe his warnings refer to that. Or maybe he's mirroring what he
thinks she's like.

LT. RHODES: Or maybe it's just Barry being Barry. Next?

HOLLAND: Amy Lemaire. As you'd expect, she took a mollifying stance. Trish,
she said, wants to give. "You want to give to others—to the world—great
literary criticism. Then you want to be given in return, in the form of admiration or the great teaching you've experienced, admired, and told us about."
She quotes examples from Trish's papers. "When you have this mutual
giving, as you perhaps did at Yale, then you have a kind of total bliss."
Among other things, she points to the trance of the snake handlers and
Feder's seminar that she so much admired.

LT. RHODES: But it's an angry sort of bliss, isn't it?

HOLLAND: Not according to Amy. "When you're given to and can give, then you
feel at one with the world." She ends up giving her advice. "Work with
that, Trish," she writes. "Work with that strong, giving part of you, the
happy part, the part that can partner."

LT. RHODES: Do you think she means this?

HOLLAND: I think Amy believes what she's written. It's very characteristic of her.

LT. RHODES: That's true of all these readings, isn't it? Each, so far, says as much about the interpreter as Hassler.

HOLLAND: Inevitably, Justin, as I've been telling you.

LT. RHODES: Penza?

HOLLAND: As you'd expect, there's a lot of verbal whizbang, but he concentrates on her body. He surprised me with that. "I admire your body, Trish," he writes. "Now don't misunderstand me. I'm not coming on to you. I admire your body as a presence in our deliberations. You're so absolutely and solidly *there*. Years from now, when you all are distinguished professors and I've won the Nobel Prize, we will think back to this seminar, and who will we remember? Patricia Hassler, sitting there, big, loud, and telling it like it is. You have a voice that we'll not forget. You're center stage, now and always."

LT. RHODES: That last bit sounds almost as though he knew she was shortly going to exist only in memory.

HOLLAND: You're reaching, Justin.

LT. RHODES: Isn't he? "I admire your body." Come on!

HOLLAND: I think that was Paul saying something that he knew would grab our attention.

LT. RHODES: Which brings us to Wally Sisley.

HOLLAND: Wally took the tack that she wasn't really angry. "I think it's an act," he writes. "I think you like to come on hard-boiled, but you're really gentle underneath. Deep down, you're just pretending."

LT. RHODES: How on earth does he arrive at that?

HOLLAND: He picked up her rhapsody about Phil Feder, for example.

LT. RHODES: Did you get a squib from the interloper about her?

HOLLAND: No. And I was surprised not to.

LT. RHODES: Do you see any consensus in all this? I get the feeling there's more ingenuity than insight.

HOLLAND: I think consensus and even insight aren't useful ideas here. Because they each see Hassler through their own ways of seeing things, through their own cognitive styles, they can only see *their* Hassler. There's no way they can see some real, true, "objective" Hassler "out there," separate from them.

LT. RHODES: But surely they agree on something. That she was an angry person, for example.

HOLLAND: Yes and no. Sisley and Amy seem to move her away from being angry. Ebenfeld didn't mention it. Nor did Ireland, of all people.

LT. RHODES: Are you telling me there's *no* right answer in this? Not one true thing we can say about Patricia Hassler? Don't you even think your own reading is right?

HOLLAND: It's right in that it's the best I can do within my cognitive style, just as Amy's or Anne's, say, are the best they can do within their cognitive styles. We all see her through our own ways of seeing the world.

LT. RHODES: So there's no final reading of Patricia Hassler.

HOLLAND: No reading independent of somebody's way of seeing things, no. That's an impossibility. But what we now have, as a result of these different readings, is a way of talking to one another about Hassler. You can learn from Amy's or Anne's readings—I mention them because I get the most out of theirs. You can use their readings to add to your own.

LT. RHODES: This all seems so radically subjective.

HOLLAND: But everything *is* subjective. We see everything through our way of seeing things. "Subjective" doesn't say anything we didn't already know.

LT. RHODES: Radically relative, then.

HOLLAND: Better. Relative to each person's way of seeing things, to each culture's way of seeing things, to each historical era's way of seeing things, to our physiological ways of seeing things.

LT. RHODES: Relatives. Speaking of same, would you join me in an old family custom of the Rhodeses, a martini before dinner?

HOLLAND: Sounds good to me, but, look, I've finished my interpretation of Aval. Do you want to read it now?

LT. RHODES: Yes. That young man interests me greatly. Martinis will have to wait.

State University of New York at Buffalo
Department of English

Dear Justin:

Let me preface by saying that Chris Aval seems as deeply opposed to the premises of this seminar as Trish Hassler was, but unlike her, he's always been the soul of courtesy. Here is his squib on a trait of his. I think you'll find it quite different from Hassler's or the mystery student's. Keep an eye on his references to *place,* particularly how he shifts himself in and out of places.

English 6121

February 15, 1984
Christian AVAL

My Dear Colleagues,

You say, Professor Holland, tell us something about yourself. I will tell you about the game of _boules_. Whether this is about me, you and my fellow students will have yourselves to decide.

Boules is a favorite game in the south of France from where I come. There are two teams of one or two or three each. To start the game one tosses out <u>le cochonnet</u>, a little wooden ball, about six or seven meters. The idea is to throw or bowl metal balls, <u>boules</u>, as close as you can get to the <u>cochonnet</u>. If you have one ball closer than the opposing team's closest ball you get one point, two balls, two points, and so on.

The game is not just one of skill but of strategy and rhetoric and, perhaps, psychology. You can either "point" your ball as close as you can to the <u>cochonnet</u>, or you can "fire" your ball to knock your opponents' ball away. You can even "fire" at the <u>cochonnet</u> to move it away from theirs and closer to yours.

All the team (and sometimes the onlookers) consult about each throw. Also, you must be able to anticipate what your opponents are likely to do after your last shot--hence, psychology. You must try to know, in your terms, Professor Holland, the opponents' identities. Hence, like all good games, <u>boules</u> enacts not only skill, but persuasion, politics, and drama. Textuality, for postmoderns.

I was born and grew up in the small seacoast town of Cassis near Marseille. It used to be a fishing town, and there are still a few who fish, but now the town mostly profits from the tourists. My parents owned a modest old hotel that overlooked the harbor and the small sandy square of park that separates the streets of the town from the sparkling blue of the sea. The running of the hotel depended mostly on my mother, because my father was the <u>maire</u> of the town. (I find it interesting that the English word, <u>mayor</u>, from the Latin, even sounds the same in English, may-r. Are you listening, Amy, to your ancestry?)

Every afternoon, after the long dinner hour--the

climate is like that of Spain or Italy, and there are
many who follow the custom of the lunchtime sleep--my
father would go out of the hotel to the little sandy
square and play boules. There were always at least two
games. There was one for the big men of the town (like my
father) and then there were one or more games for the
lesser people and even the occasional tourist. The bigger
game was the one the townspeople watched. Even among the
casual visitors to Cassis it always had the bigger audience. It was not easy to move from the lesser game to the
bigger one, for this one game of boules was really the
political center of the town.

It was here that the important men, les grands chefs,
kidded each other about their play or insulted each other
or played at insulting each other. After the play, in the
cafés nearby, they developed their real estate deals and
the sales of businesses and issuing the restaurant permits and giving out the contracts for cleaning the
streets and the plans to attract the tourists and their
money. But it was in boules that the men measured themselves against one another, testing their skill and their
wit and their ability to withstand criticism and their
courage in betting and firing. It was here that, playing
every afternoon, my father had attracted the support--the
admiration, in fact--to make himself mayor. I did not
need psychoanalysis to tell me of the law and the name of
the father. I saw it every afternoon in that big broad-
shouldered man with the long jaw and the broad cheek-
bones, the clever, forceful, swarthy mayor of Cassis.

I used to watch this game from the balcony of the
dining room on the first floor, you would say the second
floor, of our little hotel. As a boy, I admired my father
greatly, at first for his skill with the balls, then as I
grew a little older for his skill with the other men, and
then, I learned, with the women who watched. He would
joke and cajole and wager and persuade, on the one hand
keeping everybody in a good humor and on the other letting them notice that M. le maire was very much in
charge. Occasionally, if I crossed the street and stood
among the watchers for quite a while, "M. Fernand's son"
would be allowed to take a turn. The other men would make
a small fuss. There would be much counseling me, much
discussion of whether I should point the ball or fire,
and much comment afterwards on the frequent failure or

the occasional success of my shot. But I was never really "in" the game. I remained, finally, a spectator, across the street, at home with my mother in our home which was not a home but a hotel.

My father and mother assumed that, when I would have finished school, I would assume the management of the hotel and take my place in the town. But I never became any good at the game of <u>boules</u>. I was never at home with the jokes, the gossip, the aggressive masculinity, or the scheming. I did not feel I was, so to speak, there.

School turned out to be my forte. Year after year I was the first in the Lycée Thiers in Marseille. Yet, even as I was succeeding in school, I had this lingering feeling that I ought to be succeeding in the world of my father. That involved money and politics, and school seemed petty by contrast. But when I tried the the games of my father, money and politics and <u>boules</u>, I longed for school. When I tried school, I longed for the games of my father. Lacan has written of the game of our destiny. I would translate him this way. "The game plays on, until it breaks up, in its inexorable finish, there where I am not because I cannot place myself there."

Perhaps in this text Lacan has explained why I so often defeated myself. I was good at school, but I did foolish things that abased my scores. I would fail to study or I would leave an exam early or deliberately I would answer a question in an unacceptable way. The night before the all-important <u>baccalauréat</u> I stayed up all night drinking with my pals, the sons of the men in the game of <u>boules</u>. Indeed, we sat on the benches in that very <u>parc</u> and pretended to play a noisy game of <u>boules</u> with the wine bottles, leaving a mess of broken glass facing the town fathers the next morning.

As a result I did not even try to be admitted to <u>Normale sup.</u>, <u>l'Ecole Normale Supérieure</u>, where my future, be it in academics, business, government, or journalism, would be assured for life. Instead I went to the regular University of Paris, the Institut d'Anglais on the rue Charles V.

Even there, just as I was about to graduate, I was seized with the strange idea of transferring to America, to Yale, which I had learned was the principal seat of French literary criticism and theory in the U.S.A. Yale gave me a scholarship, and I combined it with a legacy from one of my aunts. I abandoned my French studies. Somehow, when I was at Yale, I found a happiness I had not known at home, yet I continued to defeat myself in my studies, and I ended up here, not as distinguished as <u>Normale sup</u>. or as Yale. And so here I am. Or am I? Am I really just standing on the edge, hoping for a shot in the game of <u>boules</u>?

An interesting essay, isn't it, Justin? Polished, yet coming to grips at the end with his special style of life and study. He interprets his life in terms of where he is, moving himself here and there as he changes roles.

Here's the other response, to Levertov's poem. You'll see in the opening paragraphs what has happened to the fine art of literary criticism. Again, keep an eye on his treatment of place and—I should have mentioned this—his references to language.

English 6121   February 15, 1984
                                                Christian AVAL

Professor Holland, my fellow-students—

I see this poem as an interrogation of Otherness. Forgive me, Professor Holland. I know you demanded us not to analyze the poem, but to talk about our feelings. That is easier for you Americans to do than for me. My culture and my <u>formation</u> tells me the opposite. (You would say "education," but ours seems the more psychological word.) These things are private, scarcely knowable even by the subject, and certainly not to be iterated unthinkingly. I will try to do as you say, however, but in my own way. As your great poet said, we must by indirections find directions out.

This is a poem about the incommensurable alterity of the Other. The poet tries to be at one with the snake, but she is not. She has only the "desiring to hold you," and desire, as we know from the teaching of Jacques Lacan, is the signifier of our own inner lack. Moreover, the snake is not a snake. It is gold and silver, materials that matter to humans, not to snakes. It is "a long wake of pleasure." It is harmful or harmless, once more a reference to what matters to the poet or her friends, not to snakes, which, after all, are neither harmful nor harmless to one another. The snake is being, in the teaching of Jacques Derrida, differed/deferred from itself.

So, too, is the poet. She seeks to be at one with the snake in the rich, heavy moment of confrontation, but she is only liminably herself after that moment. She believes she is "I" again when she returns to her dark morning, to the desk and study, perhaps, where she has written this poem. But she is smiling and, even more momentously, haunted. She is still intersubjectively connected to the snake. She is problematized. So that at no point in the poem is she purely herself, and at no point in the poem is the snake purely a snake. This is, as I said, a poem that makes present the absence of the Other, that deconstructs both snake and poet.

And what of my feelings, Professor Holland? You ask for those, and I do not choose to debate your right to them although it seems to me very debatable. Get at your feelings by memories, you suggest. Yes, I have a memory. Or it has me.

I see my mother. She has come out of the sitting room of the small apartment our family had on the first floor (you would say the second floor) of our hotel. My mother has been gossiping with some of her friends who have called when, through the glass doors of the family's sitting-room, she sees a strange woman standing in the reception area. My mother naturally comes to see what the woman wants. I was standing there, at the head of the stairs leading up from the street to the desk, because I had seen my father come in. I was eleven or twelve years old, old enough to understand at least some of what was going on.

My mother looks at this woman, and yes, like the snake in the poem, the woman is wearing a green and gold dress. (That is why I am remembering this event.) I could see that suddenly my mother recognized this woman. She looks her up and down, judging her, assessing her as if she were a jeweler studying a brooch that someone had brought in to sell, looking at its weight, its design, the purity of the metal, just as the poet Levertov assesses the gold of the snake. My mother's chin goes up, and although she is not as tall as this woman she looks down at her. She

turns on her heel and walks back to her sitting room.
Deliberately she leaves the door open, and she says
loudly to her friends, who watched this confrontation, <u>Il
y a du monde au balcon</u>, loudly so that the woman can hear
it, and she makes the gesture of the hands that goes with
that saying so that the woman can see it.

This saying in French, there is a crowd in the balcony, you could understand as referring to this woman
standing on the first floor, but it is also a joking way
of saying that a woman has a big bosom. My mother had
looked at this woman and reduced her to just that, tits,
you would say. She was saying this woman is not a threat
to me or anybody. My mother laughs out loud, her friends
laugh all very loudly, and my mother looks back at the
woman who was blushing hard and very angry. At that
point, my father comes out of the w.c., rubbing the palms
of his hands on his trouser legs. He sees the women
laughing and realizes something of what had happened. He
quickly takes the woman's arm and pushes past me down the
stairs and into the street.

Let me explain. My mother knew that my father was
having an affair with this Parisian tourist. For a long
time, I had known that my parents had an understanding
about such things. It was, after all, the custom. An
important man in the town was expected to have a mistress
or affairs. My mother accepted that, but she had required
that my father carry on these affairs outside the hotel.
With all the rooms and the beds, it would have been too
easy and humiliating. My father respected and obeyed my
mother in this. This once, however, while he was walking
with this woman, he had to go to the toilet, so he
brought her upstairs for a moment.

It was a moment like the one that exposed the otherness of the snake. This moment exposed the duplicity of
my father, and the power--the weight, the gravity, the
size--of my mother. She had said, in effect, to the other
women (who all also accepted their husbands' affairs) that
she was not threatened by this tourist. She was no threat
to my mother or to anyone. This woman was just a pair of
tits. At the end of this scene, my mother was smiling.
Like the poet, she had triumphed over a danger, but she
was also haunted. It was, however, not a dark morning.
Rather, the Mediterranean sun was shining brilliantly, and
the sea sparkled with silver and gold and moved.

Surely, in those opening paragraphs, Christian is writing far more intellectually than simply free associating. But there is no way to hide one's self. His very artistry, his very intellectuality, say something about the man Christian Aval that even his frankness at the end of the first response does not say.

He is crafty. His responses are rather carefully crafted, quite artful and literary. He writes about the game of *boules* much as a travel writer might, not like a student being asked to ramble on about himself. In the "snake" response, the first three paragraphs are full of dreadful litcrit jargon, exactly the kind of analysis I did *not* want for the assignment, as he points out. Then he shifts from the jargon to a rather literary little sketch. It insulates him from the inquiry that this seminar poses and that he regards as alien and un-French.

The second thing I notice is how his thoughts run again and again to *place,* of being in or out of some particular place. He tells us about being on the balcony of the hotel or in the game of boules. In the episode with his mother, he almost draws a floor plan to place the woman, his mother, his mother's friends, himself, his father, and so on. The theme of that little story is itself place. The father was not supposed to bring his women to that particular place, the hotel. When he speaks of himself in the trait essay, he tells us that he has always been in the wrong place. He shifts from *boules* to school and back. He moves from Cassis to Paris to Yale to Buffalo, always feeling that this—wherever it is—isn't the right place to be.

Would I be too neat and literary if I pointed out that the game of *boules* is itself a game of place? Winning or losing depends on place. The teams are constantly negating one another's moves, pushing balls into and out of place, finally moving even the target. Balls. Fathers. Do I have to spell it out?

So too, I see his references to the Mediterranean as symbolic. The sea is undeniably there, but the colors and especially the sparkle are fleeting, always disappearing. So I see Chris. He is in the wrong place, constantly moving out of place, disappearing like the glint on a wave, his goals being moved like the *cochonnet.*

I see a third thing in his responses. Place substitutes for self. It is as though he weren't so much a person as someone whose identity depends on his location. In part, I guess this comes from his French litcrit jargon, where the term "situate" is often used to explain causal relations. Such-and-such is "situated" in a certain place means that such-and-such was caused to be a certain way. If you look back at the first three paragraphs of his snake response, you'll see what I mean. He speaks of the inner lack, of being deferred from oneself, of the presence and absence of the self and the other, of the deconstruction of the I. All this, I know, is fashionable jargon, but it is also a way of denying oneself. The story about his mother also shows people denying selves. His mother negates the mistress, but the mother and her friends have already been negated by their philandering husbands. And the boy is negated by this overpowering father.

Often in his papers or when he speaks, Christian will suddenly stop to call attention to how something is phrased in English as opposed to French. It is as though he were substituting a little lesson in idiom for what he was going to say. Again, shifting.

I see this shifting and denial of himself as related to the alleged plagiarism at Yale. When Trish accused him of plagiarism, what was being questioned was his presence in his language. I think Aval is someone who deep down inside does not believe his own self is there. He could hardly be in tune with a seminar whose basic assumption is that we can interpret selves for one another. And he uses, as Trish did, current literary theory to express and support his opposition.

He says over and over again in a variety of ways, I am not here. I do not want to be here. I want to be elsewhere than where I am.

This says nothing about the murder, though. It does make me, however, far more suspicious about him as a plagiarist. Plagiarism would act out the I'm-here-but-I'm-not-here of his personal style. But plagiarism, as you point out, would give Hassler a motive for murdering him, not vice versa.

That's as far as I can get with him, Justin. The rest is up to you.

/Norm/

LT. RHODES: So it is, Norman, so it is. You've given me a lot to think about. Now, how about that martini?

HOLLAND: If you'll let me make it white wine.

LT. RHODES: *De gustibus.* Why anyone would drink the doubtful flavors of jug wine when they could have a slug of honest gin beats me. But there's no coercing tastes. Where can we get either a decent martini or a decent white wine around here?

HOLLAND: Can I take you to the faculty club?

LT. RHODES: Rather not. I expect I'll want to talk about the case, these students, and you. I'd just as soon not have interested parties hanging about.

HOLLAND: Do you know Westward How? They have booths, and there won't be anybody there at this time of day. It's just a couple of blocks from here.

LT. RHODES: That's a student hangout, isn't it?

HOLLAND: Yes, but it doesn't get crowded until nine o'clock or so.

LT. RHODES: Westward How it is, then. END OF THIS SECTION OF TAPE END OF THIS SECTION OF TAPE END OF THIS SECTION OF TAPE

from the journal of Norman Holland

The Westward How lived up to my modest expectations. Three silent, sepa-
rated topers sat at the huge bar, having a couple on their way home from work.
Otherwise we had the big barnlike room with the booths along the walls to
ourselves. The place felt cool and cellary, and despite sawdust the tile floor
smelled of last night's spilled beer. The long bar and the panelling on the walls
and ceiling were dark and Victorian-looking. I've never understood why, in our
cold, dark climate, people don't want rooms that are bright and cheering, but
they don't. Go with gloom. Buffaloons like doors and wainscoting and beams
stained as dark and serious as a concert grand. Westward How determinedly
follows this pattern, conceding only a few blue and gold college banners be-
hind the bar and the copper hair of Sheila, slightly aging Sheila, gleaming in
the big mirror behind her. Sheila and the Westward How are on the west side of
Main Street right across from the university, specifically the student infirmary
with its mental health clinic. There's no doubt in anybody's mind who does
more for the scares and stumbles of undergraduate adolescence.

Sheila's eyebrows mutely inquired, and I replied, "White wine." In one
practiced swoop of the jug, there was my glass of wine. Justin stood back for a
moment to smile round the room, no doubt approving (Buffaloonly) the somber
mahogany (or whatever) and the long bar, it too as brown as tobacco juice. He
sauntered up and plunked himself down on one of the stools. "Martini. Straight
up," he said, "Beefeater's, Noilly Prat, seven to one, and an olive. Don't shake
the brine off the olive before you drop it in."

Sheila laughed. "You are a perfectionist, aren't you!" She fetched a bottle
of Beefeater's from the back of the two rows of bottles in front of the mirror. "I
haven't done one of these in a while," she said, smiling as she towelled dust off
the bottle. She found the vermouth he'd asked for, and lingeringly made it ac-
cording to his specifications. I'd noticed that just about everybody did things
according to Justin's specifications. To my complete surprise, she had a chilled
glass with an edged stem ready. She set it in front of him and poured.

Sheila watched him take a slow, savoring sip. "Ver-ry nice," he murmured.
"Very nice indeed. Your talents are wasted, squirting draft beer into under-
graduate glasses."

"Thank you kindly, sir," she said, curtseying and looking down coyly, play-
ing the Victorian parlormaid, and then she opened her eyes a little wider at the
three ones he left on the counter. Not usual in a student bar.

"Let's go over here," said Justin, leading me to a far corner booth. "I
want to talk to you some more about this seminar of yours." He settled, loung-

ing comfortably with his back against the wall and his legs stretched out on the
banquette, cordovan loafers dangling off the end. (Evidently he kept a replace-
ment for the Timberlands in his police car.) I reminded myself: policeman. I sat
upright with my elbows on the table, my chin in my hands, my feet on the floor.

"No tape recorder?" I asked.

"No tape recorder," he replied. "I want to have a literary conversation
with you, and we can't have the taxpayers paying to transcribe that."

"You know," I led off, "I suspect your being a playwright is the reason they
sent you out on this case. You majored in English. You even did some graduate
work—in creative writing. The police department would use you to understand
the peculiar workings of students and papers, graduate seminars, professors,
teaching assistants, all the stuff that makes up an English department. Even the
preciousness and the unreality."

"Maybe, but let's face it, a call came in that someone collapsed and died.
Such calls the Communications Center automatically routes to the Homicide
Unit. Most likely they sent me out on this case just because it was my turn in the
computer."

"Now, there's a divinity that shapes our ends."

"You too? I suppose so." He looked around the room. "This place is quiet,"
he said.

"You should come back around ten tonight."

"Let me just imagine it. Look," he went on, "as a playwright, I'm really
troubled by what you're telling me. You're saying that I don't have any control
over my audience. But that's not so. I control how they respond. I can see it
happening. I write a funny line, and they all laugh. There are rows and rows of
people sitting there, and I make them start laughing as if I'd pulled a trigger."

"But what exactly happened? When you ask members of an audience—
and I've done this—when you ask them why they think something's funny, you
get all kinds of different answers."

"You can't say what's funny?" He raised an eyebrow.

"When you ask, Why is 'it' funny?, the question is wrongly posed. 'It' isn't
funny. People find it funny."

"Explain."

"A lot of quite different people can find in your funny line a way of satisfy-
ing their different senses of humor. We do each have a personal sense of humor,
each different, maybe only slightly different, maybe a lot different, but in every
case different. How can so many different people find the same thing funny?
That's a mystery. I don't think we can know that."

"We can't know? Why not, Professor?" He was smiling—I suppose at my
having mounted the lectern. But I care about these things.

"*Because we can't see 'it.' We can't see your play as it 'really' is. We can only see what our different psyches can see. That's why no one can say what the 'it' is that enables so many different people for so many different reasons to enjoy the same play. That's why we'll never be able to say what 'great' art is.*"

"*You're not concerned with literary value, then?*" he asked, a bit testily. "*So far as you're concerned,* The Taming of the Shrew *is no better than* Getting Gertie's Garter.*"

"*A play I don't know.*"

"*Consider yourself lucky.*"

"*Look, I don't think the value* is *literary. That is, I don't think it's* in *the work of literature. Whenever you say something is better or worse, those are only words for some human way of experiencing it.*"

"*That's so relativistic,*" said Rhodes. "*Besides, aren't you trying in your seminar to get them to see one another's individual senses of what's funny, what's tragic, what's beautiful, and so on? Aren't you trying to get above this totally relativistic, individual level?*"

"*But you see, Justin,*" I said, "*they can only read each other through their individual ways of reading. All any of us perceives is what our particular psyche perceives. In fact, I'll bet you've already seen this principle in action. You asked all of us in the seminar to describe what we saw when Trish Hassler collapsed, didn't you?*"

"*You were there.*"

"*Then you've seen it. I'll bet, Justin, that when Amy Lemaire told you about Hassler's death, she saw it in terms of some form of dependency or mothering. Anne Glendish said something about being looked at, Ireland something about violence and death, Max Ebenfeld something about her body or her weight, something like that. There's no such thing as a raw fact, unfiltered through some human being's way of seeing facts. I'll bet they even remembered—why am I saying they?—we even remembered what Trish said to Aval differently.*"

"*Eyewitnesses are proverbially unreliable.*"

"*Right,*" I shot back. "*Why? Because we see even 'objective facts' through these personal processes of interpretation. We humans cannot get outside our own heads.*"

"*Anyway, I was listening for who was where, who went where, who did what, things like that. What you call 'extrinsic evidence.'*"

"*Let me translate that, Justin. You were listening, so to speak,* through *their language to some event. That's fine for you. You're a detective. You want facts. But you can also listen to these people by listening to the words they use* as *words, not as representations of something else.*"

"*And if I do, what do I hear?*"

"*You hear—you build, really—a sense of how they see things. You learn what's important to them. For Trish it will be taking in something and spitting it back. For Chris, shifting. For the mystery student it will be power in hiding—"*

"And that's what you gave me this afternoon when you analyzed Hassler's and the interloper's responses."

"Right."

"He's a wild card! A loose end. I don't know where he is or what he's doing, but I'll bet he's doing something that's going to pop up when I least expect it and knock this case into a cocked hat. I just know that."

"You don't feel you control him."

"That means trouble coming up. He said just, The poem is phony. What do you do with a response like that?" He leaned back and sipped his martini. *We were going to relax and talk about my problems, not his.*

"We use the different responses in a method of reading that I call 'poem opening.' We pass the response back through the poem and see if we can share something of that other person's experience."

"What does 'pass the response back through' mean?"

"Let me give you an example. From Hassler's response." He nodded. "She talked about speaking in tongues, the half-language coming out of the snake handlers. Once I've gotten the idea from Hassler's squib, I can read all the phrases about the throat and neck, about the snake hissing and whispering at her ears, in what is, for me, a new way. As about—what shall I call it?—a prelanguage, a nonlanguage, that makes a deeper, a more spiritual communication possible."

"She gives you an idea."

"That's it. I take the personal themes she developed back to the poem, and I read the words again through that new light."

He humphed and shook his head. "It's a little like detection. Each thing someone says, you pass back through—" He broke off. "Say, shall we make it dinner as well? Do you think we can get something to eat here? Something quick? I've got to check out Hassler's books and her apartment again."

I remembered ancient lore. "It's the law in New York State. If you serve liquor, you also have to serve food."

He laughed. "I suppose I should know that, being a cop, but I never heard it before." He held up his empty glass, and Sheila of the long coppery hair glided over to our booth. "I'd like another of these. Another wine, Norman?" I nodded. "And what can we get to eat?"

"To be honest with you," said Sheila, "I wouldn't recommend anything more complicated than a hamburger. Our cook is student help. Maybe he could rise to a cheeseburger, but I wouldn't ask for beef Stroganoff."

"A hamburger it shall be, then," said Rhodes. "Same for you, Norman?"

I agreed. I had no desire to go back to an empty house to eat, and I supposed *he didn't either. I was surprised to realize I hadn't thought about Jane's mother since this morning. I wanted suddenly to call Jane, but it was only seven. She wouldn't be back from the hospital yet.*

"Tomato and lettuce?" Rhodes asked. "We need our vitamins."

"Sure," said Sheila, moving off to the kitchen. "He's up to that."

"And the interloper?" he said, turning back to me. "Could you do this 'poem opening' even with his limited response?"

"Why not?" I said. "In principle you can take any response back to the poem and try it, pass it through. He talked about Levertov's poem as a scam. Can I read the poem as about falsity? Of course. What could be a better symbol of falsity than a snake? And she does deceive her companions."

He laughed and shook his head. "And this becomes a different poem from Hassler's version. You create from one poem as many poems as there are people to read it. Then you can take any one of their readings and create still another batch of readings from it. The permutations and combinations are endless."

"As we've always said, poems are inexhaustible."

"But you're not saying the poem can have infinitely many meanings," he said.

"No. It isn't the poem that means, it's the reader that makes meaning. Then, meaning isn't the whole story. I'm talking about the experience *of the poem. There are as many experiences of the poem as there are readers. Infinitely many."*

"That seems reasonable enough, I suppose, but it still leaves me nervous."

"Why don't you try it yourself?"

"Me?"

"Yes, you. Why not?"

"Why not indeed?" He took my letter, turned to the text of the poem on the second page, and read it over a couple of times. Then he just shook his head again. "My, that's a lovely poem. I can feel it turning my mind around. It's as though I'm first in the snake's body, feeling Levertov pick me up. Feeling help-less, taken, captured. Then I'm in her body, feeling the weight of the snake and and her power over it and her fear of it. She moves it this way and that, as she wants to. Then she puts the snake down and it escapes, back into its own place, the grass."

"Strictly speaking, Justin, it's an illusion that the poem is turning your mind around. By reading it, you turn your own mind around. But what comes to your mind when you read it? Memories? People? Ideas?"

"All right," he laughed. "You've hooked me. I'll play your game. What comes to mind? What I bring to mind, I guess you'd say." He paused. "I re-member a kid I went to prep school with here in Buffalo. Herbie Zimmer. Herbie was totally fascinated by snakes, and Herbie had a collection. None poisonous,

of course. His parents were annoyed enough at the nonpoisonous ones. King snakes. Garter snakes. Boas. Several boas."

At that point, the fair Sheila clacked two hamburgers down on the formica, and the second round of drinks. We passed the ketchup back and forth and finally bit in. "All right," he said. "A ver-ry decent hamburger. What's the waitress's name, Norman?"

"Sheila," I said.

"Sheila!" he called out. "Sheila, give our compliments to the chef! Very good hamburger!" He waggled a thumbs-up sign of approval at her. "Classic! And a couple of coffees when you get round to it."

He ate energetically, while I waited for him to go on. "Yes, Herbie Zimmer. I'd go over to his house to play, and we'd take the snakes out of their aquarium tanks and let them slither around the room. It was always fairly dicey, because we knew we'd have to catch them and pick them up and put them back in the tanks. That always scared me a little. More than a little. The snakes were awfully fast, and they were good at getting on surfaces where you couldn't see them clearly. They'd head for corners and little gaps in the wainscoting, and they had a special fondness for the hot air grilles in the floor. I was afraid the snakes would escape and then there'd be hell to pay from his parents. If one of them had ever gotten into those hot air ducts! The snakes, I mean, not the parents," he laughed. "And the nervousness about picking them up. Even if they're not poisonous, you can get a nasty infection from a bite, so we had to be careful. It was this feeling of holding them and letting them go and then grabbing them again, before they could get away. Giving up control and getting it back." He stopped abruptly. "I think I'm beginning to hear myself."

"Are you stopping there?" I asked.

"Frankly, it makes me a bit nervous to do this, but actually something else has come to mind. This is a story a friend of mine told me, something that happened to him a few months ago. He and his wife were throwing a distinguished dinner party in their big, old mansion, one of the ones on Middlesex. They had a buffet supper catered, they had the university's string quartet come in to play—I think it was the Chester Quartet that year. They were to play while the guests ate. The guests arrived in due course, had a few drinks, and it was time for dinner. They went round and collected their platesful and sat down on the chairs and sofas all in proper rows. The musicians settled themselves in front of the grand fireplace with a big Yule fire blazing away. It was quite fine, my friend said. What could be more cozy and genteel than a Buffalo winter outside and a roaring fire inside and a string quartet playing and twenty or thirty old friends having dinner?

"I guess this must have been the first fire of that winter, because gradually, gradually, the head of a snake began sticking out of the chimney stones up over the musicians' bows. It must have been asleep because of the cold stone, and then the fire warmed it up, and it began to stir around. It must have crawled into a hole among the flagstones in the big old chimney during the summer when the family was at the lake.

"At first people didn't notice it, but then it began crawling further and further out of its hole. It got bigger and bigger, looking all around, testing the air with its tongue. It liked the music. It liked watching the musicians' bows sawing back and forth. It began keeping time with its head, my friend said. When the snake got all the way out, it was a big snake. A real six-footer, but a peaceful creature. He didn't say what kind, but it wasn't poisonous. It settled down in the middle of the living-room floor and just curled up there, not bothering anybody.

As soon as the musicians saw it, they stopped playing and fled. The guests began milling around in a totally crazy way. Some of the women started scream-ing and running out into other rooms, anywhere they could go. Nobody wanted to go out in the cold and snow, so they fled into the bedrooms upstairs. Then they felt trapped and screamed more. They rushed into the kitchen and yelled at the caterer's crew. Some packed themselves into bathrooms like sardines. Most of the men were edging discreetly toward the door. Nobody wanted to fool with the thing.

My friend called the ASPCA, but it was a Sunday night in the middle of November, and they weren't expecting snakes. It took them about an hour to get their snake person there. By that time, the musicians were long gone. The cater-ers were sitting in their truck. Most of the guests had gotten their coats and boots and fled. There was food all over the floor. But the snake just sat there, unperturbed by all the hullaballoo, king of the mountain—king of the living room, anyhow—until they took him away."

He shook his head. "Now there's a memory for you, Norman. Not mine. Something that happened to a friend."

"You don't think it was one of the snakes you and Herbie Zimmer lost track of and couldn't get back in the boxes?"

"Don't say that!," he said, waving his hands as if to ward off a blow. "Herbie's mother, wherever she is, would never forgive us. No. This was a dif-ferent house. And this is a story someone else told me."

"But you remembered it, and it's part of what you brought to Levertov's poem."

"Fair enough. You're saying that I made the poetic experience out of the materials of the poem plus things in my mind that I brought to the poem."

"Right."

"So, now what? What can you do with my associations?"

"To use your memory to open the poem up, I pass Herbie Zimmer and the concert evening back through the poem, not for you now, but for me. In your first story, I hear you talking about you and Herbie and the snakes all being in various places: the aquarium tanks, the room you were trying to keep the snakes in, the snakes slithering into the hot air ducts, getting lost in Herbie's house, the two of you in school in Buffalo. Places. I hear you talking, in the story about the musicale, about the snake being in the wrong place. The guests being driven out by the snake and getting into odd places: bathrooms, kitchen, upstairs bedrooms. Food on the floor. The wrong season for the ASPCA guy. Then the last thing you tell me is that you weren't there. Lots about places."

"You're not saying I'm like Aval."

"Your places are different. Chris feels he's in the wrong place, and he shifts himself. You move others. You put things and people in places, right places, wrong places. The poem turns your mind around, you say, but that's the way you've been behaving today, very much in control, turning other people around."

"Isn't that my job as a policeman? To move the perps off the streets and into the jail?"

"Maybe that's why you became a policeman. It fit you." Sheila turned up with the coffees at this point, but I was in full flow. "So I go back to the Levertov poem, and I put back through it your idea of space, of people being in spaces, the right spaces, the wrong spaces, being kept in spaces by other people, or being free."

"Go on."

"Now I hear in the poem about the ways that we can get free of people, as in the woods, and the ways that we're confined by people, the way Levertov confines the snake when she holds it, and the way she's confined by the presence of her friends and finally by the 'dark morning.' I suppose, in some way, she's confined by her readers. She has to use language a certain way to talk to us."

"Not bad," he said, and he was about to add something of his own when, as if on cue, his beeper went off. He swung his legs down from the banquette and strolled over to the pay phone.

Metropolitan Buffalo Police Department

Tape Transcription   Homicide Unit

Body: *Hassler, P.*   Tape No. *840307.032*

Place: *Telephone call*   Time: *7:37 p.m.*

Persons present: *Det. Lt. Rhodes; Det. Sgt. Yorrick*

Transcribed by: *J. Cipperman*

LT. RHODES: Rhodes here. Taping, Yorrick. How's it coming?

SGT. YORRICK: Not so good, Lieutenant. We've got no further than when we started.

LT. RHODES: How long is it now?

SGT. YORRICK: Getting on toward three hours. He's just a student. He should have softened up by this time.

LT. RHODES: You don't know the French. Talk about retentive! Okay, what's happening?

SGT. YORRICK: Oh, that Wakowski. He's a one, sticking his knobby Polish head with nothing but stubble on it in the kid's face. I thought he was gonna headbash him a couple of times. He's after him, because he's French, you know.

LT. RHODES: No, I didn't know. Doesn't Wakowski like the French any more than—well, let that go.

SGT. YORRICK: Foreigners. He's got it in for any foreigners at all.

LT. RHODES: So, have you pried anything useful out of Aval?

SGT. YORRICK: He's a caution, Lieutenant. You'd think Wakowski would have scared him by now, but no. I have a hard time not busting out laughing. Wakowski tells him to own up to the poison, tell us how he got it, it'll go easier on him. He gives the kid one of his picturesque descriptions of life in the holding pens. The kid's game, though. You've got to give him credit. He comes back with this crazy literary stuff of his. Oh, he's a one, all right.

And when he says this stuff, Wakowski looks as though somebody slapped him with a wet rag. So I come in, trying to keep a straight face. I come in good guy, with something nice and easy about how he wants us to catch this killer to make the world safe for women and children. He comes back at me with the abbess—have I got the word right? "The abbess between every crime and any possible evidence of that crime."

LT. RHODES: Abyss, maybe.

SGT. YORRICK: Whatever. Well, I tell you, they ought to try him out on one of them classes in interrogating you told me about.

LT. RHODES: Are you getting anything about the plagiarism at Yale?

SGT. YORRICK: Plagiarism! The minute I mention the word, he comes back at me in that funny precise way he has. He starts spouting the literary stuff, and he ends up, "So you see there can be no such thing as plagiarism, because there is no such thing as an author." Well, Wakowski can't let that one go by, and the next thing I know *he's* spouting Polish and telling Aval it's from that grand old Polish epic, Panty Day Hose, or something like that, and he's got his goddam nerve saying Mickey Which or Miskey Which isn't an author, and I could see that Aval had got old stubblehead Wakowski right where he wanted him.

I told Wakowski to knock it off, and I tried to get back to who did what to whom back there at Yale University in New Haven. All Aval would say was that Hassler had lost all the papers and computer files for her paper and for no good reason at all she accused him of taking it and turning it in as his own. Oh, he had nothing to do with her paper, he says. He'd written his own, didn't know what had happened to hers, and why was she accusing him? She must have had some kind of nervous breakdown, he says.

Are we getting anything, you say? Not a blessed thing. It's like arguing theology with a nun.

LT. RHODES: I was hoping you guys would clear up the New Haven business.

SGT. YORRICK: I wish we could, Lieutenant.

LT. RHODES: You might as well call up a squad car and send him home. Catch you later. Or are you off tonight?

SGT. YORRICK: Off, Lieutenant.

LT. RHODES: Well, have a pleasant evening, and take it easy on the cream ale.

SGT. YORRICK: Check.END OF THIS SECTION OF TAPE END OF THIS SECTION OF TAPE END OF THIS SECTION OF TAPE END OF THIS SEC

from the journal of Norman Holland

Justin seemed mildly amused when he sat down again. "What's funny?" I asked him.

"Aval," he said. "Aval and two of Buffalo's finest. He's got them buffaloed all right with his theory talk."

"They're interrogating him?" He nodded. "While we're talking literary theory?"

"So was he. And winning. They've given up. They're sending him home."

"The poor guy."

"I'd say he got out of it easy."

"Even so."

"They're through, but you and I are still on our break. Are you saying, Norman, that I don't shape my audience's response?"

"Think of yourself as partners with your audience."

"I'll be honest, Norman. I don't like it. If I don't shape people's responses, what am I doing when I write a play?"

"You give them the means—your play, your words, your characters, your plot—and they build the experience according to their own lights. Their conscious response to the play is only the tip of the iceberg. Underneath, half-conscious or unconscious, are all these memories and relationships and a whole cognitive style.

"And you know and believe this already, Justin. You really do, you know."

"I do?"

"Sure. If you were to write a Broadway play, you'd try it out in New Haven or Washington, wouldn't you, before you took it to New York? Or you'd have previews during which you'd rewrite? Stand-up comics try out their material little by little before they build it into an act. Hollywood checks a movie out at a sneak preview before they make the final cut. What I'm saying, Justin, is that, as an artist, you only know if it works after *it has worked. You can't predict or control your audience. If you could, you'd write nothing but hits."*

"But what's the point of writing a play at all, if you aren't shaping the audience's experience?"

"You're saying that controlling people's responses is the reason you write. I'm telling you you're only partly in control. You find that uncomfortable because being in control of situations and people is important for you."

"You're cutting pretty close to the bone, Professor."

"That's the kind of issue we get into in this seminar."

"You're really passionate about this stuff, aren't you? You really profess."

"I think my own motivation is, if I go deep enough, that I'd like to know what makes people tick, but I don't want to get close enough to find out. But yes, I'm passionate about these ideas."

He savored his coffee for a minute and resumed. *"You know, I still feel that we ought to be able to use what you're learning about these students' styles to solve this murder. If we fasten onto a suspect, then the murder should be in that person's style, shouldn't it?"*

"True, but that isn't going to lead you to a suspect."

"It might verify our suspicions."

"Only 'might.' Any given act can fit a lot of different styles."

"I'd still like you to go on analyzing these responses. For style alone, if that's all you turn up."

"All right, Justin. I'll do that. And I'll keep my eye out for the odd fact." That seemed to satisfy him, and we got up from the table. He adroitly seized the check and, over my mild demurrers, paid for both of us. Again, Justin got an appreciative smile from Sheila at the tip. We bundled up and pushed through the storm doors. It was cold, all right, pretty bad for March, but the sidewalk wasn't icy. He was wearing loafers! I was cold in my boots. While we stood in the neon glow from the Westward How, he organized my evening for me.

"Let's see. You've done Hassler and the interloper and Aval. Sisley acted oddly this morning. I'd like to know more about him ASAP. As for the other six: Ebenfeld, Glendish, Ireland, and Penza all have motives, but not very strong ones; for Lemaire I have no motive at all. No doubt then, according to the rules of detective stories, Lemaire's the guilty one. What the hell. Sisley first. Then the rest in alphabetical order. Okay?"

"All right."

"How long will this take you?"

"If I start first thing in the morning, I could probably have three done by late afternoon tomorrow."

"Um." He considered for a moment. "Can you start tonight?"

Inwardly I groaned. I hate to work after dinner, but Hassler had been murdered, and this didn't seem a good time to invoke union rules. Jane wasn't home. "Yes, I can work tonight. If I do, I should have them for you by noon tomorrow."

"Great!" he said. "I hate to work at night, too, but I have to check out Hassler's apartment and the notebooks, and we've got a meeting of the people in the seminar scheduled for 9:00 a.m. tomorrow. I have to get ready for that."

"Sounds like a busy night for you," I said, somewhat lumpishly. "A policeman's lot is not a happy one." I was cold. He must have been warmer in his Burberry than I in my anorak, although I wondered how he could wear loafers in this weather. Despite my sulkiness, he sounded enthusiastic as we parted.

"Nor a professor's," he said. "Sorry to ask you to work so late." And he started to walk off, but turned back. "Norman, I enjoyed our dinner tonight. You've given me a lot to think about, and I like that."

Maybe it was the martinis, but he seemed to have been genuinely interested in our conversation. "I enjoyed it, too, Justin," I said, and I meant it. He was a good listener. He paid attention, he was judicious, and he even agreed with me—sort of. I was as tired as if I'd been teaching, though. The inside of my skull felt as though he had scoured it out for anything of use to him. We shook hands, and I set out for my office ready to tackle the responses for him. I felt, how shall I say it?, loyal.

Metropolitan Buffalo Police Department

Tape Transcription   Homicide Unit

Body: *Hassler, P.*   Tape No. *840307.032*

Place: *48 Masling Blvd., 4-E*   Time: *7:34 p.m.*

Persons present: *Det. Lt. Rhodes; Det. Margo Maistry*

Transcribed by: *J. Cipperman*

LT. RHODES: Margo, let's put this on the tape. You got my message . . .

DET. MAISTRY: Yeah, Lieutenant.

LT. RHODES: What time?

DET. MAISTRY: I got your message about three o'clock, like, but I couldn't get here until nearly six o'clock, because they had me working on the Phillimore disappearance.

LT. RHODES: Walsh and Moonset are handling that. But it's going okay, I assume.

DET. MAISTRY: I guess so. Moonset, you know, does not inform one what he is up to. I figured there'd be no problem if I was a little late, since this Hassler is dead anyway.

LT. RHODES: So you got here at six, and you've been checking her computer and her other stuff and poking around in her course papers. I sent for you in particular, Margo, because you've been to the university. You studied computers, didn't you? You'd have a better chance of recognizing class papers from UB than I did.

DET. MAISTRY: I was in computer science, Lieutenant, and this Hassler was in English. I took some English courses—I had to—so I think I would recognize the kind of papers you are looking for. I checked out her papers as well as I could, anyhow.

LT. RHODES: And it took you an hour and a half to do that?

DET. MAISTRY: Lieutenant, this place has got paper, fucking paper, everywhere, and it took me a helluva while to go through it. Besides, I took a little time out for dinner. I figured somebody should make sure the stuff in her refrigerator didn't go bad. Anyway, I couldn't find much, either in the fridge or the computer or her papers.

LT. RHODES: Let's talk about the papers first. You got my instructions . . .

DET. MAISTRY: Look for a stack of papers or file folders an inch, inch-and-a-half thick, you said, different typewriter faces, different names, Anne Glendish, Christian Aval—did I get that right?—Barry Ireland . . .

LT. RHODES: Yeah. What did you find?

DET. MAISTRY: Zip. I didn't find anything like that. I messed up as little as possible so you'd still have a picture of her lifestyle as if she was still living it, like. But I'm sure, Lieutenant, there's no stack of paper here like what you told me to look for, different kinds of typing and all. In fact, I think I see where that stack *was,* and I think somebody just took it elsewhere.

LT. RHODES: Show me.

DET. MAISTRY: Here, on this shelf. See? There's piles of papers all along the shelf, and right here there's a gap just about nine, ten inches wide, like. These other papers're all current class notes, term papers she's writing, stuff like that. Current. From her other courses. See the dates? So I figure this's where she kept her notes for this seminar of Holland's you're asking me about. And they're not there. See?

LT. RHODES: I see. And not anywhere else.

DET. MAISTRY: Nowhere, Lieutenant, nowhere anywhere.

LT. RHODES: You're sure.

DET. MAISTRY: Sure, I'm sure.

LT. RHODES: Okay. And the computer?

DET. MAISTRY: That's complicated, Lieutenant. First, I have to explain. You know something about computers?

LT. RHODES: I try to stay as far away from them as possible.

DET. MAISTRY: That's very unprogressive of you, Lieutenant. Even this English major here, this Hassler, uses a computer. Anyway, you understand that this box here does all the calculating and other stuff. This box is called the central processing unit or the CPU.

LT. RHODES: Okay so far.

DET. MAISTRY: See? You can do it. Okay, and you understand that the CPU also contains a memory with a magnetic disk in it on which the computer writes information just like a tape recorder writes music on a magnetic tape.

LT. RHODES: Okay.

DET. MAISTRY: Now, you correctly deduced when you turned this computer on, and it wouldn't run, that it had been pretty thoroughly erased inside, its memory had.

LT. RHODES: "Thoroughly erased." Is that different from just "erased"?

DET. MAISTRY: Hers was erased the hard way. Written over.

LT. RHODES: As if, on a tape recorder, you put new music over old.

DET. MAISTRY: You got it. There are a couple ways you could do that. You could use some special program that writes over the disk or, if you want just to erase everything, you can tell the computer to format the hard disk. Then it'll write over every bit of the surface of the disk. I think that's what happened here. When I loaded in an operating system and some undelete utilities and looked at the hard disk, all I found was zeroes. Zeroes, zeroes, zeroes, written over whatever had been there.

LT. RHODES: Just like at Yale.

DET. MAISTRY: I don't know how they do it at Yale. Here at Buffalo we just do it by formatting—that'll take everything off so that no one can read the data after that without special equipment, without really working on the disk to detect the 5 percent of the original recording that might remain.

LT. RHODES: Got you. Is this formatting a big job?

DET. MAISTRY: I don't know what you mean by a big job. The hard disk, it's nothing. You just tell the machine to format drive C, and it sits there and does it. You can go get a cuppa coffee, something. Most people put a special fix in the operating system so that can't happen accidentally.

LT. RHODES: You mean somebody could put the command in the computer—that would take only a second or two, right?

DET. MAISTRY: Right.

LT. RHODES: —and they could just go and leave the machine and it would destroy all the data that the user had recorded on the hard disk?

DET. MAISTRY: Yes, you could make it do that.

LT. RHODES: The person could be somewhere else while this was going on?

DET. MAISTRY: Sure they could, but they didn't.

LT. RHODES: They didn't? Why not?

DET. MAISTRY: Because you found the computer turned off.

LT. RHODES: You can't tell the machine to turn itself off? One of these machines would be smart enough for that.

DET. MAISTRY: Not completely, no, because it's a mechanical switch. How is the machine going to flip a mechanical switch? No arms, no fingers. It won't turn itself off, not without some special hardware, and I don't see any sign of that here. Also, I suppose that if the machine was erasing itself it would erase the special program for turning itself off, too.

LT. RHODES: Deconstruction again.

DET. MAISTRY: What?

LT. RHODES: An English department joke.

Okay, suppose the person stayed around while the machine wiped the hard disk. How long would that take?

DET. MAISTRY: A machine like this writes to disk maybe one megabyte a minute. Her hard disk has ten megabytes on it. Ten minutes, say.

LT. RHODES: Ten minutes and you could write over all of Patricia Hassler's data.

DET. MAISTRY: Except for the floppies.

LT. RHODES: Floppies?

DET. MAISTRY: Sure, Lieutenant. These little square things in the plastic boxes over here. You have to back up the information on the hard disk for safety's sake, in case the machine breaks down, or the hard disk crashes, or somebody screws it up, something like that. You should have three copies of everything, one on the hard disk, two on floppy disks. You do that—well, there're different ways of doing it, but the way this Hassler probably did it was to copy all the data on the hard disk to separate diskettes. Yes, she kept back-up disks all right. She's got at least fifty floppies here.

LT. RHODES: Well, have you looked for her data on the floppies?

DET. MAISTRY: Of course, Lieutenant, and guess what—somebody has wiped every last one of these, too. Permanently.

LT. RHODES: The machine will erase its own hard disk. Will it do the same with these diskettes?

DET. MAISTRY: No. Those you have to load one by one into the machine. By the way, you would have to do them first, because once you have erased the machine's operating system—the program that tells how to format disks and erase stuff and do other housekeeping like that—it won't format the floppies any more.

LT. RHODES: So erasing the diskettes is a job the machine couldn't do by itself.

DET. MAISTRY: No. Like I say, you have to insert each floppy and then take it out. Very tedious. You have to sit there while the machine does all this.

LT. RHODES: How long would it take?

DET. MAISTRY: Let's see. She's got about fifty floppies here. This machine, it would format a floppy in about forty-five seconds. You figure it out.

LT. RHODES: About forty minutes?

DET. MAISTRY: Yeah. Thirty-seven and a half.

LT. RHODES: Wouldn't it be easier just to take the floppies with you and throw them in a garbage can somewhere?

DET. MAISTRY: Maybe yes, maybe no. You've got a couple of shoeboxes of stuff to get rid of. Maybe if the perp didn't have to be seen somewhere after this, maybe they could do it.

LT. RHODES: But if this perp had to go to a seminar, say—

DET. MAISTRY: Then they'd have to carry all these floppies with them. You throw them anywhere where people could see them, like our regular mesh trash cans, somebody'd fish 'em out right away.

LT. RHODES: Why's that?

DET. MAISTRY: You got maybe twenty-five dollars worth of diskettes here. Then the minute that person started to use them you could see what's on them. Very risky for the perp.

LT. RHODES: Look, Margo, you know what happened this morning. Is it possible somebody could have done this in the time between this woman's leaving for her morning class—we figure that at about 8:15—and the time she enters the classroom and sits down and dies—we place that about 9:10?

DET. MAISTRY: No way. It would take almost twice that time. And somebody had to be here to turn the computer off.

LT. RHODES: This was done the way it was done at Yale.

DET. MAISTRY: Yale again. What's Yale got to do with this?

LT. RHODES: The same thing happened to this woman's computer when she was a student at Yale.

DET. MAISTRY: So the same person did it both times, right?

LT. RHODES: Unfortunately, it's not that simple.

DET. MAISTRY: Anyway, Lieutenant, glad to have been of help. It's around eight o'clock. You through with me? Maybe I can get another dinner out of my guy if I get home now.

LT. RHODES: Sure, Margo, go. Go home. You've been a big help. Thank you.

LT. RHODES: *Comment.* Lots of information, but lots of contradictions at this point.

Fact one. Somebody carried Hassler's books and papers across the hall from one classroom to the other after she died. This must have been somebody from the seminar group.

Fact two. When I examined the stuff taken across the hall, I found the papers the other students had written to her about her. But I didn't find any kind of a response from Hassler to the other students. Maybe she didn't write a response. Maybe she wasn't going to talk from notes. But more likely the person who carried the books across the hall took whatever she had written for this morning. Why else would somebody risk taking Hassler's stack of books and papers across the hall? This person would have had to be somebody in the seminar group, as in fact one.

Fact three. According to Maistry's search, somebody removed *all* of Hassler's papers relating to this seminar from her apartment. Why *all?* Evidently, judging from facts one and two, somebody wanted to get at some paper of Hassler's. But why take all? That makes the theft visible immediately to Hassler and even to us, Maistry and me. Why not just take the one paper this person was after? Unless they were after them all. But why bother, since we have other collections of papers relating to the seminar, notably Holland's, which contains everything?

And when did this person take the papers out of Hassler's apartment? If it took place before Hassler left for class this morning, she'd have noticed. It could have taken place while Hassler was on her way to class—her apartment would be easy to break into. Or someone could have taken the folders after the murder, but in that case, it would have to be someone not in the seminar group because they were all at Rhodes Hall. The interloper, perhaps.

Fact four. Most puzzling of all is the erasing of Hassler's computer files. Done in the same way it was done at Yale. This points to Aval again, and very strongly, but we don't have any hard evidence that he did it either at Yale or here.

And when could he have done it? The instant Hassler started to use the computer, she'd have seen that her disks were destroyed. Apparently, Hassler did little else but work, so she'd have noticed the sabotage very quickly. Presumably, then, the computer was all right when Hassler stopped work on Tuesday night. According to Maistry, it would have taken from forty minutes to an hour to do the whole job of erasing. Was there any period when she was away from the apartment for that length of time? It would have to have been late Tuesday night, too late to start work again, when she came home. Did she go out after, say, midnight? We don't know.

Could it have been done after Hassler left for class this morning? Yes, but not by someone in the seminar. Not by Aval, for example. Because it would have taken too much time for the person to do the erasing and get to the seminar by nine o'clock. The interloper, however, could have done it.

Could it have been done after the murder? Yes, like the taking of Hassler's seminar papers. But, again, by someone not in the seminar, because they were all over in Rhodes Hall or in the bus with Yorrick. The interloper fits the bill in this case too.

There are too many contradictions here. Moving Hassler's books across the hall requires someone *in* the seminar. Erasing her computer requires someone *not* in the seminar.

I can't get my mind round this one. Time to knock off, oh fair transcriber, time to knock off for your sake, too. The tape is running out. Time to go home. Time to go home to an empty house.

State University of New York at Buffalo
Department of English

March 7, 1984

Dear Justin,

It's about 9:00 p.m. Wednesday night. I enjoyed our dinner. I felt heeded, taken seriously, always a good feeling, not believed perhaps—that would be too much to ask. To say nothing of the hamburgers. Thanks all around.

Here are the two squibs, the trait and the snake, from Wally Sisley, and my analysis. I'll leave this in your new English Department mailbox for whenever you can get to it.

As I told you, Wally has had trouble publishing enough to keep the dean happy. Instead of writing, he acts (and quite well, I might add). I find his account of being a twin fascinating, and it suggests to me a confusion about his identity (a comedy of errors that wasn't funny at all). I see Wally as wanting always to be behind someone else, a protector who is also a mask. Tell me if you see the same. Incidentally, as you read, notice the number of times and the different ways he uses "real" or "realize."

English 6121   February 8
                                                Wally

     Something I want you to know about me? Some of you already know it. I'm an actor. At least I like to act. I'm not sure I can call myself an actor, since I'm not up to professional standards. Nearly, though.

     In 1982 a bunch of us founded the Erie Stagestruck Players--ESP. That somewhat diffident name is my invention. We found an old theater at 196 Genesee Street, down among the muggers. It was part of a church complex that was pulling in on itself as the last of its dwindled Polish congregation was moving out to the suburbs. We were able to rent and finally buy the theater. And I get to act in it.

     I love to act. Somehow when I'm playing someone else, I can do all the things that mild-mannered Wally Sisley doesn't do in real life. I can be as tough as Stanley Kowalski. I can be as flamboyant as Oscar Wilde. I can be as romantic as Romeo. Isn't there a Ring Lardner story where the meek, shy clerk in a hardware store can become wild and romantic when he's given a character to act in an amateur dramatic society? That's me, I think. I can be moody and dark and fierce like Hamlet. (My Hamlet was pretty good! At least the local critics said so.) I can be brittle and witty in a Noel Coward play. I can swashbuckle like Cyrano (my favorite role). I get to be in fantasy all the things I'm not in reality.

     Maybe behind that obvious fact is a still deeper fact. I'm a twin. An absolutely identical twin. Again, some of you already know this. Norm, I know, does, because my twin, Will, once visited the department, and we put on a practical joke. At the time, I'd been wearing a mustache. When Will came up, I shaved my mustache off, and I gave him a stage mustache on spirit gum. I switched clothes with him, so that he was wearing my tweeds and corduroys and Rockport shoes, and I was wearing the three-piece blue suit. Then we trotted off to the department. As we got near to somebody, I'd whisper the name to Will. Then he'd walk up to them and say something like, "Hi there,

Norm," or Romola or whoever. "I'm glad I ran into you.
I'd like you to meet my twin brother, Will." And Will
would introduce me. I'd say things like, "Oh, yes,
Holland. I've read about you. You're the one who does
literature-and-psychology and studies readers' responses.
Well, how's it going? Had any good responses lately?
Identity still the same? Don't be afreud to let it
change." "Romola Badger," I said. "Oh yes, my brother has
told me what a wonderful job you're doing as chair. Sitting in it all the time." People would be startled and
confused. The first confuser was that we looked so much
alike. We really are indistinguishable. There are times
when we've been able to fool even our wives. No--not
that, you dirty-minded people. The other confusing thing
was, How did this character from Washington know so much
about the people in the English Department? Well, eventually we had to explain our joke, and it was all right.
People took it in good part. I hope.

It was very strange growing up as a twin, a little
like that scene in <u>Monkey Business</u> when Groucho and Harpo
disguised as Groucho are on opposite sides of an archway,
but Harpo wants to make Groucho think it's a mirror. So
he does everything Groucho does, as if he were Groucho's
reflection. Groucho can't decide whether it's someone
else he's seeing or himself. Well, it was like that with
Will and me. I think I was six years old before I realized we were two people. It was really a <u>Comedy of Errors</u>.
Our mother dressed us alike, and the grandparents and the
other relatives all oohed and aahed over us. How cute we
were--because we were two exactly alike! Ho, ho, ho! No,
no, no, not two, a half. Things were divided between Will
and me. It was as though there was enough for one, but it
had to be divided, and when it came to dividing, we
weren't alike at all.

When the aunts and uncles would come to visit and
bring us candy, Will would always get there first. When
my father at the head of the table would finally, after
all the grown-ups, offer us kids our choice of Thanksgiv-
ing turkey, Will had his plate up right away, and he'd
always get the last of the white meat. In fact, he was
born a few minutes ahead of me, so it started right out
that way. William and Wallace, they christened us. It was
going to be Willie Sisley and Wally Sisley--isn't that
cute? But pretty soon Willie got to be Will, while I
stayed Wally. Oddly, I got to like it. It took a lot of

the responsibility off me. He got the white meat, sure,
but he took all the risks as well. When other kids would
pick on us, he was my defender. When we went to a new
school--and, boy, you have to be one to know what it's
like to be identical twins in a new school--Will would
handle all the kidding and the roughhouse. He's always
been an older brother to me.

The irony is that we're both actors. I'm not supposed
to say who Will works for in Washington, but Will actually does the derring-do that I only pretend to when I
play Cyrano. I guess. He can't talk about his work, and
he doesn't. Since our politics are so different, I don't
either. As a liberal, I of course object to our insane
foreign policies. Even so, I'm glad it's Will who's out
there, because I know, no matter how awful his politics,
he's a strong, kind, decent human being.

And how did I end up with that? Norm, I expect you'll
tell me someday.

By the way, his story about pretending to be his twin brother is absolutely true. They do look extraordinarily alike, and even those of us who
know Wally well were fooled and not too happy about it. Wally made some
rather too witty comments about his colleagues. (Professors' narcissism is
all tied up in their work, and they're painfully sensitive to other people's
opinion of it. You may have noticed.)

Wally, I think, regards the world as a risky place. He tells us his
theater is among muggers and the twins faced bullies in the new school.
You'll see the same thing in the second squib. He assumes the woods are
ominous and the snake poisonous, and he contrasts them to the cozy
bungalows.

English 6121   February 15
                                                Wally

"You faded." "I returned." That's the great moment of
the poem for me. There's strangeness in it. This forest
seemed faintly sinister to me, the kind of place that
harbors dangerous things like this snake.

I realize now that I assumed without much thinking
about it that the snake was poisonous. She says it's
harmless, but she doesn't know. I know. I know it was

deadly, and she has escaped with her life. That's why the ending of the poem is the great moment for me. I get a tremendous feeling of relief, almost like after sex. She picked up the snake. She risked it, with all of them staring at her. She got away with it. And what do you do after that's over, all haunted in the dark morning, smiling? Do you just settle down at the word processor again? Not me. I couldn't.

I wonder what she was doing out there anyway. And with companions. Who are they and what is this occasion? A picnic? A hike? I imagine that she and they were all at Bread Loaf or Yaddo or some other writers' sanctuary--a reward for literary success--and everybody was taking the morning off. When she and the snake face off, I realize that Levertov is using the snake as an image for the writer. After all, the snake has a forked tongue, and doesn't the writer lie, make up situations?

They're not supposed to do that. They're supposed to sit in their cozy little bungalows and work, work, work, not walk out into dangerous woods and get in trouble with snakes. So, I'm willing to assume this never happened, not at Bread Loaf or anywhere else. The whole thing is unreal. This is a make-believe forest, and she was never there.

Except that the weight makes it real. All too real. I can feel the weight of this big snake. It must have been big and long for her to describe it this way. I see its jaws facing my face. The forked tongue comes out from between fangs that can kill. Poison can solve everything, as the Borgias used to say. The writer's forked tongue just creates a play-world. Like this squib.

What I sense from all this is that Wally thinks it's better to approach a fairly dangerous world disguised as someone else, as his brother, in the practical joke, as Cyrano or Hamlet when he's acting, or as Levertov when he feels the weight of the snake. I'd say it this way: Wally can react to danger, he can express his aggression in fantasy, when he's hidden behind someone else. If he has to act on his own in the real world, he becomes very self-conscious. Then he has trouble writing and working. He blocks.

I'll leave this in your new mailbox. I expect you'll read it tomorrow morning. I hope it's useful. Ebenfeld next, probably after the seminar meeting in the morning.

/Norm/

State University of New York at Buffalo
Department of English

March 7, 1984 / 10:30 p.m.

Dear Justin:

I can't seem to quit. Too excited? It's getting on toward eleven, and here I sit in this gloomy old building—old house, really (as who should know better than you?)—a dark, quiet, depressing space. I can see out my window toward Main Street and the greenish mercury street lights. It's cold out there—cold in here, for that matter, the university saving on heat—and I see no one on the street.

I feel this strange compulsion to write up Max Ebenfeld for you. He seems somehow to have the key to our seminar. Tired as I am, I think you *ought* to know about him. Is an *ought* the kind of feeling Max brings out? I'll leave you to judge. Here are his trait and snake squibs.

Keep an eye out, as you read, for his delight in balancing and rationalizing things. He starts by saying he has *two* things he wants to tell us about himself, another balance. Then he goes on to rationalize a whole series of balances: the virtues and the vices, pagan and Christian, past and present, body and mind.

English 6121

February 8, 1984

Max

The first thing that comes to your mind? With me, it was two things, so I'll do right and do both.

I like the Parson's Tale. Yes, I can hear you gasping, "The Parson's Tale!!!" Even Chaucer professors dismiss it as a dreary sermon on the seven deadly sins, but I think it's fascinating--once you make sense of it.

I read The Canterbury Tales as a symbolic journey, or, as Chaucer's Parson says, this voyage, is to show you the way to that other "parfit glorious pilgrimage." Chaucer starts with those thirty-some earthy, earthly pilgrims-- including himself. He puts himself into his own story, just like a postmodern novelist. Then, in that last tale, the whole grand book pivots away from earth and toward heaven. Sure, I wish that final tale were a more lively piece of writing, but we can't have everything, can we? Not on this earth--that's Chaucer's point.

The other thing I want you to know about me is that I pump iron. I flatter myself that you can take one look at these pecs and delts and lats, and you just know that that guy works out. I love that feeling of the muscles coming into play against the machines and the free weights. You feel this surge of strength against the bar. For a moment it's not clear which will win, and then you do, and it's all right. Up she goes, and then you can hold against the down stroke, and again up, and again hold against. And again and again.

The Parson's Tale builds on the idea of the seven deadly sins. Gee I LAPSE--that's my mnemonic for them. Gluttony, Ire, Lechery, Avarice, Pride, Sloth, Envy.

Gee I LAPSE doesn't give them in order, and the order is key. Pride is the worst, because when you fully understand it, it means that you're locked into your self, self-preoccupied, self-satisfied, therefore self-contained. Your fellow humans are mere objects, grist for a psychology or a novel. You cannot be penetrated by the greatest of the seven virtues--ah, the symmetry of it-- love. Indeed, you return hate for love.

The logic of the sins rests wholly on the idea of love, God's love. Why is Sloth the next worst? Because you're locked away from love another way. You're not self-satisfied, just the opposite. You're inert, like a stone, not even capable of Ire or Envy.

Ire--you act out of yourself but with the opposite of love, anger. Then come the perversions of love. Envy: love of something but coupled with anger at its owner. You can't abide the idea that anybody has more than you. Everything has to be on the same dull, even, monotonous level.

Avarice is another perversion of love--the love of stones and metals, mere things--I suppose we in this seminar could even include a lust for academic publication. Gluttony, the love of plants and animals, but more dangerously, the love of people as though they were no more than plants or animals, mere sexual objects or audiences. Lechery, the love, but wrongful love, of other humans.

The seven Virtues balance the seven Vices--but I don't want to make this paper too long. Of the three Christian virtues, faith, hope, and charity, charity, <u>caritas</u>, <u>agape</u>, is the holy love that makes the whole system work, hence the most important virtue, the nearest to the divine. Faith and hope are what Norm would call in psychoanalytic

terms, trust. Hope is trust in our human future and also
our past. Faith is trust in another plane of being, God,
if you will. But I most like the four pagan virtues:
Fortitude; Wisdom; Temperance, moderation in all things,
the Golden Mean; and Justice.

Strength acts bodily on the outside world, and Wisdom
is the mental form of strength. Temperance achieves balances inside oneself, as Justice does outside, restraint
for a purpose, related, therefore, oddly, to chastity.

The whole system is beautifully sane and right.
There's a classical psychology here, a psychology for
mental health. Not all bound up in the interior life of
the individual, like your psychoanalysis, Norm, but
reaching out to a larger, even a supernatural world.

A personal example. Last fall, they wouldn't give me a
teaching assistantship, and I had to take a temporary job
as a loader at the Natural History Museum. I'll be honest
with you, I was furious. I wanted to break things, to
hurt somebody. Why wouldn't the department give me a
T.A., when I could see others less deserving get it? But
that's the sin of Envy. Then I found a way to think
rightly about my job using the Parson's terms.

They were having a big pre-Columbian show, with a
reconstructed temple wall in the basement. They needed
people to fit huge stones and statues precisely together.
Ingeniously, they advertised for people from the local
body-building club, and I signed up. At first I resented
it terribly. Then I decided to think about it in the
Parson's terms. Heaving those ancient stones, I was using
my strength (a pagan virtue) to reach out to the human
past (the virtue of hope). And I was making something for
the people that would see the exhibit--a loving act.

See? I've told you not one, but two things about me.
Surely our symbolically named Norm will tell me--will
tell us--how they combine.

Weight and *balance*. He likes to feel the push of his muscles balancing
the downward push of the weights. He imagines the spiritual plane or an
afterlife balancing the imperfections of this life. I can't quite tell if he's religious or not. He doesn't talk about God or Jesus, but he does carry the
weight of one hell of a superego. We get more of this balancing of sin and
righteousness with the snake.

English 6121   February 15, 1984
                                       Max

   Norm, could you predict that I would like this poem?
"The weight of you on my shoulders." That's the line that
feels so right to me. The weight, the weights, that I
have so often felt on my shoulders, when I'm sculpting my
body. This is a different weight, of course. This is the
weight of the snake, a living weight, that therefore
signifies the burden, the primal curse, we all bear.
   For me, the poem dramatizes the face-to-face confrontation with the weight of primal evil, so attractive, so
green and gold and silver, so fascinating therefore, and
yet so dangerously entangling.
   The Bible symbolizes our ancient badness as a snake.
Because of him, "In the sweat of thy face shalt thou eat
bread." We are cursed with work and heaviness and imper-
fection, but out of that fortunate fall, o felix culpa,
comes the incredible balancing glory of redemption, at
least in the Christian scheme of things. II Corinthians
gives it in images of weight--naturally enough: "For our
light affliction, which is but for a moment, worketh for
us a far more exceeding and eternal weight of glory."
   You'll laugh, but sometimes when I'm working out, I
think that my pumping iron is an allegory of the human
condition. We work toward a glory like that the New Tes-
tament promises us. When we finally get on the stage,
we've worked our hardest and lifted our utmost. At that
moment we trust that we'll receive the glory of that
small contest, symbol of the much larger contest, our
life on earth. I do like to allegorize.
   I see the same thing with this poem. She's dramatiz-
ing, "They shall speak with new tongues; they shall take
up serpents." Levertov works at her poetry, and hard work
it is. By facing the snake's forked tongue, by accepting
the burden of Original Sin, the poet wins for herself a
new tongue, even in the dark and haunted morning.
   I know this will seem too "spiritual" for the rest of
you. Okay. I understand. The myths say some very silly,
strange, and crazy things, about snakes as symbols of
rebirth, for example. It turns out, though, they're absolutely right, provided we open ourselves to them and

```
listen with an understanding ear. As Levertov opens her-
self to this snake.
    NO!, Norman, I do NOT mean that the snake is a phallic
symbol.
```

I think Max is in a phase a lot of literary students go through of being entranced with their ability to provide symbolic readings of texts. Students often formulate these symbolisms in religious terms, because religion provides a ready-made vocabulary. Then, it all "feels right" somehow, and you can't quite tell whether it's religion or the interpretive skill that "feels right."

Max loves to allegorize and symbolize things, like that snake. I see this as another version of balance. He controls an emotional, even unsettling, experience of the poem by bracketing it inside an intellectual interpretation in symbolic or religious terms. He shapes experiences the way he shapes his body, controlling things, making them "right."

These two assignments have an interesting relationship. When I ask the students to write about something they want the other students to know, most feel quite exposed at first. What we see in that response are their defenses. Then, a week later, when I give them the snake poem, I get something closer to the fantasies that those defenses are keeping in place.

With Max, on the trait assignment, I got his fascination with balance and rational interpretations, the Roman Max. When he came to the snake poem, he talked about a quasi-Christian going to glory. And, as in his final sentence, NO sex!

Max makes himself into the image of a stoic, wise person, always in control, the just judge. I can imagine Max, though, bursting out of that control. We get a faint hint of that when he expresses his resentment when the department didn't give him a teaching assistantship. He felt "furious." Then, on the opposite side of the coin are those judges at the body-building contest who'll raise him to glory and ecstasy. I think what would make Max lose control is a sense that some judging person—the department, for example, but a woman could play that part—wasn't acting justly. Forgive my pun but, if he feels he's done his "waiting," "done right," he could say to hell with balancing things and act a little crazy.

I'm through (in more senses than one!). Time to go home.

/Norm/

thursday

Metropolitan Buffalo Police Department

Tape Transcription   Homicide Unit

Body: *Hassler, P.*   Tape No. *840308.005*

Place: *Telephone call*   Time: *8:07 a.m.*

Persons present: *Det. Lt. Rhodes*

Transcribed by: *J. Cipperman*

LT. RHODES: Transcriber, I'm telephoning Professor Vernor. Got an answer. Lt. Rhodes M.B.P.D. here. May I speak to Professor Vernor, please? *[Long pause.]*

SECRETARY: I'm sorry, Lieutenant. I can't seem to locate him. He must have stepped down the hall for a few minutes.

LT. RHODES: It's urgent.

SECRETARY: Shall I have him call you back?

LT. RHODES: Yes, please. 3-9-2-7-3-3-2. That'll page me. Tell him it's urgent. *[Pause.]*
      Good-bye.

SECRETARY: Have a nice day. END OF THIS SECTION OF TAPE END OF THIS SECTION OF TAPE END OF THIS SECTION OF TAPE END OF

from the journal of Norman Holland

Thursday morning. About 8:30. The paper ran its half-baked story making me look like a crank. I had to come in because of the extra meeting of the seminar. I found a parking place (eventually!), climbed up to the third floor of Rhodes Hall, checked my mailbox, and there it was. I could see the familiar, faint dot matrix printing right away. Someday he'll get a new ribbon.

I'd already stretched out my hand, when I remembered Justin had told us not to touch. By this time Paul Penza and Anne Glendish had come into the mailroom. I cautioned them, and I asked Paul to get somebody from the police—they surely had arrived by this time for a 9:00 a.m. meeting. He brought

back Yorrick with white cotton gloves on and his famous pair of tongs. He lifted the squib out and bagged it.

"Okay, Dr. Holland. Let's get the others." I went down the names with him, and he took the squibs out box by box. "And why was there just this one thing in your box, Dr. Holland?," he asked. I explained that I'd been working late last night and cleaned out my mail just before I left.

"And is there anything else, Doctor?"

I couldn't think of anything, so we walked down the hall to the somber meeting of the seminar about to begin.

Metropolitan Buffalo Police Department

Tape Transcription   Homicide Unit

Body: *Hassler, P.*   Tape No. *840308.006*

Place: *Telephone call*   Time: *8:35 a.m.*

Persons present: *Det. Lt. Rhodes*

Transcribed by: *J. Cipperman*

LT. RHODES: Lt. Rhodes, M.B.P.D., here. Please, may I speak to Professor Vernor? I called before. It's urgent.

SECRETARY: I'll see if I can find him. *[Long pause]* He was around the lab, but I don't see him now. Shall I have him call you back?

LT. RHODES: You tried that once before, miss.

SECRETARY: I don't know what to do, Lieutenant, except leave him a message.

LT. RHODES: Okay. 3-9-2-7-3-3-2. That pages me. Will he be there later this morning?

SECRETARY: Yes. He's here every day, all day.

LT. RHODES: But not just right now. *[Pause.]* Okay. Please tell him I'll be calling on him later this morning.

SECRETARY: Yes, Lieutenant.

LT. RHODES: Good-bye.

SECRETARY: Have a nice day.

Transcriber: Why on earth am I transcribing this stuff? —J. Cipperman.END
OF THIS SECTION OF TAPE END OF THIS SECTION OF TAPE END

Metropolitan Buffalo Police Department

Tape Transcription   Homicide Unit

Body: *Hassler, P.*   Tape No. *840308.006*
Place: *Rhodes Hall, Seminar Room A*   Time: *9:10 a.m.*
Persons present: *Three members of the Homicide Unit; one*
        stenographer; all members of seminar; see below

                                        Transcribed by: *B. J. Saik*

MBPD: Det. Lt. Rhodes; Det. Sgt. Yorrick; Det. Maistry; B. J. Saik
Civilians: Christian Aval; Max Ebenfeld; Anne Glendish; Professor Norman
    Holland; Barry Ireland; Amy Lemaire; Paul Penza; Professor Wallace Sisley

LT. RHODES: Thank you for coming here this morning. You've all gotten used to
    our taping, I hope. I've also asked one of our indefatigable and immensely
    capable transcribers to be here this morning. Ms. Saik will keep track of who
    goes where and who says what. You've met Sgt. Yorrick before. Finally, this
    is Detective Margo Maistry. She knows computers and the university.

    We've already had a development in this case this morning. The inter-
    loper put a set of squibs in your mailboxes last night. Detective Rollins is
    looking for fingerprints on them right now.

    Now, Professor, I see you've taken your customary seat by the win-
    dows at the head of the table. But on Wednesday morning, Ms. Hassler had
    taken your regular seat, and that's what I'm interested in, Wednesday morn-
    ing. What I'd like to do today is reconstruct the order in which people
    came into the seminar room yesterday morning. Would you all be so good
    as to step out into the hall with Detective Maistry? I'll stand here by the
    doorway. *[The six students, two professors, and Det. Maistry went out in
    the corridor—BJS.]*

LT. RHODES: Okay? Now, who was the first to come in? *[Pause.]*

PENZA: It was Trish herself, because when Anne and I came in, her books were
    at her place already.

GLENDISH: But we didn't know they were hers. She'd put her books down at
    Norm's place, and we automatically assumed they were Norm's, didn't
    we, Paul?

PENZA: Yes, I remember being surprised when Norm came in later and sat down
    near the door. Then I realized whose books they were.

LT. RHODES: Margo, put Hassler's books on that end of the table. Okay. Would you be so good, Ms. Glendish, Mr. Penza, to sit in the seats you sat in yesterday morning? Fine. That fits the seating diagram you drew yesterday, Professor Sisley. I appreciate your helping out with that definite information. Now, who was next?

EBENFELD: I was, but when I came in, neither Anne nor Paul was here. All I saw was three stacks of books reserving places.

GLENDISH: That's right, Lieutenant. Paul and I liked seeing the sun for a change. We got up early and went to class—oh, it must have been a good half hour ahead. We decided to go back outside and take advantage of the crisp, sunshiny weather. We sat on the steps of Rhodes Hall.

LT. RHODES: Did you see anything of Patricia Hassler?

PENZA: Nary a trace, did we, Anne?

GLENDISH: She must have stayed in the building somewhere.

LT. RHODES: All right, would you get up and pretend the corridor is outside in the sun?

PENZA: This is more like musical chairs than sunbathing, Lieutenant.

LT. RHODES: Mr. Ebenfeld, you came in and sat down in the seat next to Anne Glendish's. Did you realize the books and papers at the window end of the table weren't Holland's but Hassler's?

EBENFELD: I didn't think much about who was sitting where. I was in my regular seat.

LT. RHODES: Sit down, then. Who came in next?

IRELAND: Guess it was me, Lieutenant.

EBENFELD: That's right. Barry.

LT. RHODES: And you sat across from Mr. Ebenfeld.

IRELAND: Not quite. Across and one to the right—I'd have been sitting on Hassler's left if she'd sat in her usual seat. I could stand her.

LT. RHODES: And you also didn't notice that the stack of books at the head of the table wasn't Professor Holland's?

IRELAND: I didn't pay much attention to it. I was kidding around with Max.

LT. RHODES: Take your seat then, Mr. Ireland. Next?

IRELAND: Wally came in next.

LT. RHODES: All right, take your seat, Professor Sisley.

SISLEY: Okay.

EBENFELD: No, wait a minute. Norm came in next. That was when I first realized that his regular seat had been preempted.

IRELAND: Same here, but the order was first me, then Wally, then Norm. I remember because he sat next to me.

LT. RHODES: Professor Sisley, which was it?

SISLEY: I-I'm not sure. I don't remember.

HOLLAND: I do. Wally walked in just in front of me. Maybe Barry and Max're
remembering how we sat down. I didn't sit. I put my books down and
strolled over to the window, as I usually do. That's probably the source of
the confusion.

LT. RHODES: Professor Sisley?

SISLEY: Yes, that's right.

LT. RHODES: What's right?

SISLEY: What Norm says.

LT. RHODES: Well, let's leave it that there were now four people in the room, all
well away from Patricia Hassler's place at the table. All four had *by now*
realized that Professor Holland's usual place had been taken by Hassler. *[A
chorus of assents.]*

LT. RHODES: Next.

LEMAIRE: Well, now that just about everybody else is in place, it's my turn. I
took the place next to Hassler. I always prefer a corner spot, because I can
see everyone at once. I'm not sure I'd have sat there, though, if I'd known
I was going to be right next to Trish on the day she was "it."

LT. RHODES: You didn't realize the books at the head of the table weren't Professor Holland's?

LEMAIRE: He was standing, looking out the window, as he always does before
class. Gathering his thoughts, I suppose.

LT. RHODES: Take your seat, Ms. Lemaire. Now who?

PENZA: Anne and I made our entrance.

GLENDISH: I remember you all stopped talking and looked up at us.

LT. RHODES: All right. That brings us to just about 9:00.

HOLLAND: Right.

LT. RHODES: And we're still missing Aval and Hassler.

PENZA: After we came in, I remember that Norm sat down at the wrong end of
the table and started chatting with the group.

IRELAND: That's right, Lieutenant.

LT. RHODES: You remember it that way, Professor Sisley?

SISLEY: Yes.

HOLLAND: That must be right, because I was sitting down when Patricia came in.
My back was to her, but I felt the cold air from her as she stood in the
doorway behind me, and I turned around.

LT. RHODES: You've all told me that she came and stood in the door, and you've
commented on the odd look she had on her face.

PENZA: As though she were about to perform.

IRELAND: Or as if she was ready to kill us all.

LT. RHODES: Well. Professor Holland, can I ask you to take Hassler's part? Would
you stand in the doorway as she did?

HOLLAND: All right.

LT. RHODES: How long did she stand there? Let's try an experiment. When I say "Now," Norman, you come to the door. The rest of you, imagine that Hassler has just begun to stand there. When you think the same amount of time has elapsed as Wednesday morning, call out 'Now.' Okay, let's start. Norman, come to the doorway. Now. *[Pause. Then a ragged chorus of "Now's." Checking the tape, I get an average of ten seconds—BJS.]*

LT. RHODES: About eleven seconds, by my count. *[Pause.]* Now, we still have M. Aval to get into the scene. Are you still out in the hall?

DET. MAISTRY: He's right here, Lieutenant.

LT. RHODES: Would you come in now, M. Aval, just as you did yesterday?

AVAL: Yes, Lieutenant.

HOLLAND: That's right. He slid in past Patricia, almost touching her.

LT. RHODES: Just as you did now, with your hands up like that? Shoulder high? With the palms facing her?

AVAL: Yes, I remember thinking as I went past her that I very much did not want to touch her. I wanted to hold my hands in such a way as to say, No, I do not wish you any harm. It is hands off. Or perhaps hands up.

PENZA: An eloquent pair of hands.

AVAL: In the logic of representation, Paul, gesture is necessarily presemantic. I simply did not want to evoke her anger.

LT. RHODES: Did you take off your coat?

AVAL: My anorak. Yes. I put it on one of the two chairs where people had placed coats. Then I sat down.

LT. RHODES: Sit down as you did yesterday, M. Aval. Right. Now, Professor Holland, would you be so kind as to act out what Patricia Hassler did yesterday?

HOLLAND: She walked down the left side of the table like this. She stood behind Christian and faced the group—

LT. RHODES: How far behind Aval?

AVAL: I didn't see. I had not reversed myself to look. She was behind me.

LEMAIRE: I was facing her. She stood about two feet behind him—

HOLLAND: Three feet, surely, Amy.

LT. RHODES: Show me with your hands . . .

EBENFELD: This far. *[Several people put their hands between two and three feet apart—BJS.]*

LT. RHODES: Did she touch him?

EBENFELD: No.

HOLLAND: No, she was too far back.

LT. RHODES: And he couldn't have touched her?

LEMAIRE: No, not possibly.

LT. RHODES: And she spoke—

GLENDISH: She said, "Him. He's the one I was talking about."

AVAL: I beg your pardon. She said, "Him. He's the one." No "talking about." I should know.

PENZA: Sorry, Christian, old guy. I distinctly heard what Anne did. "You're the one I'm talking about."

EBENFELD: She said, "He's the one. He's the one." But she pointed at him.

LT. RHODES: I think we'll never get any agreement on the wording of what she said. Eyewitnesses!

PENZA: Earwitnesses, I should think, Lieutenant.

LT. RHODES: But they didn't touch.

LEMAIRE: No.

AVAL: No, certainly not, Lieutenant. Why should I? This is more of the police foolishness. I could not reach back to her. She did not reach forward to me.

LT. RHODES: But she said something like, "He's the one." And you disagree about her saying, "The one I told you about."

MANY VOICES: Yes.

LT. RHODES: Would you continue your journey, Professor Holland?

HOLLAND: All right. She walked to the end of the table, took off her coat, tossed it onto the heap of coats on the chair over there, and sat down. Like this.

LT. RHODES: What we've ascertained, then, is that no one touched her from the time she appeared in the door to the time she sat down.

Her death scene—you've all described.

Now, the medical examiner's report established that she was killed by a special, fast-acting poison that acts in less than a minute, perhaps within seconds of what the M.E. calls "envenomation." We believe she was given the poison by some sort of scratch on her body. *[A chorus of "scratch," "come on," "CIA," etc.]*

We've now established that no one touched her from the time she appeared in the door of this room to the time she sat down. Now it's just possible that someone could have scratched her out in the hall. Then she'd have come in the room carrying this lethal dose in her veins.

That's possible, but pretty unlikely. Hoping you'll pass them in the hall is a pretty catch-as-catch-can way to murder somebody. How do you know you're going to have the opportunity? We might have seen the person in the doorway. Furthermore, the poison acts *very* fast.

It's far more probable that she was scratched in this room. Something on the chair perhaps. Professor Holland, please stand up. Sergeant Yorrick, would you check that Windsor chair, so incongruous with this sleek modern teak table? That's right, put on those fireman's gloves. Move your hands very slowly and carefully over the surfaces of the chair. We're looking for any kind of pin or nail or even a splinter. Be very cautious. Don't under any circumstances let it break your skin. *[Pause.]*

Imagine, Sergeant, that you're a blind man passing his hands over a sculpture. Just let your hands go slowly and lightly over the surface. That's right. Run your fingertips over the arms and up and down the legs and the crossbars. Use the palm of your hand to go over the curved arch of the back. *[Pause.]*

That's right. Now curve your hands around the spokes in the back. *[A long, long silence.]*

Nothing?

SGT. YORRICK: Nothing, Lieutenant.

LT. RHODES: You'd better untie the ties and look under the mat, Sergeant. Yes, lift up the rubber mat. *[A sudden burst of ohs.]*

HOLLAND: My God, that was meant for me! You're trying to kill me. It was in my chair. It was where I always sit. It's ME they were trying to kill!

LT. RHODES: I.

HOLLAND: What?

LT. RHODES: It's *I* they were trying to kill. We are, after all, in an English department.

HOLLAND: Damn it, Rhodes, don't joke at a moment like this. You set this up! I could have been killed! You set this up, knowing that whoever and whatever killed Trish was still in the room.

LT. RHODES: Easy, Norman, easy now. That's where we found the tack, but that's not the tack we found. The lethal thumbtack we took to the lab for analysis, and we found the poison on it and traces of Hassler's blood. Yes, on Wednesday morning, there was a tack on that chair, under the rubber cushion. When Trish Hassler sat down the tack penetrated her skin, and she received the poison.

HOLLAND: But that business of Yorrick and the gloves! You made me think I was nearly killed! What the hell did you do that for?

LT. RHODES: To see reactions.

IRELAND: And were they satisfactory, Lieutenant? Did we pass your test?

LT. RHODES: Possibly.

PENZA: Jesus, what a stunt!

HOLLAND: That tack was meant for me. I know it. If I'd sat in my regular seat yesterday morning, I'd have been dead today.

LT. RHODES: That's a possibility. For various reasons, though, I think it unlikely.

HOLLAND: But I *always* sit there.

LT. RHODES: You didn't yesterday. The murderer couldn't take the chance of getting the wrong person. Of that I'm sure.

HOLLAND: Then why did you have us go through this charade? Why did you have me sit in the very chair she died in? With the tack right there? Damn you, Justin, you were playing a game with us here. You were playacting, you and Yorrick. And the students . . . ! Look at us, looking at each other, each looking more guilty than the next, each thinking, as I was, "They think I'm guilty." And, of course, *you do*. You're busy suspecting everybody, including me. And we all respond with that feeling that we've done something wrong, that inner sense of deficiency, that it's so easy for a policeman to tap into.

LT. RHODES: I'm trying to solve a murder, Norman. You must allow me my methods, as a famous predecessor of mine said.

HOLLAND: What methods? What did all that accomplish? What did you find out?

[A knock at the door.]

LT. RHODES: Sergeant, see who that is.

SGT. YORRICK: Rollins, Lieutenant.

LT. RHODES: Yes, Hy, what is it?

DET. ROLLINS: Lieutenant, I've lifted three good sets of prints from the surfaces of these new papers we got this morning. They include both thumbs and index fingers, although rather more to the side of the finger than I'd like. The next step is for Fred and me to compare them with the prints from these students and their professors. That'll take some time, as you know. But I thought Professor Holland might need this paper for his seminar, so I brought photocopies. I made as many as the originals you gave me plus one for yourself and one for Sgt. Yorrick. I didn't know you were here, Margo, B.J.

DET. MAISTRY: That's all right. Happens all the time.

GLENDISH: Right, Maistry. You get to expect that kind of thing in a sexist society.

LT. RHODES: Excellent, Hy. Let's pass those around and have a look at them. B. J., will you include this in your transcript? Thank you.

Memo

```
Date:     March 8, 1984
To:       The ninnies of Norm's nerdy seminar
From:     Yr friendly nose-picker
Subject:  Latest asininity
```

What in hell is the matter with you lead-headed people? Are you so bamboozled and befuddled with all this theoretical claptrap of Holland's that you don't believe her? Or what? She told you. She TOLD you who did it, but you

go on as if nothing had happened. Even the police do.
That's what comes of having a scatterbrained playwright-
detective. Do I have to come out of my anonymity and tell
you again what she <u>already</u> told you? If you haven't acted
by Friday morning's meeting, I will. I will. Can you face
me? Can you face her, poor Trish?

LT. RHODES: Now what? You're all specialists in interpreting. What can you tell
me about this latest squib?

GLENDISH: Our friend is calling attention to himself. Pay attention to me, he
says, as he always says.

PENZA: You've got it, Anne. He puts himself right in the center of things, even
though he's really outside of it all. We have a murder and a victim and a
detective, but *he's* the one we're supposed to pay attention to. He's always
trying to grab off the spotlight. Pushy, I call it.

EBENFELD: What I see is the way he singles out Lt. Rhodes—the "playwright-
detective" as he calls him. He's attacking authority.

IRELAND: He's sure as hell angry about something.

EBENFELD: I'm going to guess he singles out the "playwright-detective" because
both a playwright and a detective act in the open, just the opposite of this
character.

SISLEY: You could take the contrary position equally well, Max. A playwright is
always behind the scenes. It's the actor who's front and center downstage.
Our mystery student singles out Lt. Rhodes because he's hidden. He ma-
nipulates the action from above or behind what we see. Just as he put on a
little play this morning. The mystery student would like to do that himself,
I think.

HOLLAND: I like that, Wally. Clever. Amy?

LEMAIRE: I'm sorry, Norman. I can't relate to this. I'm still getting over the
business with the thumbtack. If that had gotten you, Norman . . .

HOLLAND: But Amy, there was no poison on this tack.

LEMAIRE: I'm still shaking, thinking what could have happened to you.

HOLLAND: I appreciate your caring, Amy. Chris? Anything from you? You look
troubled.

AVAL: I'm sorry—my mind wandered. I am afraid I do not understand this note.
It seems to say and yet not to say at the same time. As is perhaps inevitable
for discourse of this kind, language coming from an author whom we do
not know to exist or not.

HOLLAND: Oh, he exists all right. I see in this squib once more his fascination
with his own position in hiding. "My anonymity."

GLENDISH: Which is anything but.

HOLLAND: And if he comes out of hiding, he can change everything.

GLENDISH: Hey, maybe we'll finally get a look at this creep.

LT. RHODES: That's what I wanted to ask you. You're all telling me about the style of our interloper, his personal style, but what about the content here? He's saying that Patricia Hassler already told us something. What's he referring to?

IRELAND: Beats me.

PENZA: C'mon! She pointed the finger at Chris, sure enough. She put you right on the spot, old buddy. That must be what this guy is referring to.

LT. RHODES: I have some problems with that. For one thing, the interloper wasn't present here yesterday morning. He didn't see her point the finger, as you so accurately put it, Mr. Penza. How could he be referring to that incident?

SISLEY: Somebody must have told him.

LT. RHODES: But as far as I know, none of you knows who he is.

HOLLAND: Maybe somebody mentioned the incident casually, in conversation, and he overheard and learned of Trish's gesture that way. There's been a lot of gossiping about Hassler's death, as you'd expect.

LT. RHODES: I asked you not to.

HOLLAND: We're only human.

LT. RHODES: All right, casual, unintentional storytelling. That's a possibility.

But here's another difficulty. Hassler said to all of you, pointing to M. Aval, "He's the one," or words to that effect. The interloper says, "She told you who did it." But what is "it"? How could it refer to the killing? Hassler had no way of knowing someone was about to kill her. Therefore, she couldn't have been accusing M. Aval of that crime. So what was she accusing him of? Or was she accusing him at all? What does her statement mean? Until we know that, we can't know what the interloper believes she told us.

AVAL: At last, Lieutenant, you are on the right track. Now you are being properly theoretical. The anaphora of "it" destabilizes the sentence. By referring to what Patricia said, "it" opens up a chiasmus of intertextualities, each of which contests the meaning of the others, subverting any possibility that just one person is being referred to.

LT. RHODES: Do I understand you correctly? Are you seriously saying, M. Aval, that Hassler's sentence, "He's the one," does not refer to one person?

AVAL: Because, at the onomastic level, no one person is named. Therefore it could be any person. Therefore the phrase "the one" actually means the many.

IRELAND: That's downright ingenious, Chris, old guy, and completely unconvincing, not to say half-assed.

AVAL: Then show me the flaw in my logic, Barry, old guy.

LT. RHODES: Another time, gentlemen. At the moment, I'm trying to find out what the interloper may have meant by "She told you." Do you think it refers to her action in pointing to Christian Aval? If so, then the "it" in her sentence must refer to something other than her murder, because that hadn't happened yet—

AVAL: Therefore it could not yet become part of the discourse—

LT. RHODES: Peace, M. Aval, peace. If the phrase "She told you" refers to something else, what is that something else? [A long pause.]

HOLLAND: We simply don't know what Patricia's pointing at Chris meant, although it was very explicit. Therefore we don't know what "She told you" means or even if it refers to the pointing. It could refer to something else entirely, some other statement of Trish's.

LT. RHODES: And none of you has any idea what that other statement might be. [A mumble of noes.]

LT. RHODES: I'm tempted to conclude that the intruder got some information from Hassler. He mistakenly assumes the rest of you have it, too. Is that possible?

HOLLAND: I suppose it is.

LT. RHODES: But none of you has any idea what that might be.

PENZA: And anyway, I still think he's referring to Patricia's pointing.

LT. RHODES: We have a new uncertainty in the case.

HOLLAND: Does that mean that this stage business this morning, this frightening demonstration, served no purpose? That you're no wiser now than you were at nine o'clock?

LT. RHODES: On the contrary. I learned several important things. In the fullness of time, Norman, all will be vouchsafed unto you. For the time being, however, you must leave the professional detectives to draw our conclusions from the events of the morning. I regret any inconvenience or anxiety I may have caused. It's all in order to bring the killer to justice, so that we all—you all—can sleep easier again.

   If you haven't done so, please at once have your fingerprints taken by Detectives Bowers and Rollins. Yorrick, see that that happens right now, this morning. As you've seen this morning, it's important that you not discuss the case with anyone. Avoid gossip, questions, and the temptation to show off by saying, I was there, I saw what happened.

   You may all go except Professor Holland. Norman, may I speak to you for a moment?

HOLLAND: Sure. [Pause. Students and detectives filed out.—BJS]

LT. RHODES: Please believe me, Norman. I don't think the tack was meant for you.

HOLLAND: But it's a schoolchild's trick. Put a tack on the teacher's chair. It was meant for the *teacher,* for *me!*

LT. RHODES: I think not.

HOLLAND: Why not?

LT. RHODES: You don't go to a lot of trouble to get a fancy poison and then risk wasting it on the wrong person.

HOLLAND: Maybe the poisoner was crazy.

LT. RHODES: Please believe me. At this moment, I've a very good idea who killed Patricia Hassler—

HOLLAND: You do?

LT. RHODES: —and the person wasn't trying to kill you.

HOLLAND: If you know who did it, why don't you arrest them?

LT. RHODES: Because there are too many loose ends. I need to show that this person in fact obtained this poison. I need to show a motive. And I need to show what the plan was and how it was executed.

HOLLAND: Well, I hope what you put me through this morning was worth it.

LT. RHODES: It was. Very much so.

HOLLAND: Do you want me to go on analyzing squibs for you?

LT. RHODES: They could really help with the loose ends. You may be able to turn up a motive for me. We left it that you'd do Sisley and then the students in alphabetical order.

HOLLAND: Yes. I finished writing about Sisley and Ebenfeld last night. I put what I wrote in the mailbox Romola provided you.

LT. RHODES: I'd forgotten about that. I have a mailbox. Joy.

HOLLAND: I'll start on Glendish right away.

LT. RHODES: I'll pick up your Sisley and Ebenfeld write-ups as soon as I can. But first, I have to meet with Yorrick and Maistry to go over the morning's events.

HOLLAND: Okay. END OF THIS SECTION OF TAPE END OF THIS SECTION OF TAPE END OF THIS SECTION OF TAPE END OF THIS SECTION

LT. RHODES: Come back in, will you, Maistry, Yorrick, B.J.? Nice acting, Yorrick.

B.J. SAIK: They all seemed really, really surprised to me. I was watching them as Yorrick pulled up the rubber mat. They were all absolutely, totally looking at what he was doing. Yes, very good acting, Mort.

DET. MAISTRY: Their faces when the shiny head of the tack showed! They were surprised, all right, all right, and especially the professor. Especially him.

LT. RHODES: He seemed completely unnerved, enough so that I'd be willing to rule him out as a suspect at this point, except that we're working on our impressions of their emotional states—never conclusive.

SGT. YORRICK: You mean, he could have been acting.

LT. RHODES: Any one of them could. And don't forget, Sisley and Glendish are both actors.

Besides, we have something more conclusive. Hassler was poisoned by the thumbtack. Who had an opportunity to plant the tack? It had to be done *after* her coat and books were in place, otherwise the killer wouldn't know where she was going to sit. And it had to be done when only the killer—or killers—were in the room.

DET. MAISTRY: That was what I thought, too, but then this occurred to me. Couldn't somebody sitting next to Hassler's chair have worked the tack under the rubber mat? They could use the corner of the table to hide what they were doing.

LT. RHODES: A good point, Margo, excellent.

SGT. YORRICK: According to Sisley's diagram, the two who were sitting next to Hassler were Paul Penza and Amy Lemaire.

LT. RHODES: Lemaire, however, didn't get there until quite late. She'd have had no way of knowing there'd be a vacant place next to Hassler.

DET. MAISTRY: But Penza, on the other hand, got there very early this morning. Half an hour early. Students, in my experience, don't get up any earlier than they have to.

LT. RHODES: Hold on, people. Let's take this step by step. Go down the timetable. No one could have planted the thumbtack before Hassler got there, particularly since she was sitting in the seat that was usually Holland's.

SGT. YORRICK: Unless the target was really Holland, as he feared, and Hassler was killed by miscalculation.

LT. RHODES: Remote. Somebody'd make sure this fancy poison got to the right person.

Okay. Hassler arrives and puts her books in place.

DET. MAISTRY: Then Hassler leaves, and she takes her coat. Presumably she went outside the building.

SGT. YORRICK: The coat could have been a blind.

LT. RHODES: Don't forget that Ireland saw her on the corner of Main and Masling Boulevard around 8:45. And Holland has told us, twice now, that he felt cold air coming off her when she appeared in the doorway. Hassler went outside the building all right, but what did she do? Ireland said she was just standing there. Why did she go out and stand around in the cold?

SGT. YORRICK: And for how long was she outside the classroom?

LT. RHODES: If we can believe Penza and Glendish, they were sitting on the front steps of Rhodes Hall and didn't see her. Evidently, they didn't see her because she'd left the building before they sat down. So she had from whenever she put her books down until she reentered the seminar room.

DET. MAISTRY: Unless she snuck in the back door, like.

LT. RHODES: Possible. But why? Besides, to walk from Rhodes Hall to Main Street and stand around—doesn't that use up a good part of her time?

How long does it take to walk from Rhodes Hall to Main Street? Yorrick, check that out, will you?

SGT. YORRICK: Then Penza and Glendish come in, and that gives Glendish and Penza the opportunity of planting the tack. It could have been just one of them. One of them might have used some ruse to get the other out of the room.

DET. MAISTRY: Or they could have acted in concert.

LT. RHODES: Then Penza and Glendish went out, they say, and Ebenfeld came in. He says he found the room empty, so they did go out. He saw three stacks of books marking three places. So Ebenfeld had a chance to plant the tack, too.

DET. MAISTRY: And then Ireland comes in, and Sisley and Holland.

LT. RHODES: Sisley puzzled me today. Yesterday he seemed so decisive about what was said and who came in when. Today he seemed not to remember things.

SGT. YORRICK: Even so, once you've got four people in the room, and none of them sitting next to Hassler's seat, none of them has opportunity. So Sisley and Holland are out of it. No— Wait a minute. Holland could have done it. He was wandering around up at that end of the room, after all.

LT. RHODES: Not close enough to Hassler's chair.

DET. MAISTRY: Penza and Glendish came in again, after the two profs. Then Amy Lemaire. She sits next to Hassler and conceivably she could have put the tack on the chair.

LT. RHODES: Conceivably. You don't like her, do you?

DET. MAISTRY: Too nicey-nicey for me.

LT. RHODES: Then finally we get Aval. He appears *after* Hassler is standing in the door, and his seat is one removed from hers, so he has no opportunity.

SGT. YORRICK: He brushed by her in the doorway. Maybe he used some gimmick on his jacket to scratch her. Maybe the tack is a blind.

DET. MAISTRY: Maybe, schmaybe.

LT. RHODES: I think we have to say Aval didn't have opportunity. Who does that leave us with?

SGT. YORRICK: Penza, Glendish, and Ebenfeld, with Lemaire a remote possibility. Interesting that those are the three in the romantic triangle we heard about yesterday. Could they all have connived at revenge?

LT. RHODES: The motive doesn't feel strong enough for me, not to get three of them to agree on murder.

SGT. YORRICK: Maybe just one or two of them then.

LT. RHODES: Very maybe.

There's another problem. There was a time after Hassler had put down her things to mark her seat and before Penza and Glendish entered the room, when someone who came into the room could know where Hassler was going to sit and would be alone to put the tack on the chair. In other words, there was a period, how long or short we don't know, when anybody, repeat, anybody, could have planted the tack.

SGT. YORRICK: Ow!

LT. RHODES: Imagine it this way. The killer is trailing Hassler to the seminar, sees her go in, reserve her seat, and leave. The killer puts the tack on that seat and goes somewhere to mark time until the seminar begins.

DET. MAISTRY: This careful a killer would have to have some reason to expect Hassler to leave after she put her things down.

LT. RHODES: I can visualize the killer carrying this tack around, in a pillbox, say, waiting for a chance to play the old schoolkid's trick on Hassler in some public place. He or she keeps trailing Hassler, looking for an opportunity, and it came Wednesday morning. If it hadn't come then, it would've come later.

I think we have to admit that this morning's exercise has more or less ruled out our most obvious suspect, Aval. It leaves us with three much less likely ones. Except, and it's a big "except," for that brief, somewhat unpredictable period, when she left her seat marked but unguarded, when any one of them could have planted the tack.

SGT. YORRICK: Still, we've changed the probabilities. If it was Aval, he could only have done it during that special period, whereas Glendish, Penza, and Ebenfeld had more of a chance.

LT. RHODES: True, but I think what we really need to do now is track that saxitoxin. I'll start with Professor Vernor—if I can ever get hold of him. I can read Holland's latest write-up on the way.END OF THIS SECTION OF TAPE END OF THIS SECTION OF TAPE END OF THIS SECTION OF

State University of New York at Buffalo
Department of English

Date: Thursday, March 8, 1984
To: All Graduate Students
From: DREGS

This is a

WARNING!!!

from your unofficial, anti-official union, the Disreputable Rabble of English Grad Students. If you did not read it in Ma Badger's memo, you read it in this morning's *News-Gazette*. The police have issued orders to fingerprint all the graduate students. Not the profs snug in their bourgeois comforts. Oh no. Not the undergraduates who can scarcely wait to start developing real estate or selling gas-guzzlers. Just the graduate students. They know how we keep asking tough questions of our craven administrators. They know we are already marginalized and oppressed by our corrupted legislature. They know we make trouble, they want to keep track of us, and they are using the death of Patricia Hassler to set us up.

As your unprofessional professional association, we are warning you. If you give Rhodes your fingerprints, our beloved MBPD will send them to Albany, to cops in every state in the country, to the FBI, the CIA, the NSC, to Interpol. Every pot-bellied deputy in Appalachia is going to have a crack at you. Every dweeb in the FBI will be able to haul you in for any crime from armed robbery to spitting on the sidewalk. Even the spooks in the CIA and the NSC can have at you for espionage. They just say they found your fingerprints at the scene, and you get to try to defend yourself. This is how the establishment puts down the troublemakers.

The order has come down from Lieutenant Norman ("Justin") Rhodes, whom Ma Badger tells us is Rhodes of Rhodes Hall. We say he's Rhodes of Rhodes National Bank, Rhodes of Rhodes Investment Trust, Rhodes of Rhodes Real Estate, Rhodes of Rhodes Avenue, above all, Rhodes of your friendly landlord, otherwise known as Rhodes Property Management. That's who Rhodes represents. Rhodes of the Establishment, Rhodes of the Knowledge/Power Structure. That's who wants your fingerprints.

Don't be suckered into it! The police have no right to force you to give your fingerprints, unless they arrest you or unless they can show you have some connection with the crime—if there was any crime at all. After all, we only have their word for it that Trish Hassler was poisoned. She could have had a stroke, she could have killed herself, she could have just plain died. *Don't* do it! *Don't* give your fingerprints to the police. *Don't submit!*

REJECT!   **REJECT!**   **REJECT!**

RESIST!   **RESIST!**   **RESIST!**

REFUSE!   **REFUSE!**   **REFUSE!**

Metropolitan Buffalo Police Department

Tape Transcription   Homicide Unit

Body: *Hassler, P.*   Tape No. *840308.008*
Place: *Schafer Medical Lab, UB West*   Time: *10:34 a.m.*
Persons present: *Det. Lt. Rhodes, Professor Harold Vernor*

                                          Transcribed by: *S. Moreno*

LT. RHODES: I'm waiting in Professor "Pop" Vernor's office, indeed I've been waiting for twenty minutes now. Basically, I've got two questions. How do you get hold of saxitoxin? What can he tell us about this vial we picked up in Aval's apartment?

Vernor has me seated in front of his desk, and from time to time, he rushes in here to get some papers, he nods at me, and then he rushes off again to his lab across the hall. A tall, bony man with a little halo of disorderly white hair around his bald head, a white lab coat billowing out behind him as he scurries here and there supervising his crew of Asian graduate students. I can see half a dozen at least, seated at a long lab bench, looking into retorts and flasks and test tubes, Bunsen burners hissing out their blue heat, white mice disconsolate in their cages. Looks like something Dr. No would have set up in the old James Bond movie. I see him scurrying back and forth from his desk in here.

LT. RHODES: Professor! Excuse me, Professor, can I flag you down? I think this will only take a minute or two, and I'm in the middle of an investigation.

VERNOR: Yes, yes, Lieutenant. Just one minute. We've got an unexpected reaction across the hall. Just one minute—

LT. RHODES: Dammit. There he goes again. Maybe I should just bury myself in the latest issue of *Toxicon*— *[Pause.]*

Professor! Please! This is police business.

VERNOR: Oh, yes, Lieutenant Rhodes, isn't it? Yes, I knew your father. Very generous man. Harmon Rhodes. I used to see him at the annual dinners of the Roswell Park board. Very generous. Interested in cancer, he was. Gave a lot of money to Roswell. I tried to interest him in our work here, the possibility of using the alkaloid toxins selectively to destroy the cancer cells. The puffer fish's tetrodotoxin kills the Japanese gourmet that eats it, but it doesn't hurt the puffer fish. Why is the animal immune to its own poison? Why can't the human be immune to what would kill his cancer? But I couldn't get him to support it. Said he'd best leave it to the experts. Let them decide. Probably right about that, although it was no help to us. Or was that your uncle? Harmon Rhodes.

LT. RHODES: My uncle, Professor Vernor. Uh, I'm tape-recording this interview— This is a new procedure at the Police Department—

VERNOR: Oh yes, Lieutenant, I read all about that. If you can just hang on for a minute—

LT. RHODES: Please, please, dammit, please. I just have a couple of questions, sir, if we could—

VERNOR: Your uncle, was it? Yes, a great benefactor of Roswell Park's research, Harmon Rhodes. Not much help to us. He used to mention you, you know. Troubled that you were a playwright. Oh, yes, Lieutenant, I've read about you in the paper. Did he ever get used to the idea?

LT. RHODES: Not really, Professor—

VERNOR: And then your being a policeman. That didn't go down very well either. The Rhodeses were always business leaders here in Buffalo. Business. I don't think playwriting or policing exactly pleased old Harmon. It was like a piece of the family turning against the family, he said. Or am I remembering that right? Did you ever get that straightened out with your family?

LT. RHODES: No. Professor, how would somebody get hold of saxitoxin?

VERNOR: Saxitoxin! Terrible stuff! Why would anybody want to get hold of saxitoxin? Except the CIA. We have some, of course, but just a sample. My real work is on tetrodotoxin, which is altogether—

LT. RHODES: You have some?!

VERNOR: Oh, yes. It's a bit like tetrodotoxin, and we keep a small vial of the stuff in case we need it. Just one vial.

LT. RHODES: So someone could have gotten saxitoxin from your lab?

VERNOR: Dammit, Lieutenant, what kind of a fool do you take me for? Of course they couldn't get it from this lab. We keep all our dangerous chemicals in a drug safe, under lock and key, and only I have a key.

LT. RHODES: So you're the only one who has access to it.

VERNOR: And the department secretary. So that people can get these chemicals if I'm not around.

LT. RHODES: Swell.

VERNOR: I keep the key in my desk.

LT. RHODES: Could any of the your research assistants have gotten the key?

VERNOR: Well, they'd have to ask me or my secretary. Unless they stole it from my desk. But these oriental fellas wouldn't do that. Too scared of being sent back to do anything out of line. But that Vietnamese girl is a citizen . . .

LT. RHODES: Let me take you back to the start, Professor. I'm investigating the murder of Patricia Hassler, who was a graduate student in the English Department—

VERNOR: Yes, yes, Lieutenant, I know. I read the newspapers, you know, and your medical examiner fella, Dr. Whatsisname—

LT. RHODES: Dr. Welder—

VERNOR: —yes, that's right, Welder, was here all yesterday afternoon identifying the poison. We finally showed it was saxitoxin. Mouse blastoma test—it's a real humdinger. Fella had never heard of it. You know, these days, they don't give the medical students enough pharmacology, no, not nearly enough for what they need with all these drugs going around now. Now, twenty years ago, the medical school had a pharmacology requirement—

LT. RHODES: Professor Vernor, could we get back to the murder? I want to find out how someone, a layperson, not a professional toxicologist like yourself, would get hold of saxitoxin.

VERNOR: The CIA, they're the only people who use it, as far as I know. And, of course, the people out on the West Coast who study it for the fisheries. Rabkin, Loewenberg, Hutter—a bunch of them out there.

LT. RHODES: But here in Buffalo?

VERNOR: Nobody. We've got some, as I say, but we keep it under lock and key.

LT. RHODES: Except that your secretary or any one of your research assistants could get the key.

VERNOR: Oh no, Lieutenant, that'd be very dangerous. We keep it in a drug safe, but we keep it separate from the other drugs in a locked box within the safe, and only I have the key to the locked box. I keep it at home, in my bureau drawer. Oh, no, Lieutenant, we wouldn't leave that around loose. That'd be very dangerous. It only takes a few micrograms, you know—

LT. RHODES: I know, Professor. That's what you and Dr. Welder worked out yesterday.

VERNOR: So you know how dangerous it is.

LT. RHODES: Well, is there any way somebody like an English professor or an English graduate student could obtain saxitoxin?

VERNOR: An English professor! What would an English professor do with saxitoxin?

LT. RHODES: Commit murder.

VERNOR: Oho, I see what you're driving at, Lieutenant. You think someone in the English Department killed this woman, whatshername, and they did it with saxitoxin.

LT. RHODES: That's what you and Dr. Welder showed yesterday.

VERNOR: And someone from the English Department did it. That's odd. They always seemed to me a perfectly decent group of fellas. But they have a woman chairman now, don't they?

LT. RHODES: Or a graduate student.

VERNOR: Oh, well, a graduate student. That's different. Could a graduate student in English get hold of some saxitoxin? To tell you the truth, Lieutenant, I don't see how. The CIA has its supplies, of course, but I don't see how an ordinary person could tap those. We got our sample from a surgical supply house, but the feds have these elaborate regulations you have to comply with to get it. You have to be an accredited lab. You have to explain what you want it for. They deliver it by hand, and you have to sign for it right there in front of them. No. I don't see how somebody in the English department could ever get some. Even the anthropologists—they had to borrow my sample for their exhibit.

LT. RHODES: Excuse me?

VERNOR: That fella in the Anthropology Department, the fluttery one, he was setting up an exhibit in the Natural History Museum. Natural poisons and how native tribes here and there use them. Something like that. "Primitive Pharmacopeia," he called it. Catchy title. Yes, he had to borrow my saxitoxin for his exhibit.

LT. RHODES: The Anthropology Department had an exhibit with your vial of saxitoxin in it?

VERNOR: Yes. Didn't I tell you that? Fluttery fella.

LT. RHODES: Could someone have stolen the saxitoxin from the exhibit?

VERNOR: Oh no, Lieutenant. He returned the vial to me, and I put it back in the safe. We haven't touched it since, until just yesterday, when we needed it for some tests. That's right. Your medical examiner and I needed a standardized sample to measure against what he brought to me on the thumbtack and in the bits of flesh.

LT. RHODES: But there was a vial of saxitoxin on exhibit in the Natural History Museum?

VERNOR: Oh yes, Lieutenant.

LT. RHODES: And who borrowed it?

VERNOR: Silly man, but I wanted to help him out. Hahn. Ike Hahn.

LT. RHODES: Professor Isaac Hahn in anthropology?

VERNOR: Yes, that's right. Anthropology, not English, of course. I'll bet they still have English-speaking graduate students in English. We haven't had a native American in this lab for, it must be three years now. All these oriental fellas. One Vietnamese girl. Nice people. Hardworking. But they don't speak English worth a damn. You get lonely. It'd be nice to have some native Americans. Maybe I should go into English— You know, I knew a fella who did that, went from chemistry to English. It was back in graduate school. Fella was studying chemistry, said he liked the sciences, search for truth, all that sort of thing. He went away one summer and when he came back it was all quantum theory, all new stuff. Where's the truth in that?, he said. What we studied last semester is all wrong now. So he went over to the English department and took up Anglo-Saxon. Hasn't anything changed in Anglo-Saxon in eight hundred years, he told me. That's truth, he said. To hell with this science stuff. Heard he did pretty well at it, too. Now if I could turn that around, if I could get some students from English down here—

LT. RHODES: Maybe you did, Professor Vernor, and you just didn't know it. Somebody got hold of some saxitoxin somehow. We picked up this vial in a student's apartment—

VERNOR: Look at that, will you! It looks just like our vial down here.

LT. RHODES: Does it? Study it carefully now.

VERNOR: Let me get our vial. I had it out just yesterday. It must be around here somewhere.

LT. RHODES: Around loose?

VERNOR: Oh no, we always keep that in the drug safe. I'll get it out. I'll be back in a minute. *[Silence. The tape is turned off, then on.]*

LT. RHODES: What a way to spend a morning! He got embroiled with one of his graduate students who's holding a sick-looking mouse. The man doesn't understand what Vernor is telling him. Oh hell, this could take forever. Just a minute, he says. It's been ten now. *[Pause.]*

LT. RHODES: Professor! Professor Vernor! Please, can we finish up this interview? I've got a murderer to catch.

VERNOR: Oh yes, Lieutenant. I almost forgot about you. Let's see. Saxitoxin. I've got the vial here in my pocket. Tricky stuff. You want to be careful how you handle it. Now let's see the one you're carrying. Why, it's empty!

LT. RHODES: Yes, Professor. Empty.

VERNOR: And you want me to tell you if it ever contained saxitoxin?

LT. RHODES: If you can. But first I'd like to know if this looks like your vial. Is this the kind of vial that saxitoxin comes in? The only kind?

VERNOR: Well, there's really only one place that handles it. I don't know where the CIA gets theirs. Probably have it on hand. Now if you put the two vials side by side— Yes, they're the same size. Same printed label. They both have a control number. See, on your vial, it says, "Control No. 2719." Then on ours, "Control No. 2718." Oh no. That can't be right. The system is that the control numbers have to be divisible by 9. This isn't correct, this control number. But otherwise the label looks just like the label on ours. And the stopper. Wait a minute. See, there's a tiny line down here that doesn't appear on your label. Let me get a magnifying glass. I had one here somewhere. Myrtle! Do we have a magnifying glass somewhere?

SECRETARY: Upper left-hand drawer.

VERNOR: Yes, that's right. Here it is. Oh, it's a line of type. Of course. "Government Printing Office Contract 831213LS/01."

LT. RHODES: And there's no government printing number on this label.

VERNOR: No. God knows what that means. You know the government, all these regulations. Well, of course, you do, working for the city. Government printing always has that contract number on it.

LT. RHODES: So, is this label really from a real saxitoxin supplier?

VERNOR: I think not, Lieutenant. All of the stuff ultimately comes from the government, the CIA.

LT. RHODES: I don't understand. You said the CIA had its own supplies.

VERNOR: Congress caught them with a whole lot of the stuff and made them sell it off. Well, with the CIA selling it, nobody bothers to manufacture it. They just use the CIA supply, which is sold, thanks to Reagan, by a private surgical supply house.

LT. RHODES: So there's only one kind of label, and this is a counterfeit of that label, not genuine.

VERNOR: And the control number is fake. Now that I look at it— See, hold the magnifying glass for yourself, Lieutenant. See the word "Saxitoxin"? See how irregular the edges of the *t* are? All the letters, their edges aren't smooth. This isn't regular printing. This is something somebody did on a laser printer with their computer. Oh yes. I recognize the look of the letters. That's the way we make a lot of the labels in this lab. Most labs do the same. Wonderful things, these laser printers.

LT. RHODES: What you're saying, then, is that this vial looks just like your vial, but the label on this vial is a counterfeit? It's not possible that the vial was stolen from some other toxicology lab that makes labels the way you do, on your laser printer?

VERNOR: Why relabel the vial? Why not just leave the label the government put on it? As we did. Why try to make a label just like the government's label if you already have the government's label? This vial was never a real vial of real saxitoxin. You're a detective, young fella, you ought to be able to figure that out. And the control number is wrong.

LT. RHODES: You're a bit more familiar with these procedures than I am, Professor Vernor. Yes, what you say makes sense.

VERNOR: Even if I talk a lot. Right, Lieutenant? You didn't think I had half a brain left, but I fooled you. That's why they call me "Pop," you know. Not because I'm senile, not because I'm past retirement age. Because once you get me open, I bubble for a long time. I talk a lot, but I generally end up by saying something worthwhile in all the rest of it. The flavor lasts.

I'll check that vial for you, Lieutenant, but, like yesterday, it takes about four hours to run the mouse blastoma test. I'll get one of my grad students to do it.

You remember, Lieutenant, they used to talk about the "yellow peril" to jack up the immigration barriers? No, you're too young. But we used to be real scared about Orientals coming into this country. Now they're the only ones who study the sciences. This department would close down if we didn't have these Chinese and Japanese and Vietnamese and Korean graduate students to teach the beginning courses and run the student labs. What do you think about that? Well, no matter. I'll be retiring soon.

That label is a fake. Of that I'm sure. Is that all you wanted to know, Lieutenant? If so, I'll get back to my lab and get somebody, maybe Ah Sing, started on this, but I'm pretty sure you won't find any traces of saxitoxin in *this* vial. Why would the poisoner fake the vial if they had a real one? Hey, Lieutenant? How's that for detecting? You through with me now?

LT. RHODES: Yes, Professor. Thank you very much for your time.END OF THIS SECTION OF TAPE END OF THIS SECTION OF TAPE END OF THIS

LT. RHODES: *Comment.* God, how do his students take notes from this character! Pop Vernor indeed. I'd like to pop Vernor. Oh well.

He's telling me that he's the only person in this area with saxitoxin and that he keeps it under lock and key. Sort of. But there was an exhibit at the Natural History Museum where his vial was on display. Could the saxitoxin have been obtained then?

But why fake the vial? To incriminate Aval? That's the only reason I can see. But the person who wanted to incriminate Aval had to fix it so that we'd think he had put the tack on the chair. But he couldn't.

No, he could. Aval could have put the tack on the chair before Hassler sat on it. If he got there very early, while her books were in place but before Glendish and Penza came in. But how could anyone, anyone!, even the real poisoner, be sure that there would be that window of opportunity and that we'd fit Aval into it? I can't make it fit.

Pop goes the weasel. Pop leads me to Professor Isaac Hahn. Professors! Natural History Museum. Downtown. While I'm still on campus, I'd better check back at the English Department. Signing off. END OF THIS SECTION OF TAPE END OF THIS SECTION OF TAPE END OF THIS

Metropolitan Buffalo Police Department

Tape Transcription   Homicide Unit

Body: *Hassler, P.*   Tape No. *840308.008*

Place: *Rhodes Hall, UB West*   Time: *11:04 a.m.*

Persons present: *Det. Lt. Rhodes, Romola Badger*

Transcribed by: *S. Moreno*

LT. RHODES: *Comment.* Damn!! Damn, damn, damn! Sorry, Mary or whoever is transcribing this, but she shouldn't have done it that way. Badger, I mean. Now, this crazy student union, DREGS, is trying to stop the graduate students' getting fingerprinted. Badger screwed it up.

She is, of course, a politician, and I have to assume she had some reason for phrasing her memo as she did. Anyone would know you don't "order" an independent bunch like this to do something, particularly something so associated with the police and guilt as fingerprinting. What *is* her game? Anyway, here she comes—

LT. RHODES: Professor Badger, you've caused me a major problem. I should be doing an interview at the Natural History Museum at this point, to say nothing of reading the materials Professor Holland's been putting together for me, but now I have to deal with this.

BADGER: *I* cause you a problem? You are referring to the DREGS memorandum, I take it. I'm sorry to say our graduate students are a volatile lot. My predecessor was bent, it sometimes seems to me, on recruiting them on the basis of poetic madness.

LT. RHODES: But if you knew they were so easily offended, why did you tell them I was *ordering* them to be fingerprinted? And surely "Rhodes of Rhodes Hall" was going to slap them right in their socialism.

BADGER: Lieutenant, I can't believe that you are trying to blame *me* for the unpredictable responses of a group of immature graduate students spoiling for a fight with *any* authority figure who swims into their ken. No, Lieutenant, you cannot hold me responsible for *their* excitability.

LT. RHODES: Then, how do I proceed now?

BADGER: Let me begin by saying how immensely grateful I am that *you* are in charge of this appalling case, I mean a man of *your* sensitivity and talent.

I've long admired your plays. You have a gift for understanding how people are formed by their social setting. You are, I'm certain, one of the few detectives in this city, indeed, in the world, who could *really* understand our English department. If anyone can.

LT. RHODES: What's that supposed to mean?

BADGER: *[laughs]* Well, you have to realize that English departments are full of eccentric people. The *a*verage person would call them impossible. Here, because of ancient traditions like tenure, academic freedom, faculty governance, and the like, they have to be tolerated.

LT. RHODES: Be that as it may, your eccentric graduate students have responded with this memo. Now, how am I supposed to get the graduate students' fingerprints?

BADGER: I could, of course, threaten them with departmental retaliation, but I think we should start by making some sort of appeal to them.

LT. RHODES: That makes sense.

BADGER: I would recommend, Lieutenant, that *you,* not me, respond to the DREGS memorandum and make that appeal.

LT. RHODES: That also makes sense. They don't sound too fond of you, and you're telling me the feeling is mutual. Does it make sense for me simply to ask for their help as I did with the students in the seminar?

BADGER: As you've pointed out, Lieutenant, *I* am not a good judge of how our more im*passion*ed graduate students will react. If frankness worked with those in Holland's seminar, it might go over with the others. You can dictate your memo to Marie.

Incidentally, here are the photographs you asked me for, of the graduate students and Professors Holland and Sisley.

LT. RHODES: You're prompt.

BADGER: I pride myself on speed and efficiency.

Now, what else can I do to help your investigation?

LT. RHODES: Has anything unusual happened recently in the department?

BADGER: Professor Holland is always unusual.

LT. RHODES: People tell me you've had some unpleasant scandals in the past few years. Has he been involved in those?

BADGER: Oh, no. In that respect, Professor Holland is quite comme il faut. I have never heard anything about his private life that gave me cause for concern. He is married, happily, so far as I know. He is a professor of the highest standing in the profession. His teaching methods, in particular, have attracted a great deal of attention.

LT. RHODES: Yet, I think, you don't approve.

BADGER: No, I do not.

LT. RHODES: Why?

BADGER: That would take us on a long ex*cur*sion into the thickets of academic policy and politics, Lieutenant. But perhaps, as a man of letters yourself, you might find the question of interest.

As you probably know already, we in this department are under a kind of mandate from the higher administration. The president sees this university as, in his phrase, "poised for greatness," and he wants us, to continue his metaphor, "to take the next leap." More to the point, my immediate superior, our dean of humanities, Dean Hedge, wants the same.

My predecessor as chair, Professor Agger, felt that the way to advance the department was to recruit faculty in areas that departments in other universities either could not or would not handle. He argued that we could not make our mark by trying to do what everyone else was already doing and probably doing better than we would be able to do for the foreseeable future. As a result, he sought the original, the unconventional, the bohemian, and sometimes, I'm *sorry* to say, what was simply off the wall.

Last year, some of the senior faculty, who had been here before all this hiring, and I were able to persuade the dean to a *dif*ferent, more traditional point of view. We are a large public university. We have to model ourselves on the successful public universities, the midwestern Big Ten, for example. We cannot function like the privates, Yale or Columbia, which can afford to be idiosyncratic and original. We have to appeal to a state board of regents. Ultimately we have to obtain our budget from the legislature and the voters. As I see it, then, we have to do whatever ordinary people think appropriate for English departments to do. We make ourselves extremely *vul*nerable if we embark on novel, untested modes of teaching or, for that matter, writing and research.

LT. RHODES: I take it, then, you don't much approve of Professor Holland's Delphi seminar.

BADGER: Professor Holland is an *in*teresting test case, wouldn't you agree, Lieutenant? On the one hand he publishes a great deal, and there has been a lot of interested comment in the profession on his ideas and methods. My predecessor hired him on the strength of this reputation. But that benefits Professor Holland, doesn't it? It *does*n't benefit his colleagues in this department. We are subject to the risk that things will not go well in one of Professor Holland's extra*or*dinary seminars. The department may well be criticized for not reining in its maverick members. In short, Professor Holland gets the upside and we get the downside.

Now this *dread*ful death in his Delphi seminar. I shudder at the problems we will have recruiting young faculty or promising graduate students into a department where students are murdered. I try not to think what is going to happen to our budget. I fear I will be saying no to a lot of requests next year.

LT. RHODES: Is it very bad for you in particular, Professor Badger?

BADGER: What do you mean?

LT. RHODES: Are you an ambitious person, Professor Badger?

BADGER: *[Pause.]* Perhaps.

LT. RHODES: It cannot further your career to have this murder in your department. Some might say that you were irresponsible to let Holland go on teaching this way. That you were therefore partly responsible for the murder.

BADGER: That would be *quite* wrong, wouldn't it, Lieutenant? In this department, as in most others, what the teachers do in their classrooms is the teachers' own business within *very* broad limits. No absenteeism, no coming to class high, no sexual harassment, limits like that. Within those parameters, however, the individual teacher teaches as he or she sees fit. I am not responsible, *no* administrator at the university is, for Holland's teaching methods.

LT. RHODES: But they're inconvenient for you.

BADGER: Not inconvenient enough for me to commit *mur*der, Lieutenant, if that's what you're hinting. *[Laughs]*

LT. RHODES: It's a detective's job to be suspicious. Thank you for your cooperation. I'm sorry the DREGS memo happened.

BADGER: *So* am I, Lieutenant. *Please* believe me.
    Before you dictate your response, might I ask you something?

LT. RHODES: Of course.

BADGER: Your family has been a *great* benefactor of this university. The land on which you and I now stand was given, *most* generously!, by your family. This converted mansion in which the English Department carries on its work was once a house on *your* family's estate. I believe that you are indeed Rhodes of Rhodes Hall. Whether the graduate students like it or not, *I* shall continue to think of you that way. May I ask you to help us meet the questions that will no doubt arise from other citizens of Buffalo less informed about English departments and less sympathetic, less de*vo*ted to this university?

LT. RHODES: You can certainly ask, Professor Badger. I'll do what seems right in my position.

BADGER: Let me speak more plainly, Lieutenant. There will be those who regard this *dread*ful murder as the result of Professor Holland's teaching methods. They will say that he was doing a kind of psychotherapy for which he was not qualified and that one of these students broke down in the process and committed murder. You know and I know that is not the case. How can we make sure that the newspapers and the taxpayers also know that it is not the case? You saw the dark hints in this morning's *News-Gazette*.

LT. RHODES: I don't know how I can help you with your public relations problem,

Professor Badger. I have my hands full with this investigation. May I make a suggestion? That you put your own clever mind to the problem. That you come back to me with a proposal as to what I could do. Then I can decide whether I should do it or not.

BADGER: I have watched you at work yesterday and today. You are a master at delegating tasks. Should I assume that you are delegating this particular task to me?

LT. RHODES: You could assume that.

BADGER: Then I will indeed get back to you with a proposal.

LT. RHODES: Again, Professor Badger, thank you for your help.END OF THIS SECTION OF TAPE END OF THIS SECTION OF TAPE END OF THIS

LT. RHODES: *Comment.* All right, Ms. Badger, I'll get a memo out to the graduate students. I can't say I learned anything useful from this pontificating lady. Except that the Niagara River doesn't have more cross-currents than an English department. What was it Henry Kissinger said? That academic politics are so bitter because the stakes are so small.

State University of New York at Buffalo
Department of English

March 8, 1984

Dear Justin,

Here's my reading of Anne Glendish, although she knows herself as well as I'm going to be able to spell her out. Incidentally, over the years, that's been the general rule. The women know themselves and everybody else in the seminar better than the men do.

I'm being professorial and rambling. What about Anne Glendish? I'll give you her trait response first, and then the snake. As you'll see, hers is a world of looking and being looked at.

```
English 6121                                    February 8
                                                A. G.
```

```
    The characteristic I'll tell you about you already
know. You know it just from looking at me. I'm too beauti-
ful.
```

Okay, okay. That sounds vain to you, but it isn't. I
call it actors' realism. (Some of you know I was a theater arts major as an undergraduate at Berkeley.) People
in the theater have to look at themselves quite realistically. They have to know how they look from this angle
and that. They have to know precisely how their voices
sound. They have to study themselves feature by feature,
because they need to know just exactly what they can do
and what they can't. Can I play a society grande dame? A
mother? A streetwalker? When I say I'm too beautiful, I'm
being, quite simply, realistic.

But too beautiful? I can hear the men in the seminar
asking how can you be too beautiful? The women in the
seminar know the answer to that one.

I was a theater major, because I love acting. I like
being on stage and having people look at me, and I'm sure
you can all understand what that feels like and empathize
with it. And like most people, I don't like being upstaged. It makes me so angry, I could . . . Well.

In acting classes, I loved trying to understand and
project myself into the language of the character. Even
more I loved the challenge of trying to perform that
inner truth with my own face and voice and body.

But if you're beautiful, they want you to play ingenues. Unfortunately, theater departments in colleges have
plenty of good-looking women who can play ingenues.
Little twits, like some of the cute little freshwomen you
see around here. You have to compete against these little
cuties in unpleasant ways (the casting director's well-
known couch), and they're not very interesting parts,
anyway. I wanted to play character parts. They're more of
a challenge. Of all the people in our seminar, for example, I'd most like to act Trish.

I remember a terrific one-woman play, an hour-long
monologue by a bag lady, a honey of a part. She was angry, loving, sad, bereaved, rich, poor, crazy, sometimes
saner than you or me--you name it. You could get inside
that woman and have a whole campaign, emotionally.
"You're too beautiful," casting said. "You couldn't make
her believable." Maybe they were right, but I could have
killed for that part.

Another time, I wanted to play an old woman in a
nursing home with a great death scene. Same thing. I
wanted to do Shakespeare, Lady Macbeth, Cleopatra,
Volumnia. I couldn't even get to Ophelia or Desdemona.

"Stick to drawing-room comedy," the acting teachers said.
"Noel Coward." But who does Noel Coward these days? Who
wants to? "Musicals," they said. But I can't sing. "Go to
Hollywood," they said. Grrr. Finally I gave it up.

I shifted from Theater Arts to English, because I
couldn't stand it in the theater, and I got to like plays
simply for their own sake, as literature. I got to like
literary criticism, particularly feminist and psychological criticism.

Even in this department, though, my looks get in my
way. Nobody has harassed me--it isn't that--but you should
see my freshman English class. The men--boys really--
practically have their tongues hanging out, and the women
are all jealous. They don't know what it's like. How do you
think it feels going into that class Tuesday, Thursday
mornings, and knowing that half or all of the guys in the
class were having weird fantasies about you last night?
You can see it in their eyes, the way they look at you,
they hunger for you, but then they can't quite face you.

Believe me, when you're the subject of that much
projection, you're grateful for anyone who can just look
at you realistically. That's one reason I like this seminar. We're trying to find out who we really are. We're
doing the same kind of thinking ourselves into one another that I used to do in the theater. Norm calls it an
"identity theme." In the theater we used to call it the
"inner truth of the character." Yes, I miss being onstage.
But maybe teaching freshman comp, maybe in this assignment, I'm onstage again, in a different, better (?) way.

She's onstage. Others told stories about themselves, but Anne says, in
effect, look at me. She's right when she says she's not being vain. She's
being realistic, because her reality is looking and being looked at. She's
perfectly entitled to say, What you see is the real me, because that's what
reality is for her, seeing, but more, being seen. A theme, then: I want to see
and be seen for who I really am.

English 6121   February 15
                                          A. G.

I see this poem as a scene. The poet stands in the
center of her "companions" all looking at her as she

holds this snake. For a moment there flashes into my mind
those Cretan wall paintings of round-breasted women holding snakes, like priestesses or goddesses, showing their
power by their indifference to poison. One of the signs
of divinity is that you cannot be poisoned.

But I see this speaker as thoroughly modern, holding
the snake, looking into its eyes as its tongue samples
the air between them. I see her companions looking at
her, but this is an intensely private moment. She and her
snake are taking the measure of each other. I know that's
a strange way to think of an animal, especially one as
low on the intelligence scale as a snake. (Or are they
high on the scale? Not as high as the poet, anyway.)

A phallic symbol. No, Norm, you wouldn't be that
crude. I see that somebody could read it that way, but
I'd much rather not.

As a child I liked snakes and frogs. That was odd,
because all proper little southern blonde girls were
supposed to squeal in delighted fright and run away when
the boys held the snakes and frogs up to our faces. But
the fact was, I liked snakes and frogs. I found them
interesting. Those slit-eyes made me feel I was facing an
alien species, something from outer space.

And they me. What did they make of me? I've read
somewhere that snakes have an extra sensory organ that we
don't have, a pit that senses the warmth of the mammals
that are their natural prey. So what do I look like to a
snake? Do I look like me, the me I see in a mirror, with
a kind of warm, mammalian aura around me? Do I have a
different color? Say, a warm pink that says this is the
kind of thing you can eat? (Although that would only work
for small mammals, I suppose.) What would it mean to have
a different way of seeing things? I suppose that's my
venture into strangeness for this dark morning.

I seem to be stuck here. I can't get past just seeing
this as a scene, the two faces, the woman's and the
snake's intently staring at each other.

No, I'm not stuck. I'm turning against the poem. I
think of Levertov as rather deliberately staging all
this. I don't know who her companions are. Other writers?
Critics? Reporters? Women activists? She's walking though
the woods with them, and suddenly she bends down and
picks up this snake. "Look at me," she's saying. "Look at
how daring and arty and Dionysian I am. Poisonous? Who
cares? This is the kind of thing Poets do, and I'm doing

it, and I'm a Poet, and you should watch me and be startled, a little bit afraid, and very much in awe of me."
I'm saying this is a stagy gesture. She's showing off.

I hate to be upstaged. I just hate it. That's the
worst thing that can happen to you in a play--but it's
much harder in life. The absolute worst.

Yes, the more I read this poem, the hammier I find it,
the more cynical I get about it. At first, it was a moment of communion between her mind and the snake's. Now,
I think of it as her showing off. Curious. Doesn't this
say, Norm, that we don't just have one identity-theme
reading? That we can have more than one reading, indeed,
lots of different readings? Two, anyway.

Seeing and being seen—or, to take into account the extra organ of the
snake, being perceived by the senses. She responds primarily to looking at
the snake, being looked at and otherwise sensed by the snake.

I find it amusing in the snake paper the way she turns attention away
from Levertov to herself. She accuses the poet of putting on the whole thing
as a show-off (which is what she herself wants to do). She says she turns
against the poem; I'd say she turns against Levertov's upstaging Anne. She
can't stand the idea of another woman's upstaging her. Then she addresses
me, and says, in effect, look at what I'm doing. That way, she gets Levertov
out of center stage and puts herself there.

I've got two readings, she writes. Actually, she's doing the same thing,
staging herself, in two different ways. But the staging isn't phony, it's her.
That's the way she is.

Do you think she thought Trish was upstaging her? Trish certainly made
herself the center of attention in the seminar.

/Norm/

State University of New York at Buffalo
Department of English

To: All graduate students   Date: March 8,1984
From: Det. Lt. Rhodes

I've received the memo from DREGS urging you not to cooperate, and
I'm writing to ask you please *do* cooperate and submit to being fingerprinted.

DREGS is correct that I'm Norman Rhodes, usually known as Justin Rhodes, and I come from a wealthy family. There isn't very much I can do about that. DREGS is also right that neither the state legislature nor the world at large seems to care very much what happens to graduate students. I've been a graduate student myself—in creative writing—and I know.

DREGS is probably also correct that we don't have the right or the power to force you to be fingerprinted. In any case, it would be a prohibitive expense of police time in an already difficult investigation to try to go round and subpoena fingerprints from all 103 of you.

DREGS isn't correct, however, in saying that your prints would be made available to every deputy sheriff or CIA spook in the country. In the state of New York, you have the right to have the prints we take destroyed at the end of the investigation, and we're obliged to honor your right. Further, I personally promise you that we will play fair with any prints we receive, using them for this investigation and then destroying them.

DREGS is also not correct in saying that we would use your prints to round up English graduate students for every and all crimes. Police investigations don't work that way. Most people don't realize how difficult and time-consuming it is to match prints from police files with the imperfect, partial prints that we get in evidence. Rounding up large numbers of people from fingerprints would be both inefficient and impractical.

Therefore I'm *asking* you, not *ordering* you, please to cooperate. I'll give you two reasons why it's in your interests to do so in addition to the general wish that I assume we all share, that the killer of Patricia Hassler be made to answer for the crime. Reason one, until we catch the murderer, he or she can strike again. Until we find this killer, none of you is safe. You can bring back safety, relative safety, anyway—I know that universities are high-crime areas—by helping us bring the murderer to justice. Reason two, an individual's failure to provide fingerprints will inevitably bring suspicion on that individual. If you've nothing to hide, you can only lose by withholding your prints.

I urge you, for Patricia Hassler's sake, for ours, and for yours, help us catch this killer who has struck one of you down.

/Justin Rhodes/

from the journal of Norman Holland

My disclaimers on Wally's behalf evidently didn't work. Around 12:30 Rhodes came crashing into my office, dragging Yorrick behind him. "If I hadn't had to fool around with that damned DREGS business and Badger," he said, "I'd have read your analysis of Sisley an hour sooner." I asked him what was up, but

*he just said, "You'll see. Come. I may need you to answer some questions," he
snapped, "about the department—your department, not mine." So I stopped
the analysis of Barry Ireland I was writing for him—I had nearly finished—and
he bustled Yorrick and me into his car.*

*He parked in front of Sisley's garage doors, blocking them, and dashed
onto the front porch, where he buzzed the doorbell several times in a row. Wally
opened the door in a hurry, and I could see fear in his eyes.*

"Hello again, Lieutenant."

*"Is it 'again,' Professor Sisley?" said Rhodes. Wally flinched, but I couldn't
figure out what Rhodes was getting at. Rhodes stared at him for a couple of beats.
"I need you to tell me something about the Hassler case. I want to come in."*

*"Yes," said Wally, gulping, "by all means." Yorrick stationed himself in a
corner, while Wally sat Justin and me down on an old sofa with stuttering springs.*

*I'd been in the Sisleys' house to parties, but this time I saw it as Rhodes
saw it, through family money and a policeman's suspicions. The style was academic seedy: old oak furniture, wrought iron lamps, and oriental carpets worn
in places. Practically every wall had jerry-built bookshelves. Stacks of student
papers stood under yellowed lampshades, testifying glowingly to work Wally
still had to do. I felt sure most of what the Sisleys had was left over from graduate student purchases at the used furniture store. You couldn't sell it for anything, so it traveled with you from graduate school to your first job to your
second and so on, getting more and more beat up as kids added to the wear and
tear. At the rate poor Wally was impressing the dean it was going to be a while
before he and Abby got anything better.*

*Justin went through his routine of turning on the tape recorder. At this
point, then, I suppose I should turn my fallible narrative voice over to the infal-
lible transcribers of the real. The reel?*

Metropolitan Buffalo Police Department

Tape Transcription   Homicide Unit

Body: *Hassler, P.*   Tape No. *840308.011*

Place: *443 Keyes Drive*   Time: *12:45 p.m.*

Persons present: *Det. Lt. Rhodes, Det. Sgt. Yorrick, W. Sisley,*
        W. Sisley, N. Holland

Transcribed by: *J. Cipperman*

LT. RHODES: Professor Sisley, say again what happened Wednesday morning.

SISLEY: Sure, Lieutenant. When Norm and I got to the seminar some of the students were already there, sitting at the table. I took a chair, and I chatted with them. I don't remember what we said.

LT. RHODES: Who was there?

SISLEY: I'm sorry, Lieutenant, I don't remember.

Trish was late. She was dressed as usual. She stood in the—

LT. RHODES: She had her coat on?

SISLEY: Ummm. Yes, she'd come in from the outside. She stood sort of out in the corridor, not quite in the room, looking at all of us through the doorway. She was looking fierce, as she often did. I was glad there were others there to take the heat. She stood in the doorway for a little bit. Then she walked to the head of the table. After maybe half a minute, she started walking to the spot she'd reserved for herself—actually, it was Norm's usual seat—at the end of the table. Before she got there, she stood behind Christian Aval, and she said, uh, something like, "He's the one." Then she sat down.

When she sat down she started to lean over, and she fell down on the floor.

LT. RHODES: Did she fall to the left or the right?

SISLEY: Gosh, Lieutenant, I don't remember.

LT. RHODES: Picture it in your mind.

SISLEY: I think I'm beginning to repress the whole thing. The students jumped up, so I couldn't see much, and then Norm told us all to sit down, and he went out and called for security.

LT. RHODES: Let me quote you from yesterday morning. You said that Patricia Hassler stood over Christian Aval and said, "Him. He's the one. He's the one I was telling you about."

SISLEY: Yes, that's right. I remember now. That's what she said exactly. As I say, I'm beginning to block it out. She died so quickly, and I gather from your conference this morning that that's the way saxitoxin works.

LT. RHODES: Why are you talking about saxitoxin? That's something you get when you eat clams or oysters. Why does that come to your mind in this case?

SISLEY: But I read about needles with saxitoxin on them at the museum exhibit last fall, and they described exactly the way Trish died. Besides, you showed us this morning that a thumbtack killed her.

LT. RHODES: Yes, but I didn't mention saxitoxin by name. Norman, have you ever heard of saxitoxin?

HOLLAND: No.

LT. RHODES: Did I mention it this morning?

HOLLAND: If you did, it went right by me.

LT. RHODES: Explain about this museum exhibit.

SISLEY: The Natural History Museum did an exhibit on different kinds of poisons. They told how you could make curare from plants or saxitoxin from shellfish. They even had little vials of the finished poison. The placard alongside the exhibit said that if you concentrated the stuff enough, all it would take was a scratch, and the victim would die in less than a minute. And that's how Trish Hassler died, isn't it? I just assumed you meant saxitoxin. That's what the poison was, wasn't it?

LT. RHODES: Yorrick, are you listening? This is the second lead to this exhibit.

YORRICK: Okay, Lieutenant.

HOLLAND: Yes, I remember hearing about that show. It would've been Isaac Hahn who set it up.

LT. RHODES: All right, Yorrick, I'll check out that exhibit as soon as we finish here.

HOLLAND: It's not showing now, you know. The exhibit took place last fall.

LT. RHODES: I understand. Let me ask you a literary question, Professor Sisley. Who're "the abstract and brief chronicles of the time"?

SISLEY: Whew! You've got me there, Lieutenant.

LT. RHODES: Who holds the mirror up to nature?

SISLEY: The writer?

LT. RHODES: You don't recognize my quotations?

SISLEY: I'm in American literature.

LT. RHODES: Then how did you know these were from English literature?

SISLEY: I don't. They sound English. If they were from American literature, I'd have known them.

LT. RHODES: You're trying to tell me you don't recognize a quotation from *Hamlet* about actors?

SISLEY: As I say, Lieutenant, I'm in American literature.

LT. RHODES: How much would you say Patricia Hassler weighed?

SISLEY: Weighed? I guess about 250 pounds.

LT. RHODES: Yesterday morning you said between 230 and 240 pounds.

SISLEY: Well, it would be very hard to say with her. She was always all bundled up in her scarves and her beads like a kind of protective armor.

LT. RHODES: What color eyes did she have?

SISLEY: Color eyes! How should I know? Blue, I guess.

LT. RHODES: Yesterday morning you had it right. Brown.

HOLLAND: My God! Look who's come downstairs! It's the twins trick again! That *is* you, Will, isn't it?

WILL SISLEY: Yes, Norman. Nice try, Wally. I appreciate your trying to keep me out of this, but you don't have a professional's eye for that kind of detail just as I don't have a professional's ear for a quotation from *Hamlet*. Relax now. The Lieutenant and I can sort this out.

LT. RHODES: So, it was you, not your twin brother Wally, who was at the seminar yesterday.

WILL SISLEY: Yes. When I left your interview, Lieutenant, I tried to coach Wally on what I'd seen, but I had no way of knowing what you might ask him.

LT. RHODES: And it was you who couldn't recognize my quotations, and, worse still, who didn't know I was a playwright of at least modest repute.

WILL SISLEY: Yes, Lieutenant. When I want to read, I like history or biography or foreign affairs. Not plays or novels.

LT. RHODES: Why were you standing in for Wally yesterday morning? And why haven't you skipped back to Washington?

WILL SISLEY: The second one's easy, Lieutenant. I wanted to stay by Wally yesterday. He was all shaken up. He was afraid you'd find out about our little deception, and he didn't know what you'd do. I finally persuaded him that you wouldn't do anything. You'd look pretty foolish, thinking you were interviewing a college professor when you weren't.

This morning I felt Wally had got to a point where I could leave, but fog closed some airport down the line, and my flight was cancelled. I'm on standby for the two o'clock. I was just about to go out to the airport, when you arrived. I thought I'd better stick around in case he needed me to explain things to you. Now, unless you finish with him quickly, I can't leave until the seven-thirty flight.

LT. RHODES: You'd better hang around, Mr. Sisley. I think you do need to explain some things to me. For one, tell me why you took Wally's place in the seminar.

WILL SISLEY: You may have heard that Wally and I switched identities once before and fooled the faculty.

LT. RHODES: Why do you think I'm here? Go on, Sisley.

WILL SISLEY: It was a lot of fun. We thought we might try it again, this time with one of Wally's classes.

LT. RHODES: You're not seriously trying to tell me you came all the way up from Washington to play a practical joke on Holland's seminar. I thought you were supposed to be clever. Indeed, people tell me you work for the CIA.

WILL SISLEY: People will tell you all kinds of things. I was visiting Wally and Abby anyway, and we thought we'd have some fun.

LT. RHODES: Let me show you why the CIA connection is important. We now know that a poison called saxitoxin killed Patricia Hassler. Your brother knew that, although I hadn't told him. How did he find out?

WILL SISLEY: He told you. This museum show.

LT. RHODES: You know and I know that saxitoxin is something the CIA uses. I've been told that a Congressional committee ordered the CIA to get rid of $200,000 worth of the stuff, but nobody knows whether the agency did so.

I expect the ordinary civilian in a murderous frame of mind would have great difficulty getting some saxitoxin. You wouldn't.

WILL SISLEY: Is it your theory, then, that I came up here from Washington to terminate Patricia Hassler? No, Lieutenant, I can assure you that the firm I work for had no interest in Patricia Hassler whatsoever. Nor do I think the firm would tolerate my acting on my own, especially within the fifty states. That doesn't, of course, prove that I didn't kill Patricia Hassler, and I wouldn't blame you for not believing me.

LT. RHODES: There's another connection. Patricia Hassler studied literature at Yale, and it's public knowledge that there was a famous professor of literature at Yale who devotedly recruited dozens of graduating Yale seniors into the CIA. I read a book about it. *Cloak and Gown,* an artful title. It seems to me entirely possible that Hassler was one of those seniors, and that the CIA decided they no longer wanted her services. Maybe that's why her career at Yale ended so abruptly and mysteriously.

WILL SISLEY: Very inventive, Lieutenant. I take my hat off to you, or I would if I were wearing one. That's really ingenious. The only trouble is, it's not so. So far as I know, Patricia Hassler had no connection with my company at all. Now the company is very big, and I certainly don't know everyone who works for it. I'm sufficiently highly placed, though, so that I'd have known if one of our employees was studying in the same department where my brother teaches. Your evidence is all stuff you and I as professionals would call circumstantial or coincidental.

LT. RHODES: Skip the buzzwords. There are three solid facts here. One, the Yale connection, the Yale mystery, really. Two, Hassler's death by means of a favorite poison of the firm you work for. And isn't a poisoned thumbtack just like other CIA tricks? Like putting acid in Khadaffi's eyedrops or doping Castro's shaving cream so that his beard would fall out? Three, your presence in the seminar, indeed your presence, in disguise, at the very moment Hassler was killed. You were there, Will Sisley. To me, that adds up to motive, means, and opportunity. I think I've got enough to collar you right now.

WILL SISLEY: Not so fast, Lieutenant. I know, and you know, too, that we could get into a nasty dust-up between our two employers. Instead of muddling all three of your facts together, let's look at them one by one. The Yale connection is pure supposition on your part. You haven't shown any motive, only the suspicion of one. You don't know that Hassler worked for the company, and I say she didn't. As for means, what do you think, that the company issues saxitoxin with the paper clips? That all I have to do is go down the hall to the supplies office and pick up a vial of poison? *If* the company has that stuff, and I'm not for a moment admitting that it does, you can be damned sure they keep close track of it. You'll need more than just the rumor that I work for the CIA to provide me with the means. Third, there was no opportunity. You know as well as I do that I was nowhere near Patricia Hassler's chair Wednesday morning. At all times there was a table and a scattering of students between.

LT. RHODES: I'll try another hypothesis, Mr. Sisley. You provided the saxitoxin for someone else. Wally maybe. Or maybe you gave some to Wally, and he gave some to someone else, and the someone else killed Hassler.

WILL SISLEY: Please believe me, Lieutenant. I've never had any saxitoxin in my possession, either for my own use or for anyone else's. Will you accept my word of honor on that?

LT. RHODES: Would you accept that from someone else?

WILL SISLEY: No, of course not.

LT. RHODES: So . . .

WILL SISLEY: Look, there's no way I can prove I've never had any saxitoxin, but that isn't my job. It's up to you to prove that I did, and it's up to you to prove that I somehow got that thumbtack under Patricia Hassler's ass. If and when you've got enough evidence to go on, you'll know how and where to reach me. You take the matter up with your superiors, and they take it up with mine. Until then, Lieutenant, you and I have nothing more to say to each other. I've got a plane to catch and work to do.

LT. RHODES: O.K. Go.

WILL SISLEY: What do you mean?

LT. RHODES: I mean go. Sergeant, get him onto that plane.

WILL SISLEY: You mean you've got Wally.

LT. RHODES: Yes, I've got Wally.

WILL SISLEY: Oh, for God's sake.

LT. RHODES: Get on your plane, Sisley. Sergeant, take him.

WILL SISLEY: Wally, try to be careful of what you say.

LT. RHODES: Out, out, Sisley. If you don't want to go back to Washington tonight, don't, but don't hang around here. I want to talk to your brother by himself. We've got one crucial question we want an answer to, and he's going to give it to us.

SISLEY: *[Voice fading]* Wally, for God's sake, be . . . *[I watched burly Yorrick, suitcase in one hand, Will Sisley's elbow in the other, hustle him out the door and into our police car. It was impressive. Rhodes turned back to a shaky Wally Sisley.]*

LT. RHODES: Professor Sisley, your brother's not here now. He can't hear us. You know, I don't think he was much help to you. I think he made you look very suspect.

SISLEY: What do you mean?

LT. RHODES: His taking over this interview makes it look as though he was protecting you, as though he knew that you had something to hide.

SISLEY: Well, I don't, and neither does he. He arrived just about six o'clock Tuesday night, and he had dinner with Abby and me. We sat around and talked the rest of the evening. Then he went to the seminar Wednesday morning. Look, while he was there, he was never in a position to put that thumbtack on Trish Hassler's chair.

LT. RHODES: You know, I quite agree with you. I don't think your brother poisoned Patricia Hassler. On the other hand, that's not the only crime we have here.

SISLEY: Oh?

LT. RHODES: I think we could fairly say that your brother wasn't very cooperative with us. Obstructing justice is a crime. And, of course, if he were guilty of such a crime you'd be either a coconspirator or an accessory. We'd have to get the district attorney to say which he was going for. None of this, of course, would do the prospects of your tenure any good.

SISLEY: Frankly, Lieutenant, I think you're reaching. My brother and the people he works for wouldn't stand still for that.

LT. RHODES: Then there's the matter of that saxitoxin. We have a thing called "reckless endangerment" here in New York. It's one of the lower degrees of murder. Fourth degree, if I remember correctly. I think it's entirely possible that your brother recklessly endangered Patricia Hassler and to that extent caused her death by bringing that saxitoxin into play. With whom or to whom we don't know yet. And again the D.A. would have to decide whether you were a coconspirator or an accessory before the fact.

SISLEY: No! I had nothing to do with any saxitoxin. I have a wife and a child, and, believe me, I wouldn't have dangerous stuff like that in the house. All it takes is a scratch. You said that this morning, and so did Will. They said that at that museum exhibit last fall.

LT. RHODES: Okay, you don't have any saxitoxin. But now we come to the sixty-four thousand-dollar question. Why did Will take your place in the seminar? He dodged that, but you're not going to. I want an answer. Do you have any idea what happens to a good-looking, mild man like yourself in the holding pen?

SISLEY: Don't threaten me, Lieutenant. I'll help as best I can. Yes, I'll admit it. Patricia had threatened me, and I asked Will to take a look at the situation. He's strong and tough and smart. I hoped he could do something about it.

LT. RHODES: She threatened you? How? About what?

SISLEY: She took a seminar with me last semester. Did very well, in fact, and I thought we were getting along fine. Nevertheless, she told me she'd write a nasty letter saying I was a rotten teacher.

LT. RHODES: So? Is that so awful?

SISLEY: She said she'd write that I'd harassed her sexually.

LT. RHODES: Her? Hardly a student who'd awaken professorial lust.

SISLEY: Not that kind, not trying to date her. She said she'd say I insisted on talking dirty in front of her.

LT. RHODES: And then it's your word against hers.

SISLEY: But that would be enough to sink me. Even her claim that I was a poor teacher would be enough, in my circumstances. Lieutenant, I'm trying to get tenure. To do that I have to present evidence about my teaching. I'm just your regular, average teacher. Like most. Most people are average teachers, neither very good nor very bad. Only the very good ones and the very bad ones stand out. The rest of us are just—well, average. If you want to get tenure, you have to present evidence that you're a good teacher.

LT. RHODES: And this is enough for blackmail?

HOLLAND: That's right, Justin, this university has gotten very sensitive about teaching in the light of parents' complaints. As a result, the evidence of teaching ability has gotten rather elaborate. There are forms, for example, that the students fill out anonymously after every course is over. A lot of the evidence you have to provide yourself. People submit their course outlines, samples of papers they've graded, lecture notes. Some people even have themselves videotaped while they're teaching. Sometimes people get testimonials from former students, and sometimes the department interviews them.

That's why Hassler's threat bites. If she wrote a letter on her own, it would automatically go in the file that went up to the dean.

SISLEY: If I had letters that said I was great, maybe one letter saying I wasn't wouldn't hurt. But I'm just your average teacher, and one bad letter could sink me. Certainly a letter that alleged sexual harassment would. Then too, Badger and the dean are ready to use any excuse to get rid of me. They'd like to replace a moderately priced associate professor with a cheap entry-level part-timer. They'd focus on that one letter to do that. Hassler had figured that out. Maybe somebody told her.

LT. RHODES: But it's just her letter against the other evidence. And everybody knows that she was a vindictive person.

SISLEY: Not everybody. She was Romola's pet. Romola was committed to her, because Romola forced her admission to graduate school over the heads of the graduate admissions committee. I was on that committee, and we were pretty skeptical about some gaps in Trish Hassler's background. But Romola took it on herself to admit her over our objections. So far as Romola was concerned, Trish could do no wrong. So, Lieutenant, I'd have ended up with a negative letter in my file and the department chair even more against me than she is already.

Norm, did you know that Trish knew who everybody was on that committee and she knew who objected to her admission?

HOLLAND: No.

SISLEY: She knew I objected, and she knew you did, Norm. She told me all about it once. I think that's one reason she was so hard on you in this seminar.

I don't know how she found out, because all that happened in May, before she got here. I sometimes suspect Romola of telling her.

HOLLAND: Romola likes to fish in troubled waters.

LT. RHODES: Let's get back to this investigation. What did Hassler want from you?

SISLEY: Control, I think. She wanted to have a faculty member under her thumb, so she could find out things, maybe get exams ahead of time, maybe even influence key votes. Then there was the money. She knew I didn't have much, but she had me give her four hundred dollars a month in cash.

LT. RHODES: This is blackmail? Four hundred dollars a month? You've got to be kidding! This could only happen in academia.

SISLEY: She knew I couldn't handle any more than that. She had it all figured out. Our salaries are a matter of public record, you know, and that's a quarter of my salary after taxes. She said to me once that she didn't want to make me desperate.

LT. RHODES: But it *did* make you desperate. You wrote on February 15 that poison, quote, could solve everything, unquote.

SISLEY: Yes, but I didn't poison her. The tenure thing would be settled this spring, and then she wouldn't have a hold over me any more.

LT. RHODES: She knew that as well as you did. She knew she could only blackmail you for four hundred dollars a month for just a couple of months. Four max. Sixteen hundred dollars. That doesn't make sense. It isn't enough to justify the the trouble and the risk. Was she angry at you for something in that seminar of yours she took?

SISLEY: I don't think so. She did very well. She really was very brilliant, even if she was also a bitch.

LT. RHODES: You couldn't prove it by me, Professor Sisley. But evidently you thought her paper was very good, and you told Trish so.

SISLEY: Yes.

LT. RHODES: And she decided to blackmail you anyway.

HOLLAND: As I and a few of the students pointed out in our papers for this week, it was precisely the act of being given to that she most resented. She had to give back aggressively what she received passively, in this case, Wally's praise.

SISLEY: Motiveless malignity. Like Iago.

LT. RHODES: So now you know English literature!

SISLEY: I'm sorry, Lieutenant. I was trying to conceal Will's impersonating me. He told me you'd asked him about some quotation.

LT. RHODES: I understood what you were doing, but imagine what you were demonstrating about the education of professors of American literature.
Tell me what he was doing in the seminar.

SISLEY: I was afraid, Lieutenant. I thought that, even if I paid up, Hassler would double-cross me. Out of sheer malice, she'd destroy my chances for tenure, and I'd be out on the street. It's very hard, you know, to get a new job at my stage, just pre-tenure, unless you have extraordinary credentials. Better than mine, anyway. She'd have ruined me.

HOLLAND: That's true, Justin.

SISLEY: That's why I turned to Will. I thought Will might be able to do something, I didn't know what. He'd have figured out something. He's always been stronger and tougher than me. He had resources.

LT. RHODES: Like saxitoxin? What did you imagine? That he'd strong-arm her? That he'd kill her? Was that the idea?

SISLEY: No, no, Lieutenant. We hadn't planned anything yet. I had an idea that maybe Will could pretend to be me and get her to repeat her threats and maybe tape-record her. Then we could turn the blackmail around. Something nonviolent, believe me. It was just an idea. Will could handle something like that. I couldn't.

LT. RHODES: So you say.

SISLEY: Will agreed to come up from Washington and size up Patricia Hassler. I told him this was the session at which he'd best see her in action. Then, once he'd figured her out, he said, we'd work out a plan. As it turned out, we didn't have to.

LT. RHODES: Unless Will got enthusiastic and did something on his own, not planning it out with you.

SISLEY: That's not like Will. Besides, as he said, he didn't have the opportunity. There was no point where he was alone near Hassler's chair and could plant the thumbtack.

LT. RHODES: Except that anyone, repeat anyone, could have planted the thumbtack between the time Hassler put her books down and Glendish and Penza came into the room. Your brother. You. You, Norm. Anyone.

HOLLAND: So I'm still a suspect.

LT. RHODES: Actually, you're not.

HOLLAND: I don't understand, Justin.

SISLEY: I don't either, Lieutenant.

LT. RHODES: Tomorrow. At tomorrow's meeting of the seminar, I'll make it all come clear—I hope.

All right, gentlemen, that's enough of the brothers Sisley for now. I have to check out that museum exhibit. Come out on the porch, Norman. *[Steps. Pause.]* Best leave Sisley inside.

HOLLAND: Do you want to talk about this? Have you had lunch?

LT. RHODES: I have to check out this museum lead, and I have to talk to Pop Vernor again. All that puts a squeeze on the afternoon, and I'll have to do a press conference at eight o'clock, just time enough to make the eleven o'clock news and the morning paper. I need time to do some thinking before I have to meet the press.

HOLLAND: Poor Wally.

LT. RHODES: He could use some propping up.

HOLLAND: What did you mean about tomorrow?

LT. RHODES: Take therefore no thought for the morrow: for the morrow shall take thought for the things of itself. Right now I'd like you to keep analyzing the students for me.

HOLLAND: Give me a break. I'm tired too.

LT. RHODES: You have to do it anyway. You might as well do it now to help me settle this case. Look how useful your interpretation of Sisley was.

HOLLAND: Only because he happened to mention that he had a twin brother who could pass for him.

LT. RHODES: But that's what you and I have to get out, isn't it? Facts. Solving a murder is getting all the facts into a whole story. There's a lot I can't fit together in this case. Your analyses give the facts I develop a human sense. I want you to go on doing them. Put them in my new mailbox.

HOLLAND: Alphabetical?

LT. RHODES: Unless you see some reason not to.

HOLLAND: I've just about finished Ireland.   •

LT. RHODES: Sorry to be so insistent, but there's so much about this case I don't understand. But there's also a lot I *do* understand. See you tomorrow at nine. Yorrick, call a squad car and take him back to the university. Then, Yorrick, you find out how long it takes to walk from Main Street to Rhodes Hall. Wait there for me. I'll talk to Professor—who is it?—

HOLLAND: Hahn. Ike Hahn.

LT. RHODES: —at the Science Museum.END OF THIS SECTION OF TAPE END OF THIS SECTION OF TAPE END OF THIS SECTION OF TAPE END

LT. RHODES: *Comment.* Yes, I do know a lot. I know who did it and how it was done. I'm not sure why, though. Too many loose ends. Who is the interloper?

What did he have to do with the death? How was the saxitoxin obtained? When was the thumbtack put under the cushion?

There are too many people with motives in this case. But what I don't have enough of is facts. I have enough motives for half a dozen murders.

Yorrick's got the car. I'll have to find a cab to get to the museum.

State University of New York at Buffalo Department of English

Thursday Afternoon

Dear Justin:

Here are the two papers from Barry Ireland, who is, obviously, one of my problem children. I've been keeping my distance, trying not to antagonize Barry and especially trying to keep the other students from crossing him. I think they're all pretty sensitive to his problems. When I started this kind of seminar, I was afraid students would turn on the psychic wounded the way a flock of chickens will peck a bleeding one to death. But they're protective.

You'll see in these two responses he's pretty close to violence all the time. I think he'd have been this way even without Vietnam, but he and Vietnam sought each other out, and the experience made him worse.

There's something else to look for. In psychological jargon, I'd call it denial: an ability to ignore the parts of reality that seem threatening or unpleasant. Look at the way he says Vietnam is simply "behind him." That's all over. For a cute psychological exercise, look at his other uses of the word *behind,* Justin.

If I were to try to phrase Barry's identity theme, I'd say something like: a world of violence that I know and don't know.

```
English 6121                          8.2.84
                                      Barry


A trait I want you to know about—I know what you expect
me to say. You think I'll come on as the VIETNAM VET
(look out, look out!) and tell you about the louie I
fragged or all the gooks I killed--or raped--and all the
```

sweet dope and pussy we used to put down on those Saigon
streets. (Do you think this seminar encourages stereotyp-
ing?) That's all over with now. It was a mistake to go,
but what did a kid from the mountains of West Virginia
know? And maybe it was a mistake to come back. But that's
all behind me now.

I like cats. Hell, I love cats.

I've read this somewhere: HE-MEN DON'T KISS CATS.
Bullshit. I'm a he-man, and I kiss cats. (At least I
think I'm a he-man, he said smiling his endearing
snaggletoothed Boy Scout grin and flashing his "Mom"
tattoo.) I've got four of them: Adam the solemn; Doctor
John, the sweetie; Lord Peter, the whimsical one; Marple
the unexpected. My little tribute to Britfict.

Shiteating landlord tried to make me get rid of them.
Came to my door one day. I hear you've got a bunch of
cats in here, he goes. You know that's against your
lease. How'd you hear, say I. One of the other tenants
complained, sez he. Oh, I go, Who? Never you mind, sez
he. She sez she can smell the shit. What shit?, I go,
What cats? You want to look around? Yeah, sez he. Come on
in, say I. I locked the door behind him--that surprised
him a little--and there were the cats, sleeping in different spots in my one room. Aha, sez he. Oho, sez he.
But, say I, I keep the kitty litter out on the fire escape, so how the hell can your bitch spy smell anything?
I showed him the box, indeed I lifted him up and held his
head way out the window for a really good look. I also
showed him some of my souvenirs. Photos of our squad with
what was left of a village in the background. Viet Cong
flag, stained with something. Bayonet. He was impressed
by how sharp it was. A cattle prod--I don't know why I
hang onto that thing, and he didn't want a demonstration.
A grenade that I'm pretty sure is dead. A string of ears.
Actually, it's a string of dried apricots--I'm not <u>that</u>
crazy--but I told him ears, and he evidently believed me,
because he said I could keep the cats until the end of
the lease, but then it was out for all of us. No problem,
say I. And who was it complained? He didn't want to say,
and I didn't press the point (no pun intended). But I
sure as hell have an idea.

I think I'd die without my cats. They're the perfect
predator. Double lidded eyes, a reflecting layer on the
retina, exquisitely designed for hunting smaller mammals
at night. Come to think of it, that could be a metaphor

for certain human activities--although the mammal I'm
thinking of is hardly small.

Design. Did you ever really look at a cat's claw?
There are these little tubes of cartilage attached to the
bone into which the claws can retract. That way, their
paws can be as soft and silent as a Q-tip, retracted. But
extended, they can cut, sharp as a scalpel, into mammal
flesh.

I read a technical book on cats once, a German author.
Paul Leyhausen, <u>Verhältensstudien an Katzen</u> (although I
read it, obviously, in translation). The librarian said
it's the definitive work. That's why I memorized the
German title. He began his cat-watching career during
double-u double-u too in a POW camp in Canada. He started
by watching cockroaches in the camp, and when he got out,
he traded up to cats. It's a homely book, full of charts
and graphs and diagrams, but it's stunning, pure observation, perfect in every detail.

All the different species of cat, from a tabby to a
lion, have the same program, a run and then a pounce with
the claws hanging onto the flanks and the teeth going for
the spinal cord just back of the head. They even have a
special incisor designed to tell them when their mouths
are positioned right for the kill. The tooth is slightly
loose in the socket and has a nerve to sense its movement. When the tooth is firmly held <u>between</u> two verte-
brae, then the cat's instinct says, BITE DOWN, and it
snaps the backbone and the cord. They're completely,
perfectly designed for the one purpose.

Male cats have the same bite when they grasp females
for mating, the teeth right behind the head on the spinal
cord, but then they know not to bite down. What exquisite
programming!

Well, as Norm likes to tell us, we all boil down to
sex and aggression, and they're right there, side by
side, in that old mammalian brain, the one that does the
loving and hating, as opposed to the front brain that
takes graduate seminars like this. You can see them
hating, and you can tell that they love you--as I love
them.

We have a limbic system the way they do (and hence
emotions and play). We have nipples as they do. And we
have hair as they have fur. But theirs is so much finer
and softer. That's why it feels so good to hug a cat, and
yes, to kiss a cat. We sleep in a big old mammalian heap,

```
Peter and John and Adam and Marple and I, all fur and
tits and warm blood and sex and aggression. What would I
be without them? A thinking machine, no emotions at all?
I like it that I'm a mammal. I wish I had children.
```

Denial would include the way he makes a joke out of his threatening the landlord. (That must be one of the world's more nervous-making jobs, being Barry Ireland's landlord.) By the way, it came out, when the seminar discussed that paper, that Trish and Barry live on the same floor of the same apartment house. They are, it turned out, practically next door to each other. Barry admitted that he suspected Trish was the neighbor who complained to the landlord about his cats. (That's just the kind of bitchy thing she'd do, isn't it?) She answered, by the way, that he could damn well think what he liked. Then Barry said he was over all that. That was settled. That was behind him.

I think the cats are a kind of hope for Barry. The cats are killers but also soft, loving creatures, Q-tips. He becomes a he-man who kisses cats. When he goes to sleep with them, he snuggles down with the softer part of himself, fur, tits, and a boyish, snaggletoothed smile. It's as though he wants to protect the loving, non-violent side of him. Who knows? Barry could turn his violence toward love instead of death. Abruptly, unexpectedly, he says he wants children.

```
English 6121                              15.2.84
                                          Barry
```

```
    Hey, Norm, you must have picked this one just for your
friendly visitor from old Vietnam. We've got the jungle
here, and the weight of your pack on your shoulders, and
even the bit about camouflage at the end.
    No, I would not have hung any goddam green snake
around my neck. I saw plenty of them in those days, and
I'd have shot every damn one right in the cold, prettily
pulsing throat, except we were afraid we'd give away our
location.
    Actually one day one of the guys in the squad really
did pick up a snake--sort of. We were on recon, and base
told us to stay put for further orders. We stopped in a
clearing, and we sat down and stretched out. We had this
rich kid in the platoon. Herbie lay down flat and dozed
off. The next thing you know there was this big brown
```

snake curled up on his chest. Herbie woke up, but he didn't dare move or speak or anything. He just stared at it like a gun barrel pointed up his nose. The snake must have liked the warmth of old mammalian Herbie. It didn't show any signs of moving. The rest of us just stared. We couldn't shoot it, right there on his chest. If we poked it with a bayonet or something, it would probably bite him. Somebody giggled. We sat there for quite a while, while old Herbie sweated away. Finally, one of the Southern kids remembered he had a harmonica in his kit. He decided to see if he could charm the snake. Damned if it didn't work, too. He played something, <u>Lonesome Road,</u> I think it was, something sweet and slow and sad, and that sucker perked up and sort of shook himself and uncoiled off Herbie's chest and slithered off into the grass. Somebody went after it with a rifle butt, but it got away.

    Phallic symbol. That's why you picked this poem, isn't it, Norm? The joy, trying to hold the joy, and then there's that long wake of pleasure. Smiling and haunted after a morning quickie, I've known days like that. Then I'd spend the rest of the day looking at the yard, at the coils of rusty wire and the tan stacks of jerry cans and the rusting white washing machines and imagine somebody stalking me behind all that cover.

    So shall we say this is a poem about the environment? (Took you by surprise, didn't I! You didn't think this response would end up here.) An environmental poem: danger in all the industrial junk of our regular lives, while out there in the greenwood even a snake is harmless. It's all joy and desire and pleasure. That's what <u>she</u> thinks.

    He ends with denial again. The trouble with psychological denials is that they fail. You can't get rid of realities like landlords. You lie down to sleep, and the next thing you know there's a snake on your chest. For that reason, deniers like Barry may look indifferent, but often they're watching and spying and caring very much.

    That's how the environmentalism fits in. It's a paranoid suspicion of dangers in his surroundings. He identifies with both the watchers and with the violence, the way he identifies with his cats. They have eyes that can see in the dark. They're predators because they're programmed to be. Nothing personal. Just as Barry is violent without malice.

He's looking around for violence, and he's ready to counterattack: the rifle butt, the cattle prod. He isn't trying to hurt anyone else, as he sees it. He's just defending himself.

Could he have killed Trish? Yes and no. Yes, he was angry enough at her about the cats—I don't believe his denial for a minute. Yes, he'd be quite indifferent to the act. No, it would not be like him to do it by putting a poisoned tack on her chair. But this is all interpretation, intrinsic evidence, not extrinsic.

And anyway, you say you know who did it.

/Norm/

Metropolitan Buffalo Police Department

Tape Transcription   Homicide Unit

Body: *Hassler, P.*   Tape No. *840308.019*

Place: *Museum of Natural History*   Time: *3:16 p.m.*

Persons present: *Det. Lt. Rhodes, Professor Isaac Hahn*

Transcribed by: *M. Windham*

LT. RHODES: Professor Hahn?

HAHN: Yes?

LT. RHODES: I'm Detective Lieutenant Justin Rhodes. May I talk to you?

HAHN: The police!

LT. RHODES: Is that a problem?

HAHN: Goodness, no! I just can't imagine why you want to talk to *me!*

LT. RHODES: I'm investigating the death of the student in the seminar yesterday. You probably read about it.

HAHN: A dreary, dreadful thing! But what has that to do with me?

LT. RHODES: I've never been down here before, Professor Hahn, in the basement of the museum. As a boy, I used to come to the museum a lot. I remember the huge stuffed Kodiak bear, the African dioramas, the mummies, oh yes, the mummies. How they used to frighten us kids when it was winter and the sun would go down early and we were left alone with the mummies, their ivory eyes with obsidian pupils staring in the dusty twilight. Memories.

HAHN: You can hardly imagine, Lieutenant, how many people have told me about those mummies. I think every child in Erie County must have been frightened by them. But you said you were investigating the death of that poor dear girl in the English seminar?

LT. RHODES: You sound as though you knew her.

HAHN: Goodness, no, but it's so sad, so brilliant a graduate student dying so unexpectedly.

LT. RHODES: Yes. For the record, would you identify yourself into my mini-corder?

HAHN: I'm Professor Isaac Hahn. I'm a professor in the anthro department. Actually, I'm only half in anthro and half of me is assigned to the Museum of Natural History. I'm tempted to say the better half, but I don't have a better half. If you don't mind my little joke.

LT. RHODES: I came to ask you about last October's exhibit.

HAHN: You came to the right person, Lieutenant. I liaise between anthro and the museum. I set up exhibits of current work in anthropology. You see, it's down here in these basement workrooms where those exhibits come into being, Lieutenant, that you so enjoyed as a boy.

LT. RHODES: I understand from Professor Vernor, you had an exhibit last October in which you displayed a variety of poisons.

HAHN: Gracious! Are you telling me that poor girl was poisoned?

LT. RHODES: You'll be reading about it in tomorrow's newspaper.

HAHN: Poisoned. Is that a fact! So we're dealing with a murder . . . Gracious me!

LT. RHODES: The exhibit?

HAHN: It ran from October 4th to November 22nd. We're trying to bring forward to the public the true facts of the ecological crisis. We wanted to show right out front how nonindustrial peoples can distill from bark or plants or animals a variety of the drugs we use in so-called civilized medicine today. People just have to realize that when the industrial nations destroy, say, the Amazon forests to create grazing lands for Wendy's hamburgers, we may be losing species of priceless medicinal value.

LT. RHODES: Poisons?

HAHN: Poisons, too. Some of them have medicinal value, you know, like curare. That's used as a muscle relaxant.

LT. RHODES: And the exhibit? Where was it?

HAHN: We set the whole thing up in the rotunda of the museum, right up front where you'd see it when you first came in. For the centerpiece, in the middle, we had a medicine man leaning over several, oh, maybe twenty, bowls and jars containing various drugs. A big handsome mannequin with great back muscles.

LT. RHODES: Did you put real drugs in these bowls and jars?

HAHN: Good heavens, no, Lieutenant, what do you take me for? They'd have spoiled completely, out in the air like that. The medicine man has to make each batch as he needs it. They don't have our methods of storage. Dear me, no.

LT. RHODES: But you did have some real drugs in the exhibit—

HAHN: Of course. That was the other side of the story, you see, the industrialized side. We ran red ribbons from the bowls and jars to some vertical exhibit cases off on the walls around the medicine man's hut. In those cases, we put the regular bottles and pillboxes you'd actually see in a pharmacy or laboratory today. Absolute realism, you see, factory labels, seals, and all.

LT. RHODES: Now, where was the exhibit that included saxitoxin?

HAHN: Saxitoxin! Saxitoxin was a side issue so far as we were concerned, compared to the medicinal drugs.

We had the scene with the medicine man—or I suppose I should say medicine mannequin—in the middle of the rotunda, then some vertical display cases around the periphery. You know the kind of vertical case I mean, Lieutenant: big Sheetrock panels with glass portholes in them, and the exhibits sat in the cylindrical exhibit spaces behind the portholes. We put authentic modern containers of drugs derived from plants and animals, things like aloe and yucca from North America, opiates from the Middle East, medicinal teas from Peru and Colombia—we were extending the Amazon situation to species all over the earth.

LT. RHODES: And the saxitoxin, where did you put it?

HAHN: Saxitoxin doesn't come from the Amazon basin, either. You make it by grinding up thousands of butter clams that've been tainted by a red tide. It's associated with the Indians of the Pacific Northwest. So, as I say, it was very much at the edge of the exhibit geographically and intellectually, and therefore physically.

We simply placed a vial of saxitoxin in a porthole in one of these vertical display cases. Behind the vial one of the museum's artists had painted a truly handsome Kwakiutl Indian, looking out over Vancouver Sound. All through the water was this brownish red stain, and then the sky and the water darkened to a blue near the horizon, so that you had this band of red and a band of blue and this strong, stern Indian profile looking at this—

LT. RHODES: Was that all?

HAHN: On the right side of the porthole we had a longish explanation of saxitoxin. How it relaxes the muscles to the point of death, how it kills quickly, how the CIA uses it, what shall I say, to ease the pain of captured agents. Actually, I have the placard in storage. Would you like to come take a peek?

LT. RHODES: Your card told the person looking at the exhibit that this was a quick and painless poison?

HAHN: That's right.

LT. RHODES: And you put a vial of real saxitoxin in the exhibit.

HAHN: Yes, indeed we did.

LT. RHODES: Why did it have to be genuine?

HAHN: Credibility, Lieutenant, and ethics, for that matter. Our presentations require absolute realism. *I* require it. You have to use authentic artifacts, otherwise people begin to think of what you're telling them as just some kind of fairy story—a con. We're telling the truth, scientific truth.

LT. RHODES: But you didn't use real drugs in the exhibit in the center.

HAHN: That was different. If we'd used real plant and animal drugs, they'd have gone bad. They'd have festered and smelled. Yuck, Lieutenant, yuck.

LT. RHODES: And you got your saxitoxin from Professor Vernor.

HAHN: Yes, only established researchers in toxicology can get saxitoxin, and we hardly qualify as that, do we? Strictly amateurs.

LT. RHODES: What's that supposed to mean?

HAHN: Oh, just a joke about the way some people use drugs recreationally. Probably you don't find that amusing, Lieutenant. Anyway, Pop—that's what we call him, Pop—lent us his small vial of saxitoxin.

LT. RHODES: Now what did you do with this vial after you dismantled the exhibit?

HAHN: We brought it straight back to Pop Vernor. He was very particular about that.

LT. RHODES: Had the vial been tampered with?

HAHN: When we put the vial in the exhibit, there was sealing wax around the top. When we took it out, there was the same sealing wax.

LT. RHODES: The same? Can you be sure?

HAHN: It seemed to be the same, Lieutenant, but we weren't looking for any alteration. We had no reason to, did we?

LT. RHODES: Would it have been possible for someone to steal the saxitoxin from your exhibit?

HAHN: No, certainly not. The vertical display units had glassed-in openings, like portholes. The drugs stood on little glass shelves in these portholes in the vertical display cases. The faceplates were screwed right on.

LT. RHODES: So that anyone with a screwdriver could open them?

HAHN: Hardly. We do have guards in this museum.

LT. RHODES: Two guards for three floors.

HAHN: How did you know that?

LT. RHODES: I noticed, as I came in.

HAHN: That's only on weekdays.

LT. RHODES: So, couldn't someone have come in on a weekday, waited until there were no people in the exhibit, and opened the case? Couldn't someone simply have gone behind and opened it from the rear?

HAHN: You're joking!

LT. RHODES: How was the case secured at the back?

HAHN: For exhibits that don't contain anything valuable, we use the less expensive cases that just latch at the back. These were latched.

LT. RHODES: So somebody could simply have unlatched the back and taken the saxitoxin!

HAHN: But they didn't! After the exhibit closed, we still had it. We gave it back. No one took it.

LT. RHODES: Let's just suppose, professor, that someone looked closely at the saxitoxin on display and went home and duplicated the bottle with just water or glycerine in it. They used sealing wax that could be bought at any stationer's to make a seal. Let's suppose they then came to the exhibit a second time carrying the counterfeit bottle. One way or another, they open the case, leave the substitute and take the original. Why not?

HAHN: Why not! Because it's so unnecessary. Why go to all this trouble to get saxitoxin when you could use cyanide or aconite or any one of a number of poisons from any chem lab in the university?

LT. RHODES: Because your placard told them this was just the kind of poison they wanted. Effective in tiny quantities. Very fast.

HAHN: Well, we had to explain the exhibit, didn't we?

LT. RHODES: Professor, are you sure that, every day of the exhibit, the vial you were showing was the same one that was put into the exhibit on the first day?

HAHN: I think you're being unfair. How could I possibly know such a thing?

LT. RHODES: Could you be certain that the vial wasn't switched with a dummy at some point during the exhibition and then switched back?

HAHN: Well of course I'm not certain. I'd have to be psychic to be certain of that.

LT. RHODES: Would it have been possible for someone to remove the sealing wax, take some of the poison, and reseal the bottle?

HAHN: Possible? Of course it's possible. Anything's possible.

LT. RHODES: I think you were negligent, professor, putting a dangerous poison out where someone could steal it.

HAHN: Well I'm very sorry, Lieutenant, I just can't be responsible for that. If people take it into their heads to murder other people, I can't be responsible for that. I'm here to make exhibits that educate the public and that's what I do and that's all I'm going to say about it.

Have you finished with me?

LT. RHODES: Yes, professor. I'll find my way out. Past the mummies. END OF THIS SECTION OF TAPE END OF THIS SECTION OF TAPE END OF

LT. RHODES: *Comment.* What a tweedy little twit! He fusses over all these quote realistic unquote details, but he can't see that there's a real world beyond his exhibits, in which people find poisons useful. Clearly, this exhibit would've told anyone looking for a poison the properties of saxitoxin, and they could easily have stolen it here. Now I have no way to trace the person who stole it. It could be anybody who visited this exhibit.

I suppose I can break out the pictures Badger got me and ask the guards if they remember any of them. Fat chance! But what other possibilities do I have?

I'll also have to check Vernor's sample and make sure that it's still saxitoxin. No. It has to be, because he and Welder used it as a control in their analysis yesterday. But maybe some of it's missing. I'll have to call him. Oh joy.

Metropolitan Buffalo Police Department

Tape Transcription   Homicide Unit

Body: *Hassler, P.*   Tape No. *840308.019*
Place: *Buffalo Natural History Museum*   Time: *3:52 p.m.*
Persons present: *Det. Lt. Rhodes, Darryl Jones,*
        Terence O'Malley

                                                       Transcribed by: *M. Windham*

LT. RHODES: Mr. Jones, Mr. O'Malley, you've probably read how we're taping all our interviews with citizens.

JONES: And a damn good thing, too. I'm Darryl Jones, and I'm a guard at the museum here.

O'MALLEY: Another fucking waste of the taxpayers' money. I'm O'Malley, guard. That enough?

LT. RHODES: Your badge says "Terence."

O'MALLEY: Yeah, my friends call me Ter.

LT. RHODES: I'm checking into the death of that student who dropped dead in a class yesterday—you may have read about it in the paper?

JONES: Yeah.

LT. RHODES: Okay. I want you to think back to last October-November. There was an exhibit in the main hall about drugs—

o'malley: I knew it! All those damn students are taking drugs.

lt. rhodes: Not this kind of drug, Mr. O'Malley. Anyway, tell me if you remember the exhibit.

o'malley: That's a long time back, October.

jones: Yeah, Lieutenant, I remember that show.

lt. rhodes: I'd like you to look at these pictures and see if you remember any of these people attending that exhibit.

o'malley: Jeezus, Lieutenant. You expect me to remember individual visitors from way back in *October!*

lt. rhodes: It's a long shot, I know. Give it a try, will you, Mr. O'Malley? Here's the first one.

o'malley: No, I don't recognize him. He looks like some kind of foreigner.

lt. rhodes: As it happens, yes. How about this one? He's very big, muscular. That doesn't show in this head-and-shoulders picture.

o'malley: No.

jones: C'mon, O'Malley. He used to *work* here, for crissake. Remember? Moving those big stones around? Yeah, I remember him.

lt. rhodes: So he was around a lot? Did he show up at this exhibit?

jones: He worked here a week maybe. This exhibit? That I don't remember.

lt. rhodes: How about this one?

jones: Hey, I recognize her! She's easy to remember. And a pleasure to remember. Yeah, she came to that exhibit, more than once, I think, and I remember because I haven't seen her before or since. Though I'd like to.

o'malley: Cut the crap, Darryl. You're just saying that to get my goat. Yeah, I recognize her, Lieutenant. And I, goddam it, have a right to.

jones: Don't give me any of that cracker jive, O'Malley. If I think a white chick is fine and foxy, I'll damn well say so.

lt. rhodes: Gentlemen, gentlemen, let's stick to identifications. Let me say for the recording that you both have recognized Anne Glendish as attending that particular exhibition. And more than once, you said. I've got these in alphabetical order. How about this one?

jones: Yeah, she's easy, too. A big woman like that. Not hard to remember. Yeah, all those beads and stuff.

o'malley: Yes, I remember her too.

lt. rhodes: You're sure? Okay. You've identified Patricia Hassler, the dead woman. Did she come more than once? Like Glendish?

o'malley: Maybe, maybe not, I'm not sure.

jones: Me neither.

lt. rhodes: Let's keep going. This one?

jones: I can't be sure. He's a grown-up. The students stand out, because we don't get so many students here. But this guy—

O'MALLEY: Jeezus, what a homely guy. I hope I never look like that. No, I don't remember him.

LT. RHODES: This one?

O'MALLEY: Does he always wear that bandanna? I've never seen him before.

JONES: Me either.

O'MALLEY: No.

LT. RHODES: How about this woman?

JONES: Another grown-up. No, no bells.

O'MALLEY: Me neither.

LT. RHODES: This one?

O'MALLEY: Bingo! He was with the good-looking girl.

JONES: That's right. I remember him because he was showing off for her, scooting around the exhibits and stuff. I told him to calm down, I remember.

LT. RHODES: Okay, you've identified Ann Glendish and Paul Penza. And you're right, he's the good-looking one's boyfriend. Did he come more than once?

JONES: *She* did. And I remember seeing her without him, so maybe he only came once.

O'MALLEY: Me, I don't remember.

LT. RHODES: One more.

O'MALLEY: He's not as young as the others. No, I don't remember him.

JONES: Nor do I. Wait a minute. I've seen him before. I've seen him at that little theater on Genesee. He's an actor, isn't he? Yeah. I recognize him. He played Mack the Knife once.

LT. RHODES: And did you see him at this exhibit?

JONES: I sure did. I remember now. I remember thinking at the time, I've seen this guy before. Yes, he was here for that show.

LT. RHODES: Yes, he said he saw it. Okay, then. You've identified five of these people as being here at the drug exhibition. Let me spin through these remaining pictures once again. Concentrate. This one, the foreigner?

BOTH: No.

LT. RHODES: The prof?

BOTH: No.

JONES: Is that what he is? He doesn't look like it.

LT. RHODES: This guy?

BOTH: No.

LT. RHODES: This woman?

BOTH: No.

LT. RHODES: Okay, that's it then. Thank you very much, gentlemen. You can go back to work now.END OF THIS SECTION OF TAPE END OF THIS SECTION OF TAPE END OF THIS SECTION OF TAPE END OF THIS

LT. RHODES: *Comment.* They identified Ebenfeld, Glendish, Hassler herself, Penza, and Sisley. But it's all shaky, of course. Except for Ebenfeld. He had more opportunity than is good for him. As for the rest, it's a good six months ago. A routine encounter or no encounter at all. And they must see hundreds of people in the course of a month. And I have no way of asking about the interloper. So I still can't be sure where the poison came from.

I think I'll go back to campus. Holland has probably got some more readings for me. And I'd better call Vernor. This damn case simply won't come together.

Metropolitan Buffalo Police Department

Tape Transcription   Homicide Unit

Body: *Hassler, P.*   Tape No. *840308.019*
Date of Event: *March 8, 1984*   Time: *4:17 p.m.*
Place: *Telephone Call*
Persons present: *Det. Lt. Rhodes, Professor Harold Vernor*

                                            Transcribed by: *M. Windham*

LT. RHODES: Lt. Rhodes, M.B.P.D. here. May I speak to Professor Vernor, please? It's urgent.
SECRETARY: I saw him just a minute ago. I'll see if I can find him.
    [Long pause.]
SECRETARY: I don't see him, Lieutenant. I'm sorry. No, here he comes. Professor Vernor, a telephone call for you from Lieutenant Rhodes.
VERNOR: Who's that? The Army?
SECRETARY: Lieutenant Rhodes, the policeman you talked to this morning? About the murder?
VERNOR: The murder.
SECRETARY: The girl who was poisoned?
VERNOR: Yes, of course, do you think I don't remember?
SECRETARY: No, sir.
VERNOR: Lieutenant, what can I do for you? No, don't get up. I'll just sit on the corner of your desk here. Just sit there, Miss— Lieutenant, you still there?

LT. RHODES: Professor Vernor, I've just finished talking with Isaac Hahn about that exhibit he had up in October. He said he borrowed a sample of saxitoxin from you.

VERNOR: Saxitoxin! Isaac Hahn? I wouldn't give Ike Hahn saxitoxin! That's very bad stuff. That's the poison that killed that girl in Holland's seminar, you know.

LT. RHODES: Yes, I know. In fact, you and I were talking about that this morning.

VERNOR: Yes, of course. Did you think I didn't remember?

LT. RHODES: Not at all. That's why I called you, in fact.

VERNOR: Oh. My field isn't saxitoxin, though, but tetrodotoxin, more generally, the neurotoxins derived from fish.

LT. RHODES: Yes, but you very generously helped us identify the poison that killed Patricia Hassler.

VERNOR: Yes. Welder. That fella ought to get his own autoanalyzer, stop using ours. Yes, we used the mouse blastoma test. Very new. Very good. Yes, of course I remember all that. Did you think I didn't?

LT. RHODES: Of course not. We greatly appreciated your help, and we're going to mention you in the press release.

VERNOR: Good. That's the way to keep citizens cooperating, Lieutenant. Give 'em lots of credit. Now, if you don't mind, I've got to go round the lab here and—

LT. RHODES: Professor Vernor, what I'm calling you about is the vial of saxitoxin you lent Isaac Hahn for the exhibit last fall at the science museum.

VERNOR: Of course I remember. You have to be very careful with that stuff. I lent the Natural History Museum our sample. It's just a couple grams, but that's enough to clobber an elephant, and we got it back. Yes indeedy we got it back. You've got to be careful with that stuff.

LT. RHODES: I gave you a vial this morning that seemed to be a copy of the one you gave Professor Hahn—you were going to check it over?

VERNOR: Vial? Oh yes, I remember. A fake. I spotted the fake. Check number wrong. Yes, I spotted that right away.

LT. RHODES: Yes, but you were going to have someone in your lab see if it had ever contained saxitoxin.

VERNOR: Oh, no. That vial was a fake.

LT. RHODES: But someone in your lab was going to make sure it had never contained saxitoxin. Chinese fella.

VERNOR: Oh, we've got a lot of Chinese fellas. Just about everybody in this lab is oriental now.

LT. RHODES: Did he check?

VERNOR: Yes, of course, he checked. I told you he was going to, didn't I? Checked what?

LT. RHODES: Whether the fake vial had ever contained saxitoxin?

VERNOR: Let me go ask him. *[Three minute pause.]*

LT. RHODES: Should I just hang up and start over? I guess if I've invested this much time . . .

VERNOR: Lieutenant? Still there? Yes, just as I thought. I talked to Mr. Ah.

LT. RHODES: Yes?

VERNOR: Ah.

LT. RHODES: Ah? I don't get you, Professor.

VERNOR: I just talked to Mr. Ah.

LT. RHODES: Mr. Ah?

VERNOR: That's right. Ah Sing. Fella checking that vial you brought in. Little hard to follow his English, but I got it. He says he scraped off some of that dried stuff at the bottom of the vial and ran it through the autoanalyzer. You fellas ought to get your own, you know—

LT. RHODES: And what did Mr. Ah find?

VERNOR: Iodine. Old-fashioned iodine.

LT. RHODES: Iodine!

VERNOR: That's right. It's a poison, too, you know. But not lethal like saxitoxin. That's very dangerous stuff. It only takes a little bit—

LT. RHODES: Let me try another possibility on you, Professor Vernor. Maybe someone tampered with the vial while it was in Hahn's exhibit.

VERNOR: Tampered with the vial! I don't see how that could have happened. The vial came back sealed, just as I sent it out. I remember that very clearly. Oh yes, very clearly. We checked, you know. I may be fuddly, but I'm not fuddly about saxitoxin.

LT. RHODES: We imagine it this way. Someone broke the seal, opened the vial, and took some of the poison out. Maybe dipped the thumbtack in, maybe several thumbtacks. However. Then that someone sealed the vial back up so that Hahn and you'd think it was untouched.

VERNOR: Well.

LT. RHODES: Well?

VERNOR: Well, that's an interesting theory, Lieutenant. Do you have any proof of it?

LT. RHODES: That's why I'm calling you, Professor Vernor, to see if we can prove it.

VERNOR: Now, Lieutenant, you already took up a lot of my time yesterday identifying this saxitoxin. And my specialty's not saxitoxin, you know, but tetrodotoxin.

LT. RHODES: The Police Department greatly appreciates what you're doing for us, professor. We think we're very lucky to be able to call on a world-famous expert in these poisons.

VERNOR: Oh?

LT. RHODES: Oh, yes, everyone I've talked to about this says you're the man to consult.

VERNOR: Well, I suppose I've achieved a certain reputation in the field. So, another case of poisoning? Is it tetrodotoxin this time?

LT. RHODES: No, we want to check that vial you lent Professor Hahn for his exhibit at the science museum, the vial of saxitoxin. You have to be careful with that stuff, and we want to find out just how careful Hahn was.

VERNOR: Hahn? Isaac Hahn? Ike's perfectly honest—if not overly bright. I don't think he'd have taken any saxitoxin. But you think somebody else might have tampered with that vial.

LT. RHODES: That's right, Professor Vernor. We want to find out if any of the poison had been removed when Hahn gave you back the vial. Is the amount in the vial the same as when you gave it to him?

VERNOR: The amount in the vial— Ah. That's hard to say. The vial orginally contained two grams. That's a very small amount to the layperson, a little less than half a teaspoonful, but, like I say, this stuff packs one helluva wallop. A fella'd only have to take out a few milligrams to work that thumbtack trick.

LT. RHODES: The same amount, Professor?

VERNOR: We'd have to weigh it before and after, wouldn't we? We have the word of the company that provided us with this sample that it was two grams, but we don't know how accurately they weighed it. Then I've used some on the original experiments I got the sample for. I used some more with Robbie Welder when we checked out your samples.

Now, when we deal with substances as toxic as saxitoxin, we keep track of how much we use. We weigh it before and after, but our measurements might not be accurate to more than ten or twenty milligrams. You know how it is, you get in a hurry— Then some could have evaporated while the vial was open. There could have been a microscopic leak through the stopper. You see, the amounts needed are so small that we wouldn't be able to carry out a differential measure. Just subtracting what we know we used from the amount we started with—just as a matter of accuracy, it wouldn't necessarily match up to what is in the vial now.

You understand about the cumulation of errors? If the first measurement was good to plus or minus 10 milligrams, then you can never be more accurate than 10 milligrams after that. You understand?

LT. RHODES: Would you try, anyway? Maybe the murderer stole more than was necessary.

VERNOR: Would I try? Well, sure. That's no big deal. I'll get one of these oriental kids in the lab to have a try at it. We'll have to dig out the original weighings.

Call the company to find their margin of error. Weigh it again, under maximum safety procedures. They're very careful, these oriental fellas. Nasty stuff, though, only takes a couple of milligrams. Just smelling it'll kill you.

LT. RHODES: —and you'll call me back?

VERNOR: Of course, Lieutenant, I'll call you back. I don't want to go all the way down to headquarters, do I? That's why Alexander Graham Bell invented the telephone. I'll call you back within, oh, a couple of hours.

LT. RHODES: You want my telephone number?

VERNOR: Of course I want your telephone number. How am I going to call you back if I don't have your number?

LT. RHODES: 3-9-2-7-3-3-2. That gets my pager, and then I can call you back.

VERNOR: Good thing these pagers. Get paged, you can call back, right away, don't have to wait for messages. Good-bye. Yes, good-bye.END OF THIS SECTION OF TAPE END OF THIS SECTION OF TAPE END OF THIS

LT. RHODES: *Comment.* Could I establish that the saxitoxin came from the museum vial? Does saxitoxin have an individuality, like different kinds of paper or glass? Given the murk of Vernor's thought processes, it could take me a week to find out, and does it really add anything? This has got to be where the saxitoxin came from.

State University of New York at Buffalo
Department of English

March 8, 1984

Dear Justin,

Here's my reading of Amy Lemaire, although that scarcely seems necessary, since she's served herself up so clearly. She explains why in the opening paragraph, when she describes herself as a compulsive giver. She is so right. You won't find the other students telling things quite so close to themselves.

The opposite side of her giving is that she wants to be given to. That translates into dependency. Amy seeks and sees relationships in terms of trust and vulnerability—as you'll see from her "trait" response.

A theme for Amy? Simply, to give and to receive.

Here's her "trait" response.

English 6121

Dear Everybody:

I'm glad Norm didn't ask us for something that we
<u>didn't</u> want the seminar to know. I'd have blurted it out
right on the spot. The something about me that you ought
to know is that I'm a compulsive giver. Sundays, I have
to make sure I don't take all my money to church, because
when the plate comes by I'd put my last dollar in it.
These days, busy as I am with this seminar and everything
else, I've been working nights in the Salvation Army
cleaning up the place so that homeless people can sleep
there on cots. I don't say this so that you'll think I'm
a saint or even a particularly nice person. I just plain
enjoy giving to people. I can't not do it.

It doesn't take much imagination, particularly in this
crowd, to see that that could have gotten me in some
difficult situations. Yes, but enough said about that.
Where it helped me was when I worked as a flight attendant on USAir. The rest of the girls--women we'd say now,
and rightly so--would get tired of coffee, tea, or me,
and quit after a year or so. I went on and on. I loved
it. I loved the squawling kids, the lame old people, the
lecherous businessmen, the drunks, the dazed-out students, the ones in a hurry because they were missing a
connection, the ones in a fury because their flights were
delayed or cancelled--I had a smile for each and every
one. It must be something from my family, with whom I'm
still very close, by the way. I didn't even mind shut-
tling from Buffalo to Cincinnati to Cleveland to Minne-
apolis to St. Louis, from one gray, beat-up midwestern
city to another. I liked what I was doing. I enjoyed the
camaraderie and the parties and the feeling of belonging
with the other stewardesses and the pilots and the rest
of the crew. I was having a great time.

After seven years, I'd gotten bonus flight miles
enough to take me around the world, and I got a leave to
do just that. Used Air (that's what we used to call it)
had an agreement with B.O.A.C., and I took my miles with
them.

The first leg of the trip, Kennedy to Heathrow, was
the best, and it also turned out to be the only leg,
because I met Herbert, who was a flight attendant on

B.O.A.C. We met in Heathrow Airport, because I absentmindedly went right off to the crew's locker room instead
of the passengers' waiting room. We struck up a conversation. I'd never met a "steward" before, and I was fascinated by all the places he'd been. I was fascinated, too,
to find a man who liked the job for the same reasons I
did plus others. Herbert had a real sense of the craft of
what he was doing, as well as the helping part of it.

Instead of going on to Karachi or Shanghai or wherever, I took a flat in London and Herbert and I became
lovers. Indeed we became engaged. One of us had to work,
though, and Herbert earned more than I did, so he flew
his regular route, to Bombay, and I quit Used Air. We'd
been together for about six months, when the next thing I
knew all I had of Herbert was his body in a box and a
picture on my bureau (it's still there). He had a heart
attack, collapsed, and died on the job, in flight, somewhere over the Indian Ocean. At the funeral, I noticed
that Herbert had some friends who dressed oddly and sim-
pered in a manner I recognized from Greenwich Village.
One of them told me--Didn't you know, luv?--that Herbert
was gay, or, more properly, bi. Less properly.

I wouldn't have minded if he'd told me himself, but he
hadn't, and I never knew whether he'd stopped with his
other, male lovers when he met me or not. I couldn't ask.
Anyway, I felt betrayed. I felt that I'd lost not only
Herbert but even the time that I'd had with him. It was
all gone. If only he'd told me he was bi, I could have
taken that, but when he kept it from me, I felt as though
he'd never trusted me. I told him everything about me—he
never even had to ask. But he kept the truth about himself from me. He'd never been in love the way I had. All
I could feel was total loss, and I hit rock bottom.

I won't go into details. If you can imagine them
luridly enough, you won't be far wrong. Eventually, I had
to move back in with my family here in Buffalo, or there
wouldn't have been anything left of me. I always liked
reading, even poetry, and my dad said, Why don't you take
a course at the university? I did, I loved it, I did
well, they gave me my B.A., they admitted me to graduate
school, and here I am.

What I didn't anticipate was that the study of literature wouldn't be the study of literature. It would be
this dreary "theory." That's why I'm taking this seminar.
It has to do with real people reading books, the students

I serve, whom I enjoy so much. It's so much more fulfill-
ing than dishing out Used Air's toy food. If only this
department will grant me a Ph.D., I'll go on giving the
students my best. They need me, and I need them. Right
now, that union card is what I want more than anything.
There are times, when things get in the way, when I think
I could kill to get it. As I say, I like to give people
things, and when I can't, I go to pieces.

   Do you see what I mean about her relationships of trust and vulnerability? She needs the homeless people, her passengers, or her students, as
much as they need her. She depends on her family, on religion, on Herbert.
Herbert's not telling her was a failure of trust, of the mutual dependency that
she so needs in relationships, and that's why it devastated her.
   Something else that follows from her compulsive giving is the ease with
which she identifies with others. Here's her "snake" response. Watch how
she projects herself into the snake's mind and body.

English 6121   February 15, 1984
                                          Amy

   How do I feel when I read this poem? A little bit
scared, a little bit repelled. Scared, more. I don't
really like snakes but I'm not repelled by them. I could
take them or leave them--and, come to think of it, that's
exactly what Levertov did.
   "You hissed to me." I hear that as "you kissed me." I
don't know why, and I can't get it out of my head, but
that's what I hear. You kiss me, I kiss you. A poison
kiss? Maybe no poison. Maybe no kiss.
   But, if not, what did the snake get out of this, I
wonder? What passed between them? She says she got "joy"
and "a long wake of pleasure." But what did this feel
like for the snake? Did she give the snake any joy, any
pleasure? She could have killed that snake, snapped its
back like snapping a whip.
   She felt the weight of the snake. Did the snake feel
the lift she gave to that weight as pleasure, as a kind
of exhilaration? Maybe. She got a weight, he got a lift.
Seems fair. (I guess I automatically assume the snake is
a he--Freud was right, Norm.)
   She speaks of the snake's scaliness. The snake would

have felt her warm skin as just the opposite of his cold
dryness. It would have looked different, a pink against
his green and gold. She talks about the snake as gold and
silver, something precious. Maybe he felt the difference
of her, her smooth, squeezy human skin. Maybe he found
that just as alien to his scaliness as she found his
scaliness alien to her skin. Maybe he thought it precious
for that reason. Maybe for snakes gold isn't interesting,
because they see a lot of that, but warm, pink, stretchy
skin is, because they don't.

So with the warmth and the moisture on her skin (if she
was sweating. I sure as hell would have been). Maybe her
warmth would have seemed precious to him because that's
what snakes prey on, nice mammalian warmth. And her size
would have been like the big rock candy mountain, a whole
worldful of delicious, warm-blooded food. Maybe the snake
did feel pleasure, then. Maybe that's something she gave
the snake--whatever the snake gave her.

So there's a moment of pure and total sensual presence, they're almost at one, and then they separate. She
says she's haunted, as if the ghost of the snake stayed
with her in her dark morning. I say she's really alone.
I'd feel terribly, terribly alone. At least I would if it
weren't a snake.

I said at the beginning Amy's theme is to give and to receive. That's why
she reads Levertov as giving to the snake as well as being given to by the
snake. To put that in psychological terms, she identifies with the one to whom
she's giving. She imagines what being lifted up might feel like to the snake.
She envisions the snake's looking at Levertov's pink flesh or sniffing her
warmth and feeling her sweat. That's part of her satisfaction in giving, to
share vicariously in the feeling of being given to.

Really, then, when Amy is in the act of giving, the boundaries between
herself and the other person come down. That's why she sees Levertov's
moment with the snake as a total presence. Amy can imagine herself as
both of them. She's doubly there. Look at the two "Freudian slips" she tells
us about. She keeps hearing, "You hissed to me," as "You kissed me." Mouth
to mouth, Amy is both of them. Or her walking into the crew's locker room at
Heathrow Airport. She's both passenger and crew.

She can feel the satisfaction. She can also feel the fear the helpless
one must feel at the possibility that the giving will break down. Failure of
dependency she sees as very dangerous. Levertov, after all, could have
snapped the snake's back. If the giving fails, Amy can feel not only frustrated

but aggressive, since not giving shades over into killing. She tells us in the "trait" paper that she could kill to get a Ph.D. and continue teaching.

But, but, but. You're not to read that as a threat to kill Patricia Hassler. Just the opposite. It would be more like Amy to come to some kind of accommodation, some mutual exchange, even with someone as difficult as Hassler. As she does, in effect, with that snake. Yours,

/Norm/

Metropolitan Buffalo Police Department

Tape Transcription   Homicide Unit

Body: *Hassler, P.*	Tape No. *840308.022*
Place: *Telephone call*	Time: *4:54 p.m.*
Persons present: *Det. Lt. Rhodes to Det. Sgt. Yorrick*	
W. Sisley, N. Holland	
	Transcribed by: *S. Moreno*

LT. RHODES: You're not easy to get hold of, Yorrick. Why didn't you answer your phone?

SGT. YORRICK: Sorry, Lieutenant, I was out walking from Rhodes Hall to Main Street and back. I did it a couple of times.

LT. RHODES: And?

SGT. YORRICK: Seven minutes. Give or take a half minute.

LT. RHODES: Okay, I'll put that in the old computer and see if I can figure out who went where on Wednesday morning. Thanks, Mort. END OF THIS SECTION OF TAPE END OF THIS SECTION OF TAPE END OF THIS SEC

from the journal of Norman Holland

The morning had already begun badly when I got Romola's note. Mostly it's Rhodes. He's a steady pressure, working me this way and that. First he

scared the bejeezus out of me. Just that thin rubber mat had been between me and certain death—at least that was the way it seemed to me. Then that turned out to be just playacting. Next I had to spend the time after the meeting writing up Glendish for him, and he hadn't even read Sisley and Ebenfeld yet, although I worked late to get them done last night.

Then he yanks me off to Wally's house . . .

The morning's mail: a rejected manuscript, an advertisement for a rival's book, and the note from Romola, could I please see her in her office before the day was over, perhaps at 4:30. Smooth as syrup she was, but I knew what was coming.

Around 4:20, I finished writing up Amy Lemaire and put it in Justin's mail-box. Penza still to go—I looked over his papers for a few minutes, then duly presented myself at the department office. As always, appointment or no, I was told to wait in the straight chairs facing the secretaries. "Dr. Badger is on the phone to the American Council of Learned Societies, Dr. Holland. She asked if you could wait a few minutes." Big deal!, I glumly thought, and realized that that was exactly what I was supposed to think.

After what she must have judged a suitably humbling interval, I heard Badger's voice on the intercom, "Professor Holland can come in now." I man-aged to get to the door before the secretary's demeaning wave, strode in, and sat abruptly down in the chair facing my statuesque, silver-coifed boss.

"You wanted to see me."

"Yes, Norman. It's about this terrible business of poor Tricia Hassler."

"I thought it would be. Difficult as she was, no one would wish this on her."

"But evidently someone did, Norman. Someone was sufficiently angry at Tricia to kill her. If only this had happened in some ordinary seminar . . ."

I couldn't let that go by. "Well, of course, it could have, couldn't it? It could have happened in any seminar at all. Her death has nothing to do with the kind of seminar this was." Mentally, I crossed my fingers. I believed what I said, but one worries.

"I know, Norman, but it didn't happen in any other seminar. It happened in your *seminar, the Delphi seminar. Norman, the dean is very concerned. We're in a difficult position. Sooner or later the press will get wind of what kind of seminar this was. They and the president and the trustees will ask all sorts of difficult questions. Why doesn't this English professor just teach Shakespeare as he ought to? He isn't qualified to do this touchy-feely stuff. Sooner or later someone was bound to go over the edge, and he couldn't man-age it."*

"So? Romola, you know as well as I why I do what I do. I've written half-

a-dozen articles explaining how readers make meaning and why it's important for the future teachers we're training to have some idea of how their own minds work." To the extent they do work—inevitably, that thought flashed through the old psyche. "Besides, we don't know that the killer was someone in the seminar. We don't know that someone went over the edge. So far as my teaching is concerned, I've had psychiatrists sit in on the class and okay it. I've written this method up, and people all over the country are emulating it."

"Oh I know that, Norman. I do know. And I do admire your ideas and your work. But it's Dean Hedge. He's the one that's raising these questions."

"Well, if you know, Romola, why don't you explain it to him? I've been doing these Delphi seminars for years, and they've been a great success. Students have written me that this seminar has changed their lives, for God's sake! Besides, let's not forget that you've okayed my Delphi seminars semester after semester. Cancelling them now wouldn't look too good for you either." (Blessed inspiration!)

"Please, Norman, please don't *be angry, and* don't *misunderstand me. I'm on your side. I really am. The department doesn't* have *to announce next year's classes for another couple of weeks. I can see there might be problems whichever move we make* right now. *Just promise me you'll think about what I've said."*

I'd pushed the right button. "Yes, Romola, I'll think about what you've said." I felt like a little boy being forced by his mother to promise to be good.

"Thank you, Norman. Be well. And I am really terribly, terribly *sorry about the Hassler affair."*

As I left the office, she buzzed her secretary to come in for dictation, and I began to imagine what she'd write. "Dear Dean Hedge: I have brought up with the faculty member in question the concerns I broached to you after the chairs' meeting last week. You will remember I was worried about this man's teaching methods. The tragic death of Patricia Hassler suggests that my concerns were not unwarranted. He remains adamant, however. Can I have your advice on this? And perhaps your voice at some point?"

Yes, I'd had enough memos from Romola to imagine her style. She'd be smiling now, thinking ahead to her chat with the dean and how she could use her "concerns" to push her career along. She's been carrying on a flirtation with our glamor-boy blow-dried president. A telephone call from her to him, a troubled hesitancy in the voice, a particularly liquid set of vowels wrapped round her judgments on "Delphi" teaching, and Hedge would find himself having to answer awkward questions. I'll bet she's warming to this bonus from Hassler's death. We should set up a pool on when she becomes dean. I give poor old Hedge about another two years.

Metropolitan Buffalo Police Department

Tape Transcription   Homicide Unit

Body: *Hassler, P.*   Tape No. *840308.022*
Place: *Telephone call*   Time: *5:35 p.m.*
Persons present: *F. Vernor to Det. Lt. Rhodes*

Transcribed by: *S. Moreno*

VERNOR: Hey Lieutenant!

LT. RHODES: Professor Vernor.

VERNOR: That's right. Hey, you're some kind of hard to get hold of.

LT. RHODES: Me?

VERNOR: Yes, you. Who else am I talking to?

LT. RHODES: Anyway, I'm back in the English Department now and I'm taping this call.

VERNOR: What's that?

LT. RHODES: I'm taping this call.

VERNOR: Why are you doing that? Well, never mind. I just thought you might need this in a hurry.

LT. RHODES: What did you find out?

VERNOR: We checked the weight we've got now against the two grams we started with less the amounts we've recorded that we used in various experiments. Six times we've used that stuff. Dangerous, you know. Inconclusive. I said it would be. We should have 1.376 grams, and we've got 1.233. That means there are 143 milligrams missing. That's enough to do the job all right, but we can't say for sure that it came out of this vial. The errors in the original measurements are too large. You know error theory, don't you?

LT. RHODES: In a way, it's my profession. Okay, I hear you. I guess we'll just have to put it down as a possible source. Possible. Thanks for your trouble, Professor Vernor. I really appreciate what you've done for us.

VERNOR: Call me anytime, Sonny. And don't forget the press release.END OF THIS SECTION OF TAPE END OF THIS SECTION OF TAPE END OF

LT. RHODES: *Comment.* I wish I could be absolutely sure this was the source. It would connect everything up nicely. At least it's still a possibility and it's the *only* possibility—unless Will Sisley is lying.

State University of New York at Buffalo
Department of English

March 8, 1984

Dear Justin,

Here are Paul Penza's squibs. Have fun! I think you will. Did I tell you the creative writing people think he's their hottest property? They see a great future for him, another Barnes or Barthelme or Barth. Yes, I can see him making a brilliant career with a special language-y fiction, more schematic than human, though.

His writing for the seminar displaces human issues to language or, as he phrases the matter, language games. Like Anne Glendish (but different), he sees himself as a performer, people watching him, as he comes up with this or that verbal turn.

See what you think. By this time, you should be pretty good at this yourself.

English 6121

February 8
Pee Pee

"A feature or characteristic of yours that you would like the seminar to know about." Oh, how meticulous our Norm is with this delicate assignment. (Except for that final preposition. Wouldn't "about which you would like the seminar to know" have been just a tad more professional and professorial? Oh well.) A "feature." That could be a cleft chin (à la Kirk and Michael Douglas) or some especially glowing auburn hair or a particularly cute <u>retroussé</u> nose (perhaps turned up under the plastic surgeon's expensive little mallet). But especially attractive, an inducement. "Feature" is the plus word, although its root in Latin *factura* (a making) conveys a touch of the artificial or at least the self-made. Then "characteristic," the generic, neutral catchall basket of a term (which my <u>American Heritage</u> sez means "feature," which, of course, takes us back to where we started, but that's the way of dictionaries, isn't it?).

I know you think you know what I'm going to say. With a pirouette, a forward somersault, and a cartwheel, he came up laughing, hands high in the air, centered in the

ring, the spotlights beaming down, the tinsel on his
costume glinting in the blue glare, the faces of the
audience dim blobs behind the starry figure of the performer, all eyes upon him, standing there, his arms
raised in triumph. "I am a writer," he shouted, and his
voice echoed in the vast tent. "Write her." "WRITE her."
"Write HER." "Right her." "Rite. Er." And after that
last, faint, questioning echo, he hesitated and did not
answer, his arms came down, the klieg light fizzled in a
shower of blue sparks . . .

I'm not going to say all that, because you already
know all that. I'm going to tell you something you don't
know. I work nights at the Crisis Intervention Center,
a.k.a. Suicide Prevention Center, a.k.a. Panic Management
Center, a.k.a Rescueds Rescuing Rescuers. Call it whatever you like, nights we sit there and the big red pointy
pilot lights oddly added to the telephones flash on, and
we pick up. Just before we pick up, we have a momentary
wonder, What is this one going to be? Is this a boy with
his speech thick and his syntax sliding and his pronouns
lost and wandering who has ODed? Will you be able to get
the street and the number out of him, and will the ambulance howl and growl and clang and bang its way there in
time? Is this an old woman who is giving up at last? Take
me, love me, o death, finish me, throw me away. Is this
my dream girl, long blonde hair falling over the edge of
the pillow, while the red blood from her wrists stains
her unwrinkled sheets?

You pick up, and it's a med student who's going to
flunk out. It's a mother whose drunken husband says she's
cheating on him, and he's coming to stab her and the baby
because he can't stand the noise any more. It's a man
who's lost his job at the windshield wiper factory and
can't find another and the sonofabitch landlord says he's
going to throw him and his invalid wife out on the street
and their four kids, Maria Theresa and Frank Xavier and
you know the rest. And who the hell cares? In these '80s,
days of truly magnificent greed and hypocrisy, who the
hell cares?

Not me. You can't. That's part of the training they
give you. You're there to help as best you can. Listen to
them. Give sympathy, but don't take them home with you.
You can't let yourself care about them in the way that
you'd care about your mother or your little sister or
your lover Anne. You'd fall apart and be no use for them.

You have to care, I guess, in the way that doctors are
supposed to care.

Separate yourself. Just listen. Tell them there are
chances, possibilities, a whole big world out there of
social services, charities, churches, clinics, all kinds
of goodkindhelpful places. Goo-goos on every
streetcorner. Call University Health for the med student.
Get a county ambulance to the doped up kid. Catholic
Charities for the wiper man. We sit there with lists of
social services. We try to open a door, turn on a light,
unlock the cage. Try to get them to believe in free en-
terprise and private charities and trickle-down econom-
ics. Yeah, just try.

So that's the feature that I want you to know about
me. Now for the second attraction, the American International Pictures horror movie, when the sex takes over at
the drive-in and people don't even pretend to watch. Why
do I do this?

Two reasons. The stories and the voices. The voices
come over the phone and they slip right into my writer's
ear that comes with no heart attached. I hear those beautiful falling syllables of Afro-English. I hear the
"mahn," the "bay-buh," the "dew-in" this and "dew-in"
that, the "muthuhfuhckuh," that clicks in so, so easy for
them, so hard for me. How the hell do you make a schwa
click? I hear that Puerto Rican "fok" go off like a pis-
tol shot. Fok, fok, fok, they fire their verbal revolver.
I hear those hard midwestern slum a's, flat and angry as
a prairie in November. "Gaahd", they say, it's "haah-rrd,"
and it is, and that's the language to say it in. I hear the
age in the voices, the consonants all there and lingeringly
slow, the vowels lost in the hoarseness of their dry
throats, the sentences that stop in the middle of a phrase
for no reason at all, and you say, "Yes?," as chipper as
you please, but you know that they have left you and
wandered off into some other worry or, you hope, into
gentle memory from the big, cool parlors of childhood.

And the stories. We are supposed to listen, and I do,
waiting for the gunshots, for the diapers, for the hot
stoves and the broken toilets, for the twenty-dollar
bills, for the pulls and the pushes and the fists and the
knives, for where he stuck it, for what I saw, for all
the gory glorious imagery of life, a kind of life, a part
of it. Not life for us students, not much of the time is
it that way for us, anyway. I think I'm losing this.

Every once in a while, we do a house call, and I get to see the wallpaper, the linoleum, the frayed carpeting and the threadbare furniture that are behind the telephone calls. I remember once they called us because a mother had cut her passed-out husband's cock off while the two-year old and the four-year-old were watching, and when the cops came they knew where to take the man and where to take the woman, but they didn't know what to do with the kids. I should know? Yes, I should. I have a neatly annotated list of appropriate social agencies, and that night it was the Salvation Army that gave them room at the inn, and a strong, kind woman in, would you believe?, a navy blue and cardinal red soldier's uniform who held them and tucked them in and I think a uniform was just what they needed, although it didn't help me at all with the nightmares I had for a week after.

And I see I am being litry again. I liked that bit about the "big, cool parlors of childhood," didn't you? But you know what they tell us in creative writing classes. When you think you've written something particularly fine, cut it. No matter how hard that is, cut it.

End of paper, and ask me, ask me, What did they do with the cock?

You see what I mean, Justin, about his papers being fun to read? But I sense a hard man under all that cheer. He could teach Barry a thing or two about indifference.

Center stage, isn't he? He even gives us right out loud the image of himself as a circus performer standing starry in the spotlight. He spots himself. (As well as spotlights—I think I'm beginning to hear language the way he does.) Do you think that's why he works at the "Center"?

Language is a performance for him, a stunt, as he describes himself. His tone is that he's putting on some sort of act for me and the other students. I think it's not an act. That's the way he is, but he seems more superficial than Glendish. She writes about truth. He writes about sounds. He's always performing, and the way Paul performs is through language. And, I guess, sex, to judge from his several references to penises. (If you want to play some interpretive games, look back at how he uses "hard.")

He doesn't treat the people he meets at the center as people with problems so much as bodies, bodies for whom he has to find a place. The fraught human issues, the things he hears about at the Crisis Center, he turns into dialects, vowels, metrics. No bad thing if you want to write poetry. Not perhaps such a good thing if you want to write fiction. But we'll see.

He tells us a story, as most of the students did for the trait paper, but it's not about him. He's only the spectator and narrator of the story, not the person suffering through it.

A theme? I'd say something like, Watch me, admire me, as I split human experience into either raw body or language.

English 6121

February 15
Paul the Penman

I like it. This lady is a pro. Look at that first line:

Gree**n** S**n**ake, when I hu**ng** you rou**n**d my **n**eck
    a**n**d stroked . . .

All those **n**s! All that shape and structure in a line as easy and natural in speech as if she were just chatting on the phone. She talks to the snake. That's the poetry part, and she tells us it is poetry by using "round" instead of "around" which would make it prosy, and she knew that just as easy as pi, while I had to think about it.

Poetry is talking to a snake, scary, maybe poisonous, but sensuous, hissing. Listen to all the hissing--

and **s**troked your cold, pul**s**ing throat
    a**s** you hi**ss**ed to me,

(a little by-play there with the short **i**s in "pul**s**ing" and "h**i**ssed") and then even more--

on my **sh**oulders,
and the whi**s**pering **s**ilver of your drynes**s**
sounded clo**s**e at my ear**s**--

Green **S**nake--I **s**wore to my companion**s** that **c**ertainly
    you were harmle**ss**!

Amazing! and in language as plain as oatmeal. Look at those short **i**s in the third line or the **oh**s in the second:

and str**o**ked your c**o**ld, pulsing thr**oa**t

each right along with the stress. She does it again in the middle:

> I had n**o** certainty, and n**o** h**o**pe, **o**nly desiring
>   to h**o**ld you, f**or** that j**oy**,

and then zzzzzzzip, she lets all that tension go with the
little **ee** sound that ends the **o** of "joy"--jo**ee**--and it's
all gone. The moment is over, and that's the big break in
the poem. Beautiful! It's like watching Wimbledon. She
makes it look so easy.

I wish I could do that. Oh, sweet bleeding jeezus on
the cross, I wish I could do that. I know what the rest
of you think, that I just churn this stuff out, and maybe
that's true about papers for Norm's seminar (sorry about
that, Norm), but when I'm really writing, really trying,
oh God, it's hard, it doesn't come easy, and it hurts so
in the head and these damn chairs in this seminar, and
scratch my head and hold my pencil (phallic symbol, Norm)
and stick to it and grind and do it and do it. Then I
look at this woman's writing, and it's like she just did
it with a flip of her wrist. I could steal--oh God--if I
could make that work mine . . . Yes, if they ever send me
up for something it will be for plagiarism. Mark my
words.

Yes, I'll bet you do. I can hear you all. In the
immortal words of Our Ron, "There he goes again." Instead
of talking about what the poem is <u>really</u> about, instead
of talking about the anxious-making, hard part, the snake
as phallic symbol, he's run away to his language games.
Yes, Herr Doktor Professor Freud, thanks to you we can
all now say that the snake iss a phellic zymbol. But do I
believe it?

No, <u>goldener Sigi</u>, I'm not convinced. She's talking
about poetry, about daring to escape from the humdrum
into the magic of—what? Nature? But it's not nature for
me. It's nature rendered as **sss-sss-sss**. And **oh-oh-oh-oh**.
And **nnyuh-nnyuh-nnyuh**. Ah, the power, the skill, the
mastery, the grace. This lady is a pro.

His reading of the Levertov poem is virtually all at the level of sounds
and letters. Then, he jumps from the level of language to phallic symbols,
the snake here, the castrated cock itself in the trait paper. That suggests
what language, for him, stands for. No pun intended.

He's wonderfully narcissistic, as I see him, immensely talented, rather
selfish. I'm curious about his relationship with Glendish and where that's
going. I guess I'm more curious about her than him.

But at this point, Justin, you must have heard more literary theory than you ever wanted to. I've ended these readings. You tell me you are about to end this case. This is a double ending then. I feel a little sad. Curious.

Yours,
/Norm/

Metropolitan Buffalo Police Department

Tape Transcription   Homicide Unit

Body: *Hassler, P.* ....   Tape No. *840308.022* ....
Place: *HQ* ....   Time: *8:10 p.m.* ....
Persons present: *Sgt. Ruth De Soo, Det. Lt. Rhodes, reporters*
.........*(see below)*..

....
....
....   Transcribed by: *S. Moreno*

Reporters identified: Dolly Kellehan; Darlene Novopolk; Waldo Pressleng; "Dutch" Sidey; Leonard Tobyne.

SGT. DESOO: Good evening. I'm Sergeant Ruth DeSoo, the new spokesperson for the MBPD. Thank you for coming around to this evening's press conference on the Patricia Hassler case. I'll not keep you long. First, the department has prepared a statement with the cooperation of Lieutenant Rhodes. Why don't you read it now. Then you can ask questions of the lieutenant, identifying yourself first. Copies are available at the back of the room. *[A two-minute silence.]*

UNIDENTIFIED VOICE: Aw cut it out! A tack on the chair? Come on!

LT. RHODES: Here it is, right here in this little plastic bag, ladies and gentlemen. Take a look. This is a murder weapon. Look. Don't touch. *[A one-minute silence.]*

LT. RHODES: That last part is important, about the skillful laboratory work by Dr. Robert Welder in collaboration with Dr. Harold Vernor. If you can find space, Doc Welder would appreciate your getting in that bit about the university being the only place in the county that has the special equipment, an autoanalyzer, that the medical examiner needed for the analysis.

REPORTER #1: Dolly Kellehan, *Buffalo Morning News-Gazette*, but hell's bells! you all know me by . . . Anyway, Lieutenant, what was the name of that poison?

SGT. DESOO: We're not divulging the name of the specific poison at this time.

KELLEHAN: And just why is that?

LT. RHODES: You know the routine, Dolly. We may get false confessions. We have to know something the public doesn't know so as to check out those stories. If you need a name, just say it's a "neurotoxin."

UNIDENTIFIED VOICE: Say again.

LT. RHODES: Neurotoxin.

REPORTER #2: Leonard Tobyne, *New York Times.* Lieutenant, does this discovery that she was poisoned by a thumbtack mean you'll be making an arrest soon?

LT. RHODES: Any talk of an arrest would be premature.

TOBYNE: Why is that? Doesn't this narrow the group of suspects down to the people in the room at the time, the people in the seminar?

LT. RHODES: I wouldn't want to say that all or only the people in the seminar are suspects. I'd be naming eight persons, all but one of whom, presumably, is innocent. I don't want to subject the other seven to unwarranted suspicion.

KELLEHAN: We hear there were some pretty peculiar things going on in that seminar. Did that have something to do with the murder?

LT. RHODES: I've had Professor Holland explain the seminar at length to me. I'm convinced the special nature of the seminar in no way caused the murder.

REPORTER #3: "Dutch" Sidey, Channel Five. Can you explain the seminar to us?

LT. RHODES: It's complicated. Explaining it would take a lot of your time, and I'm not sure it would mean much to your viewers. If you want to pursue that line, you ought to talk to Professor Holland himself.

REPORTER #4: Waldo Pressleng, *Newsday.* Isn't that something we all did in school? Put a tack on the teacher's chair?

UNIDENTIFIED VOICE: Maybe you did, Waldo.

PRESSLENG: What I mean is, isn't that a pretty special way of killing somebody?

LT. RHODES: Very unusual. Yes, Mr. Pressleng, I find the method suggestive, especially in this academic setting. But what it means, if anything, we don't yet know. Perhaps we should say, how to interpret it, we don't yet know. *[Pause.]*

SGT. DESOO: Is that all? Okay. Again, thank you for coming out tonight. Drive carefully. There are patches of ice and patches of dry out there. That's the most dangerous surface.END OF THIS SECTION OF TAPE END OF THIS SECTION OF TAPE END OF THIS SECTION OF TAPE END OF THIS

State University of New York at Buffalo
Department of English

March 8, 1984

To Whom It May Concern (and specifically, Detective Lieutenant Norman Rhodes, Homicide Unit, Metropolitan Buffalo Police Department):

I'm writing this down so that there will be a record—that seems to me the only way to handle what follows, and I said I would. As I begin writing, it's 11:15 at night.

I was home, alone, when Amy Lemaire called about ten o'clock all upset and crying. She had to see me. I told her I'd meet her at my office, 36 Rhodes Hall. When she came in, she looked taut, jumpy, red-eyed, scared. This was not the brown, round Amy I was used to.

"Norm," she said. "I have to talk to somebody. Can I count on you not to repeat what I'm going to say?"

I waffled. "Amy," I said. "No way can I promise you that. Suppose you told me you'd murdered Trish. I could get in a lot of trouble if I didn't tell Rhodes. Sit down." I moved some papers off the chair. "Tell me about it, if you want to, if you think you're able to, and I'll do whatever I can to help. But I can't promise not to pass it on." She did sit down, but she sat there all angles, quite unlike round, equanimous Amy Lemaire.

"No, it's not that, Norman. I didn't kill Trish. But I had a good reason for wanting Trish—not dead, just gone, just away somewhere in time, ended. Not there to do what she was doing to me. She'd found out something about me, and she was blackmailing me."

"Blackmail?," I said. "For what? Can you tell me? If you don't want to, obviously you don't have to."

"Can I smoke?" she asked. I nodded a reluctant okay. "Of course, I don't want to tell you, but I think I have to. Norm, I'm ashamed to tell you this. I know you, and it'll change your feelings toward me. I worked as a prostitute in New York for sixteen months."

I was shocked, I admit it. For all my belief in feminism and sexual liberation, my jaw must have dropped. My first feeling was one of repugnance, I have to confess, and a series of ugly images flashed through my mind. Women in grotesquely revealing clothing on slummy streets. Then I got rid of the images, and I was just plain sorry for her. Still shocked, but sorry, and then, so like me, self-conscious. How was I to react? Friendly, concerned professor? Older friend? Should I hug her? Would she misunderstand that? The wise clinician, detached but sympathetic? I opted for that. "I'm sorry to hear this, Amy. It must have been miserable for you. But none of that needs to be part of your life now."

"That's what *I* thought. That's all over with. And by the way, it wasn't a miserable thing. I'd had a fair number of casual lovers when I realized I'd been giving away what I could get something in exchange for. It was that awful time after Herbert died—I wrote about it in my squib."

"I remember," I said.

"I'd begun to think about teaching, and I knew I'd need money. I like to be fucked, and I felt I was doing something for the men—my clients. Some were lonely. Others needed their egos salved. For others it was just fun. Whatever they wanted, they were grateful to me.

"I was working in an apartment on upper Madison, and the couple who ran the operation were very decent. No pimp was beating me up. The wife sometimes worked with us. The husband served as security. My clients never abused me, because he was very effective. The couple wouldn't have any really kinky stuff in the apartment, although some of the other girls would go out on dates and do some strange things.

"Inside the apartment was a class act. Fees were $300 an hour and up. After paying for my food and my own apartment in New York, I still made a tremendous amount of money, even giving the couple who ran it their forty percent. I spent sixteen months as a working girl, and all in all I managed to bank $30,000. After a while I realized that there was no future in what I was doing and a time limit as to how long I could go on doing it. So I quit. No problem. Everybody was very professional about that.

"I had my stash, and I knew that now I could start what I'd wanted to do for a long time. I could become a professor of English or, as I came to realize, English Education. I could go for a Ph.D. It's that $30,000, that stash from my days as a working girl, that's supporting me while I go to graduate school. I moved here, and I planned never to tell a soul about my days and nights in that Madison Avenue apartment. As far as my parents are concerned, they think that during those sixteen months I was working in New York as an airline ticket agent. As for whatever I did before I met the lovers I've had here—that's none of their business. And I'm too old to get married. I'm not sure I want to, anyway.

"One thing I do know—I want to teach. I want to help kids. I came to realize, as I found out what I liked in the program here, that I wanted to teach teachers who'd then teach kids better than I'd been taught. That way, I double what I do for kids. The money I earned will see me through to my Ph.D., or it would've, if Hassler hadn't found out about how I earned it."

"Hassler! How did she find out?"

"How did she find out!" Amy laughed sourly. "I told her. How dumb can you get?" And she started crying, trying to hold it back but sobbing anyway. I put my hand on her shoulder.

"It was after one of your seminars, as a matter of fact. I'd tried to be especially nice to Trish during seminar, trying to keep her from banging on you any more than she did. We ended up walking out together. It was getting near lunchtime, so she offered to make lunch for us at her place on Masling Boulevard. I didn't quite know what to expect, Trish being such a Turk, but that day she behaved—I have to say it—sweetly. She came up with a tuna fish sandwich and a beer. It turned out to be a couple of beers. With the week's seminar over, we both felt a little lazy, and we settled into one of those let-down-your-hair girl-talk lunches.

We got to talking about fat. What else? I'm not as bad off as Trish, but it's a problem for both of us. Or was. We got to talking about fat and pleasing men, and we got into a feminist rap where we were sharing what we have to put up with so far as sex is concerned, abortion, women earning 69 cents on the dollar, and all the other injustices. We got angry and funny, and we kept drinking more beer. The first thing I knew I was telling Trish stories about men I'd known. And the next thing I knew I was telling her how I'd earned my bankroll for graduate school."

"She was fascinated—or said she was. Where had I worked? How many men did I serve a day? A week? What about contraception? Disease? AIDS? She wanted to know everything. Especially, How much did I earn? What had happened to the money? And I'm a sucker for someone who wants to sympathize with me. First thing I knew I told her about the $30,000."

"We napped a little towards the end of the afternoon, and I went home to try to salvage a little of the day. I was doing homework when she telephoned. She threatened to tell. She told me she'd turned on a tape recorder once she got me to telling stories, and she had my career as a hooker on tape. She blackmailed me, Norm. It's that simple."

"But Amy," I said, "this is 1984. The sexual revolution is long over. People aren't that worked up any more about somebody's sexual past."

"It wasn't just people. Trish pointed out that nowadays, since all the child abuse cases, in order to teach, most states check your record pretty carefully. She said that she'd write licensing boards what I'd told her. She'd write every damn licensing board I came near, posing as the morally indignant citizen. 'You can't have whores teaching our children,' I remember she said. So cruel! Granted I'm not trying to be a classroom teacher, but a teacher of teachers. I *have* to be able to be certified. If she chose to, Trish could wreck my just-aborning career. 'Think about it,' she said. 'Call me back when you've gotten used to the idea. Call me back—or else.'"

"I have to admit," I said glumly, "she probably could cause you a lot of trouble, especially with the tape to back her up."

"You know what she was like, Norman, mean and crazy enough to do anything. It took me about five minutes to call her back. This time I was furious, and she wanted to calm me down. She reassured me. She wasn't going to try to grab off my whole nest egg, she said. She must have figured that if she made it impossible for me to teach, I'd just take the money and run. Her plan was for both of us to live on my earnings. A hundred twenty-five dollars a week, she said. She'd calculated it out. I'm a year ahead of her. She'd collect enough more than her current living expenses to bank some. I was to pay her enough to see her through four years. In the meantime, I'd have enough—barely enough—to carry me through my remaining time. She allowed me three years including this one. She thought that if I worked carefully and fast I could be sure of getting my degree before the money ran out."

Just like Trish, I thought, that mix of intelligence and meanness, turning Amy's impulsive telling back on her.

"Who's kidding who? No way could I finish my degree two years from now. I'm not as quick as she, and I don't have her kind of high-test under-graduate background. She said, I could get money from my parents. Damn her. They deserve to live a little now, not support me. They don't have the money to see me through graduate school, not if Pop retires. But what was I going to do? I decided the first thing was to shut her up while I planned, so I made the first payment. That was last week. Cash, she said, and I handed her $125 in cash on Sunday night."

"At her apartment?"

"I walked up to her door, she opened it, and I handed her the money. She told me to come in. What now?, I thought. She surprised me. She soft-ened. She said that this arrangement might not last as long as I feared. I asked her what she meant. She'd worked out the numbers, she said, and it was going to be all right. Painful but okay. She promised she wouldn't bleed me dry. She said that she'd see that there was enough to last me through to the degree. All she wanted was some help for herself. She said something odd. 'I want somebody to pay me *something,* and tonight you're it.'

"I didn't know whether to believe her or not, but I sure as hell wanted to. It's hard for me to think that there are people with not one ounce of the milk of human kindness in them. And what was I to do, anyway? She had me. So I decided to think as well of her as I could and hope for the best."

"Wednesday morning, when I saw her fall over onto the floor, I felt a sudden sympathy for the other fat woman, the other me, struggling to get the money for graduate work. At the same time, when they said she was dead, I was as glad as I've ever been about anything. So, is that detective Rhodes *not* going to think that I killed her? No way."

"But how is he going to know?," I said. "Everything you've told me so far was strictly between you and her. Nobody knows but you and me that Trish was blackmailing you."

"She was like every blackmailer you've ever read about, Norman. She said that she'd written it all out, sealed it, and put it on file with the proverbial trusted friend. This person would open the package and shout my story from the rooftops if anything happened to her.

"Trish was ever smart."

"Now, just after dinner tonight, I've gotten the first call. It was a man's voice. Soft, insinuating. Not a voice I could identify, although I thought I recognized it. That poor guy who has been slipping responses into our mailboxes, but I'm not sure. 'Aren't you sorry Trish was murdered?' he said. 'Aren't you going to be lonely? Never fear, though, I'm taking over from her. I'll bet you learned some stuff in New York that you'd like to demonstrate for me.' And then some sexual talk, worse than anything I heard in that apartment on upper Madison."

"Ouch."

"He wants me to meet him at midnight downstairs in the graduate student lounge on the first floor. He wants to talk about what he calls 'my predicament' and 'my training.' I have all too accurate an idea of what he really wants. God knows I can do that for him easily enough. I'm not crazy about giving him sex, but if it'll buy me time until the cops figure out who killed Trish, and I can figure out how to deal with that tape, it'll be worth it.

"On the other hand, if he gets mad at me, for whatever reason, and he tells that detective the story, Rhodes will be sure I did it. That's why I've come to you." And she started sobbing again. She kept on moaning, "What can you do? What can anyone do to help me?" I put my arm around her and tried to calm her down. And I had an idea.

"Amy, I owe you one," I said. "More than one—I owe you a bunch. If it hadn't been for you, this seminar would've long since fallen apart. You kept us together. You protected us from Trish's venom.

"Maybe there's a way we can handle this without telling Rhodes. You've told me about Trish's blackmailing you and about this new blackmailer. I'll write a memo or something recording what you've said. I'll use the old trick of sealing what I write and sending it to you as a registered letter, so that you can establish the date. Just hang onto the letter. Don't break the seal. If the time ever comes when you need to prove that you confessed all this before the second blackmailer revealed it, then take the unopened letter to Rhodes. Let him open it and read my formal statement that you've told me the whole story. Also, if ever it becomes important, I'll tell the authorities myself that you told me about Trish's blackmailing you, before this new blackmailer makes it public. And when the killer is caught, and you know you don't need my letter any more, give it back to me or destroy it. In the meantime, deal with this creep as best you can.

"Amy," I said, "I'm confident enough of you so that I'll take the responsibility of not telling the lieutenant what you've told me unless and until it'll help you to have me tell it."

She's left, and that's what I'm doing. Amy said she was going over to the Westward How and have a couple of strengtheners before she met this new blackmailer. I asked her if she wanted me to come with her and confront him. She said she was afraid we would just make him make good on his threats.

I've written out our conversation as closely as I can remember it. Tomorrow I'll post this letter by registered mail to Amy, and I'm keeping a copy here in my files for this ill-fated seminar.

Yet, ever the academic, I have to point out that there's a paradox here. How does Amy know what I've written? Suppose I'd killed Trish Hassler myself. I could easily set her up as the confessed murderer. I could write in this to-be-sealed letter that she'd confessed she murdered Trish. She has to trust me, that's all. But surely she must sense the risk.

Similarly, I assume she's been honest with me. Suppose she made all this up. Suppose she's had me write this letter so that she can accuse me to Rhodes of keeping things from him or fabricating evidence. Then she could set me up for obstructing justice. Indeed, she'd be making me a prime suspect in the murder.

There's some kind of infinite regression here that I can't resolve.

I suppose that's all any of us can do when we create these texts or read them or talk about them. We have to say what we believe to be the truth. We can be sincere. Otherwise no one can ever rely on anyone. Didn't Socrates say something like that? But that's all we can do.

I wish there were something more that we could trust beyond our fallible selves. And isn't it curious that this question comes up with Amy for whom trust and dependency are such important themes? Or not so curious.

As I think alongside Amy about her missteps and her fears, I begin to think of the world in her terms: giving, trust, dependency, identification, but being me, I think about how trust draws you into things. Well, I always knew that. You never know ahead of time that your trust won't be betrayed. You have to take that on faith, and I've precious little of that. But what I'm seeing here is slightly different. Here I see the utter impossibility of our ever knowing the private thoughts or writings of another. Amy cannot know what I've written in this sealed envelope. I cannot know what is in her sealed mind. Yet regardless, I just have to be honest, as she has been with me.

When I pass her concerns about trust through this situation, I experience something new for me about trust. It's not just poem opening, Justin, but world opening.

By now, Amy has left the Westward How, and she's downstairs, I assume, waiting for her meeting with the new blackmailer, the mystery student if it's really he. It's taken me about forty-five minutes to write this letter, so it's now just about midnight, just about the time Amy is to meet this viper. I wonder if she's with him downstairs now, as I seal this. An ugly thought. A thought I don't want to have. Suddenly, I feel very sleepy.

/Norman N. Holland/

Metropolitan Buffalo Police Department

Tape Transcription   Homicide Unit

Body: *Hassler, P.* .... Tape No. *840309.001* ....
Place: *Telephone call* .... Time: *12:20 a.m.* ....
Persons present: *from N. Holland to Det. Lt. Rhodes at home*
       (see below)

                                                          Transcribed by: *S. Moreno*

HOLLAND: . . .tenant, Lieutenant! I'm calling you from my office.

LT. RHODES: . . . Okay, okay, goddammit, it's past midnight. What is it, Norman? You woke me up!

HOLLAND: Something happened tonight. I think maybe I've found the mystery student. Maybe not. I'm not sure, but I think it could be important.

LT. RHODES: Okay, you're being taped. This line's recorder goes on automatically. Go ahead.

HOLLAND: Sometime shortly before midnight, I was in my office working . . . I was tired, very tired. Rather stupidly, I folded my arms on my desk and put my head down. I remember feeling how cold the formica was, and next thing I knew, some noise must have awakened me. I think what woke me was a spongy sound, like a squeegee. I realized it was footsteps coming up the stairs and down the corridor, ever so faintly squooshing on the vinyl floor. I sat there in the dark, not moving. I'll be honest, Justin, I was scared.

LT. RHODES: Fair enough. You thought you could be hearing a murderer.

HOLLAND: I heard a key slide into a lock and the click as the knob pulled the latch back. An office door, I figured. I heard a door being pushed open, but I also could hear air being sucked into the automatic closer, so it wasn't an office door—our office doors don't have closers. It had to be some public room, like a fire exit door or the mailroom door, which has a closer. Then I could hear the rubbery footsteps again and the door wheeze as it closed.

I tried to read my watch, but it has one of those liquid crystal displays, and I've never been able to read it in the dark. I'm going to guess it was right around midnight. I got out of my chair, and I tiptoed to my door. I turned the knob as silently as I could and inched the door open just a crack, and I peeked out. The night lights were on, every third light on the landing round the central staircase. I couldn't see anyone in the hall, but from under the mailroom door, about five yards from where I was, a slit of light spilled out onto the floor.

After hours, the room is locked, but your office key opens the mailroom, so it could be anyone in there, anyone with a key. Faculty. T.A.s. Most of us, whenever we come in the building, day or night, check the mail, because besides the U.S. mail, there's an endless stream of campus mail and department mail that can go in your box any time. But why at midnight? Maybe somebody pulling an all-nighter.

LT. RHODES: Tell me what happened.

HOLLAND: I inched my door closed again, but I kept the knob turned so the latch was held back, and I could open the door a crack without making any noise. I heard some vague thumping noises in the mailroom, but I wasn't about to go in after whoever it was—

LT. RHODES: Very sensible. What time was this?

HOLLAND: It couldn't have been more than a couple of minutes after I heard the mailroom door close. Then it was quiet again, until I heard the latch pull back, and the mailroom door closer breathe as the door opened, then a faint thump as whoever it was pushed the door closed against the rubber shock absorbers. The person was trying to be very quiet. I heard footsteps again going past the door where I was listening. We couldn't have been more than inches apart, and I had the door latch pulled back. I pressed my forehead against the door to hold it tight against the frame, but all the person would have had to do was push on my door, and we'd have been face to face. I waited for the footsteps to go by, and then I heard them tapping down the wooden staircase toward the lower floors, across the entrance hall, and out the front door of the building.

LT. RHODES: How did this person get in? Wasn't the front door locked?

HOLLAND: Probably it was, but, like the mailroom, our office door keys open it. I waited till I could hear the click of footsteps as the person crossed the tile entryway and the wheeze of the front door closing, and then I realized something. *This person had not tried to go into an office at all.* Whoever it was had come here for the sole purpose of going into the mailroom. They came after midnight, and I remembered that Wednesday night, last night, the mystery student dropped off a squib in the wee small hours. *This had to be the interloper.*

LT. RHODES: Why couldn't this just be a student dropping off a paper he'd just finished?

HOLLAND: Because deadlines are always before 5:00 p.m. Badger insists on that, because she doesn't want students prowling around the campus in the middle of the night. Rape.

No, I'm sure, Justin, this could only have been the mystery student. I must have been hearing him or her leaving a squib in the mailboxes. So I hurried down the hall and into the mailroom. I checked my own box, I checked a couple of the others, Amy Lemaire's, Barry's, but no squibs! Justin, no squibs!

LT. RHODES: So it's *not* the interloper.

HOLLAND: No, I'm sure it is. I have a reason for thinking so. Anyway, my office overlooks the front of the building, and I could see this person walking away. He was going so fast that his boots made little sparks when he hit a bare patch of pavement.

LT. RHODES: You say "he"?

HOLLAND: I couldn't tell. Whoever it was was all bundled up in a parka with a book bag on their back. It could have been a man or woman. In those down parkas they all look alike. And by this time the person is a couple of hundred yards away.

LT. RHODES: "Is"? You say "is"?

HOLLAND: Yes, I can still see him—or her. There's a long, clear sidewalk between Rhodes Hall and Main Street, maybe half a mile, and between the snow and the streetlights I can still see this person pretty clearly. This has to be the mystery student. Who else would come *just* to the mailroom at midnight?

LT. RHODES: Well, if you're so sure this is the interloper, why don't you follow out your hunch? Trail him. Maybe you can find out where he lives.

HOLLAND: I'm sure, Justin.

LT. RHODES: Well, then, hurry up and follow him. Be very careful, Norman. Keep a good, safe distance, mind, but see where he goes. Call me when you can. Now hang up and move. Move as fast as you safely can. END OF THIS SECTION OF TAPE END OF THIS SECTION OF TAPE END OF THIS

LT. RHODES: *Comment.* Curiouser and curiouser. It could be our interloper, but why no squibs? Chances are this is nothing at all. It must be cold out there. All I can do is wait till Holland calls again. I might as well go back to sleep. Over and out.

Metropolitan Buffalo Police Department

Tape Transcription   Homicide Unit

Body: *Hassler, P.*   Tape No. *840309.001*
Place: *Telephone call*   Time: *12:40 a.m.*
Persons present: *from N. Holland to Det. Lt. Rhodes at home*

                                             Transcribed by: *S. Moreno*

HOLLAND: Justin!

LT. RHODES: Where are you, Norman?

HOLLAND: Home.

LT. RHODES: You okay?

HOLLAND: I've got an address for you.

LT. RHODES: What? That's great!

HOLLAND: I followed him, as you told me to, and I kept my distance. I kept a good city block away all the time. It would have been easy for him to spot me, though—there wasn't another soul out—but I kept on the other side of the street, and there was a center island and plenty of distance between us, so I could see him quite clearly and where he was going. It was a straight shot. This police work could get interesting—

LT. RHODES: What do you mean, a "straight shot"?

HOLLAND: He went right down the sidewalk from the front of our building, across Main Street, and continued on down Masling Boulevard. In the third block— and those blocks are long—about the middle, he turned left into one of those big old apartment houses that've been cut up into student hives. The Shakespeare Arms. Adroitly named, for students.

LT. RHODES: What's the address?

HOLLAND: 131 Masling Boulevard.

LT. RHODES: Did you get any clue as to which apartment?

HOLLAND: I looked for a light to go on, but I didn't see one. Maybe it was to the back of the building. Maybe I was at the wrong angle.

LT. RHODES: How many people live in that apartment building?

HOLLAND: I'd say at least fifty.

LT. RHODES: Damn!

HOLLAND: Don't despair! I've carried it a step further. The English Department gives us a list of all the faculty and graduate students with their addresses. I scanned it for 131 Masling Boulevard. There are five graduate students in English who live at 131 Masling. No faculty, of course.

LT. RHODES: Good work, Norman.

HOLLAND: Here they are. Kirk Kinder, Felix Kulper, and Abe Poria.

LT. RHODES: That's only three.

HOLLAND: The other two are a surprise. They're both in the seminar.

LT. RHODES: Hey! Who?

HOLLAND: Paul Penza and Max Ebenfeld.

LT. RHODES: That *is* a surprise.

HOLLAND: But it couldn't have been Ebenfeld.

LT. RHODES: Oh? Why not?

HOLLAND: Too tall. The person I was following was of average size. Max is big.
It couldn't have been Max.

LT. RHODES: I thought Penza lived with Glendish.

HOLLAND: He does. This is the department's list and might be out of date.

LT. RHODES: And no women on your list.

HOLLAND: No.

LT. RHODES: And, anyway, we can't be sure that one of these five is the interloper, because no squibs were left in the boxes tonight. You're sure about
that, aren't you?

HOLLAND: No squibs. I'm sure of that, but at the same time I have a strong hunch
this was the mystery student.

LT. RHODES: Your nocturnal prowler is another loose end. Why was somebody
going to the English Department mailroom at midnight? Not to an office.
Only to the mailroom. And no squibs.

HOLLAND: I don't know, but I do know it was damned cold out tonight.

LT. RHODES: Take comfort. You may have found out something important.

HOLLAND: Well, if that's all, Justin, I want to get to bed. We've got a meeting at
nine tomorrow, haven't we?

LT. RHODES: We do indeed. See you then.END OF THIS SECTION OF TAPE
END OF THIS SECTION OF TAPE END OF THIS SECTION OF TAPE

LT. RHODES: *Comment.* A puzzler. Somebody wanted something in that mailroom
enough to sneak in at midnight. But not to leave a squib, evidently. Could
it have been to take a squib *out* of the boxes? Not a faculty member—
Masling Boulevard tells us that. Not a woman, he says. I don't see how to
make this relevant, but it must be. It must be.

friday

From the *Buffalo Morning News-Gazette,* March 9, 1984

Grad Student Was Poisoned by Thumbtack

Professor Denies Mystery Seminar Led to Murder

Dolly Kellehan

(CITY, March 8). Police told a startled press conference today that an ordinary thumbtack had taken the life of the graduate student who collapsed and died Wednesday morning on UB's West Campus.

Detective Lieutenant Norman "Justin" Rhodes, Homicide Unit, MBPD, showed reporters a simple thumbtack, which, he said, bore a powerful poison, a new rotoxin. Someone had placed the poisoned tack on Hassler's chair, causing her to fall to the floor dead as she seated herself in Professor Norman Holland's seminar.

Asked by reporters if an arrest would be forthcoming, Rhodes said that any talk of an arrest would be "premature." He said, however, that because the police now knew the type of poison, "the field of suspects was narrowing."

A careful police search, said Rhodes, found the envenomed thumbtack under a thin rubber cushion on Hassler's chair. In answer to questioning he agreed that putting a thumbtack on a chair was a common schoolroom prank. The method by which the poison was administered was, he said, "suggestive in this academic sitting."

Reporters pressed Rhodes to state whether the murder had been committed by someone in the seminar. Rhodes refused to say that, on the grounds that he did not want to expose innocent members of the seminar to suspicion.

Rhodes credited lab work by Medical Examiner Robert Welder, working with Professor Harold Vernor of UB's Pharmacology Department, for establishing the type of poison. Rhodes would only identify the poison as a new type of rotoxin, but declined to name the particular poison, saying that it would be important in establishing the police department's case for that information to be known only to the police and the murderer.

Professor Norman Holland teaches the seminar in "literature and psychology" in which Hassler was murdered. He declined to comment on this new development, claiming he was busy assisting Lt. Rhodes in the investigation.

Holland called the suggestion that that there was a connection between the murder and the unusual nature of the seminar he was conducting "sheer and utter balderdash." "It is unfortunate," he said, "that a distrust, represented by your question, has grown up between the university and the community."

from the journal of Norman Holland

What a way to start the day! And what a contemptible newspaper, whipping up town-gown enmity to advance their damned conservative politicos! And after that night . . .

I'd finally dozed off around dawn and had to scramble to get to Rhodes's 9:00 meeting. Everything at the house is out of kilter without Jane. I tried first thing to call her—she'd left a message on the machine that she stayed at the hospital last night. Then I tried Amy to find out what had happened at her— what other word was there for it?—assignation. No answer. What did that mean? But when I got to Rhodes's meeting, she was there. I couldn't read her expression. He, however, was in fine fettle.

Metropolitan Buffalo Police Department

Tape Transcription   Homicide Unit

Body: *Hassler, P.*   Tape No. *840309.003*
Place: *Rhodes Hall 21, UB West*   Time: *9:05 a.m.*
Persons present: *See below*

Transcribed by: *S. Moreno*

Persons present: Det. Lt. Rhodes, Det. Sgt. Yorrick, Det. Maistry; C. Aval, M. Ebenfeld, A. Glendish, N. Holland, B. Ireland, A. Lemaire, P. Penza, W. Sisley

LT. RHODES: Good morning. I'm tempted to say, "Good morning, class," you all look so bright and scrubbed.

IRELAND: I like it that you're so goddam cheerful, Lieutenant. Somebody's dead, motherfucker. Is it that you haven't noticed? That you don't give a shit? Or are you just giving us an example of keeping our morale up? You're getting more and more like a real lieutenant all the time.

LT. RHODES: Sorry about that, Ireland. I didn't mean to be disrespectful to Trish Hassler's memory. But perhaps you'll understand better when I tell you that I'm pretty sure—morally certain is the phrase I'd use—that I know who killed her. *[General hubbub.]*

LT. RHODES: Quiet down, now. I want to take you back to square one. First of all, let's put it on the record that we're taping this session. As on Thursday, I've brought Sergeant Yorrick and Detective Maistry with me and also Ms. Moreno, one of our incredibly expert transcribers.

MS. MORENO: Thank you, Lieutenant.

LT. RHODES: Let me note a further development. This morning we found another squib in your mailboxes. Sgt. Yorrick's taken it out. It's another squib from the interloper, more puzzling than any we've seen so far.

HOLLAND: Another squib! When did *that* happen?

LT. RHODES: After you and I talked last night. Another loose end, Norman.

HOLLAND: I should say so. But, as early as Wednesday night, Lieutenant, you said you were "morally certain" you knew who killed Trish Hassler.

LT. RHODES: Yes.

HOLLAND: Yet you keep talking about "loose ends."

LT. RHODES: We have *too many* clues here. I'm sure I know who killed Hassler, but there are so many clues that I have little, lingering doubts. This morning's squib, for example. But I want to start you out, not on that, but with what I think I know, and then maybe you can help me to clear up these uncertainties.

First of all, I think there's a meaning in the method of her death.

HOLLAND: You *interpret* her death a certain way.

LT. RHODES: Fair enough, Norman. Let me play the game that Professor Holland has been playing in this seminar. What comes to your minds when you think about the way Patricia Hassler was killed?

PENZA: I think of it as a schoolchild's trick, putting a thumbtack on the teacher's chair.

LT. RHODES: Anybody else?

HOLLAND: Yes, that's what I remember from long ago, school pranks.

IRELAND: I think it's a damn strange way to kill somebody. Sneaky. Getting them unawares, like a sniper. This is a land mine, but a teeny-tiny land mine.

EBENFELD: I think of it as if all Trish's anger had turned back on her in that tiny little focused point.

LEMAIRE: Me, too. I remember what Trish said, that, for her, school was everything. The whole world. It seems sadly appropriate, then, that she should die by a school prank, doesn't it?

AVAL: Yes, all these things are possible meanings of the thumbtack—or, Professor Holland, possible interpretations of the thumbtack—but what is the point of this exercise, Lieutenant?

LT. RHODES: No pun intended, I assume. I just wanted you to observe how academic, how schoolchildish, if you'll allow me that portmanteau word, this crime is.

HOLLAND: Is that perhaps why you addressed us as schoolchildren when you came in?

LT. RHODES: An astute observation. Yes, I was thinking very much how this crime has been involved with academic ambitions and rivalries and ideas.

Of course, Hassler wasn't the only one of whom we could say school was everything. Didn't you say that to me once, Norman? That you entered school at the age of five and you've never left?

HOLLAND: I may have said that. It's certainly true.

LT. RHODES: Is there anyone else for whom that would be true? Sisley?

SISLEY: I had a stint in the Peace Corps.

IRELAND: Nam.

LT. RHODES: You were a flight attendant for a time, Ms. Lemaire?

LEMAIRE: Yes, for eleven years, in fact.

LT. RHODES: Well, perhaps we can't read any symbolism into the method.

Let me tell you something else about Hassler's death. When we went over her apartment after her death, we found that her computer had been completely erased. All her work was gone. How do you read that?

IRELAND: Damn mean, say I. It's as though somebody was trying to erase Trish herself, wipe her out completely.

PENZA: Yes, that's the way I read it, too. Zzzzzap! You imagine, you scrape lovely words and ideas out of your mind, you write and you write, and here's all your beautiful language gone into the computer's nowhere land. What a bitching thing to do. You mean, there's nothing left of Trish, nothing but her body?

LT. RHODES: Whatever papers she turned in. But nothing in her computer. Nothing of the work she'd not yet turned in.

GLENDISH: I guess the moral is, if you want to be remembered, turn your work in on time.

IRELAND: Hey, Anne! You're like the lieutenant here—you think it's all a joke.

GLENDISH: Not a bit, Barry. I was thinking of how little any of us would leave behind if we were to die at this stage of our lives. Poor Trish. She was terribly ambitious to be an academic star, admired of all, and she never got her chance.

SISLEY: Wiping the computer seems to me a sneaky thing, like getting at her through a friend or her family or someone close to her.

LT. RHODES: There's a further complication to the computer business. When could this have taken place? We know that Patricia Hassler lived for her work. She was likely to start working any time, day or night, that the spirit moved her.

Then tell me, when was the computer wiped? If it had been done Tuesday evening or any time before Tuesday evening, Hassler would've noticed it. She'd have known she was in danger. It had to be done after she left for the seminar Wednesday morning.

SISLEY: You mean that, while we were sitting here Wednesday morning, someone was erasing Hassler's computer?

AVAL: Or perhaps someone set the machine to erasing itself. They will do that, you know.

LT. RHODES: Yes, we know or, more properly, Detective Maistry knows. She's our computer expert. But Maistry tells me that it would've taken some time to do the kind of erasing that was done. It couldn't have been done in the short interval between the time when Patricia Hassler left her apartment and the time when you all were together here in the seminar room.

AVAL: Does that mean, then, that we in the seminar are exonerated? That none of us could have done it? We were here, and the machine was there.

LT. RHODES: No. It doesn't clear you, because the machine could have been erased anytime between the time you were all here, when Hassler died, and the time I entered her apartment to inspect it.

AVAL: But you kept us all here, Lieutenant. We waited all morning in the room across the hall.

LT. RHODES: Not quite. While you were waiting, some of you were excused to go to the bathroom, to get study materials, whatever.

EBENFELD: Would that have been time enough for someone to erase the computer?

LT. RHODES: Probably not, but now you see what I mean by loose ends. Which brings us to the interloper. Who is he? Or who's this she pretending to be a he? Another possibility to be considered. That person would've been able to erase Hassler's computer while the rest of you were in the seminar.

You see, in that famous triad, motive, means, and opportunity, I'm asking about opportunity. Who'd have had the opportunity to erase Hassler's computer?

Who could have put the tack on Hassler's chair?

Consider the possibilities. As I see it, simply as a logical proposition, there are two times and only two times someone could have put the tack on Hassler's chair. They're marked off by the moment when Trish entered the room and put her books down. Simply as a logical propositon, whoever put the tack on that chair could have done it either before or after that moment.

If the killer did it *before* Trish put her books there, he or she had no way of knowing that she was going to sit there. If so, then the tack wasn't directed particularly at her, but possibly at Professor Holland here—

HOLLAND: Ugh!

LT. RHODES: —or it may have been a kind of random act of violence, like a terrorism. Let's kill whoever sits in that seat.

IRELAND: Are you looking at me, Lieutenant?

LT. RHODES: No, I wasn't looking at you, Mr. Ireland. Let's just note that Ms. Glendish and Mr. Penza were the first people in the room that morning, and, according to them, they came in together.

PENZA: Now just a damn minute, Lieutenant. You can't pin this thing on us.

LT. RHODES: You're right. I can't. Because, if someone were willing to put the tack on the chair *before* Hassler had used her books to mark the place as hers, they could have done so at any time, from the middle of the night on. That means anybody in this seminar, anybody in the department, indeed anybody at all.

But we also know that it's not just anybody.

HOLLAND: What do you mean?

LT. RHODES: Actually, you all saw the evidence for that particular deduction, didn't you?

But let me go on to the other possibility, that the killer put the tack on the chair *after* Hassler had put her books at that place. As I say, Glendish and Penza both came into the room after Hassler's books were in place, at least according to their account. They then had a few minutes when they were alone with the chair, and they knew this was the chair Hassler was going to sit in. They had opportunity. They could have put the tack on the chair. They'd both have had to agree to do so, of course, if we believe their account.

PENZA: And just why the hell wouldn't you believe us?

GLENDISH: Yes, Lieutenant. Are you calling us liars?

LT. RHODES: Ms. Glendish, Mr. Penza, when I talk this way, please don't take it personally. I'm just thinking out loud, trying out all the possibilities, keeping track of what we know and who we know it from.

All right. According to Glendish and Penza, they went outside to enjoy the March sun. They thus left a new window of opportunity. Hassler's books were in place. Whoever recognized those books would know that Hassler—99 percent probability—was going to sit in that chair. That person could have placed the tack.

The only person who we know saw those books while he was alone was the next person to enter the seminar room, Max Ebenfeld. Max, then, by his own account, had opportunity. Even so, before Max came in, there was opportunity for anybody to place the thumbtack.

After Barry Ireland joined Max in the seminar room, no one was alone with the chair. It would've been possible for all or some of the people involved to conspire to kill Patricia Hassler. You all resented her, but such a conspiracy is exceedingly improbable, and the improbability mounts as the number of people increases.

On this theory, you, M. Aval, are the least likely person to have killed Patricia Hassler, since you were the last to arrive except for the victim.

AVAL: Thank you, Lieutenant, for that admission.

LT. RHODES: Indeed, you arrived while Hassler was standing in the doorway. At that time, at least, you couldn't have done it, because everyone confirms that there was no physical contact between you and Patricia Hassler.

AVAL: There was none.

LT. RHODES: Nevertheless, one could read her statement, "He's the one. Remember, he's the one," as an accusation. But, of course, it cannot be an accusation of her murder, because presumably she didn't know she was going to be murdered.

AVAL: Presumably.

LT. RHODES: It might then have been an accusation of something else, perhaps something that happened between you two at Yale.

AVAL: Possibly.

LT. RHODES: And perhaps the statement wasn't an accusation at all. It could mean many things. Yes, Professor, I'll amend that. More properly, we could read it in many different ways. Again we have a loose end, a clue we cannot yet interpret.

Let me go back to the evidence that makes me morally certain I know who killed Patricia Hassler. This clue you all saw. Let's go back to the first possibility, that the tack was put on the chair before Hassler put her books down at that place. In that case, the killer would've expected Professor Holland to sit on the fatal tack, and that would indeed be just like the schoolchild's prank. The teacher sits on the tack and jumps up in pained surprise and the class bursts out laughing, although no one would have laughed at this prank.

HOLLAND: But wait a minute . . .

LT. RHODES: That's right. We had a demonstration yesterday morning of the tack on the chair, and it didn't work that way. Professor Holland sat on the chair where we, the police, had put a tack identical to the one that killed Patricia Hassler. *He did not feel anything.* Indeed he sat there for quite a while without feeling anything.

HOLLAND: But that same tack killed Patricia Hassler.

LT. RHODES: How much do you weigh, Norman?

HOLLAND: A hundred forty-nine pounds.

LT. RHODES: How much do you think Patricia Hassler weighed?

HOLLAND: Around two hundred fifty.

LT. RHODES: Actually, according to the autopsy, two hundred thirty-three. The tack on the chair was very nicely calculated. Only someone as heavy as Hassler would force the tack—and the poison on it—through the rubber cushion and into the victim. There's no one in the seminar as heavy as Hassler was, not even you, Mr. Ebenfeld.

HOLLAND: My God, I can't believe that anyone could use so subtle, so chancy, a technique for murder.

LT. RHODES: No, not murder. Only one person could know that the tack would go through under Patricia's weight but not under Holland's weight or Ebenfeld's weight or the weight of anyone else in the seminar. Only one person could have experimented with a two hundred thirty-three pound human being to find that out. Only one person could be sure that the poison would go into Patricia, and that was Patricia Hassler herself. *[General hubbub.]*

LEMAIRE: Suicide! You're saying she committed suicide!

IRELAND: I don't believe this.

LT. RHODES: Ah, but we have confirmation of my reasoning from the autopsy. There was a small puncture wound next to the fatal puncture. This other wound had healed. The fatal puncture, of course, had not. I think the other puncture was caused when Hassler tried out the tack, presumably using this chair when no one else was around. She may have tried similar tacks out on several of the chairs in this seminar room to see if others would press the cushion hard enough to drive the tack into their bodies.

LEMAIRE: Oh no!

LT. RHODES: Or she may not have bothered. She'd become very angry at everyone and everything, quite indifferent. She probably didn't give a damn whether someone else got pricked or even got poisoned.

Notice, though, how so many questions are answered by the hypothesis that Hassler killed herself, how many of the clues fall into place. We can explain the second puncture wound. We know how and when the thumbtack was planted. She did it before Glendish and Penza came in.

GLENDISH: She did sit down pretty decisively.

LT. RHODES: Notice, too, that, if Hassler killed herself, she probably erased her computer as another act of self-destruction. The fact it took an hour to erase ceases to present a problem.

EBENFELD: Lieutenant, about the tack, didn't you say there was a window of opportunity after Patricia put her books down? After Paul and Anne left. Nobody was in the room from then until the time I came in. The mystery student could have put the tack at Patricia's place then.

LT. RHODES: Or—I hate to point this out—you could have.

EBENFELD: True.

LT. RHODES: But notice what nice timing that would take. The interloper would have had to have been following Hassler.

LEMAIRE: Maybe they were friends, and he—or she—walked to class with Patricia.

LT. RHODES: And stayed in this room? Or came back? The timing is iffy again.

LEMAIRE: She could have come here with the friend very early and then gone down to the cafeteria and eaten her breakfast. If she had breakfast . . . Would you have breakfast if you were committing suicide . . .

LT. RHODES: The autopsy showed no breakfast. Besides, we have Barry's evidence that he saw Patricia standing alone on the corner of Masling Boulevard as he was walking up to class. That has to be where she went *after* she put her books down.

EBENFELD: You've settled on this, then. She came up before any of us was here, placed the thumbtack, left her books, went away, and then came back to make her entrance after we had all sat down.

LT. RHODES: All but Christian Aval. You agreed that she looked round at all of you and that she looked oddly. You couldn't agree on her expression, but you did all say it was odd. Then Christian Aval came in—last. Her expression changed again, and again, each of you interpreted it differently.

AVAL: Necessarily, Lieutenant.

GLENDISH: Then, while we watched, she sat down, knowing that she'd kill herself?

LT. RHODES: You're right to be skeptical. This is a very strange form of suicide. I've never encountered anything like it. The reason for my conclusion isn't the window of opportunity. It's the fact, which you all witnessed, that Professor Holland sat on the tack but it didn't go into his flesh. Hence Patricia Hassler is the only one who could know that it *would* go into *her* flesh. The window of opportunity is what I believe you'd call in academia a necessary but not a sufficient condition.

EBENFELD: Let me get this straight. She'd prepared a thumbtack with this poison—

LT. RHODES: Saxitoxin. She obtained it from the exhibit on traditional and modern drugs at the science museum. Witnesses at the museum said she attended the exhibit at least once and perhaps twice. It had to be twice. She could have stolen the drug on one trip and returned it on the second. Or she could have discovered the drug on the first trip and put it on thumbtacks the second time she came. But it's unlikely she knew before she saw the exhibit that it contained saxitoxin or that saxitoxin was the drug she wanted.

Saxitoxin promised a fast and painless death, so she got hold of it at that exhibit long enough to put some on a thumbtack. She'd been planning this a long time.

IRELAND: That's one sick way of committing suicide.

PENZA: Suicide *is* sick, Barry.

LEMAIRE: Poor Trish. Poor hurt Trish.

LT. RHODES: Notice how things come together. The timing on Wednesday morning, the erasing of the computer disks, her visiting the museum exhibit, the
school prank as a way of killing, indeed the very fact of suicide—you've
told me, Norman, that you read Hassler as someone who's preoccupied
with turning things against herself or against others—all these things fit
together around one central theme. Patricia Hassler committed suicide.

Look, this is the basic technique of criminal detection. Fitting facts
together to form a cohesive whole.

HOLLAND: Of course! I'd never thought of it that way. Holistic reasoning, the
philosophers call it, converging themes into an organic unity. We use it in
literary criticism. It's one of the basic modes of human thought, like logical sequences or hypothesis testing.

LT. RHODES: You're being *very* professorial, Norman.

HOLLAND: I know, but this is good for the students to realize. We're still a seminar, after all.

LT. RHODES: You once said to me, Norman, that the trick in the professorial game
is to keep the question in the air as long as you can before you bring it
down to an answer. As you're doing right now. Just the opposite of the
Homicide Department. Their regulations say, once I've come to the conclusion of suicide, I have to close the file. I want to take a little longer,
though. I have to gather in at least some of these loose ends.

HOLLAND: Of course. You judge how successful a holistic explanation is by how
many of the relevant details you can bring together with it and how easily
and directly you can connect them.

LT. RHODES: Once we conclude that Hassler was committing suicide, we can
quite readily connect most of the details of the case. But not all. That's why
those loose ends bother me so.

HOLLAND: Ultimately, one gauges the rightness of a holistic explanation against
other holistic explanations. Are you saying that maybe there's a better explanation out there that would interrelate not only the things we have mentioned, but the loose ends that don't fit?

LT. RHODES: Could be. Hassler waiting on the street corner, for example, or her
missing papers for this seminar, or most puzzling of all, why she took this
odd, odd way of killing herself.

IRELAND: She could have just taken the poison at home or taken sleeping pills or
jumped off a building.

LT. RHODES: That's the most important loose end, her motive in complicating her
suicide this way. Patricia Hassler is the only one who can say for sure what
went on in her mind. For the rest of us, her intent is a matter of hearsay or
guesswork. I have some ideas. But it wouldn't be fair to the person involved to put them forward. Perhaps you can help me.

The careful plotting of the suicide raises one question, but there are others. Forty minutes elapsed between 8:30, when Anne and Paul arrived and saw Hassler's books on the table, and her reappearance in the doorway to the seminar room. Where did she go, and why?

Mr. Ireland, you saw her standing at the corner of Main Street and Masling Boulevard about 8:45, about the middle of that forty-minute period. Most people—not you, Ms. Glendish—thought it was pretty damn cold on Wednesday morning. Why did she leave a warm building to stand out there in the cold?

SISLEY: I don't know the answer to that one, but what about her standing behind Christian and saying, "He's the one"?

LT. RHODES: So far, we've concluded that this couldn't have been an accusation of murder because she couldn't know she was going to be murdered. But if she was committing suicide, then we have to change our previous conclusion. She knew she was going to die. Maybe, by pointing at M. Aval, she intended to make us think he was the murderer in the murder, so to speak, that was about to take place.

IRELAND: God, what a bitch!

LT. RHODES: The accusation itself, however, was ambiguous. We didn't understand it as an accusation, because we assumed she was murdered. Once we know that she was committing suicide, we can understand what she was saying. *He drove me to it.* By something that happened when they knew each other at Yale, perhaps. Ultimately, the phrase, "He's the one," means something different depending on whether we know about her planned suicide or not. It could mean something that we cannot even guess at now, because we lack some equally critical piece of knowledge.

Ah, Norman, I see your smile. I've said it wrong again.

HOLLAND: It's not the phrase that means—evidently, since we can give it several meanings. Given new information, we now see that our previous interpretation was wrong, and we give it the new meanings that you suggest. At least I do.

LT. RHODES: M. Aval, you look pale. Are you going to be sick? I can imagine that this must be deeply painful for you.

AVAL: No, Lieutenant. It is just that I have had what I can only describe as an attack of irony.

LT. RHODES: How very French of you. Do you want to explain?

AVAL: No, Lieutenant, I do not.

LT. RHODES: Very well. Let's simply leave it at that. That Ms. Hassler committed suicide and by this remark she made it likely that our suspicions would turn toward M. Aval. As they did.

EBENFELD: Then the suicide was planned more as a murder than a suicide.

LT. RHODES: A suicide *and* an attempted murder, the suicide of Patricia Hassler and—perhaps—an attempt to destroy Christian Aval. Once we hypothesize that Hassler was trying to make us arrest and convict Christian Aval for her death, another clue falls into place. We found in M. Aval's apartment a vial labeled "saxitoxin." It was in a peculiar place, wedged between his computer monitor and the central processing unit. It was a place where he himself couldn't fail to see it, and, as M. Aval himself pointed out, it was so clumsily hidden that we couldn't fail to find it. But precisely because it was so clumsily hidden, it was unlikely that a person as clever as M. Aval had hidden it.

SISLEY: So you think Trish hid it there.

LT. RHODES: Yes. I also think M. Aval would've noticed it at once when he sat down to his computer—as he did when we went to his apartment with him. He would certainly have removed it. Hence he must never have seen the vial before we discovered it. It *must have been put there after he left to go to the seminar Wednesday morning.*

GLENDISH: Jesus! What a thoroughgoing bitch! So when did she do this?

LT. RHODES: She must have wedged it into Aval's computer after she placed the thumbtack here. That, I think, is what she was doing in the missing forty minutes. She waited on the corner where Ireland saw her until she saw Aval cross Main Street on his way to Wednesday's seminar. Then she let herself into his apartment—Yorrick noticed that you could get past his lock with a credit card— and planted the false vial. Then she herself came to class. That was probably why she was late.

When she arrived, she looked startled or alarmed—that expression you all interpreted differently—because Aval wasn't in the seminar room. Your absence, M. Aval, would defeat her plans. You had to be present so that she could make her accusation, whatever it meant. Then, when you came in, she felt relieved and looked it.

The usual situation is that you have a crime without clues. Here we have clues—loose ends—without a crime. That is, if you don't consider suicide a crime. I don't.

We have several clues that don't fit the idea that Hassler committed suicide. The strangest one occurred around midnight last night. At that hour, my telephone rang. It was Professor Holland. He'd been working late in his office, and he heard someone come into the mailroom. He assumed this was our old friend the interloper, and when this individual left the mailroom, he followed him—or her—but he was unable to get a final identification. All he got was the address of the apartment building that this individual entered.

We found five graduate students from the English department living at the address Professor Holland noted. Kirk Kinder—not in this seminar. Felix Kulper—not in this seminar. Paul Penza . . .

PENZA: Lieutenant, that's where I used to live, and I've arranged with my old roommate to get my mail there. But you know that I'm sharing Anne's apartment now. I listed that old address because I didn't want everybody in the department to know. But all of you know that that's not where I was living last night.

GLENDISH: He was home with me last night.

LT. RHODES: I'll buy that. Abe Poria—not in this seminar. Max Ebenfeld . . .

EBENFELD: Yes, I live at the Shakespeare Arms. But I was home last night. I went to bed early. Alone.

LT. RHODES: Could you prove that?

EBENFELD: No way, Lieutenant.

LT. RHODES: To be frank with you, Max, it may be necessary. I've no idea at this point what the significance is, if any, of this late visitor to the mailroom.

LEMAIRE: Can I suggest something, Lieutenant? That it had nothing to do with this case. It was just a student delivering a paper to some faculty member's mailbox, a student who'd worked late. Lots of us end up delivering papers in the middle of the night. We figure, if the prof set a 5:00 deadline, as they mostly do, he won't pick the papers up till the next morning. You can get a whole night's extra time to work. Profs don't go to the mailroom at night. Students do, though, lots of times. We T.A.s all have keys to get us in the front door of the building and into the mailroom.

LT. RHODES: That's the way I interpreted it, Amy, when I decided not to send someone around to check the mailroom last night. Professor Holland had checked his mail anyway. Now I regret not checking, because of the squibs that you got—or didn't get—this morning. These squibs must have been delivered *after* Holland looked. Probably, then, the person he heard and followed wasn't the interloper. But none of this fits my solution, that Hassler committed suicide.

SISLEY: It seems beside the point to me. Does the mystery student matter, now that we're sure that Hassler committed suicide?

LT. RHODES: Probably not. But it's another loose end. Why did someone take Hassler's books across the hall on Wednesday morning? Another detail that doesn't fit the explanation. And here's the most puzzling one of all. Sergeant Yorrick came by the mailroom and picked up the squibs from your mailboxes. As you know, we've been trying to identify the interloper from fingerprints on his squibs. Thank you very much, by the way, for your cooperation in that effort.

We collected this morning's squibs and checked them for fingerprints. There were *no* fingerprints. That's odd, since there were fingerprints on the squib we got yesterday from the interloper. It's particularly odd, given what this squib says. Let me pass out these photocopies of this new squib. Put your interpretive skills to work and tell me what you make of this text.

```
English 129                        March 9, 1984
                                   Joker


To my fellow hopers/hoppers? after truth, reality, the
facts

Let's push aside all the bullshit theorizing and poke
right into the core of the matter. I did it.
     Patricia had found out who I was, and she was threat-
ening to reveal my role in the seminar. She told me, and
she convinced me, I believed her, that Badger would make
a brouhaha of all this and withdraw me from the program.
End of Ph.D., end of career, end of me. She had to be
silenced. Before any of you had entered the room, the
poisoned tack was already on Patricia's chair, waiting
for her body. I could go away, knowing the inevitable
would happen. There was no need for me to be present.
There never has been, has there?
     And who am I? Never fear, you shall find out. I am, so
to speak, depositing me at the same time as this response
to you. Friday morning--tomorrow morning--my guilt will
become visible to all. Revelation!
     Nevertheless, you shall not have me, Lieutenant
Rhodes. I don't expect to sit in your courtroom or your
prison while you build up testimony and inference. The
guilty one will be punished by the guilty one, the in-
truder by the intruder. That is enough. Until tomorrow
morning, then . . .
```

AVAL: That's his printer, an IBM Graphic, I think. *[Pause for thirty seconds or so.]*

HOLLAND: Wait a minute! If Trish killed herself, why on earth is the mystery student confessing to her murder?

LT. RHODES: Now do you see what I meant about loose ends? This is a major piece of data that doesn't fit. Why indeed? But do you think this was written by the interloper? Maybe someone else wrote this and attributed it to him. Can you try your interpretive skills on this? *[They were all quiet for about a minute and a half—slm.]*

PENZA: You're all so silent— I'll speak up. It sounds just like him. "Hopers/hoppers." That's him—his playing with puns. Then all the stuff about getting to reality and facts hidden by, he says, "bullshit." That's him, exactly. You call it "fascination with things hidden," Norm. "Hopper"—haven't I heard that word used for a toilet? All his anality.

LEMAIRE: I don't know . . . If I were going to confess to a murder, would I do it this way? Playing hide-and-seek games?

PENZA: You wouldn't, Amy, but he would.

LEMAIRE: You're always so sure of things, Paul.

HOLLAND: I have to confess I'm not sure of this one. It's a little off, somehow, a little away from his usual style.

AVAL: To me, it is exactly like him. I agree with Paul. "Hopers/hoppers." He is afraid he will be revealed, as he has been afraid all semester. He is so pleased with himself as he tells the story of how he did it. "Revelation!" That is very like him. Notice, too, that he is absent, hidden, distanced. "I could go away."

HOLLAND: But not being in spaces could equally well be you, Chris. Like the ending, about not being in the courtroom.

GLENDISH: He was always showing off in what he wrote for us. How clever he was and at the same time, how illicit. How he could break all the rules. This time he got broken. This one just doesn't read like him.

HOLLAND: Justin, this seems to me the purest kind of intrinsic evidence.

AVAL: I think he is hiding there, as when he refers to himself as "the guilty one, the intruder." He always speaks of himself in the third person that way.

SISLEY: I agree with Norm. It's not quite like our mystery student's usual hide-and-seek. Maybe someone else was pretending to write like him, imitating his mannerisms.

LT. RHODES: Whoever wrote this, the intruder or someone else, how did this person know which was Hassler's chair?

HOLLAND: Good point, Lieutenant. Extrinsic evidence.

LT. RHODES: Especially since it wasn't Hassler's chair anyway, but your regular seat.
    I have to point out, M. Aval, that "brouhaha" is a French word.

IRELAND: Score one for the home team!

AVAL: I have to point out, Lieutenant, that the word has ceased to be exclusively French. "Brouhaha" has become an English word also. As "racket" has become French.

HOLLAND: I didn't know that!

LT. RHODES: We're losing sight of the question. Tell me, does this squib read to your practiced eyes like other squibs by the interloper?

HOLLAND: I don't think we can distinguish with any surety one person's writing style from a second person's imitation of it. Not without some sort of computer counting of letters or sentence lengths or adjective-noun ratios, the kind of thing even a forger is unaware of.

LT. RHODES: I suppose I have to accept that—you're the expert—but we're losing sight of this case. We have this squib. It's a confession, but I remain absolutely convinced by the method of her dying that Patricia Hassler took her own life. If she did, why is someone *forging a confession* to murder?

Another problem with this seeming confession. There are no fingerprints on the original squibs that were in your boxes. If someone is confessing, why would they take the trouble to eliminate fingerprints?

LEMAIRE: Maybe they just kept their gloves on when they came in. It was cold last night.

HOLLAND: You're telling me!

AVAL: I am not troubled, as you are, Lieutenant. What you call the loose ends are in the nature of things. The case you are working on is refracted to you through language, and language is by its nature ambiguous. The case is a text, and it is in the nature of texts to deconstruct themselves and impose on us conflicting and inconsistent meanings. The texts that we read or the texts that are the world—their meanings are, finally, undecidable.

May we leave now? I find this room a painful place to be.

LT. RHODES: I can understand that, Aval. But you need to accept that, as far as I'm concerned, Patricia Hassler committed suicide. No ifs, ands, or buts. No ambiguity. No deconstruction. No one but she could have . . . *[Somebody burst in at this point, an unidentified policeman.]*

VOICE: Lieutenant, they found a body! At the foot of the stairs. In the basement. *[At this point everybody started talking and shouting. I could only hear the lieutenant's voice shouting over and over again, "Get his fingerprints." "Get his fingerprints." Then someone turned off the machine. Me, probably. —slm]*

from the journal of Norman Holland

All of us, Rhodes, I, the students. Yorrick, Maistry, even Ms. Moreno, ran down the stairs to where they had found the body. Second floor, first floor, then down a flight of stairs I never knew existed to the eerie old basement of this old, old house and its giant furnace radiating the warm, resinous smell of oil-converted-from-coal—in Buffalo, you notice these things. At the foot of the stairs a body lay sprawled, horribly bruised, and the head full of blood with bits of what

I took to be white bone. Brain? Arms and legs every which way. I felt sick looking at it, and I had to turn my back to it. What has happened to my life that I am involved in this stuff? Rhodes took characteristic charge . . .

Metropolitan Buffalo Police Department

Tape Transcription   Homicide Unit

Body: *Hassler, P.; Kulper, F.*   Tape No. *840309.003*
Place: *Rhodes Hall basement, UB*   Time: *9:49 a.m.*
Persons present: *Det. Lt. Rhodes,Det. Sgt. Yorrick,*
     Det. Maistry, N. Holland, others

                              Transcribed by: *S. Moreno*

LT. RHODES: . . . back, back. You students will have to wait upstairs. Officer, get those students out of here. Stand outside that door so that the four of us can get to work. Yorrick, the first thing I want are fingerprints. Get your kit, and see if you can take them without moving the body off those stairs. I think it's going to be important to match those bruises to the stair treads. Maistry, go upstairs and send for Doc Welder.

DET. MAISTRY: Yes, sir.

LT. RHODES: Yorrick, as soon as you've got them, check those fingerprints out with Rollins and Bowers against the interloper's prints on those squibs. But first, Yorrick, get some uniforms and block off the area around the door leading down here. Use campus security.

SGT. YORRICK: Right away, Lieutenant.

LT. RHODES: Who's the corpse, Holland?

HOLLAND: He looks familiar. One of our students, I'm pretty sure, but I don't know his name.

LT. RHODES: His wallet says Felix Kulper. "6-A-H." What's that?

HOLLAND: Arts and humanities, year six. Wait a minute— Kulper was one of the five English students living at the Shakespeare Arms.

LT. RHODES: Tell me what you know about him.

HOLLAND: Not a thing.

LT. RHODES: I think he's our interloper.

HOLLAND: You mean this death is connected with the other one?

LT. RHODES: I think so. We'll know as soon as they check the fingerprints. I knew there were too damn many loose ends.

HOLLAND: Could this be another suicide?

LT. RHODES: Do people kill themselves by throwing themselves down a flight of stairs? Not bloody likely.

HOLLAND: An accident, then?

LT. RHODES: This is what killed him, this blow on the head. The skull is cracked—see?—but there's very little bleeding. No blood on the steps, to speak of. Death must have been instantaneous and *not* here in the basement.

HOLLAND: You mean this is another murder?

LT. RHODES: He's wearing rubber boots, those duck things with the canvas tops. That fits.

HOLLAND: I don't get it. No suicide. No accident. But how do you know this is the mystery student?

LT. RHODES: I don't *know* that. I suspect he is. We won't *know* until we get a match on those fingerprints.

HOLLAND: All right, *suspect*. Why do you *suspect* this is the mystery student?

LT. RHODES: Let's go up to your office. I need to do some thinking. Mrs. Moreno, you go find Maistry. That office is pretty small. C'mon, Norman, let's walk up.

HOLLAND: But you expect him to be.

LT. RHODES: Yes.END OF THIS SECTION OF TAPE END OF THIS SECTION OF TAPE END OF THIS SECTION OF TAPE END OF THIS SECTION

from the journal of Norman Holland

We were both pretty tired but keyed up, and I suppose he wanted the exercise. Anyway, he bounced up the four flights as though he were at a gym, and I trailed after him, puffing. Over his shoulder, he explained that he needed to think, and he thought that I could help him work out the solution. When we got to my office, I sat him down in the swivel chair, and I installed myself opposite him in the wooden chair where students usually sit. He sighed before he switched on the tape recorder.

"Sometimes I get awfully tired of this thing. I feel as though I'm on stage all the time. I feel locked into my own words. I feel like one of these criminals who have an electronic gadget strapped to their leg to monitor their imprisonment at home. Odd that they should treat the police this way as well as convicted criminals. Tell me, are they deconstructing a hierarchy, Norman?" I just

smiled. What could I say? It has nothing to do with deconstruction. He turned on his little recorder.

Metropolitan Buffalo Police Department

Tape Transcription   Homicide Unit

Body: *Hassler, P.*   Tape No. *840309.007*
Place: *Rhodes Hall 316 UB*   Time: *9:58 a.m.*
Persons present: *Det. Ltd. Rhodes, N. Holland*

                                                     Transcribed by: *S. Moreno*

LT. RHODES: Thanks for letting me use your office—and you—Norman. I want to do a little quiet brainstorming and see if we can figure out how this second death is related to the first.

HOLLAND: You're convinced they *are* related.

LT. RHODES: I am indeed.

HOLLAND: I noticed something. When we were back in the seminar room, the officer who said there was a body in the basement didn't say what kind of a body it was, but you automatically assumed it was a "he". "Get *his* fingerprints," you said.

LT. RHODES: I was pretty sure the body was the interloper, and we've assumed all along that the interloper was a he. And I'll bet Rollins and Bowers will show you I'm right.

HOLLAND: Why do you think it's the interloper's body? Why not just some unrelated person who fell down the stairs to the basement?

LT. RHODES: I had more than a hunch, Norman. Those damned loose ends. Hassler killed herself. That's clear. She apparently wanted everyone to think that Aval was responsible. *That's* clear. But we still had the interloper out there, and his mysterious, promising squib that we found in the mailboxes on Thursday. There was the unknown visitor to the mail room last night. Most important, we still hadn't explained the squib we found this morning. Not the police, but "the guilty one will punish the guilty one." That sounds to me like a threat of murder or, more likely, suicide. So, when we found a body, I thought it probably was the interloper's.

HOLLAND: But you said the squib was false.

LT. RHODES: Yes, that squib presents real problems. One, the squib confesses to Hassler's murder, but we know that Hassler wasn't murdered. Two, there are no fingerprints on the squib. Why would you eliminate your fingerprints if you were confessing anyway? Three, it's a suicide note—at least, as I read it. The writer says he won't be caught. Rather, the guilty one would punish the guilty one. And then we find a body, as promised, "tomorrow morning"—today. But it wasn't a suicide, not unless he committed suicide by throwing himself down the basement stairs with enough force to crack his skull. The squib is false three ways.

HOLLAND: Yet it was in something approximating the mystery student's style.

LT. RHODES: Right. If the note is false, that suggests—it doesn't prove, it suggests—that somebody went to the trouble of imitating the interloper's style. It had to be somebody who knew that style, so it presumably was someone in the seminar.

HOLLAND: *If* it was an imitation, and not the real thing.

LT. RHODES: Another problem. There was something extremely odd about your account of the nocturnal visitor to the mail room, Norman, something that nagged at me. I played the tape over, and then I spotted it. When you described this person coming up the stairs, you said you heard boots "squooshing" on the floor. Spongy, you said, like a squeegee. Then, when the person was leaving, you heard them "tapping" down the wooden staircase and "click" on the tile floor by the front door and finally, you saw sparks as this individual hurried along the sidewalk. Apparently this person had metal wedges in their boot heels. How does that fit with the "squooshing" you first heard, which sounds like rubber boots or galoshes?

HOLLAND: You're right! The sound *was* different. I didn't notice it at the time, because I was concentrating on not making any sound myself, but, yes, the sound of the boots leaving wasn't the same as the sound of the boots coming upstairs. What do you think that means?

LT. RHODES: You're the only one who can answer that.

HOLLAND: Me? I don't know. The person changed boots? But why would anyone do that? And where did they get them? Maybe the person who left wasn't the same as the person who came in? But how can that be? When I checked the mail room for squibs I didn't see anybody there. If there'd been two people on the third floor, I surely would've seen or heard the second one—just as I saw and heard the first. I don't get it.

LT. RHODES: Neither do I. And I don't know what, if anything, it has to do with this case. The most important thing we have to explain is this body. Why was Felix Kulper killed? Because he was the interloper? Surely that wasn't enough. Since Hassler was dead and since she committed suicide, who had anything to fear?

HOLLAND: I don't know.

LT. RHODES: That's what I came up here to try to figure out. I need some quiet and an intelligent audience.

HOLLAND: I'll do my best.

LT. RHODES: Why leave a squib this morning? Suppose there were no squib, what then? We'd find Kulper's body. For all we know, this dead person had nothing to do with the seminar or with Hassler. By producing a squib, whoever killed Kulper tied his death in with the seminar.

HOLLAND: But the mystery student was supposed to produce a squib this morning. Remember? Remember his Thursday "memo"? He said that if we didn't do something about what Trish had said, he'd do something on Friday morning. As I read the memo, he was saying he'd send one final squib revealing his own identity and whatever it was that Trish was supposed to have told us.

LT. RHODES: As I read that memo, he meant he'd come out of anonymity and come to the class.

HOLLAND: Language or presence.

LT. RHODES: Exactly what were the memo's words?

HOLLAND: I've got a copy here. "She TOLD you who did it, but you go on as if nothing had happened."

LT. RHODES: Who did what?

HOLLAND: Killed her.

LT. RHODES: But she killed herself.

HOLLAND: You were the only one who knew that.

LT. RHODES: We can't be sure. Somebody else might have figured it out. She might have confided her plan to commit suicide to someone.

Let me see that squib.

"What the hell is the matter with you lead-headed people? Are you so bamboozled and befuddled . . . that you don't believe her?"

You know, Norman, this reads to me as though the intruder thought they knew something that they didn't. Now, we could assume he was referring to Hassler's pointing the finger at Aval. But suppose it were something else. Suppose the intruder thought Hassler had told the class something else.

HOLLAND: The memo makes sense if you read it that way. "She TOLD you who did it." "Did it" could refer to something else, not her death.

LT. RHODES: Okay, let's follow that out. The intruder believed that Hassler had told the other people in the seminar something—we don't know what. Maybe the plagiarism at Yale. I'm going to guess that he somehow learned on Thursday—after he'd issued this memo—that the others *didn't* learn whatever it was they were supposed to learn.

What would that be? It was something Kulper knew, but the seminar didn't, but Kulper thought they knew it. And it was something he expected them to react to, maybe to do something about. Anyway it was something very drastic. And it was about something done to Patricia Hassler.

HOLLAND: Now how could Kulper know something the regular seminar members didn't know? And why did he think, on Thursday, that they did know it? Maybe somebody told him something, some crucial fact.

LT. RHODES: But then why would he assume that everybody in the seminar knew the fact? No, it must be some piece of information that he thought had gone to everybody in the seminar. It must have been something in one of your famous squibs. Those are the only things that go to everybody in the seminar, aren't they?

HOLLAND: Yes, except for the reading lists and the outline of the seminar they get from me at the beginning of the semester.

LT. RHODES: So we can assume that Kulper somehow got a squib that the others didn't get. How could that be? You remember, when we discussed with them how Kulper got squibs, they all said that he would take them out of their boxes, and then they'd have to ask whoever wrote the squib for an extra copy. If this hypothetical squib never got in the mailboxes, whom could the interloper steal it from?

HOLLAND: You've got me.

LT. RHODES: Wait a minute. Do you remember when the students talked to me about the different people whose squibs had been missing from their mailboxes? The one person whom nobody had missed a squib from was Trish Hassler. Do you see what that means?

HOLLAND: Has it something to do with her identity, her turning things against herself?

LT. RHODES: No, let's stick to facts—extrinsic evidence as you call it. If none of Hassler's squibs were stolen from the mailboxes of the regular members, that means that the interloper didn't have to steal them. *He was getting them already.* Who could he be getting them from?

HOLLAND: In principle, anybody. Anybody could make a xerox of a squib and put it in the mystery student's box.

LT. RHODES: But why would any of the other members of the seminar do that? It had to be Hassler herself. Somehow she knew who the interloper was, and she simply counted him into the seminar. She put a squib in his box at the same time that she put squibs in everybody else's boxes.

HOLLAND: That sounds reasonable enough. But what does that have to do with Kulper's death?

LT. RHODES: Suppose Hassler wrote a squib that somebody didn't want the rest of the students to get. Suppose it said something awful about that person, something that would damage him terribly. He might steal all the squibs and kill Hassler.

HOLLAND: Or she.

LT. RHODES: All right, I'll call this proto-killer X. X might steal all the squibs and kill Hassler.

HOLLAND: But Hassler wasn't murdered, she killed herself.

LT. RHODES: We're still at the stage of motivating X. We're still trying to see how Kulper might have known something the other members of the seminar didn't know, but he would think that they did.

Let's keep going on what we do have. Week after week, as the seminar went along, everybody got squibs from Hassler, right?

HOLLAND: Right.

LT. RHODES: But this week nobody got a squib from Hassler.

HOLLAND: That's right. Under the rules of the Delphi seminar, she didn't have to respond to what people wrote to her.

LT. RHODES: But suppose she *did* write a response. Suppose she put it in all the boxes, and then someone, someone who'd be terribly damaged by what that squib said, took all the squibs out. That someone wouldn't know that the interloper Kulper was also getting a squib, because only Hassler, on this theory, knew that Kulper was the interloper.

Hassler had put this damaging squib in Kulper's box and in the boxes of the other people in the seminar. X took the squibs out of the seminar people's boxes, but didn't know to take it out of Kulper's box. So Kulper knew something the people in the seminar didn't know, but he thought they knew, because what he got was just a squib like any other, a squib from Patricia Hassler.

HOLLAND: That's neat. You've explained both how Kulper would know what Hassler was saying about X and how he would assume everybody else knew it, too. But when would Trish have put this squib in the boxes?

LT. RHODES: You tell me. You know how this seminar works.

HOLLAND: She could have put them in the boxes anytime up to the Wednesday morning meeting of the seminar at 9:00.

LT. RHODES: But the killer has to take them out before anyone notices they are in the boxes. Right after Hassler distributes them.

HOLLAND: I see the problem. Does this help? Trish was always early with her squibs. None of us really wanted them, they were so bilious. Therefore she made sure we had them right away. She tended to put her squibs in early in the morning. This week, she might have put her squibs in early Monday morning or early Tuesday morning. If she waited until Wednesday, she could just have handed them out in the seminar itself.

LT. RHODES: Students, as I remember all too well, never get up until they have to.

So, if she was putting her squibs in the mailboxes early Monday or Tuesday morning, it's entirely possible none of the other students were around. Suppose that for some reason X, the one who'd be damaged by this squib, had gotten up early. X would find it before any of the others and remove the copies from the others' mailboxes, but fail to remove it from Kulper's box, because X didn't know about Kulper.

HOLLAND: Kulper and X dovetail logically. They both have the squib, they both know what it says, but Kulper thinks everybody else knows and X thinks that nobody else knows. Cute.

LT. RHODES: Hassler would come into the seminar Wednesday thinking they all had read her squib—I haven't worked out the consequences of that yet. Then on Thursday morning, when the seminar got copies of Kulper's squib accusing them of indifference, X would know that the interloper knew the damaging fact.

HOLLAND: But X wouldn't know who the interloper was.

LT. RHODES: X then decides to silence the interloper.

HOLLAND: Why? Hassler was already dead. She was the one making the accusation.

LT. RHODES: It must have been something that was just as dangerous in the interloper's hands as it was in Hassler's.

HOLLAND: What would that be?

LT. RHODES: We don't know yet. But it could be something Hassler found out about one of the seminar people, something that she'd shared with Kulper. Now he could take over her role as blackmailer or whatever. We just don't know.

HOLLAND: Whew! This is a long, long line of reasoning. We're pretty far from where we started, and that was already a set of assumptions and speculations.

But suppose Hassler had learned something about one of the students, X, something bad in X's past, say. Hassler could say, "X told me that she— or he—had done this awful thing." If Kulper said that Hassler said that X had confessed to this awful thing, that's once removed. It doesn't have the same force.

LT. RHODES: Maybe it does, maybe it doesn't. It depends on what the item of information is, doesn't it? At this point we just don't know. We need a text, as you might say, Professor.

What we do know is that X, the proto-murderer, now became a real murderer. X didn't have to kill Hassler because she killed herself, but X now had to kill Kulper. And did.

HOLLAND: You're absolutely sure that Kulper was murdered?

LT. RHODES: I'm as sure as I am that Hassler wasn't murdered. Suicide by throwing yourself down a flight of stairs? A probably forged suicide note confessing to a murder that wasn't a murder?

HOLLAND: Who is X, then?

LT. RHODES: A pretty problem, as the Master would say, but as we talk I'm beginning to get some ideas. Responses, would you say? Maybe.

Look at the sequence of events from X's point of view. As soon as X gets the interloper's Thursday morning squib, X knows that he—the interloper—has a copy of Hassler's squib. X knows that the interloper knows the terribly damaging thing that Hassler knew and the interloper has to be silenced. But X doesn't know who the interloper is. That's his problem. X has to kill somebody, but X doesn't know who.

All right. How can X find out? What does X know at this point? X knows that the interloper put a squib in the boxes. So the murderer knows that the interloper puts his squibs in the boxes sometime after midnight. That's the only point of contact the murderer has. So what would you do under these circumstances?

HOLLAND: I suppose X would have to lie in wait somehow for someone who was going up to the mailboxes to distribute a postmidnight squib.

LT. RHODES: That's where I come out, too. An ambush. But you've got to be sure you've got the right person.

Would you hide outside the building or inside?

HOLLAND: This time of year it's damned cold at night, as you had me demonstrate last night. Inside.

LT. RHODES: Yes, and you also want to be sure that this person is there to distribute squibs, not to work in an office at some weird hour or deliver a late paper or God knows what. You don't want to kill the wrong person, only the one person who can put into the mailboxes this information that you fear.

HOLLAND: Right. X has got to see this person is actually putting the papers in. So X has got to hide not only in the building, but in the mailroom itself and watch what anyone does who comes in.

LT. RHODES: Good point. That's the way I see it too. Now can you picture the mailroom? Where would you hide?

HOLLAND: It's right on this floor. Let's go look.

LT. RHODES: Okay. Whoever is transcribing this, we're walking down the hall to the mail room. Why on earth is it on the third floor when the secretaries are on the first floor?

HOLLAND: That's some of Badger's doing. Efficiency, she says. She knows professors are always checking their mailboxes, and she wants to save professorial time. So let's put the mail room right where the professors are. Who cares if the secretaries have to trudge up three flights of stairs every time they want to mail something or put something in somebody's mailbox? Their time isn't as valuable as the professors'.

LT. RHODES: Curious. Yet you tell me the secretaries like her and the faculty don't.

HOLLAND: I think they like a woman's being chairman—chairperson.

LT. RHODES: Let's see. It's a long, narrow room. It must have been a kind of elongated closet once. There are the mailboxes on either side of the length of the room. The door is at one end.

HOLLAND: Could X have hid behind the door?

LT. RHODES: Possibly. He might have had to stand there some hours. But look at the other end of the room. What's that big old wooden desk for? It covers about half the width of the room.

HOLLAND: I guess we leave it there so people can run the postage meter, put finishing touches on letters, fill out forms that come in and put them right back in the next mail going out.

LT. RHODES: And a swivel chair in front of it. Yes, that makes sense. X could have scrunched down into the hole of the desk, and pulled the swivel chair in after him. If X's clothes were dark, unless someone were looking down and into the desk, no one would see him.

HOLLAND: Waiting to kill. You'd have to occupy your mind. If X brought a flashlight, he could even read, like a kid under the covers after his parents have put the light out.

LT. RHODES: That's a curious image for a murderer waiting for his or her victim.

HOLLAND: I can't get used to the idea that one of my students is a murderer.

LT. RHODES: Anyway, it's a place where X could have waited. Here's how it works. X enters the building sometime in the evening, using a key available to any teaching assistant. X hides under this desk and waits. Eventually, Kulper comes into the mailroom, turns on the lights, and starts putting squibs in the boxes. X slides out from under the desk and hits Kulper with— with what? What could the murderer have used for a weapon?

HOLLAND: Maybe that big, heavy tape holder on the desk?

LT. RHODES: That'd make a blunt enough instrument to satisfy any mystery writer. I'll have to get it checked for fingerprints and blood.

Yorrick!! Sergeant!! Come here, will you?

Come to think of it, though, our murderer may have brought his own weapon. As I imagine him he's extremely foresighted, all this figuring out of who knows what and realizing that the interloper has the fatal information.

SGT. YORRICK: Yes, Lieutenant.

LT. RHODES: Sergeant, I think this may be the room where Kulper was killed. I want you to get a couple of uniforms and seal it off. Send for a site team from downtown. Nobody comes in here except you and them. Check the room for blood, skin, brains, other tissues. Use an iron test if you find anything that looks like traces of blood. The killer probably wiped up. Check particularly around the desk and in front of the mailboxes on the right side, the graduate student side. The swivel chair, too. But all over. The weapon may have been that Scotch tape dispenser sitting on the desk. Put that in one of your plastic bags and have the lab people check it over.

SGT. YORRICK: Right away, Lieutenant. You're making progress, I take it.

LT. RHODES: I think so.

SGT. YORRICK: Doc Welder has checked the body over and wants to see you.

LT. RHODES: I'll talk to him out in the hall. Let's keep this room as clean as we can. Send him up.

SGT. YORRICK: I'll get a couple of uniforms up here, too.

DR. WELDER: Justin, I've only given him a quick lookover, but I can tell you some things right away.

LT. RHODES: Go to it.

DR. WELDER: He wasn't killed by the fall.

LT. RHODES: I'd guessed that already, Doc.

DR. WELDER: Do you want this or not?

LT. RHODES: Sure. Sorry.

DR. WELDER: I don't have the evidence you have.

LT. RHODES: I know.

DR. WELDER: If I did, I'd probably have the case solved by now.

LT. RHODES: You might well, Doc. Let me have what you've got so far.

DR. WELDER: The fall didn't kill him, because the bruises from the fall don't show internal bleeding. Cause of death was a blow to the head. Proverbial blunt instrument. Very heavy blow. Enough to crack the skull. Death was instantaneous. Then he was thrown down the stairs.

LT. RHODES: Would this Scotch tape holder do it?

DR. WELDER: Sure, just the thing.

LT. RHODES: Time of death?

DR. WELDER: Can't tell yet, Justin. So far I've taken a rectal temperature and checked for rigor mortis. I'd say from nine to ten hours ago.

LT. RHODES: About twelve or one in the morning.

DR. WELDER: That's the arithmetic, yes.

LT. RHODES: That fits, doesn't it, Norman, with the time you saw X leaving this building? Okay. We have the murderer in the mail room at that time and you in your office, listening at the door. This mail room door closes automatically, doesn't it, so the door here was closed.

HOLLAND: I didn't hear anything.

LT. RHODES: The murderer slugs Kulper. It doesn't matter whether he used the Scotch tape holder or brought his own weapon. The important thing is that there's something here he might have used.

I imagine X rolling the swivel chair forward very quietly and coming out from under the desk, standing behind Kulper as Kulper is concentrating on the mailboxes. X hits Kulper and Kulper goes down.

Then X pulls the squibs out of the mailboxes—

HOLLAND: This time X checks Kulper's own mailbox—

DR. WELDER: Gentlemen, what's a squib?

LT. RHODES: It's a paper for Holland's seminar, Doc. Let's keep going—

X puts the squibs in his pocket to dispose of them later—

HOLLAND: The person I saw outside had a book bag.

LT. RHODES: —and X hides Kulper's body in the mail room, probably in the same kneehole of the desk where he'd been hiding.

HOLLAND: First X has to search the body for any extra copies and pocket those.

LT. RHODES: Right. And now we know why the boots sounded different.

HOLLAND: We do?

LT. RHODES: We got a squib this morning.

HOLLAND: Right.

LT. RHODES: The purpose in killing Kulper was to prevent us getting the squib Kulper was putting in the boxes. When you checked the mailboxes last night, there were no squibs, but we got a squib this morning. Evidently, then, the killer provided another squib for us. X must have gone to Kulper's apartment and forged the squib for this morning, using Kulper's computer and Kulper's printer, so it would look like all the other squibs from the interloper.

The person you were following wasn't the interloper, not Kulper who wore rubber boots, but someone who wore boots with hard soles and heels. After you went back to your place and telephoned me, that person brought the squibs back here and put them in the mailboxes. Then he or she carried Kulper's body to the first floor and threw it down the stairs to the basement.

HOLLAND: God! It's like the tack in the chair. I feel I came this close to death! While I was working in my office last night, this murderer was hiding in the mailroom just down the hall.

DR. WELDER: Rhodes does that to people, Professor Holland.

HOLLAND: He walked past just on the other side of my office door. If he'd heard me in there . . . If he'd caught me trailing him . . .

LT. RHODES: I'd never have asked you to trail him—or her—if I'd guessed last night you'd be following a murderer. As of last night, the only body I knew about was Hassler's, and she had suicided.

DR. WELDER: That's what *he* says.

LT. RHODES: Don't you have a body to look into, Doc?

DR. WELDER: Bye-bye, gentlemen.

LT. RHODES: On your way, Doc.

HOLLAND: Justin, this is all pretty far-fetched. You're making a lot of fancy deductions from assumptions and guesses.

LT. RHODES: But everything does fit, doesn't it? Even the boots. And this story brings together the various puzzling falsities. We did get a squib from Kulper this morning, but not, we think, a squib that Kulper wrote. And the squib had no fingerprints on it. In this squib Kulper confesses to Hassler's murder—and we know it wasn't a murder—and provides a motive for his own suicide—which we know wasn't a suicide. The squib is doubly, trebly, false! Nevertheless, the squib was written on his dot-matrix printer, so that it looked like all his other squibs. The murderer forged it, and to forge it, you have to go back to Kulper's apartment.

Let's pick up the story from there. Look at it through X's eyes. You get Kulper's keys from his pocket, because you know you have to get rid of the squib in Kulper's computer. Probably you put on Kulper's down jacket in case someone sees you leaving the building or going into Kulper's apartment.

HOLLAND: As I did.

LT. RHODES: Yes. Now we pick up your part of the story. X goes downstairs, and as soon as you hear his footsteps going out the front door of the building, you check the mailboxes, but because you're looking at the mailboxes, you don't see the body under the desk.

HOLLAND: You mean I was right there next to the body? God!

LT. RHODES: You find no squibs and you're puzzled. But you're still convinced this is the interloper.

HOLLAND: I didn't know till Amy told us this morning that students were still handing in papers in the middle of the night.

LT. RHODES: You telephone me. I suggest you follow out your hunch.

HOLLAND: So I follow this person.

LT. RHODES: You keep at a good distance.

HOLLAND: Had I gotten any closer to him, had he seen me . . .

LT. RHODES: Take it easy. You follow the person you assumed was the interloper, and you get the address of the building. You wait outside and try to see what light comes on so as to get the apartment number, or at least the floor, but you don't see a light come on.

Maybe it was in the back. Maybe Kulper's murderer used a flashlight. Maybe that was the blunt instrument.

Anyway, you get the address and you go home. You check the department list and find five English students who lived in that building. You telephone me.

HOLLAND: So the person I followed last night *was* the murderer, going to Kulper's apartment—now that X knew who the interloper was. He had an address, and a key. You've gone incredibly far on very little evidence so far. Can you go all the way? Can you figure out who X was?

LT. RHODES: Walking fifty yards in front of you, the murderer was showing you only the back of a down parka or whatever.

HOLLAND: Yes, a down parka.

LT. RHODES: I'm assuming the killer disguised himself in Kulper's parka. Wore it to the apartment and back, then put it back on the body when he put the fake squibs in the boxes, then wore his own parka away. Or hers.

HOLLAND: Yes, the parka on the body downstairs looks like the one I saw. I can't tell about the color, because it was night. So that's an important clue, isn't it? We're looking for a man—

LT. RHODES: Or woman. Couldn't a woman have worn Kulper's parka? Didn't you say that you can't tell your male and female students apart when they're all bundled up in those down jackets and parkas?

HOLLAND: Fair enough. But a middle-sized person. It had to be someone about Kulper's size. That leaves out Amy Lemaire, too small, and Max Ebenfeld, too big.

LT. RHODES: I don't think so. You couldn't be sure of the person's size at that distance in that light.

HOLLAND: But if they put on Kulper's down jacket?

LT. RHODES: I still say, for the time being anyway, that, bundled up that way and in the middle of the night and at that distance, the person you saw could have been anybody.

Anyway, we know what you did. What did the murderer do? X didn't know, presumably, that he or she had been followed. Once in Kulper's apartment, X must have taken the time to destroy any evidence of Kulper's real squib. That'd mean destroying any extra copies and making sure there was no text of the squib in Kulper's computer. Then X printed out the fake squib, took it back to the mailroom, and put it in the seminar mailboxes. Presumably X then lugged Kulper's body down to the first floor and pushed it down the flight of stairs leading to the basement. The idea was to make the death look like an accident by someone going down to the basement to commit the suicide hinted at in the squib.

The murderer wanted us to read Kulper's death this way. Kulper wanted to die. He headed for the basement where he would find lots of ways to kill himself—ropes, chemicals, plastic bags. In a suicidal state of mind Kulper could be careless enough on the stairs to fall. That would explain the skull wound. It's not the greatest script—X must have been running out of imaginative ideas. But it was enough if it didn't look like a murder.

Anyway, it was over now. X left the body at the bottom of the stairs, went home, and waited for the morning meeting of the seminar.

HOLLAND: Destroying the real squibs someplace along the way. If we could only find Kulper's real squib. Then we'd have a motive and an identity.

LT. RHODES: Yes. This all makes sense as a narrative of the murder, but it doesn't tell me who had the starring role. What it does tell us is what we have to do next. Get to Kulper's apartment as fast as we can. Yes, Hy.

DET. ROLLINS: Lieutenant, we got a match on those fingerprints. Tolerably good match. Between the left hand of the corpse in the basement and the partials on those papers you gave us.

LT. RHODES: So Kulper *was* the interloper! Fast work, Hy. You can go back to headquarters now. We won't be needing any more print work here, anyway.

DET. ROLLINS: Okay, Lieutenant. Later.

LT. RHODES: Rollins's evidence only confirms what we'd already figured out. The mind is faster than the fingerprint man.

HOLLAND: You were talking about speed before. Why is speed so important?

LT. RHODES: It's always a good idea, but in this case more so. This is one smart murderer, just as aware of these loose ends as we are—more so, probably. This killer might make a run for it.

Let's get over to Kulper's. Norman, you come. This brainstorming has been very helpful. As you must have recognized by now, you're no longer one of the suspects. I wouldn't have talked to you this way if you were.

HOLLAND: I'm not?

LT. RHODES: No. If you were guilty, you'd never have said what you did about the boots. I'll shut off the machine. My car is in the lot outside. Officer, it's important to keep everybody out of this room except Sgt. Yorrick or somebody he tells you to let in. Maistry, come along with us. We may need some computer help.END OF THIS SECTION OF TAPE END OF THIS SECTION OF TAPE END OF THIS SECTION OF TAPE END OF THIS SEC

Metropolitan Buffalo Police Department

Tape Transcription   Homicide Unit

Body: *Hassler, P.; Kulper, F.*   Tape No. *840309.010*

Place: *131 Masling Boulevard, Apt. 3-B*   Time: *10:40 a.m.*

Persons present: *Det. Ltd. Rhodes, Det. Maistry,*
    N. Holland

Transcribed by: *J. Cipperman*

LT. RHODES: . . . start recording. I'm taping our search of the apartment of Felix Kulper, the student who died. Address, 131 Masling Boulevard, apartment 3-B. Norman, don't touch anything. Let's just stand still and look for a minute.

    The apartment is strangely neat. Nondescript student furniture, cheap. Dusty. It hasn't been cleaned in a while, but no clothes lying around. All hung up in the closet. Books and papers all neat.

    For the record, the lock on this door was a sturdy Medeco D-10. It would not be possible to enter simply by using a credit card to slip the bolt back, as it was with Hassler's and Aval's doors. We used Kulper's keys which we took from the pocket of the jacket on the body.

    Maistry, look at the windows.

DET. MAISTRY: Security locks on the windows, too, Lieutenant. This kid was as careful as a surgeon in the suburbs.

HOLLAND: But so juvenile. Look at those stolen traffic signs. "Slippery When Wet." "No Right Turn." And the flashing lights from road barriers. I thought only fraternity boys stole those things.

    Oh, no! Look at the handcuffs, hanging from the arm of the floor lamp. Handcuffs! And over there, tacked up on the wall, a set of old leg irons. And look on the bureau—an animal trap.

LT. RHODES: I've only seen those things on Penn and Teller. This looks more than a wee bit sadomasochistic to me, Norman. Bondage is the game here.

    At the same time, Kulper was incredibly orderly, wasn't he? Look at these books, arranged alphabetically by author. He's got different kinds of stationery and notebooks all neatly stacked. Look. He's got ten, count 'em, ten different colored felt-tip highlighter pens all arranged in a cup. He has a file cabinet for his papers—how many students do that, Norman? His stationery all neatly set out on shelves. Look, he even has ten different colors of typing paper in meticulous little piles on that shelf. They must go with the highlighter pens.

HOLLAND: Look at all those books! Was he that much of a student? No, not when you look at what they are. Amanda Cross. Kirby Farrell. Sara Paretsky. Q. Patrick. These are just mystery stories. But alphabetized in with his copies of Barthes and Derrida and Lacan and Foucault, all the scholarly stuff. Can I pick some books up now?

LT. RHODES: Go ahead.

HOLLAND: See here, on the tags pasted into the inside back covers? Half of these are library books, but not charged out, and he's taken the tags off the spines. He was stealing books and mixing them in with books he owned. But surely that's not very good hiding. Anyone who came here would see right away what he was doing. I certainly have.

LT. RHODES: Maybe that's the tip-off. Nobody did come here. He tried to come on to the women in your seminar, but they wouldn't have anything to do with him. I'll bet he batted out with other women too. And he doesn't seem the type to have male buddies. Or maybe whatever visitors he had didn't care whether he was stealing books from the library.

Anyway, what we're looking for is the last real squib he wrote, not the one we found in the boxes this morning. How would you go about it, Norman?

HOLLAND: If he wrote this paper yesterday, chances are it's still around on his desk or his table somewhere.

LT. RHODES: Maistry, we're looking for a piece of regular typing paper with this kind of heading—Norman, show her one of the squibs you're carrying. Look on the surfaces, the desk, the table. Check the wastebasket. Look around. Try not to disturb things. Open those file folders carefully. I'll check too. *[About four minutes of silence here. Shuffling sounds.]*

HOLLAND: He'd try to hide his squibs, because he'd get into trouble if the department found out he was messing up a graduate seminar.

And besides, Kulper just plain likes to hide things.

LT. RHODES: Wait a minute. The killer came back here, and presumably he or she would have tried to get rid of any extra copies Kulper had made. I don't think we'll find any just out in the open.

HOLLAND: Maybe we shouldn't be looking for one sheet of paper. He was writing papers for this seminar every week, and the papers have to refer to previous papers.

At this point in the semester, the stack of papers I've got for this seminar is an inch and a half, two inches thick. People sort them different ways. Some make a file for each member of the seminar. Some make a file for each week. Some just stack them, week by week, alphabetical within each week . . .

Let's change our tactic. Look around for a stack of file folders or just a stack of papers an inch and a half or so thick. *[Shuffling sounds again.]*

DET. MAISTRY: I think the lieutenant is right, Professor. If Kulper's killer came here, he'd have searched the same way we're searching, and he came here first. I just don't think we're going to find the missing squib.

HOLLAND: Let's tackle the file cabinet. Boy! I remember when all my papers would fit in a two-drawer file cabinet.

DET. MAISTRY: These files are all neatly cataloged and dated. That isn't like any student I ever met.

LT. RHODES: This one is labeled "Graduate School Application," this one is "Teaching Assistant Application." These look like his personal papers.

HOLLAND: He might mislabel them, Justin. That would be a way of hiding the seminar papers. But he'd have to have some sort of system to keep the different people's papers straight and the different weeks.

LT. RHODES: Look at how sloppily the papers are stuffed back in these folders. A lot of the time you can't read the label on the file. I think these must have been searched already.

HOLLAND: If they've been searched already, I guess there's no use searching them again. If the killer came across the squib he'd have taken it. If he didn't, we're not likely to come across it either.

DET. MAISTRY: There's one place he might have left one, because it wouldn't be so easy for the two of you to find.

LT. RHODES: Oh?

DET. MAISTRY: His computer. That's where he wrote them, after all, and it's, like, automatic to "save" what you write.

HOLLAND: Right, Maistry. Exactly right.

LT. RHODES: Okay, check it out, the two of you. I'll keep leafing through his papers. So long as I can be sure that this isn't one paper in isolation. I'm looking for a whole group of squibs, right?

HOLLAND: I feel pretty sure that if you find any squibs at all you'll find the one we're looking for among them. Hey! The computer is still on!

DET. MAISTRY: Some people do that, just leave them on, to save wear and tear on the hard drive.

HOLLAND: I'll do a directory. *[Pause.]* Hey, something's wrong here. I can't get directories. The whole system is hanging up. What's up, Maistry? You're the computer expert. Look, it's just flashing. It's just flashing the IBM logo over and over.

DET. MAISTRY: I'll reset the machine. *[Pause.]* Oops! Nothing! There's no operating system available for it to come on with.

LT. RHODES: Say what that means, Margo.

DET. MAISTRY: It means that the computer has been wiped. It's just the way Hassler's computer was, except this time whoever it was left the computer on. Somebody came in and formatted the hard disk. Then, once you try to do anything with the computer, anything that requires the operating system, the machine can't do it, and gradually it hangs up. But this person didn't turn the machine off. They didn't wait for it to finish. They were in a hurry.

Maybe too much of a hurry to erase the floppies. Hey! I don't see any floppies anywhere. No back-up? Nobody but nobody runs a computer without back-up. That can mean only one thing, Lieutenant.

LT. RHODES: So, say.

DET. MAISTRY: Whoever did this took the floppies with them. They must have dumped them somewhere, garbage can, sewer, dumpster, somewhere. You probably can find them if you mobilize Sanitation and get some extra help.

LT. RHODES: We're running out of time. So did the killer, even though he had much of the night. Time to write a squib. Time to search two drawersful of file folders. But then he had to take the floppies, leaving a trail for us. But we don't have time to follow it. Let's look in the bedroom and the bathroom. Last resort.

HOLLAND: I'll check the closet.

DET. MAISTRY: Me too. What weird clothes! Elephant pants. Balloon jeans. Vests with nail heads on them. All rips and safety pins. You don't get this at The GAP. This guy is just too much!

HOLLAND: Hey, Justin, look down here! Look what I found! A safe!

LT. RHODES: A safe! Look at that, will you. One of those little cubic foot safes bolted onto the floor. Who ever heard of a student—a graduate student!—with a safe? What would he put in it, his platinum paperclips? His diamond-studded dictionary?

HOLLAND: He was always going on in his squibs about things being hidden, concealed, and the dangers if they came out. Look at the locks on the doors and windows, the handcuffs on the lamp. I read Kulper as preoccupied with keeping things inside, to himself, where others couldn't see them. Locks to keep people out, locks to keep things in.

DET. MAISTRY: Look here, Lieutenant, around the lock. See them?

LT. RHODES: Scratch marks.

DET. MAISTRY: Like from a screwdriver or something. Somebody tried to pry it open but, like, couldn't do it.

HOLLAND: They could be old marks.

LT. RHODES: I wish they were, but I doubt it. Maistry, get on the radio in the car and tell headquarters to send us somebody who can open this thing. And tell them to start searching the garbage cans between here and Rhodes Hall for those floppies. Tell them we're in a hurry. I've got a feeling whoever searched this place may have found this safe. If they did, they're making a getaway right now.

HOLLAND: I don't understand.

LT. RHODES: To it, Maistry! Norman, we know this place was searched because we saw papers out of order, the computer wiped, and the floppies taken. We assume the searcher was the killer, who wanted to find all copies of the missing squib, the one he or she had killed Kulper to intercept. We know the killer found the ones Kulper brought to the mail room and may have found others in this apartment or in the computer. If he found any, he removed them. We haven't been able to find them, anyway.

HOLLAND: Okay. Either the killer did or didn't find the squibs. That's tautological.

LT. RHODES: Now suppose, after having gotten rid of the squibs he found, the killer finds this safe. He thought he was in the clear, having destroyed the squibs. Now the killer has to assume that the safe holds copies of that paper. But he can't open the safe. He tries to open the safe, but he can't—the scratch marks. He has to figure, then, that there are more dangerous papers in the safe. They could still do damage. If that damage is sufficiently bad, the killer has to run for it.

HOLLAND: You've got another long stretch of reasoning.

LT. RHODES: True. Only the killer knows what he fears. We won't know what the damage is until we read what's in the safe. But the killer may be long gone by then. Maistry, are they sending a safe expert?

DET. MAISTRY: Yes, Lieutenant. He's on his way. They say it'll take a good hour, like, to get him here from downtown. They've got to bring him in from another case.

LT. RHODES: Damn! I don't want to wait that long. Maistry, give me your .38. I'm going to shoot it open.END OF THIS SECTION OF TAPE END OF THIS SECTION OF TAPE END OF THIS SECTION OF TAPE END OF THIS

from the journal of Norman Holland

Maistry's .38 was just the thing to open Kulper's little safe. Justin's first shot put a dent and a hole right at the space on the door between the dial and the edge of the safe. His second shot blew the door right open. "Piece of junk," was Maistry's terse verdict.

The first shot also, however, blew out Justin's tape recorder. The transcript of our search of Kulper's apartment came to an abrupt end. I wonder if the bang hurt the transcriber's ears.

And, of course, we didn't find the crucial squibs in the safe anyway. What we did find was Strips, Dr. Dominatrix, Tits and Clits, Young Lust, *comic books they sure didn't publish when I was a lad. There were some sadomasochistic photographs, and a pair of panties (!), but no squibs. At the bottom of the pile was an ordinary brown clasp envelope sealed with transparent tape, the milky kind that you can write on, and on the tape was Patricia Hassler's signature. And it had been opened.*

Hotel safe!, I thought. That's the way you wrap something up when you put

it in a hotel safe so you can be sure nobody but you has opened the envelope. I began to have a sinking feeling about that package.

"Since this was in Kulper's locked safe, but opened, I assume Kulper must have been the one who opened it," said Rhodes. *He stuck his fingers down into the envelope and took out a smaller package wrapped in a sheet of white typing paper that also had Trish Hassler's bold signature across several strips of transparent tape. This, too, had been opened.*

When he unfolded the paper, written on it in Kulper's square printing was this: "This package belongs to Patricia Hassler who has asked me to keep it in a safe place. I have promised her not to open it except in case of her death," *and Kulper's signature. The smaller package was wrapped again with transparent tape marked with Hassler's signature. It too had been slit open. When Rhodes unfolded the paper, there was an audiocassette.*

"She gave him the cassette sealed, with her signature on it. That way she'd know if he broke his word and listened to it," *said Rhodes, thinking out loud.* "Then she had him write and sign his promise to her in this childish way. That says something about Kulper, doesn't it? She knew her man all right, or her boy. She didn't want anybody to know about this. Except if she were dead. I think it's a safe guess that Kulper didn't open the package until after Wednesday morning."

I knew now I was in for it. This had to be the tape Amy'd told me about, the secret tape Trish had used to blackmail her. She was going to become top suspect and I guilty of obstructing justice or something.

Rhodes looked around until he spotted a stack of silvery stereo equipment. "Maistry?" *He handed our blonde detective the tape, and pointed to the tape deck. She began figuring out the knobs. Pilot lights went on and Maistry slipped the cassette in. Rhodes bent his head down to listen.*

Out of the big loudspeakers came two women's voices. "Bassy," *said Rhodes, smiling, as he gestured to Maistry to turn up the volume and start the tape again at the beginning.*

"I find it hard to believe about you. You just don't look the type."

"I was upset, I told you . . ."

Rhodes jumped up and hit the pause button. "Do you recognize those voices, Holland?"

Of course I did, although I shook my head no. Trish Hassler's deep, harsh alto and Amy Lemaire's small soprano. I could even hear the faint slurring of Amy's consonants from the beer she'd drunk. Rhodes started the tape again.

"I find it hard to believe about you. You just don't look the type."

"I was upset, I told you, after Herbert died and learning he was bi all the time we were together. I went a little manic, I think, and this seemed to keep me level."

"*Let me get this straight once more. You really were a hooker for sixteen months? You, motherly-looking Amy Lemaire?*" *Rhodes looked sharply at me.*

"*Why do you keep trying to get me to repeat all this? Yes, I was a hooker, and I was damned good at it, and it wasn't half bad as a way to make a living. I worked in an apartment on 70th and Madison, right opposite the Westbury Hotel. Nice clientele. Continental. Why are you making me repeat all this?*" *And Amy giggled.*

"*Not repeat, 'iterate.'*"

"*Jargon, jargon, you give me that jargon all the time, Trish.*" *Another questioning glance from Rhodes.* "*Why not 'repeat'? It's a fine old Anglo-Saxon word like some others I could mention. Why 'iterate'?*"

"*I said 'iterate' because it has a special meaning to bright young literary theorists like you and me. You remember Derrida and 'iterability,' the fundamental property of signs in an age of mechanically reproducible images. Any text can be 'iterated' in another context and it comes to mean something different.*"

"*I must have had too much beer.*"

"*I think you did. 'Iterability' in our case here, this afternoon, you and me, Amy Lemaire, over our friendly beers, means that what you said the first time may not mean quite the same when you say it a second time. The first time we were just being women together, talking about our lives and the kinds of sexist things we've gone through in this patriarchal society. The second time, it could mean something different.*"

"*I don't get it,*" *said Amy.* "*Is this some kind of deconstruction, or what?*"

"*I wouldn't call it deconstruction,*" *said Trish.*

At that point the dialogue stopped and Trish's snarly voice broke in. "*You've been listening to a tape recording of a conversation between Amy Lemaire and me, Patricia Hassler, that took place on February 15, 1984?*" *There was a long silence on the tape, and I thought it was over, but Maistry pushed the fast forward button until we heard high-pitched squeaking. She reversed to the beginning of the squeaks, and we heard:*

"*What?*" *(Amy's voice but, shrunken, coming over a phone.)*

"*Yes, Amy.*"

"*You tape-recorded me! That afternoon when we were drinking beer and I told you about my being a working girl in New York. You tape-recorded* that?"

"*You want to teach in a school of education, don't you, Amy? You want to teach teachers. These days when they're so worried about child abusers, do you think an ex-hooker could get a job as a schoolteacher?*"

"*Probably not.*"

"*Do you think an ex-hooker could get a job as a teacher of teachers?*"

"*Maybe.*"

"*Not 'maybe,' Amy, no. A flat no. You didn't get that question right, Amy.*

You flunk the exam. Just as, if I informed the boards and committees you're going to try to get a job from, you'd flunk that exam, too. You'd have a very hard time indeed getting that job."

"And why would you do that, Trish? You're tough, and I've seen you being mean, but why the hell would you do something as destructive to me as this?"

"Remember Iago and his 'motiveless malignity'? Not exactly motiveless, was it? Remember Iago and Cassio? 'He hath a daily beauty in his life / That makes me ugly.' Don't you think I know what you're doing in Holland's seminar? You suck up to him and everybody else, you do your sweet motherly Amy bit, and you make me look nasty and stupid. All I want to do is bring some intellectual rigor into that touchy-feely crap he puts us through. But you—goody-goody two shoes you—make me look mean. I'll show them who goody-goody two shoes really is, an old-fashioned whore. I'll show them what mean is, and take you down with me."

"You're destroying me, and it wouldn't take much to make me destroy you."

"What's that supposed to mean?"

"I'll kill you, you bitch, if you try to spoil my life. I've been through hell once, Trish Hassler, and I'm not going to do it again."

"Amy—"

"You make one move toward . . . You tell anybody about this and I'll kill you. I swear it, I'll kill you."

"Amy—"

"I trusted you, you mean, self-centered bitch, I trusted you . . ."

"Amy, I've worked this out. Suppose we turn this into a practical, not an emotional exercise. I've got a plan, a plan that won't destroy you. Trust me. I've got a plan that we both can live with . . ."

The voices stopped at that point, and Trish Hassler's voice came on in a flat, matter-of-fact statement.

"To whom it may concern. This is Patricia Hassler and what you've just heard are excerpts from an interview between me and Amy Lemaire on February 15, 1984, followed by a partial recording of a telephone call I initiated with Amy Lemaire on February 17, 1984. I call your attention to two things. First, to her admission in the interview that she worked as a prostitute for sixteen months in New York—and liked it. Second, I ask you to note that in the telephone call she threatened to kill me." There was a pause, and Hassler's voice said, "This is the end of the tape."

I felt there was a faint, foggy clutch of sadness in that one sentence, but I suppose I was just imagining things. Maybe not. After all, nobody was ever really supposed to hear that tape, unless she was dead. But when she made that tape, she'd already begun planning her suicide. What was going through her mind as she said that last sentence?

We all sat there, looking away from each other into neutral space.

"You're awfully damn quiet, Norman," said Rhodes. I felt him looking through me the way he looked through a martini. "Are you going to tell me again you didn't recognize those voices?" He turned and stared at me, hard. For the first time I sensed a fierceness in this seemingly casual man.

"Lieutenant," I said. "Justin. I have to tell you something."

"Yes, Norman. You have to tell me something. You have to tell me what Amy told you about this business of Trish blackmailing her."

I was flabbergasted.

"Come on. Overcome your retentive tendencies. Tell me what she told you. Or do you want to take time out and we'll analyze this block of yours?"

"You knew she came to see me?"

"Why else would you say you didn't recognize the voices? If she had anything to say, and now we know that she must have, she'd say it to you, not me. She trusts you."

"You're right. She did, and that's why I didn't tell you. Amy came to see me last night. Trish had worked out a payment plan that, as she said, they both could live with. That was the "practical" alternative she talked about on the tape. Amy made the first payment Sunday night. I suppose it would show up on their respective bank accounts."

"Keep talking."

"But Trish was killed, or so it seemed. Then, on Thursday evening, Amy got a call from a man. She wasn't sure about the voice, but she thought it was the mystery student. He said he had this information from Trish, and he wanted to talk with her. It wasn't clear whether he wanted money or sex. Both, I guess. She agreed to meet him. She felt she had to."

"Kulper didn't waste any time, did he? He finally got his date with Amy. And when was this meeting to take place, Norman?"

"Midnight last night. The graduate lounge. That's on the first floor of this building."

"That puts Amy right where Kulper was killed."

"Yes, I admit that, but Justin, you've got to believe me. She didn't do it. It's not her style."

"You told me styles don't matter. Style doesn't say what a person would actually do."

"Look. Amy came to me of her own free will, to tell me all this, to put it on the record as it were. I told her I'd witness what she said, so that it would be on record. I promised her I wouldn't tell anybody, not even you, unless it became necessary."

"A bit naïve—on both your parts. I'd say it's getting on toward necessary, Norman, wouldn't you? Wouldn't you say that Amy had a motive for killing

Kulper? And she was meeting him just about when and where he was killed. Motive, means, and opportunity, Norman. I'd say you could call your information 'necessary'."

"Just a goddam minute, Justin." Bluster had worked with Badger. "I haven't concealed anything material. By Thursday you already knew—although you weren't telling the rest of us, you kept that fact under your deerstalker—that Trish Hassler killed herself. Amy's confession to me, you admit, has no relevance to Hassler's death. It was only this morning that we learned Kulper was even dead and only a few minutes ago that I learned that Kulper was the one who took over Hassler's blackmailing Amy. I'm telling you right now what I know the very minute it has become material."

Specious? Yes, but I thought I could get away with it. Anyway, at that moment there was a knock on the door—Yorrick.

"Lieutenant, we checked over that Scotch tape holder. You were right as rain. Traces of blood and skin and two hairs. No usable prints, just a zillion blurred ones. The boys also found traces of blood on the floor in front of the line of faculty mailboxes. It had been wiped but the cyanide test picked it up."

"All right!" Justin crowed. "That confirms our reasoning so far. Kulper was the interloper. Kulper was killed in the mailroom by someone, just as he was putting some crucial, damaging information in the mailboxes of the people in this seminar. But damaging to whom? At the moment, it looks like Amy Lemaire."

"No!" I couldn't help it.

"You say, Norman, that you were going to tell me about her if it ever became relevant. It was always relevant. If you'd told me before, we wouldn't have let this time go by. You see what the situation is. After bashing Kulper in the mail room—or maybe where she met him! That would have been easier— she comes up here to try to find the tape. She doesn't find it, but she does find the safe, so she knows she's on the spot. She shows up at the seminar meeting this morning, so as not to arouse suspicion on our part, and Kulper's body hadn't been discovered yet. But she's had all the time since then to escape. She wouldn't have, dammit, if you'd told me what you knew."

"But Justin, it can't be Amy," I said. "I'm sure it was an average-sized man I followed here. The person I followed last night was too big to be little Amy."

"So you say. It was dark, and maybe you'd like to shield Amy. I can understand that. She seems unusually nice. Pretty, too."

"If she was going to kill Kulper, why would she tell me she was going to meet him? She didn't have to tell me anything."

He brushed me off. "We've wasted enough time. Maistry, get on the radio in the car. Send out an all points for Amy Lemaire; you can write the description as well as I can. Go, woman, go. Move it!"

"Wait a minute, Justin," I said. "Sergeant, wait. Please." Maistry, bless her, stopped. "If I follow your reasoning, Justin, you're saying, since Amy didn't find what she was looking for in Kulper's apartment, but she knows it's here and she knows we'll find it, she must be trying to escape. Okay, let's check. Give me just time enough to see if she's doing that. Let me at least call and see if she's at her place, before you get her name plastered all over the police records."

"Surely, Norman, you must realize that that's the first place we'll look. If she's there, we'll find her there."

"Let me telephone . . ."

"Okay, okay, telephone."

My hands were wet and shaking, partly because I was worried for Amy, but also because I was pretty sure I was in deep trouble if Amy turned out to be the murderer. I dialed Amy's number from my class list, and I waited. Rhodes stood next to me where he could hear what came over the receiver. I waited. One ring. Two rings. My teeth hurt in their sockets, I so terribly wanted for her to answer. It felt like twenty rings, but it was only four. "Hi! Amy! Norm Holland here. I just wanted to make sure . . ."

"Yes?"

What did I want to make sure of? That she wasn't a murderer? " . . . I wanted to make sure you're okay, I mean, after last night's meeting with your ominous caller."

"He never showed. He was supposed to meet me at midnight, and I waited around that damned graduate lounge with the lights out until one, but he never appeared. He must be trying to soften me up."

She must have registered the anxiety in my voice, because she suddenly gasped. "That body in the basement! It was him, wasn't it! The one who was going to meet me at midnight."

"Yes," I said. "Felix Kulper. He was a friend of Trish's. She left the tape with him."

"Oh, my god!" she groaned. "And that detective thinks I killed him."

"Maybe not. It's a good sign that you didn't make a run for it. If you'd killed Kulper, you'd be gone by now."

"Maybe I should have. Two deaths! This is all too much for me. Do you realize that in the middle of all this Phil Feder still wants us to write our Coleridge papers? Fat chance. Murder and blackmail—how am I supposed to say something brilliant about Samuel T.'s destabilizations of psychological hegemony? What does that even mean? Does it matter one iota? That poor sick man."

"Kulper? The mystery student? Feder?"

"Coleridge. A compulsive plagiarist. A junkie. And why am I thinking of Coleridge now?"

"Because you're Amy and Coleridge was a sick man."

"That detective has the tape."

"Amy, hang in. I'll get you through this somehow. For now, do your best with Feder's course. This will all work out."

"Thanks, Norm. I appreciate. I really do."

"Keep in touch, Amy." We hung up. I turned to Rhodes. *"That doesn't sound to me as though she killed Kulper."*

"To me either. But *she could be putting on an act."*

"If it's an act, it's more skilled than any of the actresses I've seen in your plays."

"A low blow, Norman."

"Justin, can you wait on your All Points Bulletin until we try something else?"

"I guess Ms. Lemaire will stay put. Apparently, she didn't realize that Kulper was the interloper. She didn't even know that Kulper was the man who tried to blackmail her. Actually, I think I'm going to have to bring all of them in, if I can."

"All of them!"

"Look at it this way, Norman. The murderer has to assume that we'll find the incriminating papers in Kulper's apartment. The murderer has to run. I'll bet you that while we're sitting here, he—yes, Norman, or she or they—are on their way already."

"Justin, give me one last chance to find the squibs. Five minutes." He nodded okay and sat back to watch what I was going to do.

Poe. I must have said it out loud, because Justin said, *"What does Poe have to do with it?"*

I explained. If a graduate student in literature were trying to hide some piece of writing, they'd almost certainly try to do it like the minister in Poe's "The Purloined Letter." Ever since Jacques Lacan used that story to demonstrate the idea that the "letter," the word, really, always gets to its unconsciously determined destination, they've all read that story. Poe's ingenious thief hid the queen's letter simply by turning the envelope inside out, writing a different address on it in a different hand, and leaving it in plain sight. The police ripped up floor boards and ran needles through cushions and looked inside chair rungs, but they never bothered with this letter, because it was so obviously not the letter they were looking for. *"I'll bet Kulper has read the story—they all have—and he'd believe that the best way to hide something is to put it out where it's obvious. Put all the papers right out in front of us, but in such a way that we'd never even think to look at them."*

"But," said Rhodes, *"we've looked in all the obvious places."*

I had to admit that that was a flaw in my theory. *"Let's try again,"* I said. *"Where in this room would some seminar papers be obvious but obviously* not

what we were looking for?" It would have to be a considerable stack of paper.
My collection of squibs at home was about two inches high by this time in the
semester.

I looked around. He couldn't hide them in the pages of the books. The
shelves with computer disks, different kinds of stationery, typing paper, even the
ten different colors of typing paper methodically arranged, they were quite open,
everything visibly not seminar papers. And then I clicked.

Ten.

Each week there had to be ten copies of the squibs, eight members of the
seminar, plus me, plus Kulper himself.

Kulper's theme was hiding things, but then the things would change radically once they became visible. Did he ever submit squibs on colored paper?
Did we see any colored paper on his desk? In the file cabinet? What does he
need ten kinds of colored paper for, then?

I rushed across the room, and damned if I wasn't right. There they all were!
I was shouting, "Hey! Rhodes! This isn't colored typing paper. Only the top
sheets are unused paper. Underneath, these are the squibs from the seminar.
Look! He just ran colored felt-tip pens around the edges of the squibs so the
whole pile of paper looks tinted." What Kulper had done was buy an assort-
ment of colored typing paper and felt pens to match. Then he'd stack the seminar papers under the blank colored paper. He'd color the edges of the squibs
that he got so they looked like one big stack of pink or blue or yellow paper.
Each person got a different color, and that way he could even tell whose papers
were whose without file labels. I was amused at the way he'd read us. He'd
made me gray, Glendish pink, Hassler orange . . . What's that personality test
where you pick two colors? "Why would he make Penza red, for example? Or
Ebenfeld green?"

"Down, boy, down," Rhodes laughed. "'Extrinsic evidence,' remember?
We're looking for the squib he was killed for."

And there it was, the top one on his own stack. (He'd picked charcoal for
his own color.) Then Rhodes wanted Hassler's last, fatal squib, and that was
the first one on her pile. And that was the end of the mystery, at least about
Hassler's death. Here they are—

English 6121   for Friday, March 9, 1984
To: The skull scourers   From: A repentant intruder

    Usually I am your friendly interloper, but I am not so
friendly today, Thursday, as I sit before the magic

screen in my hideaway. I'm repentant. You're about to
read a horrible story. She was going to put it in your
boxes Monday, but, I now realize, whoever murdered her
also took your copies away. Trish gave your Peeping Tom
member a copy too, as she'd been doing for some weeks.
Trish's murderer didn't know my name, ha, ha, didn't know
what box Trish had put the tenth copy of her squib in,
ha, ha, ha, in fact didn't know that she'd put the squib
in any mailboxes but the ones for the regular members of
the seminar, ha-ha-HA-HA-HAH! So he couldn't snatch my
copy of Trish's squib. I knew what Trish had said in that
last squib. You--all but one of you--did not.

Writing as I do, hidden from you, I had no way of
knowing that you didn't have the same squib I did. That
was why I accused you yesterday, falsely it turns out, of
ignoring her message. I apologize. Let's keep things
straight. Let justice be done. Yet I do not wish to be
the visible instrument of that justice. Professor Badger,
I hear, has said that she would boot me out of the program if she ever found out who I was. (Although perhaps
that could be fun at the hands of our well-endowed Professor Badger.)

Nevertheless, this time I'm going to make sure you get
my squib, and I'm going to make sure you all know who
killed Patricia Hassler. I'm going to put this page and
the pages that follow, which she wrote, in your boxes
myself. Just as the killer didn't know that Trish had
left a squib in my box, so I'm going to hide this, the
crucial squib, in a lot of randomly selected boxes of
people in the department, not just in the seminar. That
way, even if the killer, who is, of course, in your seminar, spirits the seminar copies away, there will be other
copies for other interested parties who will no doubt
inform the police of what they've read. The truth will
out. Murder will out. But not I. I will not out, thank
you all the same, Ms. Badger.

Let me tell you something about Patricia. As you know,
at the beginning of the semester, each of you got a list
of the people in the seminar and their phone numbers. I
happened to see a list being xeroxed in the mailroom and
picked it up. I thought it would be fun to play into the
seminar from my outside vantage point. And there were
these women I was learning interesting things about. I
called the fair Anne, and what happened? "Freeze, creep,"
she said. "Don't even think about thinking about me." She

did something to make her phone damn near blast my ear off. I called the lovable Amy, and what happened? "I'm sorry for you, I really am, but you mustn't hope for any encouragement from me." See a shrink, she said. I called the brilliant Patricia, and what happened? "You sound like an interesting nut. I think you've got a great idea for goosing up this cockamamie seminar. Sure I'll meet you."

The rest of you didn't like her, I know, but to me she was courteous, decent, and kind. She was big and strong. She recognized that I was one of the odd ones. She accepted me as I am. She understood that I needed to be treated harshly, needed even to feel pain at her hands, and she assented. She could hurt me, and she could coddle me, and she did both. I loved her for that. I simply loved her.

That's why I've gone to such lengths to get this, her last and most important paper to you. When you read it, you'll know who killed her. I hope you kill him if the State of New York doesn't. And if the State of New York doesn't, if you don't, I'm still here, still ready to punish the one who, more than anyone I ever met, deserves punishment.

from the journal of Norman Holland

We read this remarkable writing clustered round Rhodes who was holding the paper. I could see he was immensely pleased that all his furious deducing had worked out. He was glowing, but he didn't stop. "The murderer must have got Kulper before he could distribute those extra copies."

"Or else the murderer simply looked through everybody's mailboxes," I suggested. "It would take time, but not an impossible amount of time."

"Evidently," he said, preoccupied, "Kulper didn't know Hassler's death was a suicide. I wonder. Did he know something we don't know? Let's look at Hassler's."

English 6121   Monday, March 7, 1984

To: All of us in this yakkety-yak seminar
From: Another yakker, your Trish

I'm writing this before I pick up your squibs on me. What I'm writing now is untouched, so to speak, by your necessarily de-centered and imperfect surmises of my "identity theme."

You think you know me. You don't. What you see is a shell, not the real Trish at all. You only know me now. Holland thinks we get an identity in childhood and live it out the rest of our lives. Bullshit. I'm not the Patricia Hassler I was. If you think that sounds overdramatic, judge again when you've finished reading this.

It has to do with a man.

I've told you why school is _it_ for me. I'd found a life, the whole and only life for me. I didn't care about another fucking thing or person in this world.

At Yale I did my work and went to my classes and I was doing just fine. My profs were giving me A's, and I was beginning to look forward to being one of them, to being another Harold Bloom or a Paul de Man someday.

Outside of class, I was a lone wolf. I had acquaintances at Yale, but I had neither friend nor lover. I did have men--

I know what you're thinking. I wasn't always **this** fat. That came later, when, for month after month, I thought life wasn't worth living any more. I'd stuff my face with sweets and guzzle sodas and drink and drink, although I was able, thanks to god knows what in my Baptist upbringing, to fend that one off, alcoholism, I mean.

In those days I was fat, but not _this_ fat. I wasn't this huge, grotesque creature you see in front of you. "Pleasingly plump," you'd say. Zaftig, in a dialect favored in New Haven. I had a softness and roundness men liked. I was cute enough so that I had men, lots of men.

I'd pick up strays in the mean streets of West Haven, Italians, and bring them back to ever so proper Marshfield College. Sneak them in, then hump away the night, fuck, fuck, fuck, and kick them out in the morning. They never knew what hit them. Nor did they much care. They liked what they'd gotten. I liked what I'd gotten. They were the only friends or lovers I had and all I wanted.

That was before I met the man--or he met me, rather. I made a big mistake by not sticking to those sexy strangers who had nothing to do with me or literary theory or Yale. No, I'm not going to tell you who he is, although

you can guess easily enough, and I'll tell you on Wednesday. Show and tell. For this billet-doux, let's just call
him Lover.

Lover found me attractive--I thought. We had a couple
of classes together. He learned that I was the fair-
haired girl with Hillis and Geoffrey and Harold and
Shoshana and the other new, bright people. He admired
that, and he admired me as me--I thought. I was tall and
pleasingly plump and smart as hell, and I figured he
found all that attractive. He started easy, with a cup of
coffee after one of our classes, then lunch, and then a
movie, and he was so charming and admiring, and the first
thing you know he'd charmed the pants right off me, in
what is an altogether appropriate cliché. Before I knew
what I was doing, I'd scooped him up, and I'd brought him
up to my room and we were making out. He charmed me, o
god, did he charm me! Bastard! I gave him a key to my
room, a key to my computer, the key to me, really, and he
stole that key, the Phi Beta Kappa key, as it were, that
was going to open the big world for me. (Yes, Holland, I
recognize your goddamned Freudian symbolism!)

I think he really did find me attractive. Even now, I
think he was in love with me then, or at least in lust.
All through those long winter afternoons we'd screw and
screw and screw. Somehow we dovetailed--yes, I intend the
pun. I was the dominant one, on top in every sense. I was
smarter in school than he was, and in bed I brought to
bear all the knowhow I got from those deft Italians from
West Haven. He liked that. He seemed to take a kind of
strength from it. Our affair was as sweet and luscious
and suckable as a Georgia peach, and like a Georgia peach
it had a pit. The pits.

School was the problem. Our work went to hell--or
would have, if I hadn't been smart and quick enough to do
the work for both of us. That was how the whole mess
began, out of our very loving. So that we could have our
afternoons and our mornings and our evenings, I began to
tell him what this or that assigned reading said so he
wouldn't have to do it himself. Being seniors, we didn't
have exams, only papers. Some of the profs assigned short
papers early in the semester, I wrote mine, and then I'd
write his. At the end of the semester we were to write
longer papers, and we had to clear the topic with the
prof and discuss it with him. Lover would hold the re-

quired discussion with the prof, come back to the room, tell me about it, and I'd write his paper.

And I didn't mind a bit, because I was doing just what I wanted to do. I was doing beautiful work. I felt it was a sign of my intellectual power and my emotional power. I could hold him between my legs, and I could hold him, in a way, in my brain. Because I could write papers as he would write them, I owned him. Marvelous stuff. "Language, Liminality, and Absence." "Freud and the Art of Fracture." "Kristeva on the Misogynistic Lessness of Lacan." Thick, grinding, turgid, eminently satisfying thinking. I loved it. I loved the sex. I loved him.

Anyway, despite all the overheated screwing, or because of it, we kept up our reputation in that steamy hothouse of forced and pressured intellects. Then the time came to write senior theses. Academically, these would determine whether we got honors or not, and that would determine where we got into graduate school. As a practical matter, then, these papers would determine our professional futures.

I'd begun to wonder about my doing all this writing for Lover. An invisible worm of doubt had begun to find its way into my sick rose. He seemed to acquiesce so easily in my writing for him. I knew he was bright, and he could probably have fended for himself, but Lover didn't. He was getting considerably better grades on what I wrote for him than what he'd written for himself, and he was content.

I felt all mixed up. I'd been happy doing Lover's reading and writing for him. I was even proud that I could impose myself on him, for him. But now I began to feel that something was different. Before, I'd thought I was loving him, giving to him. That was a new feeling for me, and a strange, good feeling. Now I wondered, was he just taking from me?, and the thought ate away at me. Now I felt anxious and angry, both.

The senior thesis was coming due. It was a major project. A lot of people did as much as a hundred or more pages. There was no way I could write two of them in the time we had, and I told him so. All right, he said, and he set to work on his project, as I did on mine. He talked to his adviser, and I talked to mine. And we talked to each other. I shared my ideas with him, and he shared his with me. And we went on loving even more than we had before.

The deadline approached. I was using my computer, as always. Most literary types just use computers as glorified typewriters, but I'm damned good with a computer, always have been. I had mine hooked up with a modem so I could use the library's online catalog from my room. I could look up books, copy the library card (or its computer equivalent) into my machine and build up a bibliography in short order. My reading notes I put into a textbase system in the computer, and I could find anything I wanted among hundreds of references almost instantaneously. Of course, when I wanted to quote anything I never had to recopy it.

As a result, I was working very fast, very well. I rarely printed anything out on paper--there was no reason to. Anything I could do with hard copy I could do faster and better in the machine. Naturally, for safety, I saved everything I wrote to floppy disks. Every file was on two floppies as well as the hard disk, but everything was in the computer.

When I'd read through the paper, I knew it was good, damned good. It related Freud's hostility to philosophy, his death instinct, and Heidegger's idea of self-knowledge as "being-to-death." I stood them both on their heads. I showed how Heidegger was a sub-text for Freud and Freud a sub-text for Heidegger. I showed how philosophy had been inscribed, "always already," in psychoanalysis and psychoanalysis had been inscribed, "always already," in philosophy.

It was plain, pure, and simply brilliant. Really.

At Yale I'd been a promising student among many promising students, but not the best student, not the bright star. This paper was going to do that for me. This paper was going to be my magic key to open all the doors: grades, recommendations, schools, jobs, career. Well, enough of that. That's all gone now.

Eventually, the night before the project was due, I came back to my room to print out the final copy. My God, my hand shakes when I think of it even now. The computer came up blank. Somehow--I thought at first it must have been some crazy surge in the power line--nothing would start up. There was nothing on my hard disk. I managed to load the operating system from the original floppies that came with the machine, and I got it started again. I

checked the hard disk again. Completely blank. <u>My hard
disk was completely blank</u>! My heart started pounding.
Okay, okay, it's going to be okay. I've got all this on
floppies. <u>They were blank, too</u>. Nothing. I screamed. I
screamed and screamed.

Now I knew this wasn't any glitch in the power line.
The floppies were sitting in a box alongside the computer. Nothing that happened in the computer could affect
them while they were out of it. There was only one person
who could have done erased them. There was only one person who had read off the computer screen, our cheeks
touching as we read, my brilliant interlineation of
Heidegger and Freud. There was only one person who knew
that I kept everything, absolutely everything, in the
computer. There was only one person who could come and go
in my room as he liked. There was only one person who'd
been sticking his key in my lock (get it, Norman?). There
was only one person who had all the keys. And where the
hell was he? Where was he? What was this, some kind of
crazy joke?

I ran to his room. He wasn't there. I looked in the
dining room. No. I ran around the colleges like a crazy
woman. It was bitter cold, and the wind pushed and slowed
me as it whipped around those gothic corners. I hadn't
even put on a jacket. He was nowhere, of course.

Finally I gave up. I went back to my room and tried to
sleep, but that was dumb. I called his room. No answer. I
called my adviser and told him simply that my computer
had acted up, and I wouldn't have my senior paper on
time. I was ashamed and humiliated. I didn't want to say
that my "boyfriend" had taken it (ugh! what a word!). I'd
been played for a sucker. I'd been used. Or had I? I
still couldn't believe what had happened. I still kept
looking for him everywhere.

I guess while I was on the phone, he was in the office
turning in the paper. My paper. It was <u>my</u> paper. Mine,
mine, mine, goddam it. I want to swear when I say that,
swear every cocksucking dirty word you all are afraid to
put in these silly billets-doux.

I didn't realize fully what he'd done until noon, when
the papers were due. I went back to the department office. I looked at the list of people who'd turned in
papers, and there his name was. I persuaded the secretary
to let me look at the paper, and it wasn't his, it was
mine. It was mine, goddam it, mine, and he had fucking

stolen it. The doubts I'd begun to feel poured over my
mind. Inside I was raging like a tornado.

I had to calm down so that I could call my adviser,
again. This time, I told him that it wasn't just that my
computer had acted up. My senior paper had been stolen.
How can that be?, he said. Who stole it?, he said. That
was one of the hard moments of my life, but I told him. I
told him about Lover. God, how humiliated, how debased I
felt, how dumb, sheer damn dumb.

He said for me to come round to his office and explain
all this in more detail. I did. I told him the story as
I've told it to you. He asked who Lover's adviser was,
and I told him that.

No, I won't tell you any of their names. Isn't it
enough that I'm telling you how mortified I felt? I don't
have to make it worse by telling you how distinguished a
pair of minds I was shamed in front of.

My adviser told me to step outside--oh, how cautious
and "objective" and male they all were--and he telephoned
the other adviser. Then he called me back in. The other
adviser had said he'd take the matter up with Lover. We'd
have to wait.

I waited all right. Later that afternoon my adviser
called me. Lover's adviser had found him, spoken to him,
told him of my accusation. Lover had professed shock. Why
would I say such a thing? And answered his own question.
Because we'd been having an affair, but he'd broken off
with me. This was my way of getting revenge. How could it
be her paper?, he said. He had all the drafts and notes
that went into the paper. Could she produce drafts? (He
knew damn well I couldn't. He'd wiped the computer.)
Also, he'd discussed this paper--the _entrelacement_ of
Heidegger and Freud--with his adviser. Didn't the adviser
remember? Of course he did. Lover had fed what I told him
about my paper to his own adviser as if it was a paper he
was working on. He'd even printed out drafts to show his
adviser.

His adviser guardedly walked with Lover to his room,
and there Lover produced bibliographies, notes on reading, and the final paper. All this he must have printed
out the night before while he was printing the paper
itself. While I was banging on his door and rushing
around scaring up the streets of New Haven looking for
him, he'd been inside, printing out all these materials

on his expensive printer, which looked quite different
from mine.

And my adviser? Prompted by Lover's raw, shameless
lies, my adviser reminded me how little I'd told him
about the paper. You know me. You know how I like to be
independent, how I hate to have to depend on anyone else.
I'd told my stuffy adviser as little as I could about
what I was doing. I wanted to suprise them all. I wanted
it to be completely and totally mine. No one else was
even to be able to imagine that I had used their ideas.

My adviser asked me what evidence I could produce that
I'd written the paper in question. Not much, I told him.
I do all my work in the computer. Why print out hard
copy? The fact that Lover had had hard copy at all, I
said, showed that something was rotten. He was a bit
baffled by that, he said, being a pen and pencil man
himself. Asshole! He'd take the matter up with the chair
of the department, he said. Swell.

Yale was very decent. Oh yes, yes, yes, they were
honorable men. As soon as I said they ought to get a
computer person to try to undelete the files on my floppies, they immediately called someone from the computer
lab. But Lover must somehow have taken care of that.
There was nothing recoverable on them or on the hard
disk.

The chair appointed a committee. Ah, academia. What
else would a university bureaucrat do? It was a court of
three "judges"--again, I'm not going to tell you the
distinguished names the chair appointed. They are honorable men, all honorable men--or honorable names, anyway,
and men. Before them, I was shown to be a scorned, de-
luded, vengeful woman. Probably I showed myself that way,
and I still feel I could kill . . .

For the "trial," we met hastily in one of the seminar
rooms. As I glared at Lover across the long table, the
panel listened to both advisers. Mine said what an outstanding student I was, that not turning the paper in was
most unlike me, but that I had been evasive about what I
was writing. Also, I had at first told him it was a computer failure, not theft. Lover's adviser said he wasn't
such a distinguished student, but he'd been doing much
better lately, almost as well as me. (<u>Almost</u> as well as
me! I <u>almost</u> exploded.) He reported that Lover had described this senior project in several conferences with

him, not very clearly to be sure, but that was to be expected in the writing process, wasn't it? Then the three "judges" listened to Lover and me, first separately and then confronting each other. Lover played the innocent. He was the victim of this vindictive harpy. I sure as hell felt like a harpy, and I probably acted like one, too. I'm grinding my teeth as I write this, and I was damn well grinding them then.

I was sweating and crying and sneezing all at once, looking frightened and mad. In that state I tried to explain what must have happened with the computer, how he copied my floppies onto his and erased all the files on mine, how he formatted my hard disk, wiping all the data off it, and then printed out the final paper plus all the preliminary materials. I'm not sure they understood all that about the computer, but they seemed to see how it could have happened. But did it happen?

I pointed to the style of the paper and said that you could tell it was mine, not his. They replied, with irrefutable scholarly logic, that internal evidence of authorship is much weaker than external. They pointed to the near-impossibility of deciding authorship on the basis of internal evidence alone. Oh, they were in their element then. We got a real lecture. Shit! The external proofs, they concluded, Lover's production of notes and drafts, Lover's having discussed the paper with his adviser, Lover's having delivered the paper, outweighed any stylistic comparison. At the same time, they pointed out that I'd had a longer record of proven achievement than his. All in all, they had to say that there was no way to prove or disprove my accusation.

What shall we do?, these three flustered academics asked themselves. They went into a huddle while we waited outside. Lover refused to look at me, as well he might. I felt like strangling him right then, but the two advisers were there, waiting with us. I might have anyway, if he'd smiled. I could kill him now. But he wouldn't look at me. Instead he looked out the window to the courtyard below where some town kids were throwing frisbees in the April thaw. I felt he'd gone off somewhere in his head, away from me, as if I'd never existed.

Can any of you imagine how I felt? You know me. You know I'm a person easily angered. Can you imagine the rage I felt as we waited, I knowing that I'd not convinced those judges? I wanted to kill him, but more than

that, I wanted to make him feel the pain I felt. I've
told you that my whole life has been school, ever since I
was a wretched little girl in that wretched little Georgia town. School was what I was good at. School was what
made me happy. School was what got me away from home.
School was everything to me. When he stole that paper, he
stole my life, and I wanted to steal his.

In a triumph of academic reasoning, they punished us
both. I have no idea what went on in their minds. Were
they in their pre-sexual-revolution way punishing us for
our affair? Had they figured out that I'd been writing
his papers for him for the past semester and a half? That
I'd cheated for him? Who knows? Maybe they were just
being like Solomon threatening to cut the baby in two,
hoping that if they made it hard enough on both of us,
one of us would give up.

The plagiarism, they said, would affect where the two
of us were going to graduate school. I'd been admitted to
Yale's own Ph.D. program. They even gave me a scholarship, but with the usual condition that I maintain honors
work through graduation. But I hadn't turned in my senior
paper, and I had no senior paper to turn in. Zero. Hardly
satisfactory work, let alone honors. They took my Yale
away.

As for Lover, no plagiarism was proven, but my accusation plus his previous ineffective record cast doubt on
his authorship. He just wasn't good enough to produce
this paper--my paper. But the committee they put together
couldn't penalize him without proof. And without proof
they couldn't give me the A, the A++, goddam it, that I
deserved. So far as next year--this year--was concerned,
he'd been marginal anyway. He'd only gotten on the waiting list for graduate school at Yale. Now, they said,
would he please withdraw his application, and spend the
next year somewhere else. No Yale for Lover, either. Both
of us would be free to apply again during the next year,
once we'd demonstrated good and "stable" work at the
institutions we attended.

What the hell was "stable" supposed to mean? No sex?
No computers? No literary theory? And what chance did I
have of being accepted after the craziness of that day
and a half? They urged us to keep quiet about this whole
thing. He, obviously, had nothing to gain by noising it
around. As for me, I'd failed to convince them, and I
wasn't likely to get a fairer hearing from strangers to

the case. Repeating my accusation would just make me look
bad. And they were right. When I tried this fall to convince Ma Badger that my accusation was just, I could tell
she didn't believe me. It didn't do me any good at all.
But I don't give a damn anymore.

You take school away from me, you take away my life.

Exiled, in effect, from Yale, Lover and I both ended
up here. Strange? No, not at all. I chose it because it
was the next best place. Badger even gave me a scholarship. Lover chose it because he couldn't afford to let me
out of his sight. He knows I won't let go. Someday, somehow, I'll prove what he did to me. Once a plagiarist,
always a plagiarist. He'll do it again. I know it, and
I'll catch him at it and make him suffer everything I've
suffered. I'll get him, whatever it costs me. I've already lost what I have to lose. And gained.

Over the summer and fall I ate myself into the shape I
now inhabit. Holland, you would probably say in your
psychobabble that I was compensating, trying to put back
into myself something that'd been taken away. Or you'd
say I was going back to my parents, to Mom. Mom fed me,
and now I was trying to get Mom back. Bullshit. I didn't
even give my parents' right address when I applied here.
I cut every fucking tie to the past I could.

I wanted something I could trust, and you can trust
food. You take it in, and it's yours. You don't have to
give it back, and nobody can take it away. But that's
psychobabble too. You're giving me bad habits, Holland.

Let's get back to language, discourse, the final
reality. <u>Il n'y a pas de hors-texte</u>. There's nothing
outside the text. We are what we say. I hate and I hate
and I hate. I ate and I ate and I ate. Same thing. Just
the littlest <u>différance</u>, right? I couldn't stop. I can't
stop. And now I look the way I do. No more lovers. No
more thieves, you mean. Could I lose fifty, a hundred
pounds? Maybe. Why bother? I have a different purpose
now.

I want revenge. I want to prove that he stole my work.
You are my tribunal now. All nine of you. Yes, even you,
Holland. And when I've proved what he did, I want to make
him suffer as I've suffered. I want to take his career
away from him, just as he's taken my career--my life--
away from me. And he knows it. Lover sits here, and he
knows me, and he waits for my vengeance to come crashing

down on him. He fears and he waits, he waits and he fears, and he watches me and he watches me and he has to make it stop.

That's why he has to get rid of me. I don't know how or when, but as sure as shitting follows eating, he has to silence me and end this constant threat to him. I think he would go so far as to kill me. In fact I'm sure of it. If ever something happens to me, <u>HE</u> did it. That's my message to you this Monday morning.

Who is he? You all know him. You've sat in this chickenshit, crackbrained seminar with him week after week. Is that why he signed up for it? To keep an eye on me? I wouldn't be surprised. Or maybe to have an opportunity to do me in. That's more likely. Mark my words. Lots of opportunities, coming and going from here.

On Wednesday, I'll name him outright, for those of you who haven't already figured out who this narrative is about. Unless something happens to me in the meantime.

from the journal of Norman Holland

Rhodes and I scanned these two papers, and he was on the phone to headquarters in a flash. "Put out an APB for Christian Aval!" he told them, and he gave them a description. The things cops notice! Five foot seven. 140 pounds. Dark brown hair in a brush cut. Dark brown eyes. Pale skin. No facial hair. Aviator-style glasses. A scar over his left eyebrow. When last seen he was wearing . . . I couldn't have told you for the life of me, but Rhodes could. A black leather jacket, bright white shirt, black bulgy trousers, leather boots with a tap in the heel that you can hear. Has a French accent. That's important, he said. French accent. He told them to get onto Immigration. In fact, after he got off the phone with Homicide, he personally called Immigration, somebody named O'Rourke, and told them the description himself. He said he thought this man would try to get across to Canada. Watch all the bridges carefully, Lewiston, Rainbow, but especially the Peace Bridge, because it was nearest. He sat down to wait. I could see, man of action that he was, that he didn't feel easy leaving this crucial stage of the case in the hands of others. He wanted to be bustling about, giving orders, organizing things, fierce and casual.

"He had to keep us from seeing that thinly veiled accusation of murder, is that it?" I wasn't sure I understood.

Rhodes nodded. "Once he read that Monday squib, Chris could see she was going to try to send him to prison. How, he couldn't know, but he could read that her plan depended on this accusation. He had to keep us from seeing it. At all costs, even murder."

"Poor Chris." I was remembering Chris's intellectual arguments in our seminar. "He was always claiming that texts could do things, deconstruct themselves, destabilize meanings, or otherwise control us. In Chris's mind, that written accusation had power. It would do something to him."

"If we had read it, we would certainly have had to arrest Aval and probably try him and quite likely convict him, too."

I asked Rhodes why he thought Aval would head for Canada. Because of the accent, he said. "Here, it makes him conspicuous. There, the closer he gets to Quebec Province, the less noticeable he'll be."

I had a sudden insight. "But it's also Aval, isn't it? We know from his squibs that wherever he is, he isn't comfortable that he's there. Canada would be the kind of betwixt-and-between that he gets himself into. Not America, but not U.K. either. Not English, not French."

Rhodes gave me one of his I'm-being-patient looks. "I think he'll go to Canada because we don't have jurisdiction there. It's that much harder for us to pursue him. The Mounties're like the FBI here, and it's no joke about always getting their man. The provincial police departments are good, too. And I'll be riding all of them."

"You won't go to Canada yourself?"

"I don't know the turf. Better I stay here, and have them do the actual searching." But I could see he wasn't comfortable with that.

He settled into a nervous waiting, drumming his fingers on Kulper's desk. I was struck by another professorial thought. "You know, Justin, as I think about this case, much of it seems to turn on people or things being absent."

He turned to me. "Explain."

"Well, the most important fact of all was my not feeling the tack when I was sitting on it. The crucial problem on Wednesday morning turned out to be finding a time when no one was there. The files all gone first in Hassler's computer and then in Kulper's—those were important absences. Another crucial fact was the absence of the squib that Hassler had put in the boxes Monday morning. Then it was important that Aval didn't know that Kulper had a copy of that squib. It was important that Kulper didn't know the absence of Hassler's Monday morning squib in the other boxes. Crucial was Aval's not opening Kulper's little safe. His not being able to open it meant he had to run."

"Why do you call it 'absence.'"

"I get the word from another piece of contemporary literary theory, the idea that absence is presence."

"What on earth is that supposed to mean?"

"The idea is that, if you say something is absent, you thereby mention the something, and that makes it, in a way, present. If I say, Aval isn't here, then I, in a way, bring him here, bring him into our discourse."

"Rather like the Master and the dog in the nighttime."

"Henry James?"

"No, Norman. In this context, the Master is the immortal Holmes, and he's calling the attention of one of the less obtuse Scotland Yard types to 'the curious incident of the dog in the night-time.' '"The dog did nothing in the nighttime,"' says the inspector. '"That was the curious incident, remarked Sherlock Holmes."'

"So here," I said, "it's the absence of the tack-prick, the absence of the computer files, the absence of the Monday squib, and so on."

"I suppose. The end result of the absences is that Aval committed murder."

"And Trish won in the end," I sighed. "Maybe he deserved it."

"She didn't succeed in framing him for the non-murder of herself, but she did frighten him into committing murder on his own. In that indirect way, not at all the way she planned, she's destroyed him."

When he focused on Chris Aval again, something else crossed my mind. *"You could say that Aval plagiarized the murder she was authoring, just as he took over her honors paper."*

"Did he? Are you sure, Norman? Do you have proof? As far as I know, the only evidence we have that he plagiarized that honors paper is Hassler's accusation. That could be as false as her accusation that he was going to murder her. Remember, Norman? 'Extrinsic evidence?' It's entirely possible, isn't it, on the evidence we have that Aval is telling the truth? That she is just a vengeful jilt?"

I hadn't even thought of that possibility, I'd gotten so emotional while reading Trish's story. For a moment, I thought Justin had to be right, although my feelings were all against what he was saying. And then I decided he had to be wrong. Why? Because she committed suicide, for heaven's sake. *"Justin,"* I said, *"she so believed that Aval had stolen her thesis that she was willing to die for it. She must have been telling the truth."*

He laughed a little. *"Professor, what kind of evidence is that?"*

I had to think for a minute. *"Not intrinsic. Her suicide is a fact."*

"But does it have anything to do with the alleged act of plagiarism last April? It's eleven months later."

"*I guess I'd put it this way,*" *I said,* "*that what her suicide means depends on what you know. If we didn't know that she'd accused Aval of plagiarism and was willing to die to get her revenge, her suicide wouldn't say anything at all about the truth or falsity of her accusation. But knowing what we know, I think the fact that she was willing to kill herself to get at Aval proves she believed what she was saying, and who could know the facts better than she?*"

"*Not quite, Norman. She was pretty close to crazy even before she met Aval. She could have had some kind of paranoid delusion. Didn't you tell me that psychiatrists would call her a borderline case? I'm not sure what that is—*"

"*Well, I believe her story. Doesn't Shaw say about miracles that it doesn't matter whether or how they happen, so long as they create belief? And that's what Trish's suicide did with me—create belief. She made Kulper believe, too. Isn't that what proof is, anyway? What makes us believe something?*"

"*But that's hardly the extrinsic evidence you value,*" *he said, smiling.*

"*I suppose I have to admit that we really don't have any extrinsic evidence that he plagiarized. By the way, that's another odd thing, Justin, this case being so involved with questions of authorship. Who wrote this morning's squib? Who 'authored' Hassler's death, or Kulper's, for that matter? And the whole thing starts with a plagiarism.*"

"*Isn't that the primal academic crime?*"

"*It used to be but, as I think I told you, one central idea of modern literary theory is that the author is dead. There isn't any author, really. It started with Nietzsche. 'The "subject" is only a fiction.' A construction. Something we posit to make sense of events. Foucault says, what we designate as an author is only a projection of the way we think about literary texts.*

"*But then other modern literary theorists come along and claim that writing comes about through a series of linguistic codes that don't belong to any one person but to society. Roland Barthes says that the I that reads texts is already itself a composition of other texts, of linguistic codes. No one person, then, is the author. The author is doubly dead, first psychologized—our projection—and then dissolved entirely in the sea of language that surrounds us all.*"

"*I begin to feel ectoplasmic,*" *Rhodes said drily.*

"*Anyway, since Trish and Chris both believed there isn't any such person as the author, why were they so concerned about a supposed plagiarism?*"

He laughed again. "*Would I be naïve, Norman, to say that they were responding to simple, commonplace, premodern, even old-fashioned, motives of love and money? Yale had set it up, and they themselves had, too, that all kinds of consequences for their careers would follow upon a decision about authorship.*"

"*You're being very practical, Justin. Yet Yale has been for years the place that put forward such theories as deconstruction and the death of the author, as though there weren't any I, just language. Indeed it was one of Trish's most admired professors who claimed that 'the self is a linguistic construction . . . a figure or an effect of language.'"*

"I think all you've shown, Norman, is that professors are either not very practical or not very consistent. Anyway, I've got a killer to catch who was very much the author of his deed."

"That second murder was quite unnecessary, wasn't it?" I said.

"Yes," said Rhodes. "If Aval had waited until the meeting this morning, he'd have known that it was. He'd have learned that I had come to the same conclusion he must have come to."

"He must have come to?" I didn't understand.

"Sure. Aval must have realized early on that Trish Hassler committed suicide. I could only come to that conclusion from the physical evidence, but Aval had read her Monday squib. When she died, he knew that she'd committed suicide, because she predicted her own death in that paper. He knew he hadn't caused it, so she must have done it herself. On the other hand, he had to conclude that we would read Hassler's accusation literally and believe it—that he had killed her. That's why he had to steal the Monday squibs. That's why, when he realized Kulper could distribute Hassler's squib accusing him of murder, he had to kill Kulper."

"Are you saying that, if he had known your conclusion sooner, Kulper would be alive today, and he'd be innocent?"

"If, if, if."

"Justin, do you feel responsible? If you'd said sooner that you believed Hassler's death was a suicide . . . If you'd announced that Thursday or even Wednesday . . ."

"If me no ifs. I was fairly sure about Hassler's death from the time you sat on the tack and didn't spring up in pain. That was Thursday morning. But there were so many questions. I had no idea why she adopted this odd way of killing herself, and that left me with a lingering suspicion she must have been murdered. She intended us to think murder, too, didn't she? That's why she planted the fake vial in Aval's computer—and we had to take him in. Then we received that false squib this morning, ostensibly from the interloper, confessing the murder. That was Aval himself. As late as this morning, Aval himself was telling us, by that forged squib, that Hassler had been murdered."

"But," I argued, "he wouldn't have needed to circulate that false squib if he'd known what you were thinking."

"Nevertheless, it was only that squib that finally made me completely certain that she'd committed suicide. Somebody still alive wants Hassler's death to look like a murder. If so, then it isn't really a murder. It wasn't until just now, *when we read her squib, that we could be sure that that somebody was Trish herself."*

"So Aval, as he saw his situation, was caught in a paradox. Had he not circulated the false squib, you'd still think him guilty of murder. But in order to circulate that false one, he had to make himself guilty. He had to kill Kulper."

"You could say it's a paradox or you could just say it's a question of reading. The text of the squib had Kulper saying, I did it. But we, knowing what we know, have to read that altogether differently."

"'Knowing what we know?'"

"Or what we think we know. Or what we're learning as we read. Oh yes, Professor," he laughed, *"this case demonstrates your theories of reading very nicely, and how it's all a curious kind of bootstrap operation. We need to know things in order to read, but in order to know things we need to read. We read her death differently, we read her squib differently, we read everything differently, depending on what we bring to it. We could read her Monday squib as 'I'll commit suicide' or 'I'll kill him' or 'He killed me' or, what we finally believe is the correct reading, 'I'll frame him.'"*

"What you can learn is determined by what you already know."

"I suppose so. But let me, so to speak, read this case to you, Norman, as an exercise in reading," he said, smiling and relaxing into his intellectual mode. *"Confronted only with the fact of her death, we were able to read it as a suicide. The crucial fact became the length of the tack. It penetrated her skin, but not yours.*

"But, had we had, at the time of her death, this squib that she thought she'd distributed Monday, we'd inevitably have concluded that Aval killed her. The crucial facts would have been these. First, his motive, given by her squib, finally to get rid of her and the danger of her revenge. Second, his opportunity, which is his presence in the seminar, knowing where she would sit, again, pointed out by her squib. Third, the means, the vial in his apartment, planted by her."

"Do you really think she'd have succeeded if he had not intervened?"

"She was very clever, Norman. I can't imagine that the D. A. would have let me pursue any other line of investigation, or that I'd have wanted to. Conviction would have been certain."

I shook my head. *"Human nature!"*

"There's a third possibility. Had we had this Monday squib all by itself, without her death, we might well have read it as a suicide note. All that stuff about her self-destructive eating and about school being everything. She tells us that school being taken away equals her life being taken away. It sounds very much a declaration that she had nothing left and was going to commit suicide. As she did. That is, in fact, the 'true' reading of this text. But we had her death—and so we read the text differently."

"*Justin, you're getting as clever at this as a literary theorist.*"

"*Now we have both this document and her death, but the document came later, after we realized that she'd committed suicide. So we read it differently, and that's our fourth possibility. We can read the document, really and truly, that she's going to kill herself in order to frame Aval out of revenge.*"

"*So the meaning of the document depends on its reader.*"

"*Also her death. We can now interpret it as a combination of suicide and attempted murder, the judicial murder of Aval. Although she evidently didn't know that we haven't executed anybody in New York State for a long, long time.*"

"*If Aval knew that Hassler had committed suicide, why did Aval kill Kulper then? Why not point out the facts to you?*"

"*He didn't have any facts. More precisely, he didn't successfully interpret the facts he did have. He only had her squib. That accused him of destroying her. He could hardly show me that.*"

"*True.*"

"*Besides, from the moment of her death on, he thought he'd escaped Hassler's trap. No one connected him with her death, because the whole plagiarism business gave her a motive for attacking him, not vice versa. He was afraid that, if we ever got this squib, we'd pick him out as Hassler's murderer. And he was correct, as far as he knew.*"

"*What he didn't know was that we'd decided—I'd decided, because I didn't have this text—another absence, Norman—that Hassler's death was a suicide. Only she could know that the tack would kill her and not kill anyone else. Not knowing my deduction, Aval read this squib as putting a noose around his neck, and he was right. I'm not at all sure I'd have read her death as a suicide if I'd read this squib first. The whole case ravels itself up in a series of paradoxes.*"

"*You say paradox, Justin, but Aval said something else this morning.*"

Rhodes smiled softly. "*When he realized he'd murdered unnecessarily, he said he was suffering from 'an attack of irony.' How right he was. And now it falls to me to catch him for it.*"

But he didn't. Rhodes took his fingerprinters and his technicians and his "uniforms" out of the English Department. I called him once or twice to see how the search was going, but he grumbled that it wasn't going well, that he couldn't get the Canadians to act fast enough, that Aval was always one jump ahead of them. I think he felt embarrassed because Aval had gotten away— presumably while we were in Kulper's apartment, while we lost time not being able to find where Kulper had hidden the squibs. Maybe Justin blamed me. At the least I was a witness to his discomfiture.

afterward

from the journal of Norman Holland

Then came the newspapers. The Times *didn't do too badly, although I would hardly agree with the description of my ideas they got from that fop Embourbé. By contrast, the BMNG, via Dolly Kellehan, did its usual job of university-bashing and Holland-smearing.*

From *The New York Times,* March 10, 1984

Two SUNY/Buffalo Students Dead, Third Flees

Complex Case Turns on Postmodern Literary Theories

Leonard Tobyne

(BUFFALO, March 10)—The normally placid State University of New York at Buffalo was shaken this week by the deaths of two graduate students and the flight of a third.

One student, Patricia Hassler, 23, of Iron Springs, Georgia, poisoned herself Wednesday by sitting on a thumbtack coated with a highly controlled and lethal chemical. A second, Felix Kulper, 24, of Garden City, Long Island, appears to have been murdered and thrown down a flight of stairs late Thursday night or early Friday morning. U.S. and Canadian authorities are seeking a third student, Christian Aval, 24, of Cassis, Département des Bouches-du-Rhône, France. He is believed to have fled to Canada.

All three students were working toward graduate degrees in English. The incidents appear to stem from the two men's close involvement with Ms. Hassler, and do not signal a general decline in campus security, according to Detective Lieutenant Norman Rhodes, Homicide Unit, Metropolitan Buffalo Police Department. Still, the case, which involves both passion and academic intrigue, has fascinated residents of this snow-encrusted city.

Both Ms. Hassler and Mr. Aval have been part of a small, unconventional graduate seminar this spring. The class involves emotionally charged, highly personal teaching techniques by SUNY/Buffalo professor Norman Holland. Moreover, they knew each other before the class, having attended Yale University together.

Ms. Hassler's apparent suicide stemmed from that past involvement, according to Lt. Rhodes. She and Mr. Aval had been close companions while they were both undergraduates in the English Department at Yale. But shortly before both were to graduate, Ms. Hassler accused Mr. Aval of plagiarizing her senior honors paper. Unable to decide whether the accusation was true, the Yale authorities asked both students to continue their studies elsewhere. They each decided to study at SUNY at Buffalo.

Ms. Hassler's papers show she remained angry at Mr. Aval, according to Lt. Rhodes. She decided to commit suicide, but make it appear to be a murder. She put a paper in the mailboxes of the other students predicting that Mr. Aval would murder her.

She had earlier obtained a highly lethal poison, saxitoxin, and now used it to coat a thumbtack. She then sat on the tack in the Wednesday morning class she shared with Mr. Aval, and died almost instantly from the poison. "She keeled right over," said Mr. Holland.

Mr. Aval, however, had foiled Ms. Hassler's plan by intercepting the papers from the student mailboxes, and he was not immediately suspected. As a result the only person who knew of Ms. Hassler's claim that Mr. Aval planned to kill her was Mr. Kulper. He had become intimate with Ms. Hassler, and together they had disrupted Mr. Holland's seminar by circulating unidentified papers composed by Mr. Kulper, who identified himself only as "the intruder."

Mr. Kulper tried to distribute Ms. Hassler's accusation by papers intended for Friday morning, but Mr. Aval apparently moved to forestall Mr. Kulper. According to Lieutenant Rhodes, Aval attacked Kulper in the English Department mailroom Thurs-

day night, striking him in the head with a blunt instrument as he was putting the accusatory papers in the mailboxes, Lt. Rhodes said. Mr. Aval then threw Mr. Kulper's body down a basement staircase where it was found Friday morning near the furnace in the English Department building. Meanwhile Mr. Aval substituted his own papers in the mailboxes, naming Mr. Kulper as the murderer, according to Lt. Rhodes.

Lt. Rhodes's investigation of Mr. Kulper's apartment led to the discovery of Ms. Hassler's original accusation of Mr. Aval, and Rhodes ordered an all-out search for the French student. Mr. Aval, however, managed to elude the Metropolitan Buffalo police, and a search has been instituted by U.S. and Canadian authorities throughout the northeast.

Lt. Rhodes called the case unique in that both the crime and its solution rest on the methods of Mr. Holland. His seminar teaches what is called by English professors, reader-response theory. Students distribute to one another loose, narrative responses to literary texts showing that no correct readings of those texts are possible. According to Professor Baston Embourbé of the Department of Comparative Literature, Columbia University, Holland's methods are regarded in the profession as "controversial, both radical and reactionary at the same time."

Lt. Rhodes made extensive use of these response papers in ascertaining the activities and motives of the two dead students. Despite Mr. Aval's escape,

Buffalo Police Commissioner, Casimir Watzlawick, has called Lt. Rhodes's detection "brilliant." The detective is also the author of the feminist drama, "'The Militants," produced off Broadway at the St. Luke's Place Theater in 1981.

The private University of Buffalo, founded in 1846, became part of the State University of New York in 1961.

During Nelson Rockefeller's tenure as governor, from 1958 to 1974, he considerably expanded the campuses and enrollment of the SUNY system, including SUNY/Buffalo. Its English Department, under the chairmanship of Anselm Agger, became widely known for its innovative programs, including the reader-response work of Mr. Holland.

From the *Buffalo Morning News-Gazette,* March 10, 1984

Suicide and Murder in English Dept. at UB

French Student Sought in U.S.–Canada Personhunt

Dolly Kellehan

(CITY, March 10) The bizarre murder case that has shaken the University at Buffalo took a new turn Friday when the body of a second student was found near the basement furnace in the English department building and a third student apparently fled to Canada.

Felix Kulper, 24, a graduate student in English from Long Island, died from a blow to the head with a Scotch tape dispenser before his body was thrown down the stairs, according to MBPD Detective Lieutenant Norman Rhodes.

Kulper's apparent murder occurred as the death of another student earlier in the week was being ruled a

suicide. Patricia Hassler, also a graduate student in English, died suddenly Wednesday morning after sitting on a thumbtack coated with sexitoxin, a highly toxic poison.

Lt. Rhodes told reporters yesterday evening that Hassler had herself placed the tack on the chair in a bizarre attempt to incriminate the third student, Christian Aval.

With this second death, the University murders are shaping up as the byproduct of academic politics and a romance gone sour, the *News-Gazette* has learned.

The murder and the suicide were linked by the two men's, Aval's and Kulper's, connection with Patricia Hassler. Hassler, bitter about an old love affair with Aval, planned to make her suicide look like a murder and frame him for the crime, said Det. Lt. Rhodes. Aval, meanwhile, seems to have killed Kulper to keep him from helping with the framing.

Hassler and Aval had been undergraduates at Yale University. In their final semester, she accused him of plagiarizing her senior honors thesis—the equivalent of grand larceny in academic circles. Yale officials never decided if her accusations were true, but they asked both students to leave, and both decided to move to UB.

The tensions between the two students were made worse by the unconventional, controversial course both were taking this spring. The complex, emotionally charged teaching methods of English Department professor Norman Holland "distressed" the students, according to Detective Rhodes. Holland was also on the committee that voted to admit Hassler and Aval, sources said.

Holland admitted he had been on the Graduate Admissions Committee when both Hassler and Aval applied to UB's intense and often controversial English Department. But he said he had opposed their admission. A "higher authority," he said, had overruled the committee. He also said, as he did earlier this week, "My theories and methods are in no way responsible for these tragic deaths."

On finding Aval missing, Lt. Rhodes immediately sent out a call to the U.S. Immigration and Naturalization Service, the Ontario Provincial Police, the Royal Canadian Mounted Police, as well as the Metropolitan Buffalo Police Department. This colossal combination of international police forces has united in a massive personhunt for the missing Frenchman.

Police Commissioner Casimir ("Caz") Watzlawick called Lt. Rhodes's work "quick, thorough, and brilliant detection." Lt. Norman ("Justin") Rhodes is a scion of the Rhodes family, well known for its philanthropic works in Buffalo. Officer Rudger Ramczet, who discovered Kulper's body, resides in North Tonawanda with his wife Wanda and four children.

from the journal of Norman Holland

Despite Dolly Kellehan, I did get one useful thing out of the write-up. I was able to hint to Romola Badger that, if she continued to pester me about reader-response and my theories and methods, I would point out to the dean how she had overruled the admissions committee and admitted Hassler and Aval on her own initiative. She's left me alone since then. 'Twas not a famous victory, but some good came of it. And I got my seminar scheduled for a decent afternoon hour.

Aval got away. At the time, it seemed most likely that he got across one of the bridges to Canada, probably the Peace Bridge where traffic is heaviest.

American customs officers listen closely for accents coming across into the U.S., but the Canadians are much more casual. They probably didn't even notice his accent. At least that was Rhodes's opinion. He was quite annoyed that he'd been unable to catch Aval at the last minute. What he took to be the Times's hint that he hadn't moved fast enough annoyed him even more.

There were a few more newspaper stories, but they said no more than that the police had been unable to locate Chris Aval. Dolly Kellehan's Joe Steelworker and Mary Threedecker weren't much interested in hearing that, so the mammoth international "personhunt" faded rather quickly from the local press.

Jane came home, and that helped. As our seminar continued, we gave up writing to one another. We simply talked about what had happened and how these events had changed our own lives. We tried to imagine ourselves into the minds of Trish and Kulper and Chris. Above all, we said how we ourselves felt about the two deaths and Chris's flight.

Naturally, Badger had a big departmental memorial at which she blatted away. What can you do?

I think in our melancholy musings we came closer to the aim of our seminar than we had in the first six weeks (especially given Trish Hassler's disruptive effect). Perhaps that was the best memorial we could give our two theorists and one skeptic. We saw (once more!) how each of us perceived these same events in profoundly different ways.

There were the obvious reasons for this. Barry, for example, living in the same apartment building as Trish, saw her differently from Max, who knew her only in class. But there were the deeper differences that came from personality or, the term I prefer, identity.

Barry Ireland gave his usual shrug. Suicide, poisoning, head-bashing—that was just the way of the world, as far as he was concerned, and I was beginning to believe him. Wally felt fear mostly. It seemed to him that a terribly cruel, sardonic fate had struck through the defenses of all three of them: Trish's bluster and aggression; Kulper's hiding; above all, Chris's clever shiftings, his seeming ability to be in two places at once doing two different things. All had failed.

Penza and Glendish admitted they enjoyed the notoriety they'd gained among the other students by being eyewitnesses, so to speak, to it all. Amy was amazing. She could still feel pity for Trish even while she was terrified that her past would come out. It was a great relief to her—and to me—when I got Justin to agree that the tape was no longer material to the case and to let me give it to Amy. I have given her, and all of them, pseudonyms in this book.

In due course, the semester ground round to its end, and we parted for the summer. The simplest thing was to give them all A's, so I did.

The academic's life, like the farmer's, is seasonal. There is the rush of start-up in late August. Then the first semester moves along in a steady, even way, slowly building toward the unruly urgencies of Christmas. January and February return to the flatness of October and November, but are more gloomy. Then the pace begins to quicken again. All the things that one was supposed to have done in the first half of the year crowd into the last few weeks. Lecturers pass through. Theses are due. Jobs must be sought, recommendations written. In Buffalo, where the winter lasts into April, there comes a kind of inner frenzy. When will this end!! I've heard that the Eskimos go into rut in spring. In our more inhibited society, academics grumble and politic and scheme and revolt. Then the semester climaxes in exams and papers and a flurry of hurry-up grading. Finally all relaxes into commencement and the easiness of summer.

I was never so grateful for summer as this year. I went to my office rarely. I found I wasn't interested in churning out a flurry of articles and lectures. Like Ishmael, I preferred to go down to the waterside. I spent hours watching the Niagara River churning and rushing toward the Falls. I often wondered about Justin Rhodes.

I was a little surprised not to hear from him. I'd gotten to like him, and I thought he'd be a refreshing change from my steady diet of academic parties with their professorial gossip and university crises. Rhodes didn't call me, however, after my connection with the case ended. (I assumed the case itself hadn't been closed, because they hadn't caught Aval.) Neither did I read about Rhodes in the BMNG, at least about his police work. He had another play put into production, summer stock this time, but no cases that made the newspapers.

Should I have called him? Given the outcome of our case (yes, I think of it as "our" case), I felt leery. I might well be an embarrassment, the sign of a failure on his part. Finally I got an occasion for reestablishing contact.

One Friday in mid-June I went into the office, and there was a letter with a Canadian stamp. I hadn't come since the previous Friday, so the letter could have come as early as Monday the 11th. It had only the month for a date.

June 1984
Dear Professor Holland,

I do not know why I am writing to you, indeed, even risking myself considerably to do so. As you know, your seminar transformed my being in ways neither of us could have anticipated when it began. I remember the first day of it, one day, you told us with pride that a student had once written you saying this Delphi seminar had changed her life. Presumably, however, none of your Delphi seminars has ever changed its students' lives as this one

changed Patricia's and mine. Or--I can hear your voice
making the familiar correction--more accurately, as we
used your seminar to change our lives. You would say that
is more accurate. Perhaps it is, but I am of two minds
still about the matter.

You were kind to me at every point. I am sorry that
the tragic contradictions of Patricia and me wrecked your
seminar, but perhaps you and I can both take comfort in
the idea that these events taught the students--and us as
well--something about the nature of our natures, the
instability of our stabilities. We may have made this
particular Delphi the highest expression of the type.

That fateful Friday morning, when Lt. Rhodes announced
his deduction that Patricia had committed suicide, I
realized I had made a horrible error. For most of the
week, I thought I had succeeded in intercepting
Patricia's false accusations of me. First, I took the
squibs on Monday. Then, that Wednesday morning, as was my
custom, I secretly watched her building. But I did not
see her leave. Why? Because she had left already! Finally, when I started off to the seminar, I saw her
standing on the corner. I reversed direction, went back
to her apartment, broke in, and stole the last remaining
copy of that accusation so full of danger.

I was not sure exactly what Trish planned to do, but I
inferred from the squib she wrote for Monday that she was
making me look responsible for something violent and
criminal. If she spoke her accusation in the seminar, as
she evidently planned to do--and did!--I could answer
her. But the writing asserted my guilt without my being
able to reply. The writing was very dangerous.

I knew how passionate she was. I knew she was even
capable of doing harm to herself and blaming me. I could
not stop her harming herself, but I could stop her from
pointing to me as the criminal. And I did.

When I arrived at the seminar and she fell down dead,
I knew that that had been her plan. I was to be executed
for her murder. She died, and I would die. Liebestod.

Now the danger she was to me was finished. I felt as
though a giant hand had lifted me out of danger. But I
had to get into her books, for the police would surely
search them and find any copies of that accusation she had
brought with her. In the confusion, I was able to combine
her books with mine and carry the single stack across the
hall. We all waited while the lieutenant interviewed us

one by one, and I pretended to study in those notebooks.
I found four extra copies of her accusation. I mixed them
in with my own papers, took them home, and destroyed
them. It was risky having to leave Trish's books there
for Lt. Rhodes to complain about, but except for that, I
thought I had emerged, as you say, in the clear. Even the
vial of poison she placed on my computer-- True, I was
terrified when Lt. Rhodes took me down to the police
station, but I could see that even he knew that that
foolishness of the vial was not to be believed. It could
not have the same force as her words accusing me before
the death.

What a strange morning. I, stealing into her apartment
to remove her accusation, she waiting for me to leave
mine so that she could accuse me with the vial of poison.
Our paths must have crossed! Although I did not realize
that until Lt. Rhodes narrated the whole story on Friday
morning. We were both late, but only she was "the late
Patricia Hassler," in your peculiar English idiom.

I felt saved, until the mystery student's message on
Thursday. That I had to stop, because it would have been,
again!, Trish accusing me before her death. I knew of no
other way but to kill this strange person, who had been
both there and not there in our seminar.

Then, on Friday morning, the lieutenant told me, in
effect, that Trish had succeeded after all. She had
tricked me into tricking myself. I felt the dead hand of
fate crushing down on me. I understood there was no use
in trying to escape her trap any more, although I had no
intention of falling into Lt. Rhodes's.

Immediately, when we scattered after Kulper's body was
found, I told one of the other students in the seminar
that, to straighten out my visa, I had to go to Canadian
immigration in Niagara Falls, Canada. I asked this generous person to drive me across the Peace Bridge, and I
would get myself back--they should not wait while I dealt
with the bureaucrats because that could take hours. I was
surprised at how indifferent the Canadian customs people
were, unlike the Americans, preoccupied with boundaries.
Naturally, I will not tell you who did me this last ser-
vice--the person did not then know I was a fugitive--but
I feel sure that you know all of us in the seminar well
enough to make a guess that would probably be right.

You used to speak of our "identities." Both Patricia
and I were creatures of mind. Love did not come easily to

us. Neverthless, I loved Patricia (and I believe she
loved me), but somehow I could only love her as long as
she wrote for me. When the time came for us to write our
senior papers at Yale, she could no longer write as I
would write. She could no longer be me, in that special
verbal way. I found I could not love her as I had until
that time. That sounds as though I were just using her to
write papers for me, but that is not what I mean.

I mean that, as long as I was, I was, deeply committed
to her, as long as I was with her in the most intimate
sense, I could not live out another commitment. I could
not be in my papers, my writing, my words. It is as
though a principle of falsity, of self-contradiction were
built into my personality. But that is your language, the
idea of an essential, originary identity. I am not sure I
believe that. I believe that we are all false because we
are divided. There is the self of desire and the self in
the world. I learned this truth of myself all through my
childhood, but I only understood it with Patricia. If I
were true to her, and I was, I had to be false to someone
or something else important. The law of desire and the
law of the world can never coincide. Does not Freud teach
us that? At Yale, that "world" was my teachers and my
academic discipline, and my desire was for Patricia. I
was there where my words were not. To plagiarize was my
one authentic act.

With you, it was the opposite. I was true to my pro-
fession--I did good work for you, did I not?--but I was
false to her. I could not admit I loved her. I could not
try to correct the wrong I had done her. And I fell into
her trap. I know now that there was no need to kill
Kulper. Perhaps I knew then. Perhaps it was only the self
of desire that wanted to murder. Perhaps my desire was to
atone to Patricia by living out the grim plan she had
made for me. Perhaps my love for her made me need to
destroy my life to fulfill her words.

I am writing this to you to tell you what I have
understood about what happened. I am writing to tell you
that I am not a unitary person, but deeply divided. Yet I
can hear you earnestly saying, But Chris, that is you.
That is your identity. Your unity is precisely that divi-
sion in yourself. And perhaps we should simply leave it
at that. We are both right, you and I. We are all paradoxes of unity and unities of paradox.

I wish there would someday be an occasion when I could

theorize like this again with you face to face, but I
fear that will never be. Never in life, as we French say.
This letter will have to suffice. I am in the French-
speaking part of Canada, which in many ways is more
French than France itself and in other ways is not French
at all. Very strange! As I hear it, the language has
French consonants, but American vowels. Québec feels like
a place somehow between England and America, and French-
speaking Canada between France and Canada.

I feel a temptation to tell you where I will be next,
but that would be dangerous, given your evident friend-
ship with Lt. Rhodes, and, besides, I do not know. I have
noticed men in the unmistakably heavy shoes and stained
trenchcoats of the police. Sometimes they stand across
the street watching the flat where I live. Then I move.
Then they come again. Whether they are Canadian or
Interpol, I feel sure they are encircling me. I am demanded elsewhere, across a border. I do not know whether
I shall return. Within a few days, it will be decided
whether I am to be here or there, on your side of the
border or mine, in the hotel which is not a home or in
the game of boules which is.

Wherever I end up, Professor Holland, I hope you will
be so kind as to accept my most particular and cordial
sentiments.

                        /Christian Aval/

*As I say, the letter could have been lying in my mailbox for a week. Indeed, the
U. S. postmark said June 9 and it could have been mailed as much as a week or
ten days before, given the Canadian mails. As events turned out, it probably had.*

*I felt proud, in an odd sort of way, that Chris had chosen to trust me. He
knew I'd have to show his letter to Rhodes. He had written me anyway, simply
because he wanted to. He'd been careful, not naming, for example, the person
who helped him across the border. So I could show it to Justin without breach-
ing Chris's trust.*

*I called Justin at home that evening. When I told Justin that I'd gotten a
letter from Aval, he replied that he, too, had news. Aval had been living, Rhodes
said, in the student quarter of Montreal, in Saint-Denis, right near the Place
Saint-Louis. The RCMP had found him, or someone they thought was him,
through informants among the students—they're constantly trying to hunt out
drug dealers, and they vet any strangers who move in. While the Americans and*

Canadians were settling the identification, the RCMP suddenly informed Rhodes that Aval had left Montreal and headed back toward Ontario. Rhodes told them to follow him closely. Rhodes said that he'd been hoping that Aval would cross the border again, so that New York State would be spared the trouble and expense of extraditing him. Justin assured me that the letter could make no possible difference in the case, and I felt relieved that I wasn't betraying Chris. Nevertheless, he said, he'd like to see it. It was evidence, after all.

I asked him to lunch. Monday? Monday would be good, he said. I suggested the Faculty Club, but he countered and insisted that I let him take me to the Pluto Club (where the local wealthy take their guests and their ease). What the hell, I thought, how often do I get to go to the Pluto Club?

Not very often, the big doorman's supercilious eyes seemed to say as they scanned my cord jacket and Rockports. I walked through the lobby, really quite distinguished with its marble floor and walnut paneling, dark and Tudor in the best Buffalo manner, and into the bar. Justin was drinking a Perrier, on duty, I suppose. He offered me a drink, but I said I had to work that afternoon. This was, of course, not stopping the various brokers, bankers, investment counselors, and real estate dealers, who were quietly tippling and chortling at the small dark tables.

We passed into the restaurant, where about two-thirds of the tables were full, businessmen in their black suits and some mink-draped shoppers. Around me plates were heaped with meat, potatoes, and vegetables or thick sandwiches reflecting the city's German heritage. Someone had told them about nouvelle cuisine, *however, and there were a few fitful efforts at lightness on the menu. I chose a salmon with kiwi, and Justin a sole in dill sauce.*

While we waited for the food to come, Justin asked me for Chris's letter, and I handed it over. He read it slowly and carefully.

I looked around me, enjoying a kind of anthropological treat by watching the locals and their folkways. There came over me that curious sense I have with moneyed and familied people, of everything being in its place, settled, almost like a chemical precipitate slowly falling to the bottom of a beaker. There was no need to question anything, because it was all there, it had been there, and it would be there. And it was good. And they could afford it. Their voices were a bit loud, as if to say, this is ours. We belong to it, and it belongs to us. But richness here wasn't like South American richness, gaudy or cruel. There was a middle-class decency and stolidity to the thick, white tablecloths and the heavy hotel silver.

What I really wanted, though, was for Justin to react to the letter. He was still looking down at it, rereading, when he began to comment. "The letter tells me one thing I didn't know, namely, that he'd already escaped to Canada by the time we found those last squibs in Kulper's apartment."

"*I like to think,*" I said, "*that he was crossing the border at the exact moment you blasted open the safe, but I suppose that's much too neat and literary.*"

"*You do like to neaten things, don't you, Norman?*" When he looked directly at me, I could see he had an expression of great sadness, and I thought I could see his eyes reddening. I was surprised.

"*Justin,*" I said. "*I thought you'd seize on this letter as a call to the chase. I thought his oblique references about where he is would pique your hunting instincts.*"

"*I responded to something else,*" he said.

"*You see?,*" I laughed, "*Response is unpredictable.*"

"*I'm sorry for what happened to Aval,*" he said. "*He was, after all, a fairly decent person. Overintellectualized and all tangled up in the strange theories of your profession, yes, but basically a decent human being. He stole Hassler's paper, and that was vile. But he himself seems to think that that was a pathological aberration, a thing wrong with his personality. He just doesn't strike me as evil. He didn't deserve to be tricked or driven into murder. He didn't deserve to have his life destroyed. Neither did Hassler, although she's much less likable. But maybe she was a more pleasant person when she was happy in her work at Yale and her one romance.*"

He sighed. "*If only someone had been able to deal with the plagiarism in New Haven. I hate to sound like Dear Abby, but suppose there had been some counseling for them instead of banishment. Those profs at Yale were so fixed upon guarding the purity of their profession. Couldn't they have addressed the psychological issue?*"

"*Obviously, Justin, I'm sympathetic to a psychological approach, but the Yalies' problem was different. They didn't know whether there had been a plagiarism or not. They had to decide that first, before they could take any steps. You've got to realize that plagiarism strikes at the very heart of my profession, at its most basic intellectual assumptions.*"

"*Is that really so? Wouldn't it have been possible for the Yale profs to say, 'Look, we don't know whether there was a plagiarism or not, but you two have been through an obviously complicated affair together. At least one of you is suffering from the breakup. Let's set up an appointment for the two of you to talk all this over with a professional'? Don't they have psychological counseling for students? Don't I remember that there's a very distinguished psychoanalytic institute in New Haven?*"

"*Yes, the Western New England. Very distinguished indeed.*"

"*As for intellectual assumptions, you told me, these people at Yale don't even believe in authorship. Yet all they could see when presented with Patricia Hassler's accusation was, Who wrote this paper? Couldn't they have said, 'It doesn't matter who wrote this. Here are two troubled people'?*"

"But, Justin, that's just not the way professors of literature think. Writing is terribly important to us, reading is important, and a plagiarism is crucial. Language matters."

"Well," said Rhodes a bit testily, "here's a piece of language." He took an envelope out of his pocket and from it a small clipping. He tossed it cavalierly onto the white tablecloth between us. "I don't know whether you saw this or not. It was in yesterday's paper. It was only a small item in the local section. They told me about this on Sunday afternoon."

The first thing I saw was one of those peculiar BMNG headlines: "Man Leaps from Maid." It took me a second or two to realize what they were referring to.

Have you ever ridden the Maid of the Mist? If you have, you know it crosses the river back and forth, giving the tourists a thrill by making them put on thick, black, rubber hats and slickers and getting them wet with the very water thundering over the Falls. The boat sails upstream from the Canadian dock past the American Falls toward the foot of the Horseshoe Falls. It's quite exciting, really. The engine has to rev up to keep the boat from making sternway. It gets loud, and the Falls are roaring, and mist and splashes are falling all over the tourists. The boat feels as though it can barely hold its own against that tremendous current and turbulence, and when the captain lets the bow fall off toward the American side, you really slue around. It's quite a spectacular show.

You have to keep that picture in mind as you read Rhodes's clipping:

From the *Buffalo Morning News-Gazette,* June 18, 1984

Man Leaps from Maid

(NIAGARA FALLS, June 17) About 4:00 p.m. an unidentified man leapt over the side of the *Maid of the Mist,* crowded with Sunday tourists, as she pulled up under the Horseshoe Falls. The apparent suicide did not surface in the roiling waters of the Niagara River, especially turbulent at that point, and the body has not been found downstream.

The man had boarded from the Canadian side of the river. Otherwise nothing is known as to his identity. None of the other passengers could supply a physical description, everyone having been bundled up in wet gear. Another passenger, however, Charles A. Piastri, visiting Niagara Falls from West Haven, CT, had attempted to pull the man back as he was about to jump, but was unsuccessful.

Horace Hornblower, a spokesman for Horseshoe Honeymoons, the company that operates the *Maid,* insisted that this was the first time such a thing has happened since the Maid was re-designed to prevent accidents and sui-cides in the early 1950s.

At that time, Hornblower de-clared, the side and taff rails were raised to prevent passengers from fall-ing or jumping over. From time to time since then, the company has consid-ered raising the rails further but has decided against interfering with tour-ists' view of the Falls. Hornblower said that the company will not now raise the rails but will ask crew members to observe passengers more closely.

"Aval?," I asked.

"I'm almost certain it was."

Just as with Hassler, I was suddenly flooded with that awful chilling knowl-edge. Every one of us will someday be as Hassler is, as Kulper is, as Aval is. But what an awful, yes, awe-full, way to die, weighed down with the heavy rubber slicker, water thundering down from above and the river seething up from be-low. I suddenly caught Justin's words. "'Almost certain?' What do you mean?"

"Ninety-nine percent. Let me give it to you from the beginning," he said. "I told you that we were letting him come back to Ontario, in hopes that he'd cross the border himself and we wouldn't have to extradite him. Now, I regret the decision. I regret it more than I can say."

"I can see why," I said dryly.

"By Monday, he had gotten to Niagara Falls, Ontario. The O.P.P.—the Ontario Provincial Police—let him get on The Maid of the Mist. I wouldn't have done that, but I.N.S.—Immigration and Naturalization—was handling it from our side. Sometimes they don't show the best of judgment. They okayed it, and they sent Piastri on board to keep an eye on him. They planned to pick him up when the Maid disembarked its American tourists on our side. But this was a Saturday in June, and the boat was jammed. Piastri got separated from Aval. Once the passengers were all raincoated and helmeted up, it got hard to tell who was who. At the crucial moment, while the engines strained against the current and the spray poured over the boat, when everyone was oohing and aahing and staring up at the Falls, somebody climbed up on the railing. Piastri saw what was happening and pushed through the crowd toward the man he assumed was Aval. He tried to catch hold of the jumper's arm, but his hands slipped on the wet rubber, and whoever it was went over the side. The crew tossed out life preservers, but that was useless. They just swirled away on the current. You can't stay that close to the Falls for long, and they had to slow the engines and get over to the American side. Whoever jumped never surfaced.

"I assume it was Aval. I feel 99 percent sure it was Aval. But I can't be 100 *percent sure. Nobody on board, not even Piastri, could make a positive identification. The jumper had his back to him. In principle, the jumper could have been any tourist on his own, without companions who'd raise a hue and cry. If it was somebody else, Aval himself could have disembarked with the others in the hullabaloo when they were counting passengers off on either the Canadian or the American side. Piastri says that a crowd of police distracted him, so that he missed checking some of the passengers that got off on the American side. Then, too, he's only working from that student photograph I got from Romola Badger."*

"You didn't tell the papers this was the fugitive from the Hassler case?"

"I'm not 100 percent sure. Besides, they didn't ask, and why advertise our failures?"

"Is this a failure, or do you think this was just?"

"A kind of rough justice. Aval, after all, was guilty of murder one. I think he may have passed judgment on himself."

"What an incredible scene!"

"Yes, it reminds me of something, but I can't quite get it."

"Something biblical?"

"Yes, I think so."

"'Let—something, something—run down as waters.' Justice? No. I can't quite get it. Justin, did he die on the American side or the Canadian side?"

"We'll never know, will we?" he said, smiling wryly. We ate our fish in silence for a while, and then he asked, "Who do you think drove him across the bridge?"

"I don't think any good would come of my hazarding a guess," I said.

"Don't get me wrong. I'm not going to pursue this any further. So far as I'm concerned, so far as Homicide is concerned, the case is closed and a righteous judgment rendered. But I like to know who did what to whom when. I neaten too. Who do you think it was? You're the expert on their identities."

"Knowing their identities—their styles—can't tell you what they actually did or didn't do."

"Just from what little I saw of those people and your readings of them, I'd say Amy, wouldn't you?"

"But you remember, we telephoned Amy from Aval's apartment, and she was home."

"I'd forgotten. Extrinsic evidence, you'd say."

"I would indeed."

But in fact neither of us said much during the rest of that lunch. As I began to collect the materials for this book, though, Justin helped me a great deal. He provided the transcripts of the various events from Homicide. Being an author himself, he made a number of suggestions. Rather forceful suggestions.

"You didn't do a squib on yourself," he said one day. "I want to know about you and the way you react to that snake."

"And you didn't tell me why you're called Justin and not Norman."

"Well," he said, smiling. "Well, well. Loose ends. They always bother me. You and I will just have to collaborate again sometime."

I hope we do, I said.

acknowledgments

Help in writing this novel came from many novel quarters. I am grateful, for example, to my colleague in pharmacology (who shall remain nameless) for overcoming his evident suspicion that I was about to do in my wife and guardedly explaining to me several fast-acting, painless poisons. I've tried to honor and acknowledge here my secretaries over past decades by noting how lucky the Metropolitan Buffalo Police Department is to be able to draw on their transcribing skills. I thank Denise Levertov and New Directions Books for graciously allowing me to use "The Snake" for the dark purpose of character revelation. (No matter what Hassler and Kulper say, I think it's a fine poem.) Thanks, too, to my lit-and-psych colleagues and friends in France, Robert Silhol and Yves Thoret, who answered with Gallic precision my questions about boules, le bachot, *and* les grandes écoles. *I also owe a debt to the surgeons who attended John Bobbitt for providing an answer to the question on page 233 that had to remain unanswered when I wrote it.*

I especially thank Andrew Gordon, Molly Harrower, Brandon Kershner, and especially Laura Keyes Perry, who read the ms. at various stages and made many, many suggestions for improvement. You will understand, therefore, that whatever flaws that remain are entirely their fault. The same holds true for Wyatt Benner and Bernadine Dawes of SUNY Press, whose considerable skills produced the book you hold from a kaleidoscopic ms.

My first, last, and deepest debt is to Kelley Holland and Jane Holland, who know when writing can be made better and can say how to do it. They helped far beyond editing, though, by bucking up the old guy when he most needed it. So did Mihai Spariosu, Murray Schwartz, Jeffrey Berman, and Kathleen Woodward, who found the merits of this book after so many others had failed to do so. I am particularly grateful to Murray, for he and I developed together the Delphi seminar that is one of the subjects of this novel. (We described and illustrated the technique, for those of you who might want to try it, in three articles in College English in 1975, 1977, and 1978. It does not lead to murder.)

Finally, like countless other beginning writers of mysteries, I learned from Marie Rodell's indispensable how-to-write-it book, Mystery Fiction (1952), to which I turned again and again for guidance. I found particularly helpful three of her wise cautions: no fancy poisons, no identical twins, and above all, no experimental writing. They proved essential clues to the ultimate mystery of this mystery, namely, how to write it.

St. Luke's Place and   Norman N. Holland
Gainesville, Florida